I0743071

From Bullied to Beloved

Juliet Jaskolski

Copyright © 2025 by Juliet Jaskolski

All rights reserved.

No portion of this book may be reproduced in any form without written permission from the publisher or author, except as permitted by U.S. copyright law.

Contents

Chapter 1

Freshman year

"Ninety-eight... ninety-nine... one hundred..."

I take a deep breath and open my eyes and then pick a bobby pin out of my hair before pulling my phone out of my pocket to use as a flashlight to find the door knob in the dark. I poke the bobby pin into the door knob and jiggle it around until the knob pops open and it twists free. I swing the door open and step out of the stuffy janitor's closet and remind myself how to breathe. I'm kind of claustrophobic and sitting in that locked janitor's closet while counting to one hundred is really suffocating for me.

Of course, I could just get out after a few seconds of being in there, but I learned early on that getting out too early would result in something worse. For example, being thrown into a mud puddle or thrown into the boys' locker room during their shower time.

Counting to one hundred gives them enough time to get bored and walk away so I'm free to go eat my lunch in the library in peace. I pack my lunch so I don't even have to go into the cafeteria at all, I just have to sneak down the hallway to the stairs and then to my locker where I keep my lunch that usually just consists of carrots and a muffin or something.

There are four of them that I really have to look out for. There's Kevin Farrell who is the captain of the varsity basketball team here at our high school. He's a junior and he's really strong so they usually rely on him as the muscle to actually carry me to wherever it is that they're going to administer my daily torture. He's also an asshole.

And then there's his girlfriend, Bethany Hodges. She isn't the captain of anything because she's only a sophomore but she's a cheerleader and she also plays on the tennis and softball teams. She isn't as strong as her boyfriend but she's more of the verbal abuse of the group and her cackling laugh feels like a hundred daggers to my ears. She's also violent because although her boyfriend will carry me to my doom, he won't actually hit me or anything. He likes to pretend like he has morals sometimes and he doesn't hit girls so his girlfriend does that dirty work.

Bethany's best friend is Kelly Blake- also a sophomore. She's nothing special really. She's more like Bethany's shadow more than anything but just as annoying and bothersome. The last person in their four person tag team is Beckett Spears. He's on the JV baseball team and he's just a freshman like myself but he's still incredibly popular since his sister was incredibly well known in our school and she graduated a few years back and so he can get his friends into the most prestigious of parties.

He's different though because his mom knows my mom and they're actually really close friends because we're also next door neighbors. So he's not as mean as the other three are because he's afraid that I'll tell my mom who will tell his mom who will then proceed to ground him or something. He hates me though, just as much as I hate him and the rest of them. He's quiet, though, but just because he isn't the muscle or the brain, he isn't innocent considering he sits there and watches them do it as if it's his afternoon's entertainment. Never speaks up or tries to stop them and sometimes, he does step in to assist so he's just as guilty as the other three.

It's not just those four that mess with me but it's mainly them and anything anybody else does is nothing that I can't handle.

I eat lunch in the library like I do every day and then when the bell rings, I throw my trash away and scurry off to my next class. I try to be quick about it so that I don't get caught by those four terrible people because whenever they see me, they like to throw my books around or slam me into the lockers or, if they're feeling specifically terrible that day, they'll lock me in some closet or empty classroom or a bathroom stall or something.

Luckily, I make it to my next class safely without an incident and that's an incredible miracle. I stay in the back of my classes and for the most part, I just scribble some music lyrics in the corners of my pages to make it look like I'm actually doing assignments when I'm really not.

After I've made it through all of my afternoon classes, I make it to the worst part of the day out of everything. The end of the day. Sometimes, if I'm feeling particularly cowardice that day, I'll just hang out in my last period class for about twenty minutes and talk to the teacher, pretending like I have a question about the homework or something but today is not one of those days.

They know where my locker is and usually, they're there waiting for me. Praying on me like an innocent little deer. And I am innocent. Completely. I've never done anything to any of them at all but at the beginning of the year, they just decided that I didn't deserve to live a normal high school life. They decided that these four years that are supposed to be the best years of one's life will actually be my worst.

I get to my locker first today which is nice and then I hurriedly stuff all of my books and such into my locker before grabbing my one text book that I need to take home and shoving it in my back. I slam my locker shut in hopes of making it out unscathed today but as I turn to go down the hallway, they're there. I'm not surprised but I am disappointed.

"Where are you off to already, Superfreak?" Bethany wonders curiously.

They like nicknames that start with Super because my name is Jensen as in, the same first name as Jensen Ackles who is one of the main characters in Supernatural. I had a button with him and Jared Padalecki, his slightly less sexy co-star, on my bag at the beginning of the year because it happens to be one of my favorite shows and apparently, they think that it's something to make fun of. I don't know if they think that it's funny that I share a name with this incredibly gorgeous man when I am indeed a girl or if they think that it's funny that I like the show. Neither one hurts my feelings or anything though, because I am particularly proud of both facts and they can't take that away from me.

"I was actually on my way out, thanks for asking," I reply chirpily with a friendly smile. I try to side step them but I know that my effort is futile because there's four of them but only one of me. They have strength and insults but what I lack in physical strength, I have them beat in wit and I will not let them take that from me no matter how painful the consequences are.

"Well, we have other plans for you so just sit tight," She informs me with that excited smirk that she gets when she's being especially maniacal. It really makes me sick, that smirk that Bethany has perfected and I know that I'm in for some pain when she smirks like that.

"That sounds like fun, Beth. It really does," I assure her. "But I really gotta run."

Kevin steps forward as I try to walk away again and then he puts a hand on my shoulder, pushing me into the lockers behind me. He doesn't push me hard or anything, but enough to make the lockers shake with my weight and he doesn't let go of me, he just presses my shoulder into the metal just enough so that I can't escape but it doesn't hurt.

"At least buy me a drink first, Kev," I say. "Does this count as sexual assault?"

He barks out a rude laugh. "I would never sexually assault you."

"Well, you have the assault part down pat," I mutter.

"Hey Beth, you might want to give her a few pointers about hygiene after you're done with her," He calls to his equally disgusting girlfriend with a wrinkle of his nose. "She reeks of fish."

I'm confused by that joke because I thought that the whole 'you're a slut if you smell like fish' thing was funny in middle school but I thought that people grew out of that thing before high school started and yet, here we are. He's glaring at me the whole time that he's speaking so I just look back at him and I grin because I have the best comeback ever. I stand on my tippy toes so that I'm almost eye level with him and then I say it even though I know that I'll grow to regret it in the very near future. "Yeah, I'm a huge slut," I agree with him. "I am always fucking your boyfriend, Kev."

This doesn't sound like much of an insult and to me, it's not really all that mean but to Kevin, that's a whole new story because he's incredibly homophobic. "Did you just call me gay?" He wonders incredulously and his three minions start to close in on me as the tension grows.

I decide to make a run for it. Like, a real run for it. It's the only shot I've got out of this, even though I'm sure that it'll only make my predicament worse. If they want to bully me though, I'm sure not going to make it easy for them. The only defense mechanism that I know is to go for the man parts and/or kick the shin. I don't think that I can make it to his man parts so I quickly kick his shin as hard as I can. He yelps but doesn't fall or anything. It is enough to get him to let go of me so I quickly push myself off of the lockers and start sprinting down the hallway as fast as I can. All four of them are intense athletes so I'm confident that they will easily catch up to me but I have to use my brain. Our school is so big that it's basically a maze so I just have to twist and turn like I'm in the freaking Labyrinth and hopefully, that's how I'll lose them.

It's only a temporary solution though, because if I really do get away today, I'll have to deal with all of their rage tomorrow and it sure as hell will not be pretty.

I hear them behind me, chasing me, and I feel the text book weighing down my shoulders but I think of the huge mud puddle right outside and I think of how much I love this Batman sweater that I'm wearing and I don't want to get it muddy so I keep running. I turn right and then I turn left and I can tell that I have already confused them because I hear Kelly screech "Split up!" from behind me.

I run faster and look for a classroom that has an unlocked door, but they all seem locked. The teachers have a meeting after school today so none of them are in the hallways at all and if those monsters behind me do catch me, I'm hopeless. I'm beginning to lose my breath and my bag is bouncing against my back with every heavy step and it hurts but I don't stop running as I run through the maze of hallways.

I turn to my left into the science wing but I'm not really looking at where I'm going and when I look up, I see that, to my horror, I've cornered myself in a dead end of lockers. I curse under my breath before turning back around to try another hallway, but Beckett is already standing there, blocking my way to freedom.

I groan and start to catch my breath. He takes a step toward me and I hold up one of my fingers at him. "Just... let... me catch... my breath really quick," I pant, putting my hands on my knees. "Holy crap, I'm out of shape."

"Stop playing around," He snaps at me. He's usually really quiet, Beckett is, so it's really weird to be alone with him right now because that never happens. We used to be kind of close when we were little kids since our moms are friends and we are neighbors so we saw each other a lot and played together all of the time but apparently, becoming a complete asshole is part of the male puberty process that I was not aware of because in middle school, he turned into who he is now. Very disappointing, really, because he was the only person that could ever challenge me in a soccer game.

"Not playing," I correct him. "Hyperventilating."

"They'll be easier on you if you don't take so long," He informs me, stepping closer to me again.

"They?" I wonder with an incredulous laugh. I stand back up, separating my palms from my knees and I glare at him. "Don't pretend like you aren't part of them, you little shit."

He rolls his eyes at me and steps forward again, close enough to grab me. "Come on, let's just go. I got her!" He yells into the empty hallways as he moves forward to grab my elbow but I yank it back just in time.

"What I lack in speed, I make up in reflexes," I pipe. I side step him and move to run past him in hopes of getting out of there before they all convene in this little dead end.

"Hey," He starts to speak up and as he does, he grabs the loop on my bag and pulls me back. I was so close to my escape but with the momentum that I had going forward, he adverts that momentum to going sideways so I jerk to my right and hit my head on the bank of lockers right there. There's a loud bang of metal to flesh and it hurts a lot so I put my hand up to it and when my hand comes back down, it's covered in blood. It's not just a little drop, it is a river of dark blood and I'm sure I'll pass out soon. Probably not, but by the amount of blood and excruciating pain, I think that this'll need stiches.

I hear the others' footsteps in the distance though so I don't have time to whine about it right now. I scramble to my feet and without another look at Beckett, I take off down the hallway. Down another hallway, I find an unlocked classroom that probably belongs to one of the younger teachers that usually forget to lock their doors and I wait out there for about twenty minutes before I carefully stand and walk to the door. I'm feeling dizzy but I still make it out of the school uncaught and alive. I don't live incredibly far from the school and it's just a fifteen minute walk and I spend the whole time wiping blood from my cheek so that it doesn't drip onto my sweater. Blood is worse than mud in my opinion. It stains worse.

My mom is home- she sometimes is when I get home- so I sit on the front porch instead of actually going inside because that's what I usually do when she's already home. I take my Batman sweater off to reveal the white tank top underneath and then I use my beloved sweater to wipe the blood from my face because I don't see any other options.

I sit on the stairs to my porch and wipe the blood from the side of my face and then hold it to the cut where it's still oozing blood. It burns so bad but when I tell my mom that I think I may be concussed, I don't want it to look like I just got hacked by an axe murderer with blood all over the place.

I also don't want her to see me cry, which is another thing that I always do as I sit out here on the porch. I make sure that Beckett's car isn't in his driveway next door first though because I obviously don't want him or any of the others to see what effect they really have on me. That's why I'm so hilarious and carry myself with a faux confidence when I'm around them. I won't let them destroy me, but that doesn't mean that dealing with these horrible people every single day isn't wearing on me. It wears on me every day and it hurts.

It hurts to feel afraid of waking up in the morning because I know that the day will be hell and it hurts to feel afraid of going to sleep because I know that the next day will be just more of the same. This desperation for somebody to notice my pain, it hurts even more. But I don't want to tell anybody- especially not my parents because it'd absolutely crush my mother and I couldn't do that to her. I just want them to notice on their own.

I sit out here on the porch so that my mom won't see me crying but a little part of me wants her to come out here right now and see me crying and showing my pain. I want somebody to notice but I also don't.

When I'm done crying and bleeding, I stand up and go inside.

I don't want to show my mom the cut because I don't want to freak her out but the blood still isn't stopping and I really need it to stop, which is why I think that it'll need stitches, so when I go inside, I walk into the kitchen where she's working on her laptop at the table and just like I knew she would- she freaks.

It takes two hours to get to the hospital and back home, now with twelve stitches on the right side of my forehead and a freaked out mom. Although I tell her that I just fell on my way home, she is still freaking out about it but that's just what she does.

My head still hurts when I finish ordering the sweater online and I'm really irritated at today because of getting probably-concussed so I decide to take my aggravation out by making a video. It's just something stupid that I've been doing for a few years, just grabbing my guitar and a camera and then I'll set it up and play a song as if I was some super famous YouTube god.

This time, I sit on the edge of my bed and after I press the play button on my camera standing on a tripod, I sing Mean by Taylor Swift into my camera as if a million people were about to watch it when in reality, I will most likely be the only person to ever see it. Ever.

I take choir in school and I can at least carry a tune and I used to take guitar lessons but after I learned the basics with an instructor, I learned the rest by myself pretty much. I've learned a lot of my favorite songs on guitar and playing it is just really amazing and the sound of a guitar is perfect.

This song really feels appropriate for the day that I've had, which is why I've picked it and I'm pretty happy with it because I've already memorized the words to it and the notes on the guitar. Well, it feels appropriate almost every day of my life nowadays but I don't usually have to get stitches, so this one is specifically cruel.

I post my favorite videos to YouTube under a fake name but it's not like I'm trying to stay anonymous or anything. I mean, my face is in them but at least it's not like somebody can search my name and find them or anything so that's kept people at my school from seeing them. Nobody ever views the videos except for a couple here and there but it's still fun to do. I don't do it for other people, I just do it for my inner narcissist.

When I'm done with the song, I'm still not really feeling incredibly relaxed so I decide to actually talk to the camera, which is something that I've never done before at all but I figure that it's worth a shot. Maybe it'll be like a tiny free therapist that just listens to my problems and doesn't judge or something.

After putting my guitar away, I sit back down on the bed in front of the camera that's now off and I just stare at it for a minute. I decide what I want to tell the camera because I'll probably watch it years from now and remember who I used to be so I want it to be good. With one last long breath, I reach forward and press the 'play' button.

"Hi there," I say awkwardly. "So, I've decided that I'm done. I'm done just taking all of this shit from everybody at school. I don't deserve it. Hell, nobody deserves it. And if you were a real therapist, you'd ask me 'how does that make you feel?' well, it makes me feel fucking shitty. I feel alone all of the time. Just... so freaking alone. And pathetic. It's pathetic of me that I have to sit here in front of a camera and talk to it like it's my best friend. I'm not okay with it anymore though. I'm going to change. I am. They think that I'm just going to sit here and let them push me into a corner of self-hatred and doom? No sir, I do not think so. My cousin on my mom's side, he's a football player for some college team up north. He can teach me how to get stronger and self-defense stuff. I'm going to hold my head up higher. I'm going to sing louder. I'm going to be Jensen and I'm going to fuck everybody else. Figuratively, of course. Okay, that's the end of my rant so I'm going to go now. I'll see you when I can bench press a Kevin."

I turn my camera off and put it back in its little bag before disassembling the tripod and posting the Mean video to YouTube but I don't post the rant because that is not meant for the public eye at all. I'm sure that I didn't even mean any of it anyway. I just needed to get some steam out.

Throughout the rest of my freshman year, I begin to get more views on my videos and I have no idea how. So much so that I actually consider deleting my account because they really weren't meant for other people to see but after about 100 views on my Mean cover, I get my first comment ever and it's both nerve-racking and exciting at the same time, igniting my narcissist inside.

You have the voice of a Goddess! Can't wait to hear more!

And so I keep going. I tell my mom about it and she thinks that I should keep going too, so I do even though she's my mom and she pretty much has to say that to me. I post a new cover every two weeks despite my hell-ish experiences at school. Singing to my invisible audience makes Kevin and his clan more tolerable most of the time. I'll tape a rant here or there but I never post them at all. Just covers.

By the time spring break rolls around, my most popular video is my cover of Mean and it has a total of 700,000 views. I honestly have no idea how that happened at all but my mom starts to suggest that I may go viral. I think that's absolutely ridiculous but she really is pretty adamant about it.

"That's insane," I inform her with a roll of my eyes as I shut my laptop on the kitchen counter one night after announcing that I've surpassed the 700k mark.

"It's not insane," She laughs. "Going viral means one million views which means that you're only 300,000 away. Considering you have 700,000 already, I don't think it's insane at all. My baby's going to be star!"

And the craziest thing about the whole thing is that she's right. By the end of a very terrible freshman year, I am viral.

After I hit one million views, my whole world kind of changes completely. About a week after I celebrated the one million mark, I get an email from a guy named Chris Warner and the email reads:

Dear CandyCane (My under cover username is CandyCane because my last name is Cane... get it?),

You're becoming really popular and congratulations on that, I'm sure you're really excited. Anyway, I'm an aspiring singer and I think it'd be really cool if you did a cover of one of my songs? I just really need the publicity and you seem like you'd be open to helping out. The attached file is my demo so I hope that you like it. Thanks for your time.

~ Chris Warner

I blink a few times at the screen- this guy thought that I was popular? Wow. That's really cool. I go to his YouTube page that is attached to the email and I listen to his songs that are actually amazing so I end up doing a cover to one of them. After getting another email from him, it turns out that it really did work out in his favor because he's getting a lot more attention because of me which is incredibly insane.

I'm going to be somebody.

Chapter 2

Senior Year

"Hello my favorite people! JustJensen here and today I need to talk to you about Chris Warner. Most of you know him as one of the best singers that there is and has ever been and I am so excited to announce that Chris has contacted me, inviting me to his concert this weekend. I know that I've said this before but not only will I be in the audience to see this totally awesome guy perform his totally awesome songs, but before the show, I will be outside of the stadium signing stuff and meeting people and taking pictures with all of you amazing people. We are going to be at the Nationwide Arena in Brooks Town, Florida on January 17th so don't miss it because I want to see all of your beautiful faces!"

I grin into the expensive camera in front of me and then continue speaking as I hold up a drawing that somebody sent me of my face that they drew with colored pencil and it was really impressive.

"On another note, I want to thank everybody for sending me all of this wonderful artwork. They are all going onto my Wall of Awesome Fan Work right behind my back over there. I will look at every single thing that you send me at the PO box posted below in the info box. So, we talked about Chris and art which means that the only other thing that I need to tell you is that my lovely behind-the-scenes guy that you all know and love, Elliot, is going to be hanging out with me all week so that we can shoot a new video for you guys that will be posted on Tuesday of next week and that's all I have for this little update video. If you have any suggestions on covers that I should do next, go ahead and throw those into the comments section or you can tweet them to me like always. While you're at it, you can follow me with the link that is below. So that's definitely everything and I will see all of your lovely faces on the 17th. Bye for now!"

I lean forward and turn off the camera that's standing in front of me before running my fingers through my hair and then I pack up my tripod before plugging my camera into my laptop to import the video that I just made so that I can edit it and then I'll post it to YouTube like I do with all of my videos.

Well, most of the time, Elliot will edit my videos but because this one is pretty short and it's not an actual song, I can manage it. I met Elliot sophomore year when I decided that I should try doing music videos so I went to the AV club because they're good with technology and stuff and Elliot was the best video guy that they had. He helped me pick out a good camera and he helps me make my music videos and he edits them too so he's really amazing. He's also pretty much my best friend because we spend so much time together and everything and usually, he's here with me when I film my videos but today is Friday and on Fridays, he has work at his mom's diner along with Tuesdays.

When the video is posted, I close my laptop and go downstairs to where my mom is working at the dining room table like she usually is when she's at home and my dad is at work like he always is.

"Jensen, can you do me a favor and go get your sister? It's time for gymnastics practice," My mom asks me when I walk into the room with plans of making some food for me to eat because I'm hungry but that will obviously have to wait.

"Where is she?" I ask with a sigh of longing for something to eat. I don't eat at lunch because I usually spend my lunch hours in the AV room with

Elliot hanging out with his computer geek-like friends so I haven't eaten all day. I've never been a fan of lunch rooms to be honest. For the most part, I've recovered from my terrible freshman year but my lunch room PTSD still stands strong.

"Out back with Sara," She tells me without even looking up from her computer.

"Sure thing," I confirm, going towards the backdoor. I open it up and see that my backyard is empty so I look over to our neighbor's yard (Sara's yard) and see both ten year old girls playing around on the playground thing that the Spearses have. We have a trampoline in our yard and I think that the trampoline is so much cooler than some swings and a slide but whatever. Ten year olds are weird creatures.

"Kaitlynn!" I call my sister's name from our back porch but she doesn't hear me so I groan and hop off of the few stairs that separate our wooded porch from the grass below and I start the short journey over to Sara's house. "Kaitlynn, it's time for gymnastics."

This time, she looks over at me from where she's swinging and then she giggles for a reason that I don't understand. "Jenny, can I go to Brooks Town with you?"

"What?" I wonder with a laugh. "Why do you want to go to Brooks Town?"

"Are you seriously asking that?" Sara shrieks. "Chris Warner... hello?"

"Oh, you guys want to meet Chris?" I ask them stupidly. "That's adorable but no, you cannot go to a concert with me. Mom would definitely say no to that."

"But we can both go and then it'll be the buddy system," Kaitlynn tells me, motioning towards Sara, who is on the swing beside her.

"So you want me to take two little girls to a concert and a meet and greet?" I clarify. "Do you expect me and Elliot to watch you? Because that's not going to happen."

Kaitlynn rolls her eyes at me. "We are not babies anymore, Jen. We don't need babysitters. We just need you to get us into the concert."

"Oh, sweetie, that's adorable," I tell her with a small laugh. "Now come on, you don't want to be late for gymnastics."

"I bet Beckett would take us," She huffs irritatedly but she still stops her swing by scuffing her sneakers on the dirt below her swing as she motions towards the house.

I turn to see Beckett sitting on the stairs up to their backdoor even though I hadn't noticed him before because I was facing the other way. He's looking down at his phone but when he hears his name, he looks up and his eyes land on me. I awkwardly look away and turn back to my sister because I don't like looking at him. I haven't spoken to Beckett Spears since sophomore year and I'd like to keep that streak alive. Because our moms and our sisters are best friends, we see each other a lot but I keep it my top priority to never be stuck in a conversation with him at all.

The bullying of freshman year was really awful but after I got help with self-defense from my cousin over the summer, they realized during sophomore year that I could fight back so they left me alone most of the time but I still got called names in the hallways sometimes. After I changed my YouTube name from CandyCane to JustJensen in the middle of sophomore year, things got even easier because people started recognizing me a lot in school. When Kevin graduated at the end of my sophomore year, my junior year was super easy and the only two people that still remembered my terrible past was Bethany and Kelly but from what I could tell, Beckett stopped hanging around them when Kevin graduated. I feel completely normal now though, since I'm a senior and both of those trolls are now gone too so I'm pretty much completely free.

"Well, he's not invited either so you can all grieve together. Let's go, I have stuff to do," I call to my sister as I turn around and start walking back towards our house.

She follows behind me but she's obviously upset that I won't take her to the Chris Warner concert with me. We live in Florida but Brooks View is still a three hour road trip that I will be making on Saturday with Elliot and thankfully, both of our parents have agreed to let us stay the night at a hotel that night so that'll be really fun, especially since I've been friends with Chris for a while but I've never actually met him.

"Go ahead and ask Mom," I tell my sister as we walk into the kitchen where my mom is shutting her laptop to get ready to take Kaitlynn to practice.

"Ask Mom what?" My mom wonders curiously.

"I know that you're going to say no," Katy sighs with a sad frown. "I just wanted to go to the Chris Warner concert."

"Oh, yeah you're right. I'm saying no," She confirms with a nod.

"But Jensen gets to go," She whines as she stomps her foot childishly.

"Jensen is seven and a half years older than you," My mom refutes. "And when you're seventeen, you can go to any concert in a four hour radius as much as you want as long as you pay for the tickets."

"Jensen isn't paying for her tickets," Katy says.

"Mine are free, Squirt," I tell her, going for the fridge to make myself a salami sandwich. "Have fun with gymnastics."

"Ugh. Whatever," She mutters. I make a mental note to ask Chris for an autograph or something for Kaitlynn because I do feel kind of bad that I get to go meet him but she doesn't.

After I have my sandwich made, I carry it upstairs and watch reruns of some MTV shows on TV. I open my laptop and start looking through some of the comments on my new video and I respond to some of them. I can't really respond to all of them because there's so many but I try my best. I check my twitter too and respond to some of the ones that are on there and I screen cap some of the questions that they ask me because I'll answer them in a FAQ video that I'll do later.

My phone rings after a while of me just sitting there and replying to stuff. On the caller ID, I see that it's Heather, who is another YouTube singer and we're pretty good friends. The thing is that she lives in New York and that's pretty far away from where I live down in Florida so we rarely ever get to actually hang out. We started talking when she messaged me last year to see if I wanted to do a duet with her because she was coming down to Florida for a family vacation and I eagerly accepted. I've done duets with a lot of YouTubers throughout my two and a half years of being pretty big but I'd say that I'm closest to Heather.

"Hello?" I answer the phone while managing my Tumblr account.

"Guess who's coming to Florida," She sings in my ear without even a hello back which is just how she is.

"You are?" I wonder with a small laugh.

"I am!" She confirms. "Well, I convinced my mom to let me fly down there but I do need a place to stay. You know, if you know any good places."

I know what she's hinting at so I just roll my eyes. "Of course you can stay with me. I'll ask my mom when she gets home but I'm sure she won't have a problem with it. When are you coming?"

"In three weeks, on the 3rd and I can stay for the weekend," She informs me. "Can I stay for the weekend?"

"Darling, you could stay forever if you didn't have a life up there in New York," I say with a laugh.

"And a strict mother," She adds. "But all is well because I'm going to Florida. I am so excited for this, I need a break from this freaking snow."

"I am also excited," I grin, pulling out my 12 Breeds of Puppies calendar for 2014 that my grandma got me for Christmas and I scribble down Heather's name on the 3rd of February and then draw a line through that weekend with an arrow so that I know that she's staying for those few days.

"What do you have planned for tomorrow?" She asks me randomly.

"Um, we're having a party thing to celebrate five million subscribers. It was my mom's idea and I'm not all for it but there was no way out of it," I explain. "Why do you ask?"

"Because I know that you just passed five million and I was curious as to what your mom was going to do. I really do love Mrs. Cane."

"She's embarrassing," I grumble.

"She's excited," Heather corrects me. "And congratulations, by the way."

"Thanks," I sigh. "I mean, it'll be fun, I guess, except that she'll invite Margaret and I love Margaret but that means that Beckett will probably be there too."

"And Beckett is your neighbor that you don't like?" She wonders.

"Correct. The neighbor that used to make my life hell. It'll just be awkward and I don't want him to be there. My mom will probably make me sing too and she just doesn't understand how much I do not like this kid."

"You sound like a pre-teen right now," She laughs. "Your mom is embarrassing... she just doesn't understand. You better love your mother, missy."

"I do love my mom, she's amazing, she's just difficult sometimes," I sigh. "Anyway, I'll call you back tonight when I get a response from my mom but I wouldn't be too worried about that. She loves you so she won't have an issue with you staying here at all."

"Good," She chirps. "Because I already bought my plane ticket. Au revoir!"

I'm about to say goodbye but she hangs up before I can so I just put my phone down on my desk beside my laptop and continue to fish through my Twitter, Tumblr, and Youtube news feeds. I try to respond to as many comments and asks that I get because I don't want people to feel like I'm ignoring them or anything but it's also just really hard and it takes a lot of time and there's really only so many ways that you can say 'thank you' without sounding like a broken record.

The things that I get the most though, are letters from aspiring singers and songwriters. Thanks to the cover I did of Chris Warner's video years ago, people started asking me to do it for them. If I liked their song, I'd learn it on my guitar and play a cover of it while leaving all of their info in the info section of the video and then they will light up into the music industry. It's an intense amount of pressure on my part because if I don't do a cover of somebody's song then their dreams might not come true. That's actually what I'm known for now, doing covers of people that aren't actually famous and then turning them famous.

Because I'm home alone, I'm about to blast my music and maybe dance stupidly around my room because that's what I do when I'm bored but before I can do that, my mom kills my plans by texting me and telling me that I should start getting the backyard ready for the party that we're throwing tomorrow. I think she's just throwing this party because she likes to do this sort of thing because she knows that I don't find it necessary to have a party just to celebrate my amount of subscribers. Although, I do find this accomplishment completely amazing, I don't find it something that I want to brag about so blatantly.

However, my mom is excited about it and I know that if I don't go into the backyard and prepare things for tomorrow, I'll get a lecture on how she's doing this for me and how ungrateful I am and she'll just get very irritated and then I'll get very annoyed.

I let out a long sigh and then go downstairs to the large backyard. My dad hires somebody to mow the lawn every week because he doesn't trust me to do it with all of those blades going at such a fast speed and whatnot and my parents are too busy most of the time. Anyway, the grass is already cut so really, the only thing that I need to do is set up the speakers on the back porch so that when music plays, everyone will be able to hear it. I mean, it's not like a rager or anything, it's mostly just going to be my mom's friends because there is nothing that my mom loves more than showing off her kids. But there will be music so we need the speakers to be set up.

Nobody is better with technology than Elliot though, so as I'm lugging the two heavy speakers onto the backyard from our garage, I have my phone wedged between my cheek and my shoulder, waiting for him to pick up.

"You do realize that I'm at work, right?" He wonders as he answers the phone.

"Your mom is your boss, Elliot," I remind him with a laugh. "I don't think that she's going to fire you over answering your phone. Especially when it's me. Your mom loves me."

"She'll still yell at me," He defends. "What's up?"

"I need your nerdy brain to help hook up the stereo for tomorrow," I inform him. "When do you get off of work?"

"I get off at eight. You mean for the party tomorrow? Am I invited to that?" He wonders.

"Of course you're invited to that and it's exactly what I'm talking about. Also, you're muscly arms will come in handy with these freaking speakers because they weigh a ton. I don't understand why you have muscles considering you are lazier than a bag of rocks and it's really not fair, but I need to take advantage of your terribly wonderful metabolism."

"Don't hurt yourself, Jen," He laughs on the other end. "I'll be over at eight but it's only because I feel sorry for you."

"You love me!" I call into the phone as I eventually get the first speaker onto the porch. My arms are noodles now though, so I plop down on the wooden deck and decide that it's time for a break because I cannot deal with too much physical activity at one time. "And if you maybe teach me how to hook up this sound stuff, you won't have to do it for me anymore."

I hear him laugh again and that makes me smile. "I don't mind doing it. And I've tried to teach you but your attention span is world breakingly short when it comes to this stuff."

"Yeah, because it's hard," I explain to him. "And you're super-good at it."

"Sure, well I have to go before my mom catches me on the phone so I'll see you tonight and there better be pizza," Elliot tells me.

"Okay, I will order pizza even though you work at a diner you lazy pig," I joke as I stand up from the wooden porch and jump from the porch to the grass, skipping all four stairs.

"Good," He chirps. "Goodbye."

"Goodbye," I say before slipping my flip flops off of my feet and jumping up onto the trampoline that's in my backyard. My mom won't be too happy when she gets home and nothing is done but I think she'll feel better about it when I tell her that Elliot is coming over to fix everything. And then she'll get upset again when I tell her that she doesn't get any pizza.

Chapter 3

"I really don't want to do this," I whine to Elliot the next day.

"I know you don't," He laughs. "But you have to."

"Why?"

"Because your mother said so," He teases me. "So you have to do it."

"That's dumb," I inform him. "I don't really enjoy having conversations with my mother's friends who just ask me the stupidest questions all of the time."

"At least they're nice, Jen," He says as I slip my light pink heels onto my feet and I stand up. I used to detest heels but after I realized that kind of being in the public eye is dependent on image, I sucked it up and now I don't mind them so much. Now, I'm ready to go downstairs and face the party in my honor which makes it incredibly ironic that I really do not want to go down there. "It'll be fine."

We walk downstairs and out to the backyard where everybody has already congregated but we stay on the patio beside the long table of finger foods to stay out of the way of all of the adults.

"You should probably go say hi to people, you know," Elliot informs me as he takes one of the boiled eggs from the platter and starts eating it. "It is your party whether you like it or not."

"I'm not as polite as you, El," I tell him. "If people want to say hi to me then they can come over and say hi to me. I do not want this party to happen because my mom's friends are-"

"Talk quieter."

"Are really boring," I whisper. "I mean, they're nice, but we should be shooting a music video right now."

"I think you'll survive, Jensen, I promise."

"I guess so," I sigh. "At least my mom hired a good caterer."

"That's the spirit," He laughs. "It probably won't last all that long either."

"That's probably right," I concede, looking out at the crowd of people in my backyard. When my eyes land on Beckett standing beside his mother, pretending to be engaged in a conversation that Margaret is having with one of my mom's other friends, I make an unpleasant face and look at Elliot.

"What's the matter now?" He asks me with a laugh.

I point in Beckett's direction without an explanation. "I was hoping that he wasn't coming."

Elliot looks over and frowns as well when he sees Beckett. "Man, I really don't like that guy."

"I know that you really don't like that guy," I mumble. Elliot knows about my ugly history with Beckett and his dumb friends and he's also gone to my school all four years too so he saw firsthand some of the stuff that Beckett and Kevin had done to me. Since Elliot is so protective of me (and I'm protective of him too), it's just natural that he isn't Beckett's number one fan. "I'm not a fan either."

"Why would he even come?" He asks rhetorically.

"Be nice," I warn my best friend. "If we have to talk to him, just be nice."

"Yeah," He sighs with an eye roll.

"Now who's being a party pooper?" I tease him with a small laugh. "Come on, let's go jump on the trampoline."

"Don't you think your mom will want you to talk to people?" Elliot wonders even as I loop my arm through the crook of his elbow and pull him down and off of the patio towards the trampoline that is currently vacant. I'm wearing pink floral shorts and a lacy white tank top so when I take my heels off, I can jump freely without a problem.

"Probably," I shrug. "But we can jump until that time comes."

Elliot lets me take him over to the trampoline and we actually get five minutes of jumping randomly before my mom walks over with Margaret and (no surprise but a lot of disappointment) Beckett. Kaitlynn and Sara are sitting in the grass near the patio playing with something that I can't make out but usually when I'm this close to Beckett, it's because we're watching our little sisters and they give us a distraction so that we don't have to talk to each other but this is super awkward, especially because I know that Elliot really hates the guy for what he did to me freshman year and both of our mothers are incredibly oblivious to everything. I mean, my mom knows that I had trouble at the beginning of high school but she doesn't know that her best friend's son was part of it all.

"Hello, Elliot," My mom chirps as both me and Elliot stop jumping but we don't get off of the high trampoline. "Jensen, why don't you come down here and mingle? Everyone is here for you, you know."

"Okay," I mumble. "But they're your friends, Mom, I don't know what to say to them. I really cannot hold a conversation with people, especially when that conversation will be about me."

"You know everyone at this party," She reminds me with an eye roll. "And they're excited for you so go say hi."

"Alrighty then," I sigh, hopping off of the trampoline right before Elliot does the same.

"Congratulations, Jensen," Margaret says before I walk away to go find somebody to talk to in the mix of people. She pulls me into a slightly expected hug before pulling away with a grin. "Five million is a super huge accomplishment."

I smile at her softly. "Thank you, Mrs. Spears."

"How are you, Elliot?" Margaret wonders, looking over at him and it's kind of humorous, because Elliot wasn't expected to be brought into the conversation so he kind of jumps a little at the mention of his own name.

"Oh, I'm good, thanks," He replies politely.

"Are you two still 'just friends'?" She asks, motioning between me and Elliot.

I blush immediately and look down at my bare feet even though I know that she asks this question every time I talk to her with Elliot around, I still get embarrassed every time. "Yeah. Just friends."

"That's a shame," She sighs sadly and my mother nods in agreement.

Tell me about it, I think to myself before grabbing Elliot's elbow in my hand and pulling him away from my mom, Margaret, and Beckett. "Well, we're going to go mingle and whatnot. Thank you for coming, Mrs. Spears."

She says something behind us but I can't make it out before hurrying into the crowd of people in my backyard. I leave my heels by the trampoline just because I don't feel like putting them back on right now but I'll come back for them later.

"Why does she refuse to believe that we're not going to date?" Elliot wonders with an amused laugh as I lead him back over to the food table.

"She's a hopeless romantic," I supply with a shrug. "So is my mom, that's just how they are."

"Well, are you going to go talk to people?" He asks me. We're standing on the patio again because that's where the food is and I munch on some black olives, careful not to get the green ones because they taste like pee.

"No," I shake my head. "I'll just talk to them with the microphone."

"What do you mean?" He wonders.

I grin at him and go over to where the speaker is at the side of the patio and then I grab the microphone that's perched on top of the speaker, flipping it on. It catches everybody's attention because it lets out a rather loud screeching sound because it's so close to the speaker so I hurry over to the center of the patio to seize the screech and wait for everyone to look up at the stage. I figure that it's easier to just thank everybody at once instead of going around and thanking everybody individually so that's what I'm going to do.

"Hello, everybody," I greet into the microphone. "I just wanted to thank everybody for coming to celebrate with us. I have just passed five million subscribers on my YouTube channel and that's pretty huge so a big thanks to all of you because, even if you don't have a YouTube account to subscribe with, you're still here supporting me in your own way which really means a lot to both me and my family. And also, a big special thank you to my favorite nerd because he's always there for me and helping out with the computer stuff that I will never understand for the life of me." I wrap my arm around Elliot's neck and pull him close to my side so that everybody knows who I'm talking about and then I continue speaking.

"I mean, I think everybody knows that I had a super crappy start to high school. My freshman year was really terrible," For some reason, I find Beckett in the crowd and we make eye contact for an uncomfortably long amount of time. "Bullies are just terrible people but I was one of the fortunate ones that was able to get out. Not everybody can find a way out like I did. Anyway, my point is that I am so grateful for everyone- not just at this party, but around the globe- that promoted my YouTube channel because every subscriber and every view and like on my videos pushed me forward, out of that terrible place that I had been in for so long."

Everyone starts to cheer and I look away from Beckett to grin to all of the people in the yard as they applaud my totally made-on-the-spot speech.

"That was impressive," Elliot says from beside me with a small laugh. "Are you going to sing now?"

I shrug. "I guess so."

"I'll get off of here now then," He decides, hopping off of the patio to leave me up there by myself.

Looking out into the crowd, I can see that everyone is already expecting me to sing because they're all still looking up at the patio that I'm standing on, elevated in front of them. Elliot is standing by the stereo thing right in front of me but off of the patio so that he can start the music so I give him a thumbs up and then he nods, pressing the button that starts the background music for the song that I'm going to sing, which is Firework by Katie Perry. It's a little old and a little cheesy but it's still a cute song with a good message so I like to sing it when I'm in front of a live audience, which is rarely ever (thankfully).

After the song is over, I do a little bow while the guests applaud my small performance and then I hop off of the patio to join Elliot by the sound system as he shuts down all of the speakers and everything.

"Wasn't your best," Elliot shrugs teasingly.

I roll my eyes at him and shove his shoulder. "Shut up, I'm fabulous," I joke back.

"Yeah," He laughs and mimics me by rolling his eyes at me like I did to him. "Keep telling yourself that, Jen."

I stick my tongue out at him. "You are my best friend, you're supposed to boost my self-esteem, Elliot."

He wraps his arm around my shoulders and I rest my head on his shoulder as we walk. "No, I'm your best friend, I'm supposed to keep you humble and I do a great job at it, thank you."

"Jerk," I laugh. We approach my mom, who is standing with Margaret and Beckett.

"Jensen, your speech was absolutely beautiful," Margaret gushes.

"I didn't know that you were practicing a speech for today," My mom adds. "I'm impressed."

"I wasn't planning it," I say with a shrug. "I just felt like I should say something."

"What was your inspiration then?" Margaret asks me. "I would never be able to think up something like that so quickly."

"Oh, I ad lib most of my videos so I'm pretty used to it," I explain with a slight blush because, while I'm pretty good with addressing online compliments, I'm not so good at the face-to-face stuff.

"And I'm sure it's pretty easy for her to find inspiration with a great crowd like this one," Elliot says from beside me with his arm still around my shoulders. I can hear the malice in his voice as he speaks and I know that he's subtly referencing Beckett and how I talked about being bullied. Neither one of the adults get it but Beckett clears his throat and crosses his arms over his chest so I assume that he understood Elliot's meaning as well.

I can't hold back a small laugh as I softly elbow Elliot's side. "Now is not the time for your sass," I inform him, still giggling a little bit at his comment.

"You guys are adorable with your insiders and everything," My mom informs me and then Margaret eagerly nods, agreeing with my mother because they are forever trying to push me and Elliot into a relationship. They're not invasive or annoying or anything though, but they both fell in love when they were young and they both are pretty intent on keeping that streak alive with me.

"You guys are going to Brooks Town this weekend, aren't you?" Margaret wonders. "Is it just going to be you two?"

"Yes," I sigh. "But it's completely innocent, I can assure you. We'll be so busy meeting people, we probably won't even be talking to each other that much."

"The day will come, I'm telling you," My mom says more to Margaret than me or Elliot and I roll my eyes at her and her rambling on about this.

"Yeah, well we're going to go. Thanks again for coming, Margaret," I chirp, desperate to get away from my mom and her hopeless romantic best friend because this is seriously humiliating right now even though I'm sure Elliot is just laughing at them on the inside because he thinks that it's so funny.

"Isn't there somebody else you'd like to thank as well?" My mom wonders. I hope that she knows that she's incredibly un-subtle with her suggestion and to make it worse, she nudges her head in Beckett's direction.

I let out a sigh before forcing my gaze over to Beckett, who looks up at me when my mom says that and we make eye contact for the second time today and it's really uncomfortable. "Um, thanks for coming."

He gives me an expression that tells me it wasn't his decision- his mom made him come- but that was obvious to me this whole time because whenever we are in a room or gathering together, it's because our mothers force us to go and be in that room together. Especially if that gathering is specifically in honor of me. "Sure," He mumbles with a sigh of his own.

"Trampoline is open," Elliot announces from my side, obviously just as eager to get away from the situation as I am.

"Yes!" I cheer, taking his hand in mine as we race for the trampoline before somebody else can although, I'm sure nobody else here would even try to jump on it because they're all older and uninterested in this magnificent trampoline.

When we're alone on the trampoline, out of everybody's range of hearing, I start jumping and give my best friend a pointed look. "See? I told you that this party would suck."

He laughs and rolls his eyes. "Poor little celebrity."

"Yes," I agree jokingly with a laugh of my own. "Poor little me."

Chapter 4

"Elliot," I greet my friend on the phone.

"Yes, Jensen?" He sniffles.

"Why are you not at school?" I demand, standing in front of his locker which is usually where we meet up in the morning but he isn't there and that worries me. Elliot never misses school.

"Because I'm sick," He informs me, his voice noticeably nasally and weird. "I called myself out."

"But you'll be healthy again tomorrow, right?" I wonder frantically since tomorrow is Friday, the day that we leave for Brooks Town, to go to the Chris Warner concert which is on Saturday. He's the only one going with me and I can't go alone. Even if I could, my mom wouldn't let me. It's a two or three hour drive from here and then we're staying at a hotel for two nights as well.

"I don't think so," Elliot tells me. "My mom said that she thinks that I have mono or something so I have to go to the doctor later today to see what it is."

"But you were totally fine yesterday," I whine softly as I start to make my way to my first period class.

"I felt a little bit off yesterday," He corrects me. "I just woke up and it felt like the devil himself had forced his way into my skull and started to make a second hell or something."

"Okay, well I'm going to get off of the phone now so that you can go and get better literally over night because I need you on this road trip," I inform him. "Seriously, you chose the worst time ever to get sick, Elliot."

"It's nice to know that you're so concerned for me, Jen," He laughs in that painfully nasally voice that he has now that he's disgustingly sick.

"You know that I love you and I want you to get better too but seriously, if you were going to get sick, you could have done it literally any other weekend."

"I know. Mother Nature must have given this illness to me this weekend just to make your plans more difficult," He teases me. "I'll talk to you later."

"I expect frequent updates," I pipe before hanging up and going to class. I don't really have any other friends that I can ask to go with me on a two hour road trip so if he can't go... I don't know what I'll do. I have to go though. This is probably going to be my only chance to actually meet Chris and he was my first success story. I have to meet him!

I'm hoping for good news by the time that lunch comes around but the only text Elliot sends me is a text that confirms that it's what his mom thought- he has mono (but it wasn't from kissing, he claims). He doesn't have a girlfriend and he isn't the type of guy to mess around so I'm sure that it wasn't because of kissing, but I do tease him through text by asking about who he's been kissing.

I don't eat lunch during my lunch period, I usually go to the computer lab where Elliot's computer smart friends hang out during lunch and they're all pretty nice so I don't mind spending my lunch with them. It's a little bit weird since Elliot isn't there and he's kind of the cushion between me and his other friends, but they still invite me into the lab with a friendly welcome.

"Have you talked to Elliot?" Marcus asks me curiously as he is furiously searching a piece of code for one missed character that is apparently messing up the main function. I have no idea what that means so I just try not to pay attention to his screen. It's beginning to give me a headache, all of the dashes and colons and partial words and numbers.

I nod, sitting at the computer beside his but the only thing I do is check my email, which isn't nearly as cool as what he's doing. "He says that he has mono."

"Wait, but aren't you going to some concert tomorrow?" Gary, who is sitting on the other side of Marcus, wonders with raised eyebrows.

I nod again. "We're supposed to but if he's sick, I don't know. Do any of you fine gentleman care to take a weekend off and join me on a road trip?"

"There's a convention downtown this weekend and it only happens every two years," Marcus explains.

"Didn't think so," I laugh a completely humorless laugh. "I'm sure I'll figure something out in the next twenty-four hours though."

"I'm sure," Ian, who is sitting to my right, confirms with a nod. "You're pretty smart."

"Yeah," I snort with an eye roll. "Says the guy who can successfully hack pretty much any website out there. I'm not that smart."

"You're smart, just in other ways," He assure me with a crooked smile. "I'm sure you'll figure something out."

"Your confidence in me is refreshing," I mutter. "I'm just hoping that Elliot miraculously gets healthy overnight. I mean, maybe it's not even mono. It's just some illness that looks like mono but it's really only a twenty-four hour sickness. That can happen, right?"

"I don't think so," Gary shakes his head at me with a sympathetic frown. "Can't your mom take you?"

"She has to work," I say. "Anyway, enough about me. How's life with you guys?"

"Just the same as it was yesterday," Marcus tells me as he glares at his computer screen. "I still can't find the dang bug and I've gone through this thing about five times by now."

"I'm sure you'll figure it out."

"Where's Mom and Dad?" I ask my sister when I get home. My mom isn't in the house but her car is in the driveway so I know that she's here but she's just not inside. My dad is probably still at work though, because I didn't see his car at all.

Kaitlynn shrugs from the couch where she's watching reruns of The Jersey Shore which I think that she's too young to be watching at all but my mom lets her so I don't do anything about it. "I think Mom's out back with Margaret."

I make a bee line for the back door to go find my mom. Being the super problem solver that she is, I'm sure she'll be able to help me find a way past this Elliot Having Mono obstacle so that I can still go to the concert and to the signing. The signing that I have been promising my fans for about a month now. People are coming from all over the Eastern side of the country to see this concert and I might not even be there.

"Mom!" I call to her. She's sitting on the back porch with Margaret and they are both drinking some fancy alcoholic beverage, which is something that they do to relax sometimes- but only rarely.

"What is it, sweetie?" She wonders as I step onto the wooden patio and shut the door behind me.

"I have a major problem," I breathe. "Elliot is sick with mono and I don't think he'll be able to go tomorrow. Puh-lease tell me that you can think of a solution for this problem. I cannot miss out on this concert."

"Oh no, that's terrible," She sighs with a frown. "How's Elliot doing?"

"He has a super high temperature and his stomach feels like the Titanic sinking to the bottom of the ocean. I would go over there but he told me not to and he also said that if I tried, he would lock the doors so that I can't get in because he doesn't want me to get sick," I explain. "But I'm texting him just to make sure that he's okay. Anyway, can you take the weekend off or something? Please, Mom?"

"Honey, I don't think I can. We're supposed to be having this huge case coming in over the weekend. I would, Jen, but this just isn't something that I can miss."

"Then let me go alone," I plead desperately. "I promise, I can handle it. It's only a weekend, right? That's nothing, I'll be perfectly fine."

"You know that I won't let you do that. It's not that I don't trust you, I just don't trust other people," She explains apologetically. "There's nobody else that you can ask to go with you?"

"No," I sigh. "I've asked all of the people that I can."

"What about Beckett?" Margaret pipes from her chair, saying the first thing that she's said since I came out here. "Did you ask him?"

"Oh, Beckett! That's a good idea," My mom agrees with her friend as if they're totally oblivious to my and Beckett's mutual avoiding. I mean, I guess they are pretty oblivious to it though, because they always try to put us together in situations such as this one but usually, it's easier to get out of.

"Uh, no, I didn't ask him," I mumble. "I'm sure I'll figure something out."

"Beckett will go with you," Margaret tells me. "He doesn't have plans this weekend and I think it'll be good for you two to be forced together for three hours in a car together to finally get to know each other."

"Yes, that is wonderful. You should go ask Beckett," My mom nods enthusiastically. "I think it'd be fun for you two to spend that time together."

"But I thought you guys wanted me to end up with Elliot," I tease them with a small smile when in reality, I will not end up with either one of them but it's funny to tease them about it a little bit.

"We don't want you to date Beckett, we just want you two to be friends," My mom explains. "I mean, it'd be cute if you dated Beckett, don't get me wrong, but we are just simply asking you two to just talk to each other and try to be friends at least."

I try to think of a reason to say now that doesn't seem offensive towards Beckett. I have no idea how to get out of this without just flat out saying "No, I don't like Beckett" because that would be rude and I try my best to not be rude. I flounder for something to say, trying to think of somebody else that I can ask to go with me but for a semi-celebrity, I really don't have any real friends except for Elliot.

"I'll text him and have him come over here," Margaret suggests as she pulls her phone out.

I have to say something. If I don't say something right now then she really will call him over and then it'll all rely on him to say no. However, I really don't know what to say so I just helplessly watch as Margaret texts her son from the house beside ours and then about five minutes later, the backdoor opens and Beckett walks out, making his way over to my back porch. I'm leaning against the house with my arms crossed, obviously unhappy about this plan but trying not to let it show too much.

I notice Beckett send me a confused look, probably confused as to why I'm there on the porch, and then looks at his mom.

"Yeah, Mom?" He wonders.

"Do you have plans this weekend?" She asks me.

He shrugs and then shakes his head, which is dumb because I was really hoping that he'd nod and say that he's actually incredibly busy this week-end. I don't know which one is worse- taking this road trip with Beckett or not taking the road trip at all and disappointing a lot of my fans. "Not really. Why?"

"Great," She chirps. "Jensen needs a road trip buddy for the weekend and I think you'd be perfect for the job. Where is it that you need to go, Jen?"

"Uh, Brooks Town," I mumble as my cheeks turn red and I advert my gaze to the gray sky above us. There's no sign of rain but the sky is just kind of cloudy- that's just how it is a lot of the time during the winters here.

"Right, Brooks Town," She nods. "So get your bags packed- you leave tomorrow after school."

"All weekend?" Beckett wonders with raised eyebrows and I perk up, excited that he might have some kind of excuse to not be able to go. "I can't be gone all weekend."

"You just said you didn't have any plans," Margaret reminds him and I start hoping that he can talk himself out of having to go. Maybe I can talk my mom into letting me go by myself or maybe my dad can go. He's always working but maybe he can make an exception for me this time.

"Yeah, but-"

"Okay, well then you can forget about the cabin," She threatens him in her don't-mess-with-me voice.

"Mom," Beckett sighs to try and talk himself out of it again but the look she gives him just makes him roll his eyes and accept defeat. I can't help but glare at him for being such a quitter and not being able to talk himself out of this. "Fine. And what will we be doing in Brooks Town?"

"You can probably just hang out in the hotel the whole time," I finally speak up, biting my lip to refrain from sounding so grumpy about how terrible this situation has turned. I haven't been in a room alone with Beckett in... I don't even know how long but I'm sure that it can't end well. Whenever we're together, we have our parents to talk for us but I have no idea what's going to happen when we're in a car together and alone. Just thinking about it brings a bubble of anxiety burning in the bottom of my belly. "I'll be doing signings and stuff at the Arena. You can come if you want, I guess, but it'll probably be boring."

"Isn't there one more thing you'd like to add, Jen?" My mother urges me after taking a sip from her martini.

I sigh and close my eyes so that I can roll them without being noticed. "Thanks," I mumble before turning and going into the house. Kaitlynn is still sitting on the couch watching TV so I go into the kitchen and grab a snack before going upstairs into my room to make a video. I brush my hair and touch up my makeup just in case it has rubbed on my eyes during the day and then I set up my camera. Since Elliot is sick, I'll obviously make this video by myself and it's just going to be an announcement, so it'll be easy to make, I just have to edit out some parts and then make it one video and then post it. Elliot taught me how to make simple videos a while ago.

When I'm finally situated, I start recording and then grin into the camera. "Hello, you awesome people out there! This video is going to be really short but I just wanted to remind all of you Chris Warner fans out there that I'm going to be at the concert on Saturday night and before the show, I will be available for pictures and autographs. It is all completely free so even if you don't even go to the concert, you can come over and see me. I really don't bite and I love to see all of your beautiful faces. Now, the plans have changed- and by that, I mean my wonderful camera guy, Elliot, is now sick with mono and his replacement isn't up to par with the video equipment- so I probably won't be able to make any uploads while I'm away but I'll record some videos and make it all one video that I will post when I get back. To be honest, I'll probably ask Elliot do it when he gets all better. Anyway, wish me luck on this road trip that will probably end disastrously. Seriously, I can probably use all of the luck I can get."

Chapter 5

"You have to make sure that you take that medicine," I instruct. "And sleep a lot."

"Jensen," Elliot laughs in a painfully raspy voice. "I've already got a worried mother, I don't need another one."

With my phone wedged between my cheek and my shoulder, I tossed my small suitcase for the weekend into the trunk of Beckett's car. I don't know why I'm not driving but honestly, I think I like it better that he's driving because I can do some work on the way there. My car is pretty small too, so we'd be cramped in there for three whole hours and I think I'd lose my mind. "I just feel bad that I won't be here to make sure that you get better. Like when I was sick and you brought me soup."

"You had a cold, not mono," He reminds me. "It's completely different. Trust me, you do not want to be anywhere near me right now."

"Yeah, I know," I sigh as I step back so Beckett can put his suitcase in the trunk as well. We are both ready to go now but we have to wait for our mothers to come out and say goodbye to us before we can leave per their instructions. "But if you need any moral support for when you're throwing up or anything, just call me and put me on speaker. On my way home from school today, I left some soup on your porch, did you get that?"

"Yeah, I did," He laughs and then he coughs a lot and it sounds really painful. "Thanks. It was really good. You didn't have to do that though."

My mom and Margaret start walking towards us from my house along with Kaitlynn and Sara walking behind them as they giggle about something. "What can I say? I'm a good friend. Anyway, I think we're about to leave so I'll talk to you later. I won't call you tonight or anything because I don't want to wake you up if you're sleeping."

"Alright, have fun. And good luck with Beckett. Don't take his shit," Elliot warns me protectively.

"Please," I scoff. "I don't take anybody's shit. Feel better!" I hang up the phone just as all four of them approach us and my mom gives me a hug as if she won't see me for a year.

"I'll miss you," She tells me.

"Yeah, you know that we're only going to be gone for the weekend, right?" I tease her.

"Yeah, well I'm your mother so I will miss you. You better be good. Don't get arrested or kidnapped or murdered, okay?" She warns me with a warning look as if I could help any of those from happening. Well, maybe I could not get arrested but the other two are kind of out of my hands.

"Sure, I'll try my best," I nod anyway.

"And be nice to Beckett," She tells me, motioning towards Beckett, who is being lectured by his mom like I am with mine on the other side of the car and she's probably telling him something identical to what my mom is telling me.

"I'm always nice," I assure her with a sideways smile.

"Of course. And you have enough money? For food and gas and everything?"

I nod. "Yeah, I have everything."

"Good," She sighs and then pats Kaitlynn on the shoulder to get my sister's attention. "Katy, say goodbye to your sister."

"Bye," Kaitlynn mumbles from beside Mom. She's still really bitter about the fact that she isn't allowed to go with me to the Chris Warner concert. It's really not my fault though- my mom would never let her go with me without any adult supervision- so I don't know why she's upset with me. I'll get something autographed for her but that's really all I can do, I guess.

"Bye, Katy," I laugh at my unreasonable little sister.

"Okay, you two should get going. Have fun," Margaret chirps. I nod in agreement and then say one last goodbye to my mom and sister before getting in the passenger seat of the car with my small bag that has all of my music-related papers in it so that I can work on our way there. Beckett gets in the driver seat and then starts up the car as the awkward silence begins and, I suspect, will continue for a full three hours.

I pull my purple binder out of the bag that's decorated with a few pictures on the front. One of me and Kaitlynn, another one of me with Spencer Sparks, who is another singer who became famous after I did a cover of one of her songs and I met her last summer, and then two of me with Elliot. I open it up to the part where I have three music scores for three of the songs that I'm looking at doing next. They're all from people who emailed me, asking me to do their song, and I've narrowed it down to these three but I still have to choose by Tuesday, which is when I'll start practicing the song and then on Friday (if Elliot is feeling better) we'll start filming either a music video or just me singing it and then it'll be edited by Elliot and then it'll be posted on Tuesday so the whole thing is a week process after I choose a song.

Before I start working, I pull my phone out and put my ear buds in. Not only does it take away the awkward silence between me and Beckett, but I also have all three songs saved onto my phone. Along with the score, they also emailed me audio files of them singing their songs so I can listen to them and decide which one I want to cover.

The first one that I listen to is from a girl from Nebraska named Andrea who sings songs that are light and happy and they're pretty uplifting to listen to. The song that she sent me is a love song that she wrote and she also plays guitar for it. The lyrics are really cute:

How beautiful, to love like this,

In a world that will someday end.

We've all arrived here just to go away,

But I love this love every single day.

The second one is an alternative band from Ohio that has five members in the band and two lead singers, one boy and one girl. I explained to them that it'll sound different if I sang both parts because their songs have more depth when there's a guy and a girl singer so they emailed me a track that just has the guy's vocals so that I can add them to my track and it'll sound full. The song that they sent me is about a troubled girl and it's pretty sad, a major contradiction to the first song that I listened to. I think it's cool that it's in third person but the girl sings the chorus.

Guy:

And she's so lonely but she's not alone,

And she's so empty but the room is full.

And she's so sad with words unspoken,

Because darling, her heart was made to be broken.

Girl:

Yeah, my heart was made to be broken,

There must be a sign above my head.

It says, 'break this girl to pieces',

And they do it every damn time.

The third one is another girl and her name is Miranda and her song was about the loss of somebody due to the Army. It's really sad and she only sings it with a guitar so it makes it sound even sadder and more personal. She never specifies if it was her father, brother, or lover or somebody else who she's singing about but it feels really personal.

There is no warning or goodbye to be said,

Just a man in a suit with the bad news.

And I cry for every time that you bled,

In your camo green and cargo boots.

I'm so sorry and you deserved more,

Than a folded up flag and dust on the drawers.

This wasn't your fight, this wasn't your war,

Who were you even fighting for?

Who did you even die for?

As I'm listening to the three songs, I write down little notes on the scores for the songs so that I can make sure I remember some things that could change or that are really good. Hopefully, I'll be able to make a decision by the time that we get to the hotel. I keep making little notes, weighing the pros and cons of each song as I make a phone call. I know that it'll disrupt the silence in the car, but I figure that I should just keep working, despite the fact that Beckett is right beside me. It's been about twenty-five minutes already and I think we're doing a pretty great job so far. Anyway, I have to call Jencks's Technology which is a place that will rent out specific equipment that is too expensive to buy. Elliot usually makes this call but since he's sick, I guess I'll do it.

In the binder, I have a form with Jencks's number on it, so I flip to that paper and dial the number, keeping the headphones in so I don't have to hold the phone up to my ear, I can just sit it on the binder and it'll be fine since there's a speaker built into the hear buds.

"Jencks's Technology, how can I help you?" The voice on the other end answers the phone after a few moments.

Jencks is a pretty big corporation- nationwide, actually- so the people that I talk to are always different so I have to use my professional voice, which is annoying and which is another reason that Elliot makes these calls. This isn't something that can be done with a mom and pop place though because they have crappy equipment most of the time and they don't ship it to us for free.

"Yeah, I'd just like to confirm my order for this week on Tuesday," I explain. "The name is Jensen Cane."

"Okay, I'll look that up for you," The man chirps in a friendly voice.

"Thanks," I sigh as I turn to another page really quickly and right down that I've called this place so that I don't do it again later.

"Okay, Miss Cane, I have an order that is going to be shipped to you on Tuesday at seven P.M.. It says that you have two umbrella shades, a jib, a shotgun microphone, a shoulder support rig, a matte box, and a 4-socket adapter. Is that correct?"

"A rig? Are you sure?" I wonder, remembering that Elliot already has one of those. However, I look down at the form where Elliot has already highlighted everything that he ordered and I see that everything on the list was mentioned in the guy's list and Elliot highlighted the rig. However, something that is un-highlighted seems like something I want and, because we have a membership to this place, ordering something extra doesn't cost anything until we order over ten things at once. "Oh, yeah, you're right. Sorry. Can I actually add something too?"

"Of course. What would you like?"

"A warming filter please," I request.

"Alright, we can do that. Everything else seems good?"

"Yep," I confirm as I circle the warming filter on the list so that I don't forget that I ordered it. "Thank you."

"No problem. Have a good day, ma'am," He chirps before hanging up the phone.

After that call, I have to call Chris's person to figure out where I'm going to be before the show and when I need to be there.

"Tim Griffith," Chris's manager answers the phone as I turn back to the scores and continue making little notes on the paper to remember for consideration.

"Hey, Tim," I greet him. I've only spoken to Tim a few times but he seems like a nice guy and he insisted that we're on a first name basis, so I should call him Tim instead of Mr. Griffith. "It's Jensen Cane and Chris told me that I need to talk to you about the tent arrangements?"

"Yeah, great. Okay, so you are going to be at the East entrance of the arena," He informs me and then I scribble that down on an empty sheet of paper. "And we'd like you to be there by four. The concert starts at seven and the doors open at 6:30 and your booth will open at 4:30 so that gives you some time to get situated. After the concert, there's going to be an exclusive after party that you're invited to and you can bring your guest."

"That sounds awesome," I grin excitedly. "I'll be there. And I'll see you at 4 tomorrow."

"Awesome, see you then, Jensen," He chirps and then the conversation is over. That's enough phone calls for now so I start writing little things to remember and start drawing up plans of random things. After that, I start planning ideas for a music video for all three songs just to see which one I can create a better video for although that probably won't play a huge part in my decision.

"Do you want something to eat?" Beckett randomly asks me after a little while. I look up and see that he's pulling up to a McDonald's and I was so into my work that I didn't even notice it.

"Um, sure," I nod as I pull my wallet out of my bag.

"I'll pay," He says, pulling up to the speaker to place the order. "What do you want?"

"A twenty piece chicken nugget meal with a large fry and a sweet tea," I request, noticing how hungry I am since I haven't eaten since breakfast and I usually have an after school snack or something but today, we just put our stuff in the car, said goodbye, and then we were gone.

He repeats that into the microphone thing and then he gives his own order before pulling up to the first window to pay.

"Uh, thanks," I mutter quietly, obviously surprised at his offer to pay. If I was more polite, I probably would insist that I pay for my food but I'm not going to argue against getting free food- that just seems ridiculous to me. Like, of course I want free food.

"You're welcome," He states, awkwardly clearing his throat as he moves up to the second window and gets our food. Instead of driving off, we park in the parking lot to eat so that he doesn't have to eat and drive.

Without my ear buds in, the silence is killing me. I know that Beckett had the radio on when the car was on but now that the car is off and my ear buds are out, we are officially drowning in a stilled awkward silence. The strongest one that we've ever been in because usually, our parents are there, talking to each other so it's not really silent, but this one is absolutely silent. It's agonizing and before even ten minutes pass, words begin to bubble behind my lips and I know that I'm going to say something whether I like it or not. "So it wasn't my idea to make you come with me... just so you know."

He looks over at me as he eats a fry and I'm too embarrassed about breaking the silence to make eye contact with him so I look down to my lap. "Yeah, I kind of figured that. I don't mind it though."

"Sure," I scoff quietly as I continue to eat. "Well, I couldn't think of a reason to say no. Anyway, I know that you aren't doing this for me but thanks for coming."

"Did your mom tell you to tell me that?" He wonders, a slight smirk appearing on his lips.

"She may or may not have," I shrug vaguely and I can't help but laugh just a little bit. And then we fall back into another uncomfortable silence. After Beckett is finished eating, he gets back on the road while I continue to eat. When I'm done eating, I put my ear buds back in to deal with the awkward silence. The radio is on but the ear buds are an added measure to distance me from the awkwardness. I listen to one of my playlists while I fill out some more forms and work some more on the music video ideas.

Looking up at the clock, I see that we've been in the car for about two hours so we still have another hour to go and I'm getting bored. I still have to keep working on the music video plans though so I keep at it for a while and then I start practicing my autograph because I assume that I'll have to sign a lot of autographs tomorrow night.

My music is interrupted when my phone starts ringing so I push the green 'answer' button when I see that it is Heather. "Hey," I greet her.

"Hey you," She chirps.

"Hello," I sing. "What's up?"

"Okay, so I may or may not be at the Chris Warner concert tomorrow," She informs me.

"Well, I think you should make up your mind," I laugh. "It's coming up pretty soon."

"Funny," I can pretty much hear her eyes roll on the other end of the phone. "So yeah, I convinced my mom to let me fly down just for the concert tomorrow but I have to go back up to New York on Sunday. I honestly have no idea how I swung that but I think that she's a lot less uptight now that she's got a new boyfriend or something."

"Wow, that really is great. I'll text you tonight when I know my room number so that we can hang out before the concert. Your mom is incredible," I say with a small laugh.

"Amazing! I'll see you tomorrow then," She informs me. "Are you at your hotel yet?"

"No, I'm still on the way there," I inform her. "About an hour away probably."

"Oh, so are you with Elliot?" Heather wonders excitedly. "Tell him that I say hi!"

"It's not Elliot," I deny. "He has mono so I had to get a replacement."

"That stinks," She huffs. "Well, who's his replacement?"

"It's a long story and I will tell you later," I say when I realize that if I tell her that it's Beckett, she'll go on a rant about how much she hates him since she knows most of the stories from my gruesome freshman year and I don't feel like hearing a rant about Beckett while sitting right beside Beckett. That'd make this situation even weirder and I don't want that to happen. "Just text me when you get to the stadium and I'll try to get you into the after party."

"You got invited to the after party?!" She shrieks in excitement.

"Yeah," I laugh. "But I don't know if Chris will let me bring you though. He's really nice, so I'm sure he'll be okay with that but I should ask him first."

"Okay, just try your best because I really want to go," She teases. "I have to go now but I'll see you tomorrow!"

"Yeah, see you tomorrow," I confirm before hanging up and pulling my ear buds out of my ears and then I look down at the calendar and start moving some things around so that I can accommodate Elliot's mono so that he has enough time to rest and get better before he starts working on the video again. I doubt we'll be filming on Tuesday since Elliot is so sick. I think start jotting down ideas for a duet that I can do with Heather while she comes to visit for the weekend. We've always wanted to do a duet so this is our chance.

"You seem busy," Beckett speaks, trying to start a conversation for some reason but I'm not sure why. The radio is still on but it's quiet and not loud enough to make our silence not awkward now that I'm not on the phone anymore.

"Yeah, this stuff is a lot of work," I mumble as I erase filming from this week. All of that video equipment will have to wait until Elliot feels better. We can keep it for a month before there's an extra fine so we should be good, I hope. "Choosing a song and then turning it into a video and keeping up with all of the fans and everything."

"Well, if you're having trouble picking a song, can't you just pick one randomly?" He wonders from the seat beside mine.

"I could do that," I nod, pursing my lips and reminding myself to be as polite as I can possibly be. "But it's kind of a lot of pressure when you think about it. The two that I don't choose, their dreams probably won't come true. I am their only hope to make it out there and that's kind of a lot of weight to hold for me. I can't just randomly pick with their dreams on the line."

"Oh. Yeah, I never thought of that. Why do you do it if it's so much work then?" He continues to try and keep the conversation alive and I'm not sure if I'd prefer the silence or the awkward conversation. Either way, it's awkward.

"It's better than the alternative," I mutter.

"What would the alternative be?"

I bite my lip and close my eyes to hide them so that I can roll them without him noticing, which is a habit of mine, and then I try to decide what to say although I'm pretty sure I end up saying the wrong thing because my patience has dramatically thinned after that question that he just asked me. "Do you really have to ask me that?"

"What?" He wonders cluelessly.

This time, I don't even try to hide my eye roll as I feel word vomit coming up just like Cady when she told Aaron Samuels that Regina George was cheating on him. "You are the alternative. You and your friends. It was either work hard and change how people looked at me or continue to be your play toy for four whole years. The work is definitely worth it."

He doesn't say anything for a while and the awkward silence is back but ten times more awkward and then, after maybe ten minutes, he speaks up, "Sorry."

I don't know if he's just apologizing for bringing it up or if he's trying to start some deep conversation about how he's sorry for making my life a living hell for a year and a half with the help of the upperclassmen. Either way, I'm done with this conversation so I put my ear buds in and pretend not to hear him.

When we finally get to the hotel, I immediately get out of the car and stretch my legs and my back. Being in a car for exactly three hours and eleven minutes is not very fun- especially with Beckett as my companion. Once I'm done stretching, however, I realize something that makes this trip even more awkward than it already is: I ordered a room with just a king bed. I don't say anything to Beckett though because I'm hoping that I can convince the lady at the front desk to switch our room to one with two beds instead of one. I grab my bag from the trunk and Beckett does the same and then we make our way into the hotel. It's a really nice hotel because Chris is paying for it (he insisted no matter what I said) and he insisted on one of the nicer hotels in town that's just around the block from the arena.

"Hi," I chirp at the front desk. "We have reservations under Cane."

The lady smiles at me and then starts typing on her computer. "Yep, I have you here."

"Great, so is there a way that we could possibly switch to a room with two beds?" I ask her. "Or one with a pull out couch or something?"

She frowns apologetically at me and shakes her head. "Sorry, Ma'am. We're all booked for the rest of the weekend because of the Chris Warner concert. If an availability comes up, I will have somebody let you know."

"Thanks," I sigh as she hands me two room keys that actually look like credit cards with the hotel logo on it and then I turn away from the desk and head for the elevators, assuming that Beckett will follow me, which he does.

"You got a room with just one bed?" Beckett wonders as we get into the elevator and I push the button for level five, which is the level that our room is on.

"It wasn't a big deal when I thought Elliot was coming," I mutter and when he gives me a strange look, I decide to offer an explanation even though I know that I don't need to. "It was cheaper. If I wanted to have sex with my best friend, I wouldn't have to book a hotel room, I could do that just fine at home."

The elevator doors open on the fifth floor so I walk out and look at the signs posted on the beige walls that direct me to the rooms with numbers between 500 and 550, since our room is 534. In all honesty, I was right. If my mom found out that I hooked up with Elliot in our house, she'd be more ecstatic than angry. She'd buy me more condoms, put me on birth control, and tell me 'I told you so' about five hundred times but she wouldn't be angry at all. She'd probably celebrate. It's my dad that I'd be worried about.

"I mean, It's pretty obvious that you have a thing for him," He states as we walk down the hallway towards the room.

"A thing?" I echo with a laugh. "What would you know about my relationship with Elliot?"

"I know that you like him more than he likes you," Beckett counters and I'm not sure why he thinks that this conversation is a necessary one to be had, but it's absolutely not. "The way you act when you're around him, the way that you talk to him. Do you even try to hide it?"

I push the card into the slot by the door marked with the 534 with a little bit more force than necessary because this topic of conversation is invasive and infuriating and completely unnecessary. "I don't like him like that. I care about him but that's it. And even if I did like him, it's not really any of your business."

"You're right, it's not," He agrees. The room is pretty large, which is good. The bed sits across from a TV and beside the TV, there's a desk and to the left of the bed is where the bathroom is but unfortunately, there's no couch or anything to sleep on.

"Yeah, so tomorrow, I'm going to leave here a little before four to get up to the arena for a meet and greet and then the concert happens and then there's an after party. If your heart is intent on coming with me and sitting through two hours of me signing stuff and meeting people then you can come, I guess, but if not then you can just do whatever. Chris invited you to the after party so you can go to that if you want. It'll be in the ballroom downstairs and it starts at 9:30," I inform him as I toss my bag on the right side of the bed, closest to the bathroom. I'd rather share a bed with Beckett than sleep on the floor (besides, if he gets too close, I'll have an excuse to punch him in the face). I pull out my dress for tomorrow and hang it up so that it doesn't get wrinkled and then I pull my phone out and call my mom, telling her that we made it to the hotel room okay.

She tells me to be safe and to be nice to Beckett and I promise her that I will and then that's the end of the conversation. After I put my phone away, I pull my laptop out and connect it to the hotel's Wi-Fi before going to my YouTube channel and I read through some of the comments from my last video. I sit at the desk so that Beckett can sit on the bed and we don't have to be next to each other which makes this less awkward and it makes it even better that Beckett turns the TV on to the Sci-Fi channel to watch Sharknado. It's hard for me to not get distracted to watch it too because it's such a funny movie but I don't want Beckett to think that I'm into the same thing that he's into.

After about twenty minutes of me on my laptop and Beckett watching Sharknado, my phone starts ringing on the desk beside me. The caller ID tells me that it's Elliot, so I immediately answer it.

"Are you feeling better?" I chirp as my greeting into the phone.

"No," He grumbles in a miserable groan. "I feel a lot worse, actually."

"How long does mono usually last?" I wonder with my phone wedged between my shoulder and my cheek as I reply to a comment on the video.

"My mom said that it'll be two to four weeks," He mutters. "Anyway, let's not talk about my impending doom. Are you in Brooks Town now?"

"I am. We're in the hotel and everything," I inform him.

"And you haven't murdered Beckett yet?" He wonders in a painfully raspy voice.

"It's been okay," I sigh, not wanting to talk about it in front of Beckett because that'd just be weird. "I'll tell you about it later. You should drink some tea."

"I am drinking tea," He assures me and then coughs.

"Elliot, just listening to you makes my throat hurt," I tease him. "Please just go get some sleep or something. You sound like you're dying."

"Yeah, yeah," He mumbles. "I've been sleeping almost all day."

"Well fine then. While you're on the phone then, may I ask you why you ordered a rig from Jencks?"

"Oh, mine's broken. I can fix it once my head doesn't feel like a freaking volcano though. When does the order come in?"

"On Tuesday. It'll be waiting for you when you feel like you haven't swallowed all of Hawaii though," I assure him. "Now go and save what's left of your voice for when I have amazing details about the party for you tomorrow, okay?"

"Yeah, sure, Jen," He tries to laugh but it's just a breathy rasp and then he starts coughing. Without another word, he just hangs up, which makes me laugh a little bit. Poor guy. I've never had mono and the way Elliot's acting, I'm pretty thankful that I haven't.

"He seriously doesn't know that you like him?" Beckett wonders incredulously from behind me.

"No, he doesn't. For the last time, I do not like him like that. He's my best friend," I defend irritatedly without even turning around to face him as I respond to another comment. "I mean, if you want to tell him your stupid theory, you go right ahead. He hates your guts, he'd never believe you."

Chapter 6

Getting up the next morning is incredibly weird. I wasn't willing to sleep on the ground just to avoid sleeping in the same bed as Beckett and he didn't offer to sleep on the ground either so, as a result, we had to share the bed. When I wake up, we're thankfully on completely different sides of the bed and it helped that I ordered a second blanket so we didn't have to share one. I tried to make it as unawkward as possible but it was still pretty awkward. When dealing with Beckett, everything is always undoubtedly awkward.

I wake up first, which is another bonus, and looking at the time, it's only ten in the morning so I have a while before I have to get ready for the concert tonight. I want to take a shower before Beckett gets up though, so I go into the bathroom with my lounging clothes and my hair products to take a shower. Once I'm out of the shower, I brush my teeth and wrap my hair in a towel so that it doesn't drip everywhere and I put my clothes on, which is just some shorts and an old t-shirt because I don't want to put my concert dress on yet.

When I return to the bedroom, Beckett is still laying down but he's texting on his phone so he's obviously not sleeping anymore. I decide that I don't want to be in the same room as him when he's showering because, although I didn't really think about it while I was showering, I now realize that the proximity of him and me is way too close for one of us to be naked, even if there is a wall between us.

"I'm going to go get breakfast," I inform him. "Do you want anything?"

"Where are you going?" He glances over at me and then slowly sits up in the bed.

"There's an iHop across the street," I say, grabbing my bag from the chair that I left it on last night. I figure that since he paid for lunch yesterday, I'll just pay for breakfast today.

"Um, sure," He nods. "Anything without chocolate is fine."

I nod in response and then slip on my flip flops before leaving the hotel room, not forgetting my room key so that I don't get locked out or need Beckett to open the door for me. I walk across the street and have to wait half an hour to get my pancakes before I make my way back to the hotel room with two bags of to-go containers full of pancakes and bacon and little syrup packets.

As I skillfully put the key into the slot with both of my hands full, I quickly pull it back out and swing the door open to get into the room. Beckett is in there but he's not in bed anymore, he's on the phone with somebody and sitting down on the edge of the bed. I'm kind of surprised when I see that he's shirtless though.

I try not to stare- I really do- but as much as I dislike Beckett, I have to admit that he's really tan and really attractive. He's still talking on the phone though so even though he notices me come in, I don't think he realizes that it takes me a few long seconds to blink away from staring at his abs. I walk into the room completely and sit down on the opposite side of the bed as Beckett before sitting down his bag of food beside him.

"Alright, Mom," He says into the phone. "Yeah, I love you too, bye."

The TV is already on, so I just watch that and eat my pancakes. Once he hangs up the phone, he stands up and pulls a t-shirt out of his bag and slides it over his head before returning to the bed to eat his food.

"I got you blueberry," I say as I'm cutting up my apple cinnamon pancakes.

"Okay. Thanks."

And then we eat breakfast in silence as we watch reruns of Law & Order. It's still an awkward silence but at least the TV occupies my thoughts so that makes it better, I guess. I begin to wonder how we're going to survive all day until four in this room together with nothing to do and nothing to talk about. This may be the definition of hell.

After I'm done eating, I throw away all of my trash and then pull out my laptop after posting a selfie on Instagram that announces that I'm in Brooks Town, excited for the concert tonight.

On my laptop, I reply to a few comments from some of my videos and go through all of the social networking sites as well, retweeting and reblogging and liking things. Being famous on a social networking site means that I have to be in tune with all social networking. It's exhausting but it's interesting to hear from so many different people.

I make some coffee and sit back down on my side of the bed but the lapse of conversation is again becoming too much, so I begin talking without my brain's consent. "So do you know if you're going to go to the party tonight?"

Beckett looks up at me and seems to be thinking before his eyes flash with something that looks like realization. "Oh wow, that's smart."

"What's smart?" I wonder with a small laugh considering I have no idea what he's talking about.

"You don't really want me to go but this way, at least you can tell your mom that you tried, right?" He wonders with raised eyebrows. "So now, if I don't go, it looks bad on me and not you."

"I didn't think about that at all," I lie. "But it does seem pretty smart."

"Well, now I have to go," He tells me. "Because if I don't, then I'll get nagged."

"We need to have an intervention or something with our mothers," I suggest, only slightly joking. 'Something to make them realize that we're actually not friends."

"Yeah," He sighs in agreement and then pauses a little bit before asking, "Why don't you just tell your mom the truth?"

I stop typing on my laptop and look over at him and he's looking back at me curiously. "Because it would fucking kill her," I say. "She feels bad enough about the part that she does know, that it took her so long to find out. She'd just lose it if she found out that you were there. And then she'd tell your mom and it'd bring up a lot of crap that I've spent a very long time trying to forget."

He bites his lip and looks away. "I guess I didn't really think about that."

I stand up and go over to my bag where all of my makeup and stuff is and pull out my bag full of nail polish. "Yeah, well it's a good idea in theory but it'd just cause a lot of problems."

"I guess it would be really hard on my parents too," He adds.

"Yeah, I can imagine," I mumble softly as I pull out a deep red color and sit at the desk to start painting my nails just for something to do while I wait until it's time to start getting ready for tonight. "Which is why we have to put up with them trying to make us become friends. Just half of a year left though, and then it'll be over when we graduate. After putting up with it for three and a half years, I think we can suffer through another five months or so."

"That's the spirit," He jokes, which ends our small little conversation and I put all of my focus into making sure that I do a good job with painting my nails. We still have a forever while before it's time for me to leave and I really wish that I brought a bikini or something so that I could go swimming in the hotel pool but I really didn't think about it while I was packing. There's really nothing else to do around here while I wait though, so after I finish painting my fingernails, I text Elliot to see if he's awake but he doesn't respond so I assume he's not or he isn't with his phone so then I text Heather and she texts back that she's going to arrive early which is awesome so then I pretty much beg her to come hang out at the hotel room with me for a while, which would totally take away a lot of the awkwardness that's suffocating me right now, even with the TV on and even with me on my laptop.

Sure enough, just after noon, there's a knock on our hotel door. Beckett looks super confused because I didn't tell him that Heather was coming, but I jump up from the bed and squeal a little bit with excitement. Heather is a really good friend of mine but we rarely get to see each other in person, so this is really exciting for me to be able to see her.

I eagerly swing the door open and I'm immediately attacked by a squealing blonde girl and then I attack her back, wrapping my arms around her thin shoulders.

"You're not dressed yet," Heather states after we hug for a long few minutes and then she steps back and realizes my t-shirt and shorts. "Why aren't you dressed yet?"

"We have four hours," I remind her with a laugh. "Come on in, I should probably start getting ready soon though. I assume you want to do my hair?"

"Of course I'm going to do your hair," She scoffs, walking farther into the room and when her eyes land on Beckett, her eyes widen and then she grins. "Jen, who's your friend?"

"Um, yeah so that's the thing," I say slowly. Heather doesn't know what Beckett looks like but I've told her the stories of my freshman year, so she knows his name. I sit down on the bed as far away from Beckett as I can get, but close enough so that if Heather tries to attack, I can intervene before anybody gets seriously hurt. "When Elliot got sick, my mom helped me find a replacement and he was my last resort. So, um, Beckett, this is Heather and Heather, this is Beckett."

Heather's flirty grin turns into a gaping dropped jaw and narrowed eyes as she looks at Beckett, who still hasn't said anything this whole time. "The Beckett?" She wonders, looking over at me now.

I purse my lips awkwardly and then nod. "Yeah."

"Wait, what does 'The Beckett' mean?" Beckett finally speaks up. "Do you talk about me a lot?"

I let out a long sigh and roll my eyes. "No, I don't talk about you a lot."

"But she has told me about you," Heather informs him, preparing for a very long and very sassy rant about how terrible he is and how much she wants to ring his neck because Heather is viciously protective of her friends.

"Heather," I interrupt her before she can say anything else and then I go to the small empty closet that's across from the bathroom which is where I hung up my dress for the concert tonight so that it didn't get wrinkled too badly in my suit case. "You have to be nice. Back onto the subject at hand though, this is the dress that I'm going to wear."

It's white on the top with a light brown belt and below the belt, the dress flows in navy blue chiffon to just above my knees. It's a cute day dress that will be comfortable to be wearing all evening.

"Cute," She smiles, glancing apprehensively over at Beckett before turning her full attention to me and the dress. "Shoes?"

"Boots," I inform her. "No heels."

"Smart. But what about makeup?" She wonders. "Your makeup style makes me nervous sometimes."

"Just basic stuff," I shrug, walking over to my suitcase and pulling out my makeup bag. "Here- Investigate for yourself."

She starts emptying the contents of the bag onto the desk to approve of all of the makeup that I brought. "What's this?" She wonders, holding up a small tube of white cream.

"It's to hide this scar," I say, moving my bangs to reveal a long scar on my forehead, a little longer than half an inch wide. "I don't like to show it off in public," It's the scar that I got when I was running away from Beckett freshman year and he grabbed my bag which resulted in my head making hard contact with the lockers. It needed a few stitches and it left a nasty scar that I use makeup to cover up when I do events like this to meet fans just because I'm kind of self-conscious about it.

"Okay, so you only have a few hours to get ready. I'm going to go get lunch while you start and then when I get back, I'll do your hair," Heather explains. "Does that sound good?"

"Yeah, that sounds awesome," I confirm with a nod.

"Two large pepperoni pizzas," Heather decides before glancing over at Beckett and then back to me. "Does he like pepperoni?"

With a small laugh at the fact that Heather won't directly address him, I turn to look at him. "Hey, Beckett, do you like pepperoni on your pizza?"

He looks up from his phone and shrugs. "Sure."

"Yeah, that sounds good," I say. "You're the best, Heather."

She scoffs as she moves back towards the door. "Don't I know it."

When she leaves the room, I pull my hair up into a messy bun and then start to organize my array of complicated makeup. I don't want to get makeup on my dress since it's white and I could easily drop my lipstick or have eye shadow dust drop onto my chest at any time, so I stay in my t-shirt and shorts while I decide exactly how I want to put my makeup on.

"So how much did you tell your friend about me?" Beckett wonders from the bed as I finally start the makeup process which is start by pinning my hair away from the scar and covering it in a thin layer of the white cream. After it dries, I have to cover it with foundation and blush and then it'll be invisible.

"How much our mothers try to force us to be friends and how awkward it is," I explain. "I didn't have to tell her much more than that. She's friends with Elliot too, so he shared a lot more."

"So do all of your friends hate me?" He wonders with raised eyebrows.

"My only two close friends, yes," I nod. "More so Elliot than Heather."

"Does he like you back?" Beckett asks. "Because that's probably why he's so protective over you."

"He's so protective because he-" I stop myself when I realize that what I'm about to say is definitely not a good idea. Telling Beckett that Elliot is so protective because he was there at the beginning, during freshman year. We didn't know each other, but he went to our school so he saw how Beckett and his friends treated me every day. Of course, being a computer nerd, he got his own share of humility but it wasn't nearly as bad as how I was treated. I don't say any of that though because I think that it'd just make this whole trip even more awkward than it already is and bring up old, unwanted drama that doesn't need to be brought up.

"He what?" Beckett wonders as I stop mid-sentence.

"Nothing," I sigh, turning back to the mirror to see of the scar remover stuff is dry. Luckily, it is, so that gives me something to do instead of just sitting there doing nothing.

"You were saying something," He accuses me with a pointed look that I can see in the mirror. "What was it?"

"It's nothing," I say again, turning back to the mirror to check the makeup on my forehead to see if it's dry. It is, so I put most of my attention into doing my makeup and successfully hiding the scar.

"What's that?" Beckett randomly asks me after a few minutes of silence. I finish putting eyeliner on the eye that I'm working on and turn around to see what he's looking at, which oddly seems to be my belly.

"What?" I ask in confusion, looking down at my t-shirt that his ridden up my waist a little bit, showing some of my pale-ish skin between the shirt and my shorts and then the black ink that is etched into my skin there.

"Is that a tattoo?" He wonders almost incredulously.

I turn back around to continue with my makeup, careful to talk only when it won't mess up my steady hands. "Yeah."

"What does it say?"

To say that I'm surprised about Beckett's random interest in me would be an understatement. For the longest time, we've had a silent agreement to just not talk to each other and to avoid each other at all costs but now just because we have been basically forced into a hotel room together, he is acting like we're just normal acquaintances or something and it's weird. "It's a John Lennon lyric," I tell him, moving my shirt up a little bit more so that he can read the cursive black letters scrawled out on my side.

"Yeah we all shine on, like the moon, and the stars, and the sun," He reads it out loud. "It's nice."

"Thanks," I sigh, putting all of my attention back into my makeup as I try not to think too much about Beckett's unnecessary friendliness.

Soon after that, Heather returns to the room with pizza and Beckett successfully stays out of our way as we get ready for the concert tonight. Makeup, hair, outfits and all of that stuff that needs to be taken care of before I walk over to the arena to meet up with the people that will set me up in the booth for the signing.

Finally, after a long day of waiting, it's time to go over to the arena so I walk over there with Heather after politely saying goodbye to Beckett.

"You have much more patience than I do, my friend," Heather tells me on our way there. "I would have pounded him into the ground by now if I were you."

"I know," I chuckle. "He's doing me a favor by coming here with me so I should at least try to be nice to him. Really, it's fine. We mostly just avoid each other."

"Okay well if you want me to kick his ass, just say the word," She tells me and I don't doubt that she's completely serious.

With a small laugh, I wrap my arm around her shoulders. "That's why I love you, Heather."

Once we get to the arena, Heather disappears as I'm talking to one of the employees so I just assume that I'll see her later and we can meet up before the concert. She didn't want to go to the booth with me because she didn't want to "steal my thunder" as she said, which is nice of her, I guess, but I wouldn't have minded if she went to the booth with me. When I arrive at the booth with two security guards, there's already a long line of people-mostly teen girls and some parents. When they see me walk into the booth, they all erupt in excited screams which makes me grin from ear to ear. I mean, if there's hundreds of people screaming for you, I think it's almost impossible to not grin. I excitedly wave at all of them and then the security guard starts motioning for people to approach the table that separates me from the crowd.

Some of the girls are crying just because they're meeting me, which is kind of insane to me because I still don't consider myself famous or a celebrity or anything like that. I'm just a teenage girl who likes to make videos of myself singing. However, the girls that aren't crying are either jumping with excitement or taking a selfie with me. I see a few homemade t-shirts that have my name on them or something like "I love JustJensen!" or some kind of insider that I have on the show like my sign off saying and stuff like that.

A lot of the girls tell me that I'm their role model, which is another insane thing that I hear a lot because I never meant to be anybody's role model but apparently, the way that I stood up to my bullies really made an impression in a lot of girls, which is really amazing but also pretty surreal even though I've heard it a lot throughout the past few years.

After a few hours, I feel exhausted and my hand hurts from signing my name so many times and my head hurts from inhaling so much Sharpie but it's all worth it because talking to all of these girls who look up to me is really something that barely anybody ever gets to experience and I am incredibly lucky to be able to influence so many people in a positive way. I sound like a cliché right now but I can't help it. It's all true.

Once the concert is about to start, the security guards announce that I can't take anymore autographs so I wave goodbye to them as the guards lead me back into the building. Heather is waiting for me inside, so we go in and find our seats at the front of the arena, pretty close to the stage, and wait for the concert to begin.

I dance around with Heather some but I sit down for a lot of the concert because of my exhaustion from being outside meeting so many people. Like I said, it's totally worth it but it's still pretty exhausting. I listen to the music and I sing along and when my favorite songs come on, I'll stand up and dance with Heather but I really want to save my energy for the after party.

Once the concert is over, I walk with Heather back down the street to the hotel because the after party is in the ballroom downstairs.

"Chris said that he put you on the list," I tell Heather. "So you can go on in. I have to wait for Beckett because he's not on the list, he's just listed as my plus one."

"You're letting him into the party?" She asks incredulously. "Leave him in the dust, Jen. He's such an asshole."

"I had to invite him or my mom would yell at me," I explain. "And he had to accept or his mom would yell at him. We didn't have a choice."

"Fine," She sighs sadly as if I'm a lost cause or something. "Well, I'll go in then and I'll see you in there."

I nod and pull my phone out to see that it's 9:20 and I told Beckett to be down here at 9:30 so I'll probably have to wait here for ten minutes before he gets down here. The lobby of the hotel room is pretty big but it seems really crowded right now with all of the important people from the concert that are eager to attend the after party. The ballroom is already loud with people and it's still ten minutes from actually starting.

I find a bench near the ballroom doors, where there's a bouncer checking to make sure everybody who comes to the door is on the list, and I sit down to wait for Beckett.

"Jensen Cane?" I hear somebody say my name so I look up and see a girl who looks to be maybe fourteen standing in front of me, towering over me since I'm sitting on a bench.

I smile at her and nod. "Yeah, that's me."

"Wow," She breathes. "Hi. It's so amazing to meet you. You're seriously like, my idol. I love you so much."

I stand up because I feel like that's the polite thing to do and grin, "Thank you, that's so sweet."

"Can I ask you something?" She asks me, seeming pretty timid about whatever it is that she wants to ask me.

I nod. "Yeah, of course."

"Well, my name is Cassie and I have a blog- I was wondering if I could do a quick interview before the party. Please? It would honestly mean the world to me," She pleads.

"Sure, I have a few minutes," I tell her.

"Awesome," She grins, pulling out a thick purple notepad. "You were bullied, right? I remember hearing you say that sometimes in your videos, that you used to be bullied in school," The girl tells me, swiping some of her blonde hair out of her face.

I nod again. "Yeah, a few years ago, I was."

"Well, I was just wondering- and I know that this is totally personal so I understand if you don't want to tell me this- if you had ever considered suicide?" She rushes out that last part so fast that I hardly was able to hear her, but I made it out. "I'm asking because a lot of teenagers face similar problems and I think that you are the perfect role model for them. If you can survive this, then so can they and I think that they should hear that from you."

I sit back down and offer her the seat beside me on the bench, which she slowly takes. "Sometimes, I would think about it. I think a lot of people in this situation think about it. But I could always talk myself out of it because of my family that loves me very much. And then I would realize that if I did that- if I killed myself- then all of those jerks that made my life hell, they would win. It made me sick to think that after all of the hell that I'd been through, that they'd just win like that."

"But it's really hard," She tells me. "To think like that, not a lot of people can think like that."

"I know," I tell her honestly. "You just have to show them that you're better than them. Show them that their taunts and insults don't matter. I know it's hard but you can't give them what they want. They want you to be humiliated so just show them that you won't go down without a fight. You have to be strong."

"How bad was it for you?" She wonders, looking down at her notepad as she continues writing her notes.

I shrug. "Pretty bad. There were these guys who thought it was funny to throw me in mud or into the guys' locker room and then the girls would beat the crap out of me for no reason at all. I lived for a long time just being afraid. I was afraid to close my eyes 24/7, I was just living in fear and it was agonizing. But I never let them win. Sure, they could kick my butt physically but I never let them see me cry. And you need somebody to talk to. A therapist, a friend, a parent, you just need somebody."

She nods and keeps writing on her paper. "Okay, one more question. Do you know who that is?" She asks, pointing behind my shoulder.

I turn around to see what she's talking about and I see Becket standing there, leaning against the wall and looking down at me with an intense, unreadable look on his face. Turning back to the girl, I tell her, "Just a friend. I actually have to go now but it was nice meeting you."

"It was nice meeting you too. Thank you so much for your time," She tells me, standing up from the booth and scurrying away.

I purse my lips and turn towards Beckett, who obviously heard probably that whole thing, which makes things awkward. Well, even more awkward than they already were.

"Ready?" I ask him, deciding that the easiest way to avoid the awkwardness is to pretend like nothing ever happened.

He takes a minute to flounder for some type of response before he finally says, "That was an intense interview."

I shrug and adjust the front of my dress. "Most of them are like that. Anyway, let's go. I have people to find."

"It wasn't that bad," He says quietly, looking at me with a determined look on his face as if he's determined to believe that what he just said is true but he knows that it's not.

"Really? Which part of that wasn't true?" I hiss at him in irritation because I feel like he expects me to agree with him just so that he can feel better about himself, which is really crappy because it is not my job to sugar coat things for him like he's five years old. Like I owe him anything at all. "You know what? No, I'm not having this conversation with you. It was years ago- it's buried- and I've spent a lot of time burying it. I only answer questions like that for journalists and bloggers because I think that it could help other people but that doesn't mean that I want to get into it with you. Okay, so let's just get to the party."

He starts chewing on the inside of his bottom lip before silently walking past me towards the ballroom.

I tell the bouncer man my name and he lets us through and I immediately walk away from Beckett and he doesn't bother to follow me, which is fortunate because I don't want to be around him. I never want to be around him.

Chapter 7

"You're just going to give up like that?" Kelly wonders with raised eyebrows.

I sit up from where I've just been tossed via Kevin and Beckett into a mud puddle behind the bleachers at the football field. It had rained earlier today so it was really fresh and vast too (lucky me). "I don't consider it giving up, I look at it more as a passive resistance," I tell her. I can feel my anxiety peaking because I can just tell that today is going to be extra rough just by the look on Bethany's face. I suspect that Kevin and Bethany got in some sort of fight and they feel like it's an amazing idea to take out their anger on me. My heart is beating out of my chest but I keep telling myself to breath- it'll be over soon- never let them see you cry.

"Do you ever get tired of the bitchy comebacks?" Bethany snaps at me before stepping forward and angrily kicking my side, causing me to topple over again. I could have gotten up and tried to run but this time, they have really covered their basis and tied my ankles and wrists. I bite my tongue so that I don't cry out from the sharp pain but I can't hold back a small grunt.

"From you? Yeah, they do get kind of old," I reply sharply.

"Okay, I don't have time for this today," Kelly says, rolling her eyes as if beating the crap out of me is such an inconvenience to her. "Just kick her ass, Kevin."

"I don't hit girls," Kevin tells her with a glare before he bends down and shoves my shoulder so that I fall back into the mud yet again. My hair is soaked in the clumpy mud along with all of my clothes, my face. I'm lying in a puddle of mud so there is literally mud everywhere, including in my ears, eyes, nose, and my mouth. I think that I'm lucky that the puddle isn't deep enough for them to push my face under because with the way that they've been acting lately, I'm sure that they'd consider drowning me in it. "Although she is just begging for it."

"I am," I agree with him sarcastically. "It's my dream to get my nose broken by you, Kev."

It's Kelly's turn to get violent so she steps forward into the mud, grabs the collar of my shirt with her left hand and then throws her right fist into my jaw. "We weren't talking to you."

I want to say something else snappy but my jaw is throbbing and all I can do is groan in pain and remind myself to breath. Never let them see you cry.

"Where do you have to be right now?" Bethany hisses at Kelly. The water is filling my ears and swirling around a lot of sounds so I try to sit up but she just uses her foot to push me over by my shoulder and I'm down again.

"It's my brother's birthday," Kelly tells her. "Seriously, look at her- she looks even more pathetic than usual and it's depressing. I'm going home."

"I'm with Kelly on this one, Beth," Kevin adds with a long sigh as I focus on not swallowing any of the muddy water or any of the goop. "You're acting crazy right now."

"I'm not crazy!" Bethany screeches, again taking her anger out on me by kicking my side, sending water splashing everywhere. I let out an inhale so quickly that I squeak but they're barely even paying attention to me anymore so I don't think that they hear it. I don't think they see me start choking on the mud water either, which is somewhat fortunate, I guess. I make it a point not to cry though. Never.

"Please, Beth," Kevin scoffs. "The only thing more pathetic than the fucking dirt ball is you. So what if you have beef with her dad? This is stupid. I have mud on my jeans. I have a game tomorrow. I'm going home."

All I can think to do is breathe and try to pretend like the pain isn't there so I don't have any mind space to come up with something snappy or sarcastic remark and after all of the mud and the punching, I just feel deflated. But I don't cry.

I vaguely remember seeing Kevin and Kelly walking away but I don't care anymore, I'm just going to lay here until it's gone and then I'll walk home at a very agonizingly slow pace, but I'll make it. I always make it home. No matter what they do to me, I will always make it home at the end of the day.

There's too much muddy water in my ears to know what she's saying but I can see Bethany lean over me and she says something before she raises her fist to me. I can't help but flinch just before she slams it down on my nose. I don't hear it crack but it still hurts so bad that I wonder if it's broken. I don't know what a broken bone feels like, but I think that this might be how it feels.

And I'm so cold that I'm shivering in the inches of water that I'm lying in but I will never let her see me cry. I pinch my lips together with my teeth and look up just in time to see her fist coming at me again and then again and then again. She's screaming something but I can't hear her because of the water in my ears and the splashing is really loud and I think that there's a low hum coming from inside of me because of how cold it is and every time she hits me, I let out an involuntary yelp, but I do not cry. Never let them see you cry.

I wake up when Beckett has a grip on my arm and he's shaking me awake. I'm so startled that I let out a little yelp and jolt up in the bed, clutching my chest. I'm covered in a sheen of sweat and I'm struggling for breath as I look around the room, assuring myself that I'm okay. It was just a nightmare. Well, it was a flashback that came to me in a dream, as if experiencing that day just once wasn't good enough.

I remember it like it was yesterday- it was the worst day of my life. Bethany beat me to a pulp and I couldn't fight back because my hands were tied together and so were my ankles and she didn't stop until I blacked out. The next thing I remember is waking up on my porch, laying down in my soaked and stinky clothes in a puddle of my own blood and dripping mud water. That's how my family found me when they got home so that's the day that they found out about the bullying.

"Calm down, are you okay?" Beckett asks me.

I'm sure you can imagine how seeing his face right now doesn't make me feel any better about the situation. I cringe away from him and slide off of the bed, making a bee line for the bathroom. I lock myself in there until I can finally breathe regularly and then I turn the sink on and splash some water onto my face to calm me down. I sit on the toilet to gather my thoughts for a minute before I finally leave the bathroom again and as I walk through the room, I can feel Beckett's eyes on me.

"What's going on?" He wonders.

"Nothing," I say quickly, hating how shaky my voice is. I grab some sweat pants from my bag and slip them on over my shorts and then pull on my jacket before running my fingers through my hair.

"Jensen, where are you going?" Becket asks me with a tired yawn.

"Out," I supply vaguely. "I'm going to get coffee or something. I don't know, I just need some fresh air."

"Do you realize that it's three in the morning?"

I shrug and slip on my boots. Since we were at the party for a while, we didn't get back to the room until 12:30, so we haven't been asleep that long.

"iHop is open 24/7. Don't wait up," I say as I'm leaving the room with my purse in the crook of my elbow.

The iHop is completely empty except for a few truckers eating some pancakes so I'm quickly seated in a small booth and the waitress takes my order. I only order a coffee and it shows up pretty quickly but I still have to wait for it to cool down. I run my thumb along the rim of the mug, watching the steam leave the cup, as I try to get my mind off of that day because the nightmare won't stop echoing in my mind.

After waking up on the porch at my house, I remember hearing Katy scream my name and then I blacked out again and the next time I woke up, I was in the hospital. I remember my mom crying as I had to tell her that it was these kids at school and that it's been happening for a while. It was a few months after the incident with Beckett and the lockers but when I needed stiches for that, I told her that I'd just fallen at school but in the hospital, I told her what really happened only I left out names of course. She was so heart broken and I felt terrible. She took me out of school for a few weeks while I got better and then a few weeks later, the year was over so my mom flew us up north to see my cousin, who taught me a lot about self-defense and everything.

Beckett doesn't say anything, but I see him in my peripheral vision as he walks into the restaurant and walks over to the booth that I'm sitting in. He silently sits down across from me but he doesn't say anything.

"You didn't have to follow me," I say in a quiet voice.

"You can't just run around a strange town alone at three in the morning," Beckett tells me as if I'm crazy for even considering it.

I look up at him with a glare on my face. "Oh, and you're supposed to protect me? I'm as good as dead then."

He gives me a look of surprise but he doesn't respond and I'm pretty sure that's because he doesn't know how to. Especially since last night, I had told him that we were not to talk about it at all. "Jensen..." He trails off.

"What? Is that not fair?" I wonder with a quirked eyebrow.

"It was years ago," He reminds me in a low voice. The waitress comes by and he orders a marshmallow hot chocolate so she hurries away to bring it back for him.

"I still remember it," I snap at him. "I mean, we can make nice and drown in awkward silences all we want but it's still there. I still remember it."

"What do you want me to do?" Beckett asks me. "Do you want me to apologize or something?"

"Apologize?" I echo with raised eyebrows. "No, I definitely don't want you to apologize. I just want to drink my coffee and then go back to sleep."

"I mean... I don't know, maybe we should talk about it," He suggests softly. The waitress comes back, putting a hot chocolate in front Beckett and then hurrying away again.

"I don't want to talk about it," I tell him. "In about six hours, we're going to go back home and pretend like none of this happened, okay? We're not going to talk about anything."

"Do you have nightmares like that a lot?" He ignores my 'not talking about it' statement.

I roll my eyes at him and take another drink of my coffee. "No."

"Well, what was it about?" Beckett continues to prod but when he sees me glaring at him, he leans forward over the table. "Hey, I'm just trying to help here."

"What makes you think that I need your help?" I hiss. "If anything, you need my help. You just want me to talk about it so that you can tell yourself that you're doing better now. You're not the same person that you were at the beginning of high school. You just want to help me so that you can feel better about yourself and all of the shitty stuff that you've done. But I don't need your help. I'm completely fine. Like you said, it was years ago."

"Yeah, well I still remember it too," He replies, keeping steady eye contact with me.

Finally, I break and look down at my cup of coffee, taking another drink of it. "It was about that day in May. The 13th, I think it was."

His eyes flash with recognition and he leans back in his seat, as if distancing himself from the memory so I know that he knows exactly what I'm talking about. "Oh."

"I told my mother that I didn't remember anything after the first few blows, which is probably what she told your mom who probably told you, but I was just sparing her. I remember everything until I passed out. I thought that I was going to die."

"I wouldn't have let that happen," He says quickly.

"I don't believe that for a second," I tell him with a shake of my head. "But I don't want to talk about it. It's all in the past so it's useless to start digging up crap that happened three years ago."

"You think that I'd just let them kill you?" Beckett wonders incredulously as if that's the craziest idea ever.

"Why wouldn't I think that?" I refute. "You sat by and let them do just about everything else. And you know, you say 'them' like you weren't part of 'them'. It wasn't a 'them', it was a 'we'. Distancing yourself from it doesn't mean that you weren't actually part of it."

"I know that," He sighs.

"I don't know why you'd even want to distance yourself from it. You used to be so proud," I mutter sarcastically.

"I was never proud of that," He grumbles, his eyes glaring at me for a moment before looking back down at his coffee. "I never wanted to be a part of what they- we- did to you."

"That doesn't make anything better," I croak, deciding that we've taken a long enough trip down memory lane. Now, all I want is to just to back to sleep so that I can wake up again, back in the awkward silence of how we usually act. It's more comfortable than this. And then, I want to go home and talk to Elliot about everything that's happened and go back to normal. "Look, nothing will change what happened so let's just stop talking about it, okay?"

"Yeah, fine," He yawns. "We don't have to talk about it."

I purse my lips before taking another drink of my coffee and waving to the waitress for the bill. I don't respond to him because I don't know what else there is to say and apparently, Beckett is okay with that because he doesn't say anything either so we just sit there silently until the waitress returns with the bill and then we pay and leave (he pays for my coffee although I'm not sure why).

When we get back to the room, I'm tempted to sleep on the floor just to get away from him but I know that my back would be sore in the morning and it's not worth that, so I swallow a little of my pride and tuck myself in on my side of the big hotel bed. Beckett gets in on his side too and then flicks off the light, swallowing the room in darkness. I know that I'm going to cry- I can feel the tears heating up behind my eyes and they're so heavy that I can't just bat them away but luckily, it's dark and Beckett can't see me. A tsunami of tears is threatening to burst out of me right now so to stifle an unwanted sob, I shove my face into the pillow and face away from Beckett, hoping that he's already asleep although I seriously doubt that.

I'm sure that he hears me sniffle but if he does hear it, he pretends not to.

Quickly, I hiccup my way out of my silent sob fest and tell myself to suck it up, because I will never let him see me cry.

Chapter 8

A week later, everything is back to normal. Elliot is feeling better again and he's back to school and everything. Beckett is back to pretending like I don't exist and I eagerly return the favor. It's as if that weekend never happened, which is what I was really hoping for.

"Okay, so Heather is coming down next weekend and I think that we should do a video then," I say to Elliot as we're hanging out in my backyard after finishing the last shoot of the music video that I just finished. I decided to go with the band from Ohio and the video is going to turn out really well so we've decided that Elliot and I will start editing it tomorrow on Saturday, and just hang out for the rest of today.

"We just finished a video," Elliot reminds me with a laugh.

"I know that, but I don't ever get to see her and I've always wanted to do a video with her. Please, El?" I plead with him, jutting my bottom lip out like a two year old.

"Do you know what song you're going to do?" He wonders.

Grinning at him, I shake my head. "We're still discussing it."

"Alright, well we have to plan that one out fast if it's going to be next weekend," Elliot says. "We can worry about that on Monday."

"Good plan," I nod.

"Anyway, did I tell you that my grandma is making me go to her scrapbooking meet up on Wednesday?" He wonders with a small laugh as I slip my sneakers off of my feet and when Elliot sees me doing that, he does the same thing and we go over to the trampoline.

"No way," I say with a loud laugh. "How'd she get you to do that?"

"My mom is making me," He sighs. "My grandma needs somebody to help her carry in all of her pictures- she has boxes of them by the way- and since I'm the oldest and probably the strongest, I was elected for the job. It's basically a convention for scrapbooking. Jen. A convention."

"That sounds absolutely miserable," I say with another laugh, jumping up and down on the trampoline and trying to time my jumps with Elliot's so that he doesn't jump and then spring me all the way to the moon.

"Yeah, I mean, how much can one person possibly scrapbook?" He wonders rhetorically. "It's insane."

"Tell her that she should make a scrapbook of all of your baby pictures," I tell him with a teasing giggle. "Because I definitely want my own copy of that one."

"You're an awful human being," He scolds me. "The worst person on this whole planet, you don't even have a soul."

"A little dramatic there, El," I say. "I'm sure that you'll be fine. And look at it as a chance to spend time with your grandma, which is awesome because your grandma is so nice. I love Patty."

"You should come with us," Elliot offers.

I laugh at just the ridiculousness of that offer. "Definitely not going to happen but I appreciate your effort. I'll just be a text away the whole time though."

"Laughing your ass off."

"Of course," I agree with a laugh. "Nobody could possibly picture you sitting in a room full of middle-aged to elderly women cutting out little shapes on pink flowery paper and talking about hemorrhoids and menopause without laughing their ass off. It's impossible, it can't be done."

"Maybe it won't be that bad though," He says optimistically but I think he's trying more to convince himself of that instead of trying to convince me.

"Sure, buddy," I tease him. "Whatever you want to tell yourself."

"Okay, just shut up," He grumbles teasingly as he falls to the trampoline on his back and I follow suit so that my head is resting on his abdomen (I shamefully take a moment to admire how firm it is under my head and how I just want to turn around and lick his abs all day) as we take a break from jumping. "You're making it so much worse."

"Only because I love you," I sing.

"You don't act like it," He mumbles, lazily running his fingers through my hair.

"You'll get over it."

"Yeah, I'll get over it," He laughs. "But it's good that it's on Wednesday because you post your video on Wednesday so it'll give you all afternoon to do that without me there distracting you."

"But the people love you!" I exclaim with a laugh but I'm not kidding. The people who watch my videos really do love it when Elliot makes an appearance because he's so shy and adorable in front of the camera. "The Jelliot shippers will be so disappointed."

"Don't even use that word," He says and I can almost hear the grimace in his voice. "Jelliot is a myth created by your mother that feeds your fans' desire to believe in romance when there is none."

"Is it really that bad to believe in romance, El?" I ask him, trying not to sound affected by his words. He talks like Jelliot (Jensen and Elliot together) is just the craziest thing ever and it's never, not ever, going to happen. Over his dead body will he ever look at me like that.

"No," He admits. "But between you and me, it is. It's weird. You're like a sister to me."

Awesome.

"Right. Same," I mumble lamely.

"But I guess they don't really get that," He adds. "I still think it's weird."

"I think we'd make a cute couple," I tell him but I add a small laugh just to make it sound like I'm kidding. "You know, if we weren't so symbolically related."

"What constitutes as a cute couple?" He wonders.

"Jeez, Elliot," I say with a small laugh, looking up at the bright sky above us. Today really was a beautiful day. "Not everything is so explainable. You just look at two people and you just know if they're cute together or not. You just know."

"Well then I don't think that we'd make a cute couple," He decides.

I roll my eyes and do my best at not looking affected, which I do very well because I've been perfecting my act for the past six months. "You're biased."

"And you aren't?"

"Touché. I still think that you-"

"Asshole alert, eight o'clock," Elliot interrupts me, sitting up on the trampoline and effectively knocking my head off of his tummy. I sit up too, not really having a choice, and see Beckett walking from his house and in our direction.

I haven't talked to him since we got back from the road trip last weekend and I was kind of hoping that our mutual avoidance would go back to normal so I'm very disappointed to see him walking toward me right now.

"Have you seen Sara?" He asks me, avoiding any type of polite pleasantries and I'm relieved that this is about his sister and not about anything else.

I shake my head. "She's not here, Katy's at gymnastics practice."

"Okay," Beckett sighs. "Thanks."

I expect him to turn around and leave but he just stands there for a minute, glancing back and forth between Elliot and I. With an annoyed sigh, I say, "Is there anything else that you'd like?"

"Nope," He clears his throat and I might just be paranoid but it kind of sounds like he only clears his throat to hide a laugh. "That's it."

And then he turns around and walks back to his house, effectively ending the short conversation.

"Have I ever mentioned how much I hate that guy?" Elliot asks me.

"Only a few hundred times," I say back with a small laugh.

"Well, I really hate him."

"I'll add one more to the tally."

"Seriously. How does he just come over here and talk to you like nothing ever happened? Has he ever even apologized for what he did to you?" Elliot wonders, pretty annoyed at just the idea of Beckett's existence.

"Kind of, I guess. During the Brooks Town trip we kind of talked about it but not really," I shrug. "We're both over it though, El, it was three years ago."

"It's still so fucked up."

"More fucked up than Jelliot?" I ask him.

He pauses for a moment to think. "Even more fucked up than Jelliot. And that's really saying something."

"Yeah," I sigh. "It really is."

After a while, Elliot has to get home to finish some homework so we say our goodbyes for the day and he drives off to his house that's about a fifteen minute drive away from here. I stay outside for a little while longer before I go inside to follow Elliot's example and actually do my homework so that I don't have to worry about it during the weekend that lies in front of me. I'll be working on editing the video with Elliot tomorrow anyway so it'll just make my life easier if I get this homework done tonight.

Just before I go into my room, I hear some movement coming from down the hallway, which is alarming considering I'm home alone. I walk toward the sound, just like what any serial killer would want, until I'm in front of Katy's door. She's still at gymnastics though, so whoever is in her room isn't my little sister.

I swing the door open, knowing that if it's a serial killer, I'm already dead. However, it isn't a serial killer, it's Beckett's little sister, Sara.

"Sara!" I exclaim her name when I see that it's her. She jumps about a mile out of her skin and turns to look at me with her mouth hanging open.

"I thought you were outside," She mumbles.

"What are you doing here?" I ask her incredulously.

"I'm not stealing!" She insists quickly and then she sighs heavily and says, "Katy has the first season of Gossip Girl on DVD and I wanted to borrow it. She knows that I'm borrowing it, I already asked her. I swear that I'm not trying to steal it."

"Your brother was looking for you earlier. How long have you been here?" I wonder.

She shrugs meekly. "Well, I came for the DVD but then I saw her collection of Adventure Time stuffed animals and I had to take a minute to admire them. I'm sorry."

"It's fine," I say with a long sigh, motioning her out of the room. "But I've got to take you back to your house and you better pray that they haven't called the cops and filed a missing persons report."

"Okay," She grumbles, looking very apologetic as we walk together down the stairs so that we can get to her house. "You don't have to walk me over there. I know that you don't like Beckett."

"I have to explain what happened," I tell her. "I don't want them to think that I knew that you were over here, housing a fugitive or something. And what makes you think that I don't like your brother?"

"How about the fact that you don't like him? Please, Jensen, I'm ten. I'm not blind," The blonde little girl tells me with a roll of her eyes and a little scoff.

"I don't dislike him," I lie. "We just aren't friends is all."

"He watches your videos, you know," She tells me with a girlish grin as we walk across the grassy lawn between my house and her house. "Every single one of them."

"Really?" I ask her before I can even stop myself.

"Oh yeah," Her grin widens. "He denies it but I can hear him listening to them sometimes. I think that he wishes that you guys were friends. Or, you know, more than friends."

"That's disgusting. Both because you're ten and you shouldn't even know that 'more than friends' exists and also because we don't get along at all," I mutter before knocking on the back door of their house.

Sara giggles. "You're a bit goofy, Jensen. But really, don't tell Beckett that I told you that because he'd kill me."

"I won't tell him," I assure her just as the door swings open and Beckett is standing there with a curious and concerned look on his face.

"What did you tell her?" He wonders, looking at Sara.

"Nothing!" She says quickly, pushing past her brother and into the house. "You'll never catch me!"

Beckett turns to watch her run up the stairs and then turns back to me for an explanation.

"She was in Katy's room looking for something," I explain to him, hating that he was the one to answer the door. I'm so tired of running into him that I'm considering trying to convince my mother to move to Nevada. I'm not sure why Nevada but it's far away from Beckett. Just anywhere far away from Beckett because I'm so tired of running into him and it being incredibly awkward. "I didn't know she was in there but when I found her I brought her over."

"Thanks," He says. "I thought she went down to the park."

"Right. You're welcome," I say quickly before turning on my heels to leave.

"What'd she tell you?" He asks me before I can really get away.

"What?" I play dumb because it's my last resort panic mechanism.

"I heard her tell you not to tell me that she told you something," Beckett reminds me. "What was that?"

"Nothing," I say quickly although that's obviously not very believable but I don't know what else to say except for the truth, which I don't want to do. "It wasn't anything."

And then I'm turning to leave again and this time he doesn't stop me but after he closes the door, I can hear him yelling at his sister. "Sara! Get down here! What did you tell her?!"

I hurry back to my house but with what I just heard, it makes me wonder just how many secrets he has that he doesn't want me to know about. Of course, it's none of my business but I'm still curious. Like the fact that he watches my videos? That's not really something that I find to be believable but I don't think that Sara would have said it if it wasn't true.

No. Stop thinking about it. It doesn't matter. Beckett doesn't matter.

I'm not going to try to figure him out, he's just my stupid neighbor that I generally try to avoid at all costs. And nothing is going to change about that.

Chapter 9

"I have great news," Elliot tells me on Wednesday over the phone.

"You made a beautiful and memorable scrapbook at the scrapbooking convention?" I wonder teasingly as I push myself on the swing. Nobody is home at the Spears house so I decided to come get some fresh air and sit on one of the swings. Even if they were home, they wouldn't mind if I used their swings but the important part is that Beckett isn't there. His car is gone and all of the lights are off in the house.

"Well, yes, but that's not the great news," He says.

"Please tell me that you got me the baby scrapbook that I want so bad," I beg jokingly with a small laugh. "I will pay big bucks for that scrapbook."

"Still no," Elliot tells me. "I don't think that you'll believe it when I tell you."

"Alright, I can't guess. Tell me," I say, laughing at how excited he sounds.

"Okay, well when I went to the scrapbooking thing with my grandma tonight, I was helping my grandma out like I had been forced to do and then when we sat down, this girl sat down beside me with her mom. This girl, Jensen, is completely and utterly gorgeous. Like, it looks like somebody pulled her out of a Victoria Secret catalogue or something. So I'm sitting there, trying not to sound like an idiot and then she asks me if she can use my glue.

"So of course, I let her use the glue that was in front of me and then we started talking. Not only is she gorgeous but she's into all of this stuff that

I'm into. Video games and computers and all of that stuff that you think is too nerdy."

"I don't actually think it's too nerdy, El," I defend myself as I start to feel ping after ping of jealousy for this girl that is competing for Angel status. And every ping is stronger than the one before. It just keeps getting worse as he keeps talking. "I'm just really good at teasing you."

"I know," He assures me. "Anyway, the end of the story is me getting her number. And it wasn't even out of sympathy either, like she seemed legitimately into me, Jen. Isn't that so great?"

"That's... insane," I assure him, forcing myself to sound happy for him. I am happy for him, so happy. Over the moon, really. But it is insane because Elliot is so awkward when it comes to girls and he always starts fumbling over his words. He'd done it when I first approached him and asked him to help me with some video stuff. It took about a week for him to stop going red faced every time that we talked face to face.

"Right? I know. But she's so awesome," He gushes. "But I don't know when I should text her. Like, is tonight too early?"

"I don't know, El," I mutter quietly, trying not to let him hear how incredibly stupid I feel right now.

"Well, if it were you, when would you want the guy to text you?" If it were me? I'd be the happiest girl on earth right now. I wouldn't want him to wait at all, I wouldn't even wait for him to make a move because I know how nervous he gets. I'd drive over to his house and I'd kiss him like crazy. But it isn't me.

"Tomorrow, I think," I tell him. "What's her name?"

"Cara," Elliot says and I'm so fortunate that he is telling me this over the phone instead of coming over here to tell me face to face because it's hard enough to sound as ecstatic as I should be but it'd be nearly impossible to look ecstatic as well. I guess that I should count my blessings. "You'll love her."

He expects me to meet her? Of course he does, I'm his best friend, practically his sister. Not his hidden lover or whatever it is that I'd put in my own mind to make me believe that there was something more there. "I'm sure that I will," I say before I pull the phone away from my face quick enough to sniffle in silence and then put the phone back to my ear.

Oblivious to my emotional destruction, Elliot goes on to on about how Cara has been featured in film festivals and how they're not just films. They're activist movements against cosmetic animal testing. How cool? So cool. Incredible, really. I feel my chest caving in and I feel so... broken. I always knew that this day would come though, that he'd finally find the guts to ask a girl out and that it wouldn't be me. I'd known this whole time. I could have told him earlier about how I felt, but it just was never an option.

When I'd first grew a crush on Elliot, about four months ago just randomly out of the blue, I thought about telling him. But then my mom and Margaret had been teasing us about being a couple and he seemed so disgusted by the idea of it that I could just never tell him. I don't know how he would react, if he'd laugh or cringe or just never talk to me again. And I was never willing to find out.

"I'm going to ask her out but I'm just not sure when. We should talk for a while first, right?" Elliot wonders over the phone after he's done talking about how awesome she is. "What do you think?"

"Whatever you want to do, I'm sure she'll be okay with it," I assure him because I don't know what else to say with my mind hazing over like it's doing right now and I'm finding it harder and harder to really think straight.

"Of course, I'll wait until after this weekend because we'll probably spend the whole weekend filming with Heather and I'm not going to bail on you. Maybe next weekend. Do you think that's too soon?"

"No, next weekend is fine. You worry too much, El," I tell him, trying to force out a laugh but it's dry and awkward. I just hope that he doesn't notice.

"Well, you know me. This never happens," He says with a long sigh. "I'm just excited."

"I know. It's adorable."

"Oh, God," He groans. "You don't think that she thinks that I'm adorable, do you?"

"Of course not," I assure him quickly. "She probably thinks that you're handsome and charming in your own quirky way. She'll love you, Elliot. She'd be stupid not to."

"Okay," He sighs. "Maybe you're right."

"I'm always right," I remind him jokingly as I wipe a stupid tear from sliding off of my cheek bone.

"I know," He jokes. "Anyway, I've got some homework to get done before tomorrow so I'm going to go. I'll see you tomorrow?"

"See you tomorrow, El. I'm really happy for you," I say, kicking my feet from underneath of me so that I swing a little bit on the swing that I'm sitting on.

"Thanks, Jensen. I love you, you know," He tells me and I start to cry harder so I take a moment to try and sober up a bit before I respond.

"I love you too," I say quickly and then I hang up the phone before he can hear me crying. Although I'm not sure that he'd even realize that I'm crying even if I sniffled and sobbed into the receiver considering how over the moon he is with this girl and how distracted it makes him and also how naturally oblivious he is to that sort of thing.

I'm distracted by the phone call and my self-pity to realize that the house in front of me has started to come to life. I can tell that the kitchen light is on now and there's a few lights on upstairs too. I wonder how I didn't hear whoever came home pull into the driveway but I guess I was too distracted with my heartbreaking phone call with Elliot to realize that somebody had come home to the Spears' house.

I quickly put my phone in my jeans pocket and stand up from the swing. I feel a sense of mortification when I start to see the backdoor start to open just as I stand up and instead of staying there and facing whoever it is, thinking that it's either Margaret or her husband, Josh, I start taking off running to my house in fear of it being Beckett.

I notice, however, as I'm climbing the porch steps to get into the safety of my own house, that the only car in the driveway is Beckett's.

I get back to my room, passing both of my parents sitting in the living room watching TV, and start editing the video that I'd made today, which is what I was doing before Elliot had called and I went downstairs to talk to him.

It's a short video with me talking about Heather coming this weekend and Elliot being rid of his awful mono. I render the video and then post it to my channel before I start re-watching it and it starts to make me cry all over again because I look so happy in the video. I recorded it right after school today so I'm wearing the same blouse that I'm wearing now and my hair is in a fishtail braid down my back. I look so happy. So naïve to the storm that I have coming.

I shut my laptop, deciding that it's just upsetting me even more than I already am, and then turn on the TV that's in my room to watch a movie or something while I calm down. I'm not crying anymore but I want to get my mind off of what just happened outside with Elliot.

About ten minutes into watching the movie though, I realize that it isn't working as well as I had hoped so I decide to go for a run. I don't run that often because I'm generally a pretty lazy person when it comes to physical effort but tonight, I think that it'll help to get some fresh air without feeling suffocated in these walls.

I pull on a pair of black leggings and then some jogging shoes before changing into a tight razor back tank top and pulling my hair into a pony tail. With ear buds in my ears, I trot downstairs and both of my parents give me a strange look.

"What are you doing?" My dad asks me.

I shrug. "Just going for a jog."

"Right now?" My mom wonders. "It's dark outside, Jen."

"I'll be fine," I assure her.

"You never run," My dad reminds me.

"I'm running now," I respond with a sigh. "Getting some fresh air and all that. I won't be out long."

"Be careful," My mom warns me as I leave out the front door. I assure her that I'll be careful and then close the door behind me. I turn my music on, drowning out the world around me, as I jog down the driveway and then down the sidewalk. I pass the Spears home where Beckett's car is still the only one in the driveway so I'm pretty sure that he saw me crying on his swing set earlier, which is humiliating but I'm just going to ignore that and tell myself that it didn't happen. I have too many other things to worry about right now.

But I don't think about any of it now as I jog down the sidewalk, feeling the air hit my face and letting my feet hit the pavement with the beat of the song that's flooding my ears.

I don't know how I'm going to face Elliot tomorrow when he's talking my ear off about Cara some more. Or when he tells me that she agreed to go on a date with him. Or when he tells me about their first kiss, their first 'I love you', their first time in bed (which he will tell me about because he's a virgin and that'd be something that he'd tell me) and I'm going to have to be happy for him about it all. I'm his best friend, it's my job to be happy for him about this kind of stuff. I'll have to smile and laugh and tease him just like I normally would. As if it doesn't feel like it's ripping my insides apart.

I shake my head, telling myself not to think about it right now. I'm jogging, I'm peaceful. I look up and see the stars and I focus on their beauty for a while. They are so beautiful.

And I don't think about how pathetic I feel and I don't try to picture what this Cara girl looks like in my head. And I don't feel numbingly jealous of this girl that I don't even know.

I just stare at the stars and I run and I tell myself that everything will be okay.

Maybe now that I can see that Elliot is getting a girlfriend that there's really absolutely no chance for us and it'll help me move on. I'll get over Elliot once and for all and everything will just go back to normal. Everything will work out just fine.

The dark emptiness of the neighborhood is a bit creepy considering it's so dark and there's absolutely nobody else around and I'm a vulnerable teenage girl prone to bad luck. However, I'm not worried enough to turn back and go home. We live in a wealthy, calm neighborhood with security and everything so there's almost a zero crime rate. I highly doubt that pedophilic kidnappers/serial killers are going to be on the prowl on the exact night that I've decided to be athletic.

For a brief moment as I'm running, I suddenly want to keep running without turning to go around the block. To just go straight and to just keep going until I reach a highway or something and then to just keep going until I find a new town where there's no Elliot unintentionally tugging on my heart or a Beckett looming over me next door just by existing.

But then I mentally smack myself because that's such an ungrateful thought to have. My life isn't something to run away from, it isn't terrible. I have a best friend that loves me, I have parents and a sister that love me. I have my fans that love me (or at least moderately like me) and I have a nice house and I get nice grades. So I have an unrequited love. Boo hoo. I'll get over it. I have to.

When I get back to my house, I stop on the sidewalk in front of the house and then start walking up to the front door. I'm not ready to go back in there, to face reality again. But I can't jog anymore, my knees are wobbly and my lungs are starting to burn because I'm so out of shape. So I suck it up and head for the door. Just as I'm stepping into the grass, I see Beckett standing out front of his house but I ignore him until I realize that he's both looking at me and walking toward me.

I close my eyes and let out a long 'why me?' sigh of self-pity before pulling one of my ear buds out so that I can hear whatever he has to say and I also subconsciously wonder how sweaty I look right now, especially under the glaring street lights.

"Hey, I was just coming over to give this back," He says, holding out a thick DVD case.

I take it and look down at it, seeing that it's the Gossip Girl that Sara had taken on Friday. I wonder why Sara couldn't return it herself but refrain from asking. "Thanks," I say, still a bit out of breath as I turn around to start walking back to the door.

"Are you okay?" Beckett wonders before I've even taken one step toward the house. "I saw you earlier on the swings and you looked kind of messed up."

I flinched, not expecting him to bring that up. For so long, we've done so well with the avoidance thing. Even if we noticed something about each other, it was ignored. If I saw him fighting with a girlfriend in the front yard, I didn't ask him about it. If he saw me cursing out a camera on my porch because I couldn't get the shot right, he never talked about it. We avoid each other. It's what we do. And he's messing it all up.

"I'm fine," I mumble, not even trying to put any effort into convincing him that it's true. I don't care if he believes it or not, I just needed to say something so that I could get out of this conversation as quickly as possible. "Goodnight."

I don't leave any room for discussion as I turn on my heels and hurry into my house as Beckett glances back at me once and then turns back to his own house.

"How was your jog?" My father asks me when I get inside.

I don't even stop as I go to the stairs and reply with. "Oh, it was just awesome," And then disappear upstairs.

Chapter 10

"HAVEN!" I screech when I see my New York friend coming out of the terminal looking very tired from her long flight from New York to Florida.

"JENSEN!" She grins, running toward me and then we're hugging. We rarely ever get to see each other in person so this is really exciting for both of us. She's one of the very few people that I know that can really relate to being a big YouTuber while also being in high school because most of us have already graduated. So it's cool to be able to talk to her about the struggles of balancing the two lives of being both a high schooler and a YouTuber.

"You look so much taller in person," I tell her jokingly as we walk toward the temporary parking lot that I had parked in to pick her up here. I wasn't allowed that far into the airport without a ticket, so I met her right outside of baggage claim to take her back to my house for the weekend.

"You look shorter," She fires back laughing. "And it's so hot down here. It's January for crying out loud, and I'm sweating."

"It's really not that hot," I tell her teasingly as we go outside. "It's actually kind of chilly outside."

"Shut up."

"I'm serious," I insist, motioning down to the black hoodie that I'm wearing.

"I can't believe you," She shakes her head at me in mock disappointment. "Anyway, tell me how you've been. Boyfriends, friends, any kind of drama at all that is just so crazy that you have to tell me in person?"

"Nope, nothing that exciting," I shake my head at her, thinking about Elliot in my mind but I don't want to tell her about that- I don't want to tell anybody about that. I just want to pretend like nothing is happening until I really believe it and then it all goes away. "What about you?"

"No," She laughs. "Between school and the internet, I'm not trying to make my life any more complicated by adding a boyfriend to the mix. YouTube is my boyfriend."

"That's a very good way of looking at things," I say with a small laugh. "Anyway, Elliot is going to be by the house tomorrow to start filming the collab. He's busy tonight though, so we can spend tonight just not thinking about the video."

"Elliot's busy?" She wonders with raised eyebrows. "How is Elliot busy? He has absolutely no life outside of hanging out with you, I thought."

"It used to be that way," I confirm with a long sigh. "Me and sometimes his techie friends, but he's got a date next weekend, so he's going shopping for something to wear."

"Really? A date. Wow, I really didn't see that one coming," She tells me as we get in my car to go back to my house. "I always kind of thought that you two would end up together."

"Yeah?"

"Yeah," She confirms. "I think that you'd be cute together. But anyway, why aren't you going shopping with him? Lord knows he needs the help."

I shrug. "He asked me to but I said no. I wanted to be here to come pick you up and I'm not the best for fashion advice anyway."

"Please tell me that he didn't take his mom."

"He went alone," I say, laughing as I back out of the large parking lot. "And he'll be fine. His fashion sense isn't that terrible. He's really excited about this date though, so I'm sure he's a nervous wreck right now, trying to find the perfect outfit."

"Why didn't he just wait until after you picked me up so that we could both go help him pick something out? Elliot nervous about a date sounds so amazing to me, I really want to see it in person."

"You'll see tomorrow," I assure her. "If you just say her name in front of him, he'll turn as red as a tomato."

"What is her name? Do you know this girl?"

I shake my head at her. "I haven't met her, but her name is Cara. She's apparently Victoria's Secret gorgeous."

"Wow," She breathes.

"Yep."

"Way to go, Elliot," Heather says with a wide grin. "I wish that I could meet the girl."

"I'll let you know how she is if I meet her," I tell Heather, wanting to talk about something else now because I can't hold up my nonchalance efforts for much longer. "Anyway, everybody's demanding a release date for the collaboration. I didn't even announce what song we're doing, have you?"

"Nope. Total secrecy," She says. "I like the mystery factor. I announced that we'd be doing a collab but that's literally it. No release date, song, not even a hint."

"It's turned into a big thing," I tell her. "My Twitter is blowing up with people wanting to know what's going on."

"I love it," She grins. "We're taking this world by storm."

"We're taking teenagers by storm, not the whole world."

"The teenagers are a pretty huge chunk of the world, I think," Heather defends and I just laugh at her. "So yeah, we're pretty awesome and I think that it should concern us that we enjoy putting all of our fans in pain."

"It isn't like we're torturing them," I defend. "It's called suspense."

"Either way, it's fun," She decides with a maniacal laugh. "I think that when we get to your house, we should practice the dance thing that we created so that we know that we've got it in sync before tomorrow. After just a few hours of working, we can hang out for a while though."

"That sounds good," I confirm with a nod.

And so that's what we do. It's a Friday afternoon- I'd left school an hour early to pick Heather up at the airport- and when we get back to my house, it's empty. I think Katy's over at Sara's house or something. We get dressed in work out-type clothes even though the dance that we made up isn't very athletic. We aren't professional dancers or anything, so it's not that great but it's cute. Anyway, I'm wearing yoga pants and a cropped top while Heather is wearing shorts and a tank top because it's just oh-so hot outside.

"So, that jerk is your neighbor, right?" Heather wonders when we get out back.

I nod with a quiet sigh. "Beckett, yeah, he lives there," I say, pointing to Beckett's house.

"Scummy."

"Not the whole house is scummy," I say, laughing. "His family is actually really nice."

"But his scum is so scummy that it covers the house in scum," Heather informs me with a disgusted look on her face. "I can smell it from here."

"You never told me that you were this weird," I fire at her teasingly.

"Oh, hush. Let's just get to work," She says, dramatically rolling her eyes at me before I plug my phone into a small speaker so that we can listen to the song as we do the dance. It's Primadonna by Marina and the Diamonds, which is a really catchy song and we both love Marina and the Diamonds, so it was pretty easy to agree on this song.

After about only five minutes of practicing, Katy and Sara appear out of Beckett's house and they start running over to my yard looking very excited.

"Hi, Heather!" Katy grins at my friend.

"Um. Hello, tiny person," Heather greets her, looking very confused.

"My sister, Katy. What are you doing?" I ask that last part to my sister, looking annoyed that she's over here now and not over there at Sara's house so that she's not bothering us.

"We just want to watch you guys," Sara interjects, staring at Heather. I wonder if she's a bit star struck to be meeting Heather because I know that my sister watches her videos and because the two girls do almost everything together, it's safe to assume that Sara watches them as well. "Just carry on like we're not even here."

"We can teach you guys the dance!" Heather exclaims excitedly.

"What? Why?" I wonder with raised eyebrows.

"Yes! Please? Oh, pretty please, Jensen?" Katy pleads with me, her eyes big and pleading and Sara actually juts her bottom lip out pleadingly like a pathetic puppy.

"I have an even better idea than that," Heather tells me with a wide grin and I can immediately tell what she's thinking, and I don't like that at all.

"No," I say quickly. "Absolutely not."

"Oh come on, it'll be fun," She insists but I just shake my head in distaste. "And it'll be so cute!"

"I don't like it."

"You'd make your little sister and her puny friend's dreams come true," She sings at me and I just roll my eyes at her.

"What are you guys talking about?" Katy wonders, looking very confused between Heather and I.

I let out a long sigh, not really believing that I'm agreeing to this because I've made it a firm rule to never do this at all ever. "Do you guys want to be in the video with us?"

"ARE YOU JOKING RIGHT NOW?" Katy shrieks at me and Sara looks like she's about to pass out right there in the grass.

I can't help but laugh a little bit at their reactions. "Yes, I'm serious. You better not make me regret it though."

"Oh my God. Oh my God. Sara, this is for real. This is real. THIS IS NOT A DRILL," She screams at her friend and both me and Heather start laughing at her as she starts fanning herself in the face.

"We don't have to do anything embarrassing, do we?" Sara wonders hesitantly. "You never let us in your videos, what's the catch?"

"The catch is that I'm here, and I am very convincing," Heather pipes. "Now, let's find something for you girls to wear."

"I know the perfect dress. I've had this planned for the past year, I have it all figured out. I have been waiting for this moment for so long, you have no idea," Katy starts to rant. "But Sara needs something too. What about that purple dress?"

"No. But I do have a few prospects. Come with me," Sara pipes, starting toward her house and then Katy follows her, waving us to come with them into Sara's house. I let out a quiet groan, hoping that Beckett isn't home, and follow them along with Heather.

"Don't touch anything or you'll get scummy," Heather whispers to me just as we enter the house. Sara and Katy start running through the kitchen and then into the living room where the stairs are that lead up to the second floor where Sara's room is.

"I thought that you were going over to Katy's house," I hear Beckett in the living room just before I step between the threshold between the living room and dining room, he looks up at me from the couch, looking incredibly surprised. "What's going on?"

"Beck, you aren't going to believe this," Sara says with a grin as I subtly elbow Heather beside me so that she doesn't give any snide comments like I know that she was about to do. She hisses at me but doesn't say anything, which I'm grateful for. "Jensen's going to let us be in her next video. Isn't that so great?!"

"Uh, yeah, I guess," He trails off, glancing over at me and Heather, who are awkwardly standing by the threshold of the living room waiting for Sara to stop talking to her brother so that we can go upstairs. "Did you ask Mom?"

"Not yet, but she'll be fine with it. This is a once in a lifetime opportunity, you know. Jensen has never let us be in a video before but HeyItsHeather is here and she talked Jensen into it. How long will it be until HeyItsHeather is going to be here again to convince Jensen to let us star in the video?"

"You aren't starring in the video," I interrupt with a shake of my head. "I said that you can be in it, not star in it. And you can just call her Heather."

"Well, let's go, children. We've got shenanigans to get into before nightfall that don't involve playing dress up with tiny people," Heather breaks up this awkward situation by pulling me by the elbow towards the stairs and urging Sara and Katy in front of us so that Sara can take us to her room.

Just as we're going up the stairs, Heather turns around to face Beckett an before I can censor her, she loudly whispers, "Scummy," And I slap her arm, pulling her faster up the stairs to avoid Beckett's reaction. This is going to be a long weekend.

"This is amazing," I say in awe as Elliot pulls into the huge driveway in front of us. We're now parked in front of a huge mansion of a house that's about half an hour away from my neighborhood for the music video. Since the song is about being a primadonna, I wanted it to be shot in front of a mansion so Elliot, working his magic, got us a mansion for the day to shoot the video. Well, it's more of his father's magic considering his father is a realtor and he knows the guy who owns this house. The guy rents it out most of the time but right now, he's in between rentals and he has a heart of gold so he's letting us film here for free. It looks so regal and amazing and I'm so excited to be able to film the video here.

"Yeah, it really is," Elliot breathes. "Remember not to actually touch anything that has the potential to be broken. If it breaks, you're paying for it."

"But if we don't break anything and leave everything in good condition, he'll let us come back and film here again?" I wonder hopefully, thinking of a million things that could be shot at this beautiful house and I've only seen the front of it.

"This. Is. INCREDIBLE." Katy says as she steps out of Beckett's car as he parks right behind Elliot. Because of all of the video equipment that Elliot has in his car for the video and my mother needed to use my car today because hers is in the shop, Katy and Sara needed a ride or they weren't going to make it into the video and because all of our parents work today, Sara guilted her mother into forcing Beckett to drive them. Of course it had to be Beckett. The universe has recently been finding many ways to get us in some situations together and it all started with that road trip to the Chris Warner concert. Hopefully, it ends today because I'm tired of it.

"Don't touch anything," I warn her, giving her a look. "If you break anything or even scoff the floor of this place, I'm going to end you."

"Relax, Jen. I'm not two," She says with a roll of her eyes. "Can we get dressed now?"

"Yeah, let's go find somewhere to do that," I sigh, grabbing my garment bag that's holding my dress. Heather has a fancy garment bag for her dress too but Katy and Sara aren't wearing fancy dresses, so they just have a bag each that holds the outfits that we'd helped them pick out yesterday.

"I think that we should do the outside shots first, before it gets too dark," I tell Elliot.

He nods in agreement. "I'll start setting up."

"I can help you do that," Beckett adds, probably not wanting to be dragged inside to deal with the dresses and makeup stuff that's about to go on in there.

Walking toward the house with Heather and the two girls, I call back to them, "Play nice. We'll be back soon."

We find the bathroom easily and, not willing to leave Katy or Sara alone for even two seconds in this regal, fancy mansion, I take Katy with me into the bathroom to get dressed while Heather and Sara go to find another bathroom to use.

My dress is short and pink and under the bust area, it poofs out dramatically. The top has some pink jewels on it between the boobs and it's strapless, exposing my slightly bony shoulders and collarbone. Katy is wearing a gold tutu skirt that poofed out a lot, like my dress but hers poofed out more, and it went down to just above her knees with a gold sequin tank top and a fur thing that went over her shoulders like a scarf. I know it has a special name but I don't know it.

"I want to wear heels too," Katy pouts, looking down at my black bejeweled heels and then down to her black flats.

"Mom said no," I remind her. "And you know that she's going to watch the video. I'm not getting in trouble just so that you can feel like a grown up. I'm letting you be in the video, aren't I?"

"Yes, but still," She pouts.

"You look beautiful, Katy," I assure her as I start on my makeup. "Really, you don't need heels until you have boobs."

"I have boobs."

I laugh a little bit, careful not to mess up my makeup. "Not yet. Just give it a few years."

I do my makeup and then I do Katy's as well before I push all of our everyday clothes into the bag that she brought in here with her and then we walk back out to where Elliot and Beckett are finishing the video setup out in the wide backyard, facing a huge in-ground pool with a tall fountain at the other end of it that's now trickling clear-bluish water.

"I thought that the pool would be a cool background," Elliot explains when I get out there, grabbing my usual camera from the bag and I start to turn it on so that I can get some behind the scenes video. The screen on it rotates around so that I can hold the camera and film myself easily, which is really nice.

"Yeah, it looks really good," I confirm with a nod. "Fix your hair, I'm about to start filming."

"What's wrong with my hair?" He wonders as I'm walking over to him.

Rolling my eyes, I stop in front of him and lean forward, fixing the part of his hair that looked flat compared to the rest of his hair. Since I'm wearing heels, it's easy to reach but he's usually unfairly taller than me. "There, it's fixed."

"Well, you look... a lot fancier than I expected," Elliot says, turning around to finish adjusting his video camera on its tripod.

"Primadonna, perhaps?" I wonder jokingly, twirling in a circle on the pavement that I'm standing on by the pool. "This was my homecoming dress."

"It was?"

"Elliot, we went to homecoming together. You don't even remember what dress I was wearing? What kind of date are you?" I wonder jokingly, noticing Beckett start silently laughing in my peripheral vision as he's tightening the screws on one of the tall light boxes. I ignore him.

"That's a very ill-timed and mean joke," Elliot tells me and I think it's because his date with Cara is in exactly one week from today and he's very nervous about that.

"If you don't remember what Cara's wearing on your date, you can kiss a second date goodbye," I warn him, seeing Heather and Sara coming out of the mansion and around to the pool area where I'm standing with Katy, Elliot, and Beckett.

"I will engrave it in my brain," He assures me with a firm nod.

Rolling my eyes at him, I hold up my camera and prepare to start my behind the scenes video. Once I press the record button, I grin into the lens and I can see me grinning back at myself from the camera's screen. "Hello my favorite people! JustJensen here and today, I'm filming the Primadonna video with the second best YouTuber out there. Heather, who you all know and love as HeyItsHeather."

"The first best better be Tyler Oakley," She calls to me, just before leaning into the shot and sticking her tongue out at the camera before disappearing again.

"Sure is, buddy," I assure her sarcastically. "Anyway, this video is not only special because it's my very first collaboration with my very favorite Heather which is so incredibly exciting, but it's also special because we have two more special guests!"

I turn the camera to Katy and Sara, who are conversing to each other near where Elliot is preparing the camera. They both see me turn the camera to them and offer the camera a sweet little wave.

"It's my weird little sister!" I cheer for the audience. "And her weird little friend! So cute, isn't it? They've finally convinced me to let them in the video, so let's hope it's not a disaster."

"Jensen!" Katy snaps at me. "Edit that out. We're not weird and you can't just call people weird on the internet. Especially not when you're famous. And especially not when that person that you're calling weird is me."

"Or me," Sara adds, crossing her arms over her chest.

"Weird little humans," I say to the camera, shaking my head. I then turn the camera to face Elliot because my fans always love to get glimpses of Elliot when they can. Like a precious gem or something. "Elliot, are we almost ready?"

"Uh, yeah. Just about," He confirms with a nod.

"Well, you heard him, so I'm going to go now but I'll let you know how it goes," I promise the camera before turning it off and putting it back in the bag.

"Okay, so just stand on the tape right there," Elliot says, pointing to the little blue tape X's on the concrete in front of the glistening pool.

"What about us?" Katy huffs when she realizes that there's only two X's.

I stand on top of the one on the right and Heather stands on the one to the left and we prepare for the camera, making sure that our hair is in place and our makeup isn't smudged and I mentally go over the dance moves in my head again even though we aren't filming that part right now.

"Next scene," I tell her as she stands with Sara and Beckett behind the camera that Elliot is now operating. "You aren't going to be in the whole video, you know."

"Fine," She groans dramatically.

"Okay, are you guys ready?" Elliot asks, looking to his right where the laptop is that holds the audio for the song so that we can sing along to it and then he'll cut out the audio and replace it with the sound track that we'll record separately later.

"Never been more ready," Heather pipes and I just nod my head.

Elliot starts counting down from four and then at zero, he pushes play and then the song starts and I start singing the lyrics since the vocals start right as the song starts so it's immediate and the first few lines are mine to sing before Heather sings the next few lines and then we come together after that and sing some of the song. When I sing, I start dancing around in my spot too, getting into the music and selling the whole 'prima donna' thing.

The next scene that we shoot is the dance part where we're in the regal looking ballroom of the house- why a house needs a ballroom is beyond me but it's really gorgeous with beautifully painted walls and marble floors.

"Okay, so we're inside now," I tell my camera after pushing the recording button. "And Heather still hasn't adjusted to the heat."

"I feel like the devil just farted in my face," Heather pants into the camera. "This air conditioning is heaven right now, oh my gosh."

I give a 'she's really weird' look to the camera and then say, "Anyway, I guess she didn't know that Florida is usually a pretty warm place. Okay, so while Elliot is doing his thing over there, I'll show you around this beautiful ballroom that we've stumbled upon."

"Yes, we've just stumbled upon it like freaking Goldie Locks," Heather adds sarcastically with a small laugh.

"That's exactly what happened," I confirm with a nod before turning the camera around to face the floor and then the wall as I speak. "Anyway, under our feet, there is fancy marble floors. Over there is the fancy painted walls and the fancy drape-y curtains that look like they cost more than my life. And beside me, you can see Heather."

"I am Heather," She confirms with a nod.

"Moving on, there's little Katy and Sara preparing for their fifteen min- utes of fame," I point the camera to the two little girls as they go over the dance with each other. Katy's in gymnastics, so she picked up the dance pretty quickly yesterday and helped Sara out with it until they both got it down solid. "And then Elliot working on the camera, naturally. And then we have-"

I'm about to show the camera the gorgeous view from the window, which looks toward the pool and the tree line behind it but before I rotate all the way around, I see Beckett leaning against the wall of the ballroom, looking at his phone.

"Beckett," I tell the camera. "Clearly, this is not his natural habitat."

"It's fur coat time," Heather tells me, holding up our two heavy fur coats in her arms.

"Oh, I almost forgot about the fur coats," I say, remembering that we'd grabbed the two fur coats at a thrift store earlier today so that we look over-the-top and stereotypically rich for the video. "Okay, so get this. These coats aren't only hot and stuffy but they itch like crazy."

I put the camera down on the laptop cart so that it's pointed at Heather and I as we put on the fur coats and I make a disgusted face. "I hate it."

"But we look so rich," Heather says grinning, twirling around in a circle in her short gold dress and white fur coat. My coat is black, matching the pink and black thing that I have going on.

I let out a loud laugh. "You look like you're trying to be rich."

"I am," She reminds me. "And I'm doing a wonderful job with it, thank you very much."

We stand there laughing at each other for a few minutes in front of the camera in our uncomfortable fur coats until Elliot tells us that it's time to film so I turn off my camera and we get to it, standing on the tape marks that Elliot has lined up for us. I stand farther back beside Heather and Sara and Katy stand in front of us, looking like they're about to explode with excitement.

"You have to look snobby, not excited," I remind them just before Elliot pushes the 'record' button.

"We've got this, Jen," Katy informs me.

"Totally," Sara nods, adjusting some of her blonde hair and then she turns completely around to face the camera with Katy.

"Okay, we're rolling," Elliot announces before counting down from four like he always does and then it's go time.

Chapter 11

"Oh, hey there, internet. It's me, Heather. And my awesome friend Jensen but you guys might know her as JustJensen. I'm with Jen in Florida right now and we just finished a collab music video that's going to be so awesome and exciting and it'll be posted eventually. Anyway, it's Sunday now so I've got to get back to New York but I still have a few hours left before I have to get to the airport so in honor of our weekend slumber party, we're going to do a slumber party video."

"This is going to be so weird," I say with a laugh from where I'm sitting beside Heather on my bed. We're wearing the tackiest pajamas that we could find- Heather in a grownup onesie and I'm wearing teddy bear flannel pajamas.

"Indeed it will," Heather agrees with me. "Anyway, the first thing you do at a sleepover is have a pillow fight."

We just sit still for a minute so that Heather can later edit the video so that it shows her hitting me with a pillow and then I say 'ow' and that's our pillow fight. We already filmed that part though, so she just has to edit it into the right area later.

"And after the aggressive pillow fight, we're going to do truth or dare and to help us out with this fun little game, I've downloaded an app on my phone that gives us truths and dares. So, Jensen will go first. Truth or dare?"

"Truth," I decide, wanting to play it safe because I have no idea how this app works or how weird the dares can be.

"Alrighty," She taps the truth button on the app on her phone and then reads, "If you were given the chance to become invisible for one day, what would you do with this ability?"

"I would pull the best pranks ever. Move things around, make things float. I'd have the best time messing with people," I decide with a laugh at just the idea of all of the pranks that I could pull on Elliot if I were invisible. "Now, truth or dare?"

"Dare," She pipes and then I press the dare button.

"Lick the bathroom floor," I say with a disgusted frown. "That's so gross, why would they make you do that? I'm going to pick another one."

"No!" Heather shouts, taking the camera off of the tripod. "I'm gonna do it. I'm not a cheater, and I'm not going to lose this game."

"I didn't know that it was a competition," I say with a laugh, following her out of my room and then toward the bathroom.

"Well, it is, and I'll win," She decides.

She screams and whines the whole time, but she really does lick my bathroom floor before we go back into my room and that's really disgusting so clearly, I made the right decision to choose truth. "I suppose that you're going to force me to do dare this time," I sigh once the camera is situated again.

"Right you are, Jensen," She nods before pushing the dare button and reading, "Put lipstick on another player but you are not allowed to use your hands."

"I hate this app," I decide but I still get up and grab a thing of bright red lipstick from my dresser. "Who created this thing?"

"I don't know, it's just the first one that I found. I didn't really vet the app before using it," She says with a shrug. "And don't you dare use your feet."

"I wasn't going to, but that would be very funny," I say with a laugh before biting down on the end of the lipstick tube and then I try my hardest to apply the lipstick to look somewhat normal on Heather but it ends up on her left nostril and halfway down her chin. It takes four minutes until I finish and by the end, we're both laughing so hard that the lipstick falls out of my mouth and onto my lap before it's Heather's turn again.

"I'll do truth this time," She tells me.

"Okay, the question is..." I push the truth button on her phone and read out the question, "What is the first physical feature you look for in someone you are attracted to?"

"Pretty eyes," She responds quickly. "But you're right, this app is lame. Which is why, I've brought a backup plan. A few weeks ago, I asked you guys to send in some dares and I've picked out some of my favorites."

"Oh god," I groan, knowing that Heather is going to choose the weirdest dares to do. Although she's a singer, she's more into the actual YouTube videos, making people laugh and all of that stuff. So she really goes out of her way to give her viewers a show. Unlike me, who is more focused on the music aspect of YouTube but I still do some videos, they just aren't super entertaining.

"Don't be such a worry wart," Heather rolls her eyes at me before she stands up and walks over to where she has a suitcase full of supplies for this video. She really prepared for this thing.

And so it starts.

"Swallow a spoonful of flour," Is the first one and that's just absolutely horrible because my mouth gets so dry and the flour turns to glue in my mouth. After swallowing it all and guzzling some water, Heather and I move on to the second dare.

"Prank call a fellow YouTuber," Heather reads from her phone. "And pretend to be a crazed fan."

"Who would go for that?" I wonder, trying to think through my plethora of YouTube associates. I haven't met most of them in real life because unlike most YouTubers, I'm unable to travel all of the time for collaborations or to go to conventions where all of the YouTubers go considering I'm still in school. Hopefully, after I graduate, that'll all change.

"I'm thinking Wells," She says, referring to one of the guys that lives in London and he's a pretty big YouTuber and insanely hilarious too. I've talked to him some by phone and IM and he's really cool to talk to but I know that Heather met him when he went on a trip to New York and she did a collab with him a few months ago.

"Okay, let's call Wells then," I agree, pulling my phone out and finding his number in my phone.

"Hello?" He answered the phone, which is really good because some people don't answer blocked calls but he obviously isn't one of those people.

"AHH!" I shriek into the phone. "Is this Wells Jefferies?"

"Um. Yeah? Who's this?"

"AHH!" I shriek again and Heather cups a hand over her mouth to stop herself from laughing. "I'm such a huge fan, you literally have no idea. I-I can't believe that I'm talking to you right now."

"Oh. Thank you, love," He says on the other end with an awkward little laugh.

"I love you so much," I say, pretending to hyperventilate. "Oh my gosh."

"I love you too," Wells assures me in a polite voice but then he pauses before saying. "Wait, hang on a minute, you sound a lot like Jensen. Is this you?"

"Oh fuck," I mutter, laughing, and Heather bursts out laughing beside me. "You're such a wanker, Wells, how'd you know that it was me?"

"You aren't very good at prank calls," He informs me with a teasing laugh.

"Well, anyway, say hi to Heather," I pipe. He says hello to Heather and then we say goodbye to him after a failed prank call.

"That didn't go as expected. Next time, I'll take control of the prank call," Heather assures me before she scrolls down to the next prank in her phone. "Okay, the next dare is to cover ourselves in whipped cream. However, because that would leave us acne ridden and sticky, I've changed it to shaving cream."

"You're kidding," I tell Heather, not really thinking that she expects me to actually cover myself in shaving cream. I'd be spending weeks trying to get that stuff out of my ears.

"I'm not," She grins at me. "Come on, I even have the shaving cream. We'll just have to do it outside and since you Floridians have such nice weather, that won't be a problem. Right?"

"Fine," I mumble as she pulls six cans of shaving cream out of her suit case of doom- the same place that held the flour and also holds some other things that I'm afraid to ask about.

So then we get changed into sports bras and shorts so that we don't get our actual clothes or pajamas covered in shaving cream as well and then we go outside so that we don't get shaving cream all over my room because I'd be very annoyed if that were to happen.

"This is such a bad idea," I say but I'm laughing as I hold the first can of shaving cream in my hand with my brown hair now up in a messy bun to try and save it from the mess that is about to ensue.

"This is such an amazing idea," Heather counters from beside me with her own can of shaving cream prepared. The camera is standing on its tripod in front of us, filming this disaster but I guess that this will be an interesting memory to have. One that'll definitely go down in the history books.

"Okay, so how do we do this? On the count of three?" I ask her, shaking up the can of shaving cream. I'm not sure if that does anything to it but it feels like something that I should do to amp up the pressure.

"Yeah, I'll count down and then we just go at it until you can't see any skin. None at all. And no cheating," She warns me and I just nod in understanding. "Now, three... two... one!"

We spend an hour filming these different dares that Heather will soon edit into a fifteen minute video for her channel and even when Heather announces that this is the last one, I still have shaving cream crusted on my cheeks and shoulders but we'd successfully hosed off most of it. The smell is still haunting my nostrils though, but at least it smells alright.

"Okay, this last one is really deep, so get prepared," Heather warns both me and the audience before she reads the last dare. "Talk about love- do you believe in it? Who do you like right now?"

"Do I believe in love?" I echo in shock, not really wanting to answer that question and especially not on camera. "Wow, well I guess talking about boys does go along with the sleepover theme."

"It does," She agrees with a nod. "I believe in love. Of course I do. I mean, I don't like anybody right now because I just love you guys so much and it really does take a lot of time to love you guys as much as I do. So in a way, my fans take the place of a boyfriend right now. But someday that'll change and I'll grow up and I'll fall in love. It'll be so romantic. What about you, Jen?"

"No," I admit with a shake of my head. "I don't think so. I mean, I believe in love, but not true love or romantic love or that kind of thing. The whole thing is rigged, you know? You can like somebody with your whole heart, you can give them your whole being but they could just turn around and ignore you altogether. It's such an unfair game, and it's stupid."

"So you don't believe in love at all?" She wonders with wide eyes.

I just shrug. "I don't know. Not right now, I guess. But maybe I will someday. It's so complicated, the whole idea of love and whatever. It's too stressful to even think about for long periods of time."

"Well, that's enough deep talk for one video, so we're going to go now. Don't forget to give this video a thumbs up and subscribe and go over to Jensen's channel and subscribe to her as well, I'll put the link to her channel in a link below. We have the collab video coming out soon on Jensen's channel, so don't forget to look out for that one as well," Heather gives the camera her sign off.

I grin wildly at the camera as Heather says her goodbyes and then we sign off together before she turns off the camera and I start helping her pack up.

"This weekend was too short," She huffs, zipping up her evil suitcase of evilness. Lemon juice, syrup, cotton balls, and a bunch of other very simple household items were found in her bag but they all were turned against us for very evil purposes.

"I know," I assure her with a sad sigh. "But after graduation, we'll see each other so much more."

"Exactly," She chirps with a nod. "I'm thinking a summer in London. You know Wells and Indie could help us find an apartment- or, you know a flat or whatever- and we can meet all of those awesome people over there and do all of those collabs that we've been wanting to make for what feels like forever."

"That'd be really amazing," I smile at just the idea of getting out of here for a whole summer. Not that I don't love my family and everything, but it'd just be really cool to go to London, to be on my own and with Heather and a bunch of other YouTubers for a whole summer. It sounds like it's too good to be true though. "I don't know, maybe it could happen."

"Think about it, at least," Heather says. "I think that I could convince my mom to let me go alone but I really want you to come with me."

"I will think about it," I confirm. "I'm not sure if my mom'll go for it, but yeah, I'll definitely bring it up. London. That sounds like so much fun."

"Doesn't it?" She grins at me. "A nice 'what the hell' kind of trip before college starts and we really have to start acting like adults."

"Don't tell your mom that it's a 'what the hell' trip though, I don't think that she'll let you go. She'll duct tape you to your dining room table or something so that you'll miss your flight," I warn her with a laugh, considering how strict her mother can be. It's a miracle that she let Heather fly out here just for the weekend.

"Of course, I'll keep that part a secret," Heather assures me with a laugh. "But London. How crazy, right?"

"Yeah," I say with a sigh but now that she's put the idea in my head, the more and more that I really want this to happen. Maybe my parents won't like it too much but I have a lot of money saved up from my videos on YouTube and they sell in iTunes as well. I'm not sure if it's enough to buy an apartment (a flat?) in London, but it's worth a shot. "London. Wow."

Chapter 12

"**Y**ou look amazing," I tell Elliot with a forced smile. "Cara's going to love you, I swear."

"You really think so?" He wonders, obviously nervous about his date tonight. That's why I'm over here at his house, to help him calm his nerves and also to help him look nice, his tie is straight and tied properly and to make sure that everything is on time.

"Of course I think so. She'd be stupid not to," I assure him, standing in front of Elliot as I tug on his tie to make sure that it's straight. He's wearing a nice button up shirt with a tie and dress pants and black shiny shoes. His hair is gently tousled in that effortlessly yet totally full of effort kind of way that I love and he just looks really nice. Any girl would be the luckiest girl on earth to be the reason that Elliot dresses up like this. He looks so gorgeous and I absolutely hate it.

"I think that I should leave soon, I have to pick her up at seven," Elliot tells me, checking the fancy watch that his grandpa gave him for Christmas that he rarely ever wears because it's so fancy and expensive. He's obviously trying to impress this girl in a way that he's never tried to impress me. Of course he doesn't try to impress me, we're best friends. I try my best to shake any delusions out of my head but I can't help but pretend that he's dressing up so nice tonight for me. Oh, God, I'm losing my mind.

"Yeah, you don't want to be late," I confirm, taking a bottle of cologne from his dresser and sniffing the knob to make sure that it smells good. I don't like the smell of that one so I grab the other one on his dresser and smell that one. Liking that one much better, I spray him with it a few times so that it isn't too strong but still noticeable. "Good luck. Don't be nervous. If she's a total bitch or if it gets awkward or anything, just call me or text an SOS. I'll come storming in pretending to be your girlfriend or something to get you out of it."

"I don't think that it's going to go bad unless I mess it up," He laughs at me, jokingly rolling his eyes as he grabs his car keys from his desk and then I pull my purse over my shoulder so that I can leave too now that Elliot is leaving and my work here is done. "She's seriously amazing. I know we only met that once but we've been talking over the phone and everything and she's so great. She's smart and funny and absolutely beautiful."

"I'm just saying, there's always that option," I tell him, pursing my lips together and purposefully walking behind Elliot so that he can't see the pained look on my face.

"Are you leaving?" Elliot's mother asks when we get downstairs.

"Yeah. I'll be back by one," Elliot tells Mrs. Stoner, who stands five inches shorter than her son but she's wearing a wide, excited grin because Elliot going on a date is about as rare as snowfall in Southern Florida.

"Alright. Be safe, and have fun," She says, hugging Elliot. "You look so handsome. Jensen did a good job."

"I did, didn't I?" I gloat jokingly with a bright laugh. "Anyway, I've got to get home, so call me after and let me know how it goes, alright?"

"Oh, you don't want to stay for coffee and talk about Elliot after he leaves?" Mrs. Stoner asks me with a disappointed frown on her face and Elliot gives her a dirty look, which she easily ignores.

"Although that sounds like a blast, I can't tonight. We just posted a new video and I've got to get home to go through some of the comments and everything," I explain with a quick apologetic frown. "Take a rain check?"

"Sure, darling. Drive safe," She sings as I give Elliot one last reassuring 'you've got this' smile and then I'm hurrying out of the house to just get away from Elliot. I feel like I can breathe a little bit more once I'm in my car with the windows down driving back to my house but I still feel a little bit suffocated.

I just spent an hour and a half with Elliot as he talked on and on about this Cara girl. I helped him get ready for the date that I wanted to be going on. Sure, it makes me sad that Elliot doesn't know how I feel about him and it also makes me sad that I'm pretty positive that he doesn't feel the same way in return. But it mostly sucks because it makes me feel so freaking pathetic. I haven't felt this pathetic since I was trapped in the janitor's closet during freshman year or getting the crap beat out of me in a mud puddle.

And I hate feeling like this. I absolutely hate it. I worked my butt off to get out of that part of my life and yet, here I am, feeling just like I did back during freshman year when I was constantly running from Kevin and his Goons. Although Elliot isn't a direct threat to my physical health, he sure is destroying my mental stability and that's not okay with me.

I need to get over this. I will get over this. It'll take some time, maybe a week or two or maybe a month, but I'll get over it. I always do. It'll be okay.

I repeat this to myself like a mantra in my head as I drive all the way home. When I get home, there's a note sticking to the fridge that reads:

Date night tonight, Katy's at a sleepover. We'll bring leftovers. XO—Mom and Dad

I crumple up the note and toss it in the trashcan before grabbing a bottle of water from the fridge and trotting quickly up the stairs to my desk where my laptop sits closed, ready for me to start my work. I'm relieved to have something to get my mind off of Elliot and how he's probably picking up Cara right now, right as I'm sitting at my desk moping about him. Pathetic.

I sign onto my laptop and then open up my YouTube channel where the collab video with Heather is now posted and I start skimming the comments. There aren't a lot yet because I only posted it this afternoon but there are still a plethora of them and I won't be able to get through them all but I want to get through as much of them as possible and maybe even respond to some of them.

Most of the comments are nice but others are critiques, which are kind of annoying. I mean, I know that I'm not perfect and neither is Heather and sure, there are things that we can improve on but it's not like we're professional singers and we don't claim to be. We just like singing and so we do it. I don't want to read a bunch of comments nagging me about what's wrong with my singing, but there will always be those people that have to point out my flaws so that they feel smart or better than me or maybe they just want to help. Regardless, it's annoying.

I focus on the nice ones. Especially right now when I need as much uplifting mojo that I can get to try and get my mood to improve even just a little bit. Reading what my fans have to say helps some, but not a lot. I love them to death but I'm feeling so ridiculously sad right now that not even their nice comments can cheer me up.

I still read them though, until I can't read anymore because the tears in my eyes are blurring my vision and whenever I try to wipe them away, even more just take their place. Eventually, I'm sniffling and tears are rolling down my cheeks so I just give up on the internet all together and shut my laptop, going back downstairs to look for something down there that might cheer me up.

Although that's pretty impossible right now considering I'm now in full-on pity party mode and the only way that I could feel better right now is to not be myself. And the only way to not be myself is to get drunk or something. The idea makes me laugh. Me, getting drunk by myself in my empty house just because of Elliot going on a date with another girl. As if I ever thought that we had a chance. He's always made it so clear how Jelliot is repulsive to him, I've always known that he isn't into me like that. I guess this stupid date kind of solidifies that though, and it hurts more than I thought that it would.

I walk around my house a little longer but nothing can get my mind off of Elliot and Clara. Sitting at the restaurant that Elliot is taking her to, laughing about something funny, talking about computers in the technical way that I've never understood.

And as I get deeper and deeper into my self-pity, the alcohol idea doesn't sound so bad anymore. Sure, it's pathetic but isn't that the theme of the night? I'm just a big ball of self-pity and pathetic-ness. Sure, I'll get over Elliot, but not tonight. The pain burning in my chest will go away, I know it will, but tonight, it's burning like my whole body is on fire.

And so I go into my dad's study and I find one of his bottles of vodka. He has a whole cupboard of the stuff but he rarely ever drinks it so he won't notice that it's missing. Just to be safe though, I'll drink what I want and then fill whatever I drank with water before putting it back in the cupboard since the liquid is clear and he won't notice it until he drinks it, which won't be for years probably.

Not wanting to make the house smell like alcohol, I know that I have to go outside to drink it so I grab a glass and the jug of orange juice from the fridge before trudging out to the backyard. I know that it's likely that Beckett is home tonight and he'll probably see me out here being drunk and sad but I'm hoping that he won't think much of it. He'll think that it's just me with a very weird craving for orange juice.

Although I'm sure that the universe will find some way to throw us together because it seems that it has been having a lot of fun messing with my avoidance strategy when it came to my nonexistent relationship with

Beckett. I don't care though. I don't care about Beckett, I don't care about what he thinks of me or what he says to me or anything. I've stopped caring now that we've been forced into so many situations together lately. I've grown immune to him being around now.

Sitting on my trampoline now, I take two shots of the vile clear liquid using the bottle's lid as a glass before pouring some orange juice into the cup and then some of the vodka. It's really strong but I'm able to swallow it down in hopes of it taking my mind off of the awful night that I've had.

I can feel the alcohol doing its job after a while and I just lay down on the trampoline for a long time, just looking up at the blank black sky. No stars tonight, it's all just clouds and monotony. I hope that stargazing wasn't a part of Elliot's date plans. That'd really suck.

Once I've gotten bored of just laying down staring at a blank slate, I put the glass bottle of vodka and the jug of orange juice down in the grass so that I can jump on the trampoline, feeling like I've got tons more energy than I did before the vodka. Jumping on the trampoline, I start to sing to myself some of the saddest songs that I know. My favorite one is Not in That Way by Sam Smith because it pertains to my situation so painfully perfectly.

After a few minutes of lazily jumping around the bouncy surface of the trampoline, the inevitable happens and I get too dizzy to hold myself up. However, as I'm falling, my ankle twists underneath of me and pain shoots through my foot and ankle and then it's a dull ache. I whine about it to myself in some incoherent mumbling as I slide off of the trampoline. I want to go inside to put some ice on my ankle but I can't walk on my ankle anymore so, with my mind soaked in alcohol, the solution to this problem is to lay flat in the grass and then I start to roll toward the porch.

I crawl up the wooden stairs and then to the door where I clamber to my one good foot and try to open the door but it doesn't budge. With a loud whine, I try to push it again but I think that it's locked. And I'm pretty sure that I don't have my keys out here with me.

Stubborn about getting some ice on my ankle, I limp back to the trampoline, drunkenly falling over a few times but getting back up again afterwards and dusting off my jean-clad lings. I cradle the vodka bottle in my arms as I limp toward Margaret's house. Considering that the universe has a perverse desire to bring Beckett and I together, I'm going to use it to my advantage tonight because I know that if I knock on the door, it'll be Beckett there and not Margaret or Josh.

However, I'm passing the swing set when I fall again and this time, I feel too drained to even try to make it to the house so I just sit down on one of the swings and wait for Beckett to come to me. The universe will make it happen. It always does.

Sure enough, some time goes by and I spend that time trying to swing as high as I can, and then the back door of the Spears home glides open and Beckett pokes his head out the door and then he's walking all the way outside, looking at me with a curious look.

I know that swinging so high right now is probably a really bad idea considering how intoxicated I am. I mean, if I hurt my ankle by jumping on the trampoline then surely, I'll hurt myself swinging on the swing but I'm too gone to care about any of that.

"Splendid evening, good sir," I greet Beckett, not slowing down in my pushes to get as high as possible into the sky on the swing as it creaks and shakes below me.

"Um, hey," He greets me in response, sounding very confused as he stays on the porch, pretty far away from me.

"Are your parents currently present at this residence?"

"No," He says slowly, now taking a few steps down the porch and he starts walking toward me in the grass. "Are you okay, Jensen?"

"Of course they're not home," I say, laughing way more than I should have at that. I just find it so funny that we're alone right now, just like the universe wants, and Elliot is on his wonderful date with his wonderful girl. Just like the universe wants. "I already knew that they wouldn't be."

"You're drunk," He states the obvious, noticing the vodka bottle propped against the wooden leg of the swing set.

"No, I think that you're drunk, good sir," I negate him, still laughing a little bit. "You've even left this vodka bottle out here in the open. It's a good thing that your parents aren't home or you'd really get it this time."

"Okay, stop swinging so high, you're going to hurt yourself," Beckett says, ignoring my drunken comments.

"Are you suddenly the boss of me now?" I argue, but I still stop swinging so high and I let the swing calm down to a gentle sway.

"No, I just don't want you to get hurt," He argues, picking up the vodka bottle and sitting it on the wooden platform that leads to a plastic yellow slide. Out of my reach, I notice. "What are you doing?"

"I'm hurting myself, apparently," I inform him. "And why wouldn't I? Everybody else does and it's so easy to do, you know? I'm prone to getting hurt, I suppose."

"Jensen, let me help you home," Beckett offers me, stepping closer to the swing that I'm sitting on.

"I don't want to go home," I tell him, rolling my eyes at him as if that's the stupidest idea ever. "If I wanted to be home then I wouldn't have come over here at all."

"Why do you want to be over here and not at your house then?" He wonders.

"I need ice."

"You don't have ice?"

"It occurred to me as I was about to go into my own dwelling that, while I would like to acquire the magnificent frozen water from my own residence, I've lost the ability to gain access to said residence."

"You're locked out," He paraphrases.

I nod. "In laymen terms, yes. I'm afraid so."

"Well, I can't just leave you out here," He says.

"Join me then, won't you?"

He looks at me with apprehension before he lets out a long sigh and then sits down on the swing beside mine. I think he realizes that if he doesn't want to leave me by myself out here, this is the only way that he can make sure that I don't get hurt anymore.

"So what are you doing?" Beckett asks me after a long silence as I'm staring up at the sky, looking for the moon because the moon is supposed to be right above me, to tell me what to do with myself like it always does.

"Looking for the moon. I don't see it tonight," I mutter sadly.

"Why?"

"I enjoy talking with the moon," I inform him. "Me and the moon... oh, we go way back." I whisper, thinking of all of the times that I've been through a rough patch, I'd come outside and look at the moon and ask it to make things better. Especially during freshman year when things were really bad for me. The moon isn't having my teenage troubles today though, because he's gone behind the clouds.

Another silence ensues and again, I'm the one to break it up.

"I know that it's going to come as a huge shock to you, but I've fallen hopelessly in love with my best friend," I inform him as I start swinging again but not as high as I was earlier.

"I had no idea."

"I know," I sigh. "But sadly, it is true."

"I'm sorry to hear that, Jensen," Beckett tells me, awkwardly clearing his throat. "Are you sure that you don't just want to go inside to get a cup of coffee or something? So that you can sober up."

"If I wanted to be sober, I wouldn't have gotten drunk in the first place," I inform him. "You don't have to be worried about me though. I'll be fine on my own. Just like always."

"You aren't alone always," He assures me. "Maybe Elliot doesn't like you in the way that you'd like him to, I don't really know if he does or not, but he still loves you. He's still there for you."

"But it still hurts," I explain to him. "And it feels like I'm suffocating- I feel like I can't ever breathe. He's hurting me, and it's not even his fault. I'm that easy to hurt. Everybody does it, it must be so easy."

"Not everybody-"

"Even you, good sir," I interrupt him, glancing over at Beckett, my bottom lip now trembling and my eyes watering with unshed tears. "You spent a great deal of time hurting me, actually. And I never did anything to you. I never did anything to any of them. What is it about me? Why am I so easy to hurt?"

When he realizes that my question isn't rhetorical and that I actually want a response, he sighs, glancing up at me before looking down at the grass below him. "I don't really know how to answer that question."

"Well, why did you hurt me? Answer that question, won't you?"

"I don't know," He says, awkwardly clearing his throat again, obviously uncomfortable at the topic of conversation now. I don't care though, I'm too drunk to care about the awkwardness. "I was really dumb back then, I really wanted to fit in with the cool kids, I guess."

"Do you think that I've deserved it?"

"Most people don't deserve the bad things that happen to them, Jensen. The world isn't fair like that," He says, swinging back and forth on his swing gently.

"I mean, I'm acting like the world is ending but it isn't that bad," I continue, trying to sound more optimistic now. "It's just a broken heart, hardly even broken. I survived Kevin. I survived Bethany and she was absolutely psycho. I survived Kelly. I survived you, and I freaking live next door to you so that makes it exponentially harder because unlike the other three, you never went away. I can survive Elliot. I can. I'm freaking famous. People admire me. I'm a goddamn star."

"I don't think that-"

"And I know that I always say that I don't like to talk about what happened freshman year. I really hate talking about it honestly but I always bring it up somehow and I think that's because even though I don't want to admit it, I still think about it. Every day, I still think about everything that happened freshman year. Hell, I still avoid the janitor's closets as much as I can. If I have to pass one in the hallway, I walk on the complete other side and I hold my breath. And even today, it still kills me and I can't stop thinking about it, no matter how much I want to."

"Are you sure you don't want to just come inside to get something in your stomach?" Beckett asks me, motioning toward his house again in an attempt to get me in his house again so that I don't risk hurting myself again. "I can make you some toast or something."

"I don't want you to help me," I tell him although that's not true. If I didn't want his help, I wouldn't have come over here in the first place. I just want ice though, I don't want him to be nice to me or to talk to me about memory lane or to make me toast. I want ice and then I want to leave again.

"So you're just going to sit out here until your parents come home and find you drunk off your ass?" He counters with raised eyebrows. "I guess I can't stop you then."

"Wait. You're right. Okay. Let's go inside then," I realize that he's right about my parents. Without a way to get into my house, they'd have to come home and find me drunk and then I'd be grounded for life and my dad would lock up his alcohol cabinet which would really suck for future heartbreaks. And with me being so prone to breaking, there is bound to be many of them.

"I know that I'm right," He says with a small laugh as he stands up from his swing and then helps me out of mine. With one hand, he grabs the vodka bottle and with his other hand, he wraps it around my waist to hold me up as I pathetically limp toward his house.

"I wish that you weren't so nice. I try so hard to hate you because of the hell that you and your friends put me through but you're so freaking nice all of the freaking time and it's so hard to hate you. I just wish that you were still an asshole so that I could still hate you," I tell Beckett as we go into his house. He practically pulls me up the stairs of the porch and then through the sliding glass back door into his kitchen.

"I'm sorry. I'll try to be more hateable then," He tells me but I think that he's just being sarcastic because he laughs after saying that.

"Have you ever loved somebody who doesn't love you back?"

"No, I can't say that I have," Beckett shakes his head at me as he helps me into one of the dining room chairs and he hides the vodka bottle under the sink.

"I think that you like me," I inform him, leaning heavily on the kitchen table in front of me. "I don't mean in the way that I like Elliot, I just mean that I think that you like me."

"And why do you think that?" He wonders curiously as he walks over to the counter and grabs a few pieces of bread.

"Sara told me that you watch all of my videos," I explain. "Why do you do that?"

He looks shocked that I know that but then he turns and starts putting the bread in the toaster so that I can't see his face anymore. "I don't watch all of your videos, Jensen."

"You watch some of them?"

"Occasionally," He says with an indifferent shrug. "Just to see how you're doing."

"So you care about me."

"Of course I do, Jensen," Beckett confirms and I try to etch that part into my brain so that, if I forget about tonight in the morning, I won't forget this part. I want to remember it. "I know that it's not reciprocated because of freshman year and that's fine, I understand. But we were friends once, before high school, and I do still care about you. I can't exactly just ask you how you're doing without things being weird though, so I just watch your videos sometimes."

"That's sweet of you," I mumble softly.

The kitchen is full of silence for a few minutes until the toast pops out of the toaster and then Beckett helps me up the stairs. The alcohol is starting to fade a little bit but it's still hard for me to get up the stairs. "Is your ankle okay?" He asks me once we get into what I assume is his room and I sit on the edge of the bed, unable to stand up on my ankle.

"It hurts," I admit, taking a bite out of the toast.

"I can look at it if you want," He offers. "Do you want something to sleep in?"

I nod at him, grateful that he's being so helpful right now. When he grabs a t-shirt and some sweat pants out of his dresser, I quickly pull my shirt over my head and then drop my pants to my ankles in a few swift motions.

"Whoa, shit, Jensen, wait until I get out of the room," Beckett says quickly, tossing the clothes onto the bed and turning back around to block himself from my nearly naked form.

"You've never seen a naked girl before?" I wonder with a giggle as I throw his shirt over my head and then step into the sweat pants, tying the draw string around my waist. "I'm decent now, Virgin Boy."

"I'm trying to be polite," He defends, turning back around to face me.

"There's nothing wrong with being a virgin," I assure him. "I just didn't have you pegged as the waiting-for-marriage type is all."

"I'm not a virgin, Jensen, I'm just trying to not... you know, you're drunk, so it's weird," He explains and I let out a long yawn as I lay down on his bed. He didn't tell me that I could sleep here but I guess if he doesn't want me to, he can just carry me somewhere else or force me out of his bed but it's really comfortable so I hope that he doesn't do that.

"Okay, whatever you say," I yawn again and he walks over to where I'm lying to fix the blankets over top of me and when he does that, I pull him closer to me by grabbing his shoulder and sit I up, kissing his warm cheek before whispering, "Thank you for all of your help tonight, good sir."

Chapter 13

The next morning, I wake up to my phone ringing and it feels like a jack hammer going off inches from my face. With a loud groan, I reach over to the nightstand and push the green button to answer the phone. I don't want to do it but if it's one of my parents, I'm going to be in deep shit if I don't answer it. I guess that I could have opened my eyes to check to see who it is but that would require me opening my eyes, and that's just not going to happen.

"Hello?" I grumble into the phone.

"Hey, Jen," Elliot greets me chirpily on the other end. "Are you still sleeping?"

"Uh. Yeah," I mutter, silently wishing that I hadn't answered the phone. "What's up?"

"Don't you want to know how the date went?" He wonders, seemingly excited to tell me every romantic detail about his date and by the chirpy sound of his voice, I'd say that it went very well.

"Yeah. Of course I do," I say, pulling the phone away from my face to yawn and then I talk myself into opening my eyes and turning around onto my back so that I can sit up. However, when I open my eyes, I'm reminded that I'm not actually in my own room but I'm in Beckett's. Because I humiliated myself in front of him last night. "Shit."

"What is it?" Elliot asks me, hearing my mumbled curse.

"Nothing, just having a bad morning is all."

"Didn't you just wake up though?" He laughs on the other end.

"Yeah," I sigh. "Anyway, where are you? Do you want to meet for coffee or something?"

"I'm actually on my way to your house right now, about fifteen minutes away," He explains as I work up the courage to sit up in the soft bed that isn't mine. Looking around the room now, I can tell with great relief that Beckett isn't in here. Hopefully, I'll be able to escape without him even noticing me, that'd be really ideal.

"Okay, I'll be there... I mean here. I'll be here. But tell me now, how'd the date go?" I bend my knees and rest my elbows on my knees so that I can rest my forehead on the palm of one hand and hold the phone to my ear in the other.

"It was absolutely amazing, Jen," He tells me, sounding about as excited as an eight year old on Christmas morning. "Cara is so great. She's like, the most perfect girl that I've ever met. She's beautiful, funny, smart, adorable, she's everything. She's the best. We had such an amazing time, you were right. I had nothing to be afraid of."

"Wow, that's really awesome, El," I assure him just as I hear the bedroom door opening but I don't have enough energy to look up and greet Beckett. I'm also too humiliated about last night to even think about facing him right now. I let my ratted hair fall in front of my face so that he can't see my exhausted expression and so that I can't see him. "I'm glad that you had a good time."

"I can't wait for you to meet her," Elliot gushes over the phone. "You're going to love her too. I told her who you are and she's a fan and she's really excited to meet you. She's not a crazy fan or anything, but she's seen some of your videos."

"I hope that you didn't talk about me the whole time, El," I tell him, trying to joke even in my crappy mood. I have to make him believe that

I'm totally fine though, and so I do my best. "That's not a turn on when you're on a date."

"No, I know, we hardly even talked about you," He assures me and I don't know if I should be relieved or offended but I think that I'm both. "How do you feel about conies after school tomorrow? Cara loves Tony's Conies, so I thought that we could go there."

"I hate conies," I remind him, remembering that he said that he's on his way and I need to get back to my house because I'm not prepared to explain to him why I spent the night at the Spears house. "Anyway, you're driving so you drive without getting in an accident and I'll see you when you get here. I've got to go."

I hang up the phone and toss it onto the bed, trying to prepare myself for what has to happen next, but I'll never be prepared for this.

"I brought food and aspirin," Beckett tells me as I'm trying to convince myself to lift my face out of my knees.

Finally, I look up and I see Beckett standing beside the bed with a plate of toast and a bottle of pills and he looks like he's trying to hold back laughter, but I'm not sure why and honestly, I'm not so sure that I want to find out.

"Thanks," I mutter as he hands me both the plate of bread and the pills.

"Sure," He replies awkwardly. "How are you feeling?"

"Hungover and humiliated. I'm so sorry about last night, Beck, I honestly can't believe that I did that."

"It's fine," He says and he lets out a quiet laugh and then tries to cover it up by coughing, but I can obviously tell that he laughed.

"What is it?" I wonder, nibbling on one of the pieces of toast after swallowing both aspirin pills.

"Nothing," He says quickly, sitting down on the edge of the bed beside me. "It's just that you haven't called me that in years."

"Sorry," I say, cringing. "I'm barley awake. Where are my clothes?"

He motions to the desk where my shirt and jeans are folded on top of the back of his desk chair. "My parents are downstairs but they know that you're here, so don't freak out if you hear them down there."

"Oh my, God," I groan at the horrifying story that Margaret has concocted in her mind if she knows that I spent the night. And then she's going to go tell my mother this story and I'll never live it down. "What'd you tell them?"

"The truth, mostly. I just left out the alcohol part. You were on the trampoline and hurt your ankle but got locked out of your house so I helped out and put some ice on it and wrapped it for you and then you got tired so I let you stay here. I slept on the couch by the way," He adds at the end and if I wasn't in such a craptastic mood, I might have laughed.

I move the covers from my legs and lift up the sweat pant to reveal my hurt ankle. It is wrapped now, but I don't remember Beckett wrapping it for me. I guess I blacked out before I actually passed out, which makes me feel even more horrified about this whole situation.

"Did I do anything completely embarrassing?" I ask him hesitantly, not sure that I really want to know the answer to that question but I feel like I have to ask.

"Well, you did confess your undying love for me on the swing set but other than that, I think that you're good," He informs me with a teasing smirk and I know that he's either joking or lying because I remember everything until I kissed his cheek when we got up here to his room.

"Really? Was that before or after you admitted that you watch my videos?"

"I was hoping that you wouldn't remember that," He mutters, looking a bit embarrassed himself.

"That makes two of us," I mumble and after I say that, I realize how mean it sounds. I didn't mean it like I wish that I could forget that he told me that he cares about me, I just meant that I wish that I could forget everything that happened last night. I don't correct myself though, I just grab my clothes from the chair and awkwardly limp into the bathroom across the hallway from Beckett's room.

I get dressed and splash some water on my face before running my fingers through my ratted hair as much as possible so that I look a little bit decent. My ankle is still a little sore so I'll have to either think of an excuse as to why I'm limping or walk off the pain long enough before Elliot gets to my house so that I can pretend that it doesn't even hurt. The former, I decide, sounds a whole lot easier considering Elliot is so gullible and now that he's preoccupied about his date, he'll be even more distracted and gullible.

"I've really got to go, but thank you for your help," I tell Beckett once I get back into his room as I'm slipping my shoes on and grabbing my phone from the bed. "And I'd really appreciate it if we can both just pretend like this never even happened."

"Sure," He nods in agreement and I turn to leave the room, excited to finally escape this hell hole of awkwardness. "But, Jensen, for what it's worth- and I know that it's not worth much- I'm sorry about what's going on with Elliot. And I know that this doesn't mean much either but if you want to talk at all, I'm always around."

I try to force a smile on my hungover face but it probably looks more like a grimace. "Thanks. Again."

He nods at me and then I disappear downstairs, politely greeting Mr. and Mrs. Spears on my way out but not staying for any small talk.

Luckily, I get to my house before Elliot does. And another bonus is that my dad is at work and my mom is gone to pick Katy up from her sleepover so I have the house to myself as I try to figure out how I'm going to face Elliot after what happened last night.

My luck doesn't last that long though, because Elliot arrives before I have time to change my clothes or to even shower or brush my teeth so I probably still smell like vodka and I look like I haven't showered in months.

"You look like crap, Jen," Elliot tells me when he comes into the house. He follows me into the kitchen so that I can start a pot of coffee and he can tell me all about the best night ever.

"Yeah, I told you. I had a long night," I mutter, trying not to make my limp noticeable. It still hurts a bit but if I can make it seem nonexistent then I won't have to lie to him, which would be nice. "Anyway, so are there plans for a second date?"

"Not yet, but I told her that I'd call her today," He says. "I think that she really likes me. She laughed at all of my jokes and she was smiling the whole night and she has a really cool smile."

"You sound so surprised by that," I mention with a small, forced laugh as I lean against the counter and feel thankful that the aspirin is starting to kick in. "It really isn't that hard to believe that somebody is into you like that, El."

"I guess," He sighs with a shrug. "Are you still wearing what you wore yesterday? Exactly how long was your night?"

"Long," I repeat and he gives me a questioning look.

Not knowing what else to say, I panic and say, "I fell on of the trampoline and hurt my ankle and then continued to lock myself out of the house and it was just a huge thing. Anyway, it's all good now though. So, where are you taking her on this second date?"

"I haven't decided yet," He admits. "I feel like it should be better than the first one, so that she isn't disappointed, you know? But it should also be something a bit more personal. Like, something that I know that she'll like."

"A computer lab perhaps," I offer a joke, willing my coffee to brew faster so that I can cool it down and drink it.

"Very funny," He says with a roll of his eyes. "What are you doing today? I think I might need your help brainstorming."

"I'm going through the video ideas," I explain to him. "I've got it narrowed down to a few, but I'm still not sure yet. I think that the next video that I do is going to be a pop video- well, maybe not pop but something famous and not a small one."

"Why?" He wonders. "Tired of making peoples' dreams come true?"

"It's not that," I sigh, rolling my eyes at Elliot before the coffee pot dings when it's finished brewing so I turn and grab my coffee mug before adding some creamer and sugar. "I just feel like I don't want to do two of them so close together. I just want to have it recorded now so that I can edit it how I want it and then have it there for when I want to release it is all. You know that I like to keep busy."

"I know that but can't you just take a little bit of time out of your busy schedule to help me? I'm really freaking out here, Jen," He pleads with me, leaning against the counter beside me.

"I thought that you did all of your freaking out yesterday," I remind him with a small eye roll.

"I know but that's just how amazing this girl is- I just can't stop freaking out. I feel like I absolutely have to impress her with everything that I do," He explains, looking really nervous now.

"That's ridiculous," I inform him. "If she really likes you, then she would be okay with going to the diner downtown for waffles as a second date. Just being with you should be enough."

"That's a very romantic thought. Really, it is, but I still think that I want to do something really awesome. I know that technically, I could just take her to some diner or something but I want to... I don't know, give her the world."

"You've only had one date," I remind him in a deadpan type of voice as I grab my coffee and start walking upstairs and Elliot follows behind me.

"I know! I just like her a lot," He rants to me for about the tenth time this morning.

"I've never seen you so distraught," I say with a laugh.

"You know that I'm not good with this kind of stuff," Elliot mumbles, now looking a little bit shy. "I don't know what to do."

"What about the planetarium?" I offer him with a raised eyebrow, taking pity on my best friend and how he's freaking out about this second date. I feel kind of bad for him because this girl makes him so incredibly nervous and I've never seen him like that before. Granted, I'm sure that he's never felt this way before either because I know that he's never actually had a girlfriend before so this is all just completely new to him. "If she's nerdy like you, the planetarium is sort of nerdy, I suppose."

"That could work," He nods, his mind suddenly buzzing with the potential of taking her to the planetarium. "She really loves all sciences, not just the computer kind. And astronomy is a science, so she might really enjoy that."

"There you go, problem solved. And don't forget to bring her flowers," I remind him.

"I did that last night," He tells me. "So I shouldn't bring her flowers again, should I?"

"Oh, yeah you're right. But no matter what, just stop worrying so much. The first date is the hardest but now that you know for sure that she likes you, the rest is easy peasy," I assure him. "So just relax a little bit."

"Alright," He sighs. "What would I do without you?"

"You'd die alone, probably," I joke. Once in my room, I momentarily lock Elliot out so that I can get dressed in clean clothes and brush my hair to look decent even if I still feel gross because I haven't showered and I feel like I'm sweating alcohol from the day before and it's not a pleasant feeling. I'll have to wait until Elliot leaves to take a shower though.

"But I don't know what you should wear to a date to the planetarium," Elliot continues after I let him in. I sit at my desk and log into my computer and he walks over to my bed, sitting on the edge.

"I'm sure that you'd be fine in jeans," I assure him with a small laugh. "Just whatever you'd normally wear to the planetarium."

"But I feel like it'd be different if it was a date, you know?" He wonders, still overthinking this whole date thing, which isn't very surprising at all because with Cara, overthinking is just his thing, I guess.

"No, it's not different as a date. You'd look so ridiculous if you show up to the planetarium in a suit or something, El. You'll be fine wearing jeans. You just have to get on the planetarium site and find out when they're having shows because they aren't every night," I remind him, logging onto my YouTube account to check my notifications and everything, which is what I do every time I log on to my computer. It's like an instinct now, I guess.

"Yeah, you're right. But are you sure that you're feeling alright? You just look kind of off today," He tells me, giving me a concerned look and I know that it's wrong, but I feel myself getting a little bit excited that he noticed my bad mood. I didn't want him to notice but in a way, I'm kind of glad that he did.

"Sure. I'm fine," I reply, looking away from Elliot and putting my attention back on the computer screen so he won't be able to tell that I'm lying. "Just, you know, tired. But I'm really happy for you, El. Really, this is so exciting, you finally getting out there and going on dates and everything. It's really so exciting."

"Thanks, Jen. I must say that I'm pretty excited myself. But so nervous."

"I couldn't tell," I say with a laugh. "You just seem cool as a cucumber right now."

"Shut up," He says with a chuckle. "Wait, what are you doing?"

I glance back at him and see that he's looking at my computer screen, where I just opened my video editing software so that I can start editing through the bloopers of the Primadonna video. Elliot has taught me enough about computers so that I can edit most of my videos by myself, which I do. I edit all of the videos where I'm talking to the camera and the behind the scenes videos but Elliot mostly edits all of the actual music videos. "Editing. Why do you sound so surprised by that?"

"Do you really have to work right now though?" He wonders with raised eyebrows. "I can edit that video for you anyway."

"Yeah, kind of," I say with a small laugh. "I'm not the one going through a huge life milestone right now. I mean, I'm incredibly happy for you and everything but I still have work to do and I want to post the bloopers by tonight."

"Okay, fine. When do you want to start shooting the next video?" Elliot asks me from where he's sitting on my bed and in the corner of my eye, I see him pull his phone out and look down at the screen. He smiles down at the phone after reading what is probably a text message and what is probably from Cara, and then he starts texting back.

"I figured that I'd just do that one on my own," I say quickly. "So that you can focus on this whole Cara situation. You seem to be pretty preoccupied with it so it's fine if you want to take a break with the videos."

"What? No, Jen, don't be ridiculous," He says, looking up at me and away from his phone. "I know that I'm really psyched about Cara but that doesn't mean that I'm going to start blowing you off. You don't really think that I'm that kind of friend, do you?"

"No, I guess not. I didn't really mean it like that," I mutter, feeling my head start to throb again behind my skull and I start to rub my temple with the palm of my hand. That is really good to hear though, that Elliot doesn't want to stop doing the videos with me just because Cara is part of his life now. I know that he doesn't love me the way that I love him, but he still loves me. And that should be enough. That is enough. Everything will be okay, I just have to give it a little bit of time.

"Good. Well, let's talk about this next video," He offers me with a small, charming little smile that I'm sure that he doesn't even realize is so incredibly charming.

"Right. Yeah, okay so these are the ideas that I have so far..."

Chapter 14

"Hello my favorite people! JustJensen here and today, I'm going to share with you the crazy journey that we went on behind the scenes to make the Primadonna video happen for you guys. Elliot, of course, was there to be the backbone of this operation but what made this video special was that my good friend, HeyItsHeather was also here with me, as you may know already from watching the video, and my sister and her little friend also made an appearance so it was a really busy set. Oh, and this guy, Beckett, was there too which was weird. Anyway, we had a great time filming this video and it was so amazing working with Heather because she's so amazing and you should go subscribe to her channel by clicking the link down below and I will see you next week with a new video."

The video that I'm watching of myself fades away and then the bloopers start running. I had posted it last week but I'm just watching it again just to make sure that I've edited it well and then I scan through some of the new comments on the video before checking my phone because I hear it buzz with a text.

It's Saturday, exactly a week after Elliot's first date with Cara and they went on their second date yesterday to the planetarium and I've been spending all day working. I have a time slot at the recording studio to film a simple music video tonight and I'm meeting Elliot there but until then, I'm going to be going through the song requests that I've received from budding artists to decide on which song I want to cover next so that I can learn the guitar for it and make it a video.

The text that I've just gotten is from Elliot, asking me if I'm busy. I text him back and tell him that I'm working at home. After that, my phone starts ringing and I see that it's Elliot again, calling me instead of texting me.

"What's the point of texting me if you're just going to call?" I wonder with a small laugh.

"Sorry, I just have something important to ask you," He tells me.

"Alright then," I say, scanning through the comments still. I've been busy all week with school work so I haven't really read many of the comments on the video yet so I have to scroll all the way to the bottom. "Well, what is it?"

"Well, we're filming your video at the studio tonight, right?" Elliot asks me.

"That is correct," I confirm.

"Alright, what I want to ask you is if it's okay if Cara comes with me so that you two can meet?" He rushes out. "I know that you like to stay focused during video shoots but I promise that she won't be distracting. And maybe we can go to dinner afterwards or something. I just really want you guys to meet."

"That's fine," I assure my best friend. "I'm just dying to meet this wonderful Cara too with the way that you're always talking about her."

"I really think that you will love her and she'll definitely love you because you're both so great," Elliot informs me as I start reading through the comments on the video to keep myself busy while he sounds like he's about to go on a rant about his awesome Cara. "Anyway, thanks for letting her tag along."

"It's really not a big deal, El," I tell him, trailing off a bit when I start reading more of the comments and I realize that many of the comments are about Beckett. I was hesitant about putting that part of the video in there where he was in the shot but I didn't think that it'd be such a big deal. I was obviously wrong about that because everybody is noticing. "Holy cow."

"What is it?" Elliot asks me.

"Beckett is blowing up on my channel," I tell him, reading all of the comments about him under the video. Checking my Twitter feed, I notice a lot of people wondering who he is as well. This is not good.

"Really? I saw that he was in your blooper video, I didn't think that it was very noticeable though," He informs me.

"Me neither, but so many people are asking about him," I tell him. "I don't even know how to respond to any of this."

"Maybe it'll get the heat off of Jelliot," He jokes on the other end.

"You'd rather they start putting me and Beckett together?" I ask, raising my eyebrows at Elliot even though we're talking on the phone so he obviously can't see my surprised facial expression.

"Benson doesn't sound all that bad," Elliot laughs teasingly. "And, come on, Jensen, it's a billion times better than Jelliot."

I physically flinch when he says that so I'm really thankful that I'm hidden behind a phone call so that he can't see my reaction to that. Him saying that he prefers my fans to put me together with Beckett over him is really saying a lot considering how much he absolutely hates Beckett. I know that Elliot doesn't like me romantically and that's fine, I'll get over it. It really sucks though, when he unintentionally throws jabs at it, like us being a couple is the most disturbing, repulsive idea that has ever been thought of in the history of the solar system. It really sucks a lot.

"I still think that it's weird," I find myself saying before the silence goes on too long and Elliot gets suspicious as to why I'm being so quiet all of the sudden. "If my mom or Margaret get a hold of this, they're going to go even crazier than they already do."

"Maybe they'll get off our back too, with the whole best friend romance crap too then," Elliot suggests. "You're thinking of all of the negatives but on the bright side, it'll take the spotlight off of their delusions of us actually being a couple."

"You know," I sigh, now not only feeling hurt but a bit annoyed too. I know that he doesn't mean to sound rude or hurtful because he can be that blunt and oblivious sometimes, but it's just getting a bit annoying right now. "I actually don't find the idea of us the most disgusting thing in the universe. I didn't realize that I disgust you so much that you'd rather people want me with Beckett instead of you. Beckett of all people."

"Jensen," He says quickly, taken by surprise at my outburst. I even surprised myself really because I am usually really good at keeping my resolve, of masking my emotions from Elliot but I guess this Beckett situation is starting to really stress me out. "I don't mean it like that. I just mean that you're more like my sister than anything. And, you know, incest is kind of disturbing, don't you think?"

But you're not my brother, I want to scream at him, but I have already given away too much so I need to repair what I had just damaged. "Right. I know, you're right. Sorry. It's just that I'm feeling a bit stressed right now. The whole thing is stupid. Jelliot, Benson, it's all stupid. I'm fine without dating anybody and I wish that my fans could just understand that, you know? No Jelliot, no Benson, just Jenson. I don't need a boyfriend to define who I am."

"There you go," He chirps, sounding relieved that he diffused my ticking time bomb, even though he really didn't diffuse anything, I'll let him believe that he had. "The whole forming a relationship out of nothing is kind of ridiculous. Anyway, I'm going to go pick up Cara and we'll meet you at the studio soon, alright?"

"Right. See you soon," I mumble, hanging up the phone and tossing it onto my bed before running my fingers through my hair in frustration. I have no idea how I got to where I am right now, pining over my oblivious best friend like I am. I should think of Elliot like a brother to me, I should be repulsed by the idea of Jelliot just like he is.

But that fateful day just a few months ago, he had smiled at me one too many times and it had gotten to me. I don't remember a specific moment that I had realized that I liked Elliot like I do, I just remember waking up one day and realizing that his smile kind of lights up the room and that he's kind of beautiful and that I'd kind of love kissing him and going on dates with him. I'd kind of love falling in love with my best friend. I don't remember why or how it happened, but it did and I didn't do anything about it.

It was a harmless little crush, I'd thought, something that I'd be over in just a few weeks. I didn't think much of it until the first time that he expressed his harsh distaste of the Jelliot idea. After he left that day, I went up into my room and I cried. I cried harder than I ever should have cried and that's when I realized that I was in too deep and that I was in big trouble. I just ignored it though, and it was easy most of the time until Cara came along and messed it all up. I know that she's probably really nice and really amazing but I'm really not looking forward to meeting her today. I want to hate her but I know that she'll make it really hard today by being a really awesome person.

It doesn't matter now though because it's going to happen whether I like it or not so I just put my computer to sleep and go to my closet to grab the dress that I'm going to wear for the video today. It's black and just drapes and flows gracefully, especially the long, wide sleeves. It's kinda short, stopping about mid-thigh and I'm wearing black heels so my legs are kind of on display in this outfit but it looks somber and that's what I'm going for since the song is sad.

I do my makeup so that it will transition well on camera, which is something that I learned from a lot of watching tutorials online a long time ago because I used to be so paranoid about looking like a clown in my videos. I leave my hair down because I straightened it this morning after my shower so it looks nice and then I grab my bag and leave my room.

After letting my mom know that I'm leaving, I take off in my car toward the studio. I get there before Elliot does, which I'm a bit relieved about, so I take some time in the studio getting situated with the sound guy and testing the mic and everything before I see his dark head of hair approach through the large glass window across from where I'm checking the mic.

I grin at him before waving him into the soundproof room and the sound guy gives us the good-to-go before leaving our studio space, telling me that he'll check in in a little while but since he knows us since we come here a lot to film, he knows that Elliot can pretty much take care of all of the technical stuff. He enters the room, followed closely by a tall girl with long-ish blonde hair and an innocent smile on her doll-like pale face. Cara, obviously. She does look very pretty, even in her simple jeans and a hoodie, as she trails a little awkwardly behind Elliot into the studio.

"Hey, I have everything set up with the sound, we just need the camera booted up but you know that I suck at that," I inform Elliot when he comes in, ready to just get to work but I have to put on a happy face and be the best friend that I'm supposed to be so after I tell him that, I turn to the blonde girl and grin at her, offering her my hand to shake. "And you must be Cara. It's really awesome to meet you after hearing about you for so long. I've heard so much about you."

"Really?" She wonders in a velvety shy voice as she glances to Elliot and then back to me. "Good things, I hope."

"Absolutely," I assure her with a grin.

"I'm going to go show Cara the sound board and then I'll get started on the camera and we'll get going," Elliot announces as he starts leading Cara back out the door of the sound proof studio area and into the part that's separated with a glass window that holds the soundboard and all of the technical stuff.

"Sure," I sigh, not wanting to sound as disappointed as I feel. I just want to get this over with, really. I don't want to spend long periods of time with both Elliot and Cara together until I can either get over my feelings or learn how to hide my emotions better without randomly snapping at Elliot when he's done nothing wrong at all. I know that I agreed to go to dinner after we're done here but I'm hoping that I can get out of that somehow. I'm still thinking of a good excuse to get out of it but I can't really think of any.

I can see them through the window as Elliot shows Cara all of the high tech gadgets on the other side of the glass and I spend that time fixing my dress and going over the chords of the song on my guitar, pretending to look as busy as I possibly can before they both come back into the soundproof room.

"Alright, how many shots do you want to get?" Elliot asks me as he starts turning on the camera and hooking it up to the thing that he uses to keep the camera steady and propped on his shoulder as he films.

"Hopefully, we can just get the whole thing done in one take and be done with it," I sigh, making sure that my guitar is in tune even though I've already tuned it three times.

"Are you feeling okay today?" He wonders with a concerned frown as Cara walks around the back of the room, analyzing all of the cables and microphones that are back there. "You seem a little bit off, even on the phone you sounded weird. What's up?"

"Nothing's up," I say quickly. "I'm just kind of tired is all. The channel is wearing me out right now, especially with this Beckett crap that I unintentionally started. But really, I'm fine. I'll get over it, I just have to talk to Beckett about it and get everything cleared up and I'll be okay."

"Why do you have to talk to him about it? If he has a problem with it, he can come to you," Elliot tells me, obviously not liking the idea of me talking to Beckett more than I absolutely have to. That makes two of us there but I really should make sure that Beckett is okay with being on the channel and being so noticed like he is right now.

"It's the polite thing to do, El," I say with a small laugh. "I can't just let this go without him even knowing about it."

"Yes you can."

"I can't," I shake my head at him. "And you know that my mom wouldn't let me even if I didn't want to on my own. She'd make me talk to him anyway, so I might as well just do it willingly."

"Fine, but I don't like it," Elliot sighs and Cara returns to Elliot's side, admiring the camera that Elliot is preparing to take the video of me singing the song.

"Who's Beckett?" She wonders curiously.

"My neighbor," I explain. "He's kind of a pain."

"A total jerk," Elliot adds and I think back to that night a week ago when Beckett was the one to help me out when I got too drunk, wrapping my ankle and giving me a place to sleep and clothes to sleep in when I was stupid enough to lock myself out of my house. Maybe he's a jerk, but I don't think that he's a total jerk. Not anymore. "Anyway, Jen, remember that collaboration video you did last year with The Ready Set? Because I was talking about that with Cara the other day and she said that she's a really big fan of him."

"Yeah, I remember," I nod in confirmation and smile because that seems like what I should be doing right now so that Cara likes me. I really want her to like me even though I can't get myself to actually like her. It's nothing against her though, I'm just being jealous and maybe a bit bratty on the inside but I can't let that show. "We did I Wanna Get Better by the Bleachers. He's a really cool guy."

"That's so awesome," Cara tells me with a wide grin. "I absolutely love The Ready Set. I mean, I guess that isn't really that cool to you because you probably meet famous people all of the time. What was he like though?"

"Jordan's really nice, and totally creative and talented," I say. "And the video was really awesome because we had like, a director and a sound producer and everything."

"You have a sound producer and director too," Elliot reminds me jokingly.

"Yes but you don't have a degree in sound production," I tell him. "Anyway, he was also really funny too. I was kind of starstruck the whole time though so most of his visit is kind of a blur now."

"And you've met Chris Warner, right? I heard that you got to go to one of his after parties," She asks me.

Elliot scoffs. "Met him? Jensen invented Chris Warner."

"I did not invent him, El. He did that himself, I just... you know, gave him a little nudge. But yeah, I know Chris. We're kind of friends, I guess. I don't like, party with Hollywood A-listers or anything," I explain with a shrug.

"That's still so exciting," She insists. "You must be really excited to get out of high school so that you can really make it big."

"I don't think that I'm going to really make it big," I tell her, shaking my head lightly. "But I am ready to be done with high school so that I'll be able to travel and everything."

"We're ready to start shooting," Elliot randomly announces before gripping the camera and hoisting it to his shoulder and I quickly fix my hair and pull my guitar up onto my lap as I sit back on the black stool that I've been leaning against. I adjust the microphone one last time.

"I'll go watch from behind the glass," Clara says, making her way toward the door of the soundproof room. "Good luck!"

When she's out of the room, Elliot turns to me and I nod at him, telling him that I'm ready to go.

"Alright, we're going in 3... 2... 1..." and then he starts filming and I start strumming on my guitar and then I start singing the lyrics to Selena Gomez's The Heart Wants What it Wants.

It's a really easy video, I just play my guitar and sing into the microphone as Elliot holds the camera and moves it around a little bit to get a few angles. Most of the time I keep my eyes clothes to focus on the melody but sometimes, I'll glance up at the camera and then look back down at the microphone in front of me.

Once the video is done, Elliot plays it back with the sound and everything to make sure that we don't have to redo anything and when he decides that we're good to go, I still don't have a good excuse to get out of going to dinner with him and Cara. Even if I did, I might not have used it because I've now realized how important this is to Elliot and I should just suck it up and go with them to dinner to make him happy.

Cara chooses a pizza place just down the street from the studio and neither Elliot nor I argue against that so I get in my car and they both get in Elliot's car and we drive up the street to the pizza place. In the privacy of my car, I take a few deep breaths and tell myself to suck it up and stop being such a baby. Cara is nice and Elliot really likes her so I take another deep breath as I pull into the parking lot of the pizza place and put on a brave face, hoping that it'll stick throughout all of our dinner.

When we sit down at the table, Elliot starts out our dinner by bragging about Cara's accomplishments in the tech industry while she just blushes beside him, being so modest. She's been in competitions for programming since freshman year of high school and she's won most of them. She wants to intern at Google in Silicon Valley when she goes to MIT for college after she graduates this year.

"I've been considering London after high school," I say after she talks about how strange it'd be to live so far away from her home here in Florida.

"Wait, really?" Elliot wonders with raised eyebrows.

I nod, hoping that our pizza gets here quickly because I would love an excuse to not have to talk right now. "Yeah, Heather brought it up when she was here. Wouldn't that be really amazing, El? Going to London for a whole summer before school starts up in the fall."

"That does sound beautiful," Cara agrees with me, nodding just as the pizza arrives and I try not to look so relieved. "I've never been abroad but I've always wanted to go on a mission trip somewhere. Or maybe to Paris. Why did you choose London?"

"A lot of other YouTubers live there and because I'm stuck here for school, I haven't gotten to actually meet a lot of them even though I talk to them online all of the time. So I want to go over there to really meet them and it'll be like a summer of collaborations," I explain to her.

"So Heather's going with you?" Elliot wonders.

I nod. "Yeah. And it's just an idea right now, I haven't even talked about it to my mom."

Luckily, the conversation starts to fall flat while we eat our pizza and I try my best to take my time so that I won't have to join in the conversation.

So as I'm still eating, Elliot and Cara take turns explaining to me how they really got talking when they met at the scrapbooking convention. Cara giggling, Elliot grinning like an idiot.

Once dinner is finally finished, I feel like I'm suffocating in the awkwardness that only I'm feeling. Cara and Elliot are laughing so easily but when I laugh, it feels so constricted and forced. I just want out of this, I want to go back home and throw myself a pity party. After hearing Cara talk about how successful she is and looking at Elliot looking at her like she's made of gold, I feel about drained as we all leave the pizza place.

"Jen, don't worry about this Beckett thing so much," Elliot assures me after he walks me to my car for just a few minutes alone before we go our separate ways tonight. "He'll have his fifteen minutes of fame and then it'll all blow over in a week or so."

"I know," I sigh, leaning against my car. "It's no big deal, really."

"You just seemed so upset tonight," He explains with a concerned frown. "If he bothers you about it, let me know, alright? I won't let him mess with you."

I offer Elliot a small smile and then a quick hug. "My hero. Goodnight, El."

"Goodnight. I'll call you tomorrow," He promises before turning and walking back to his car as I get into mine. As I'm driving away from the pizza place and back to my house, I wipe away one stray tear and tell myself not to worry.

Everything will work out. It has to work out. I'm convinced that tomorrow will be my day.

Chapter 15

"Okay, so when are you going to ask her to be your girlfriend? Completely official and everything," I ask Elliot on Monday morning as we're walking down the hallway toward the cafeteria for lunch. Usually, we go into the AV room to hang out with his computer friends but I'm really hungry today, so he agreed to go to the cafeteria with me so that I can eat lunch. Saturday was rough for me, sure, but I spent all of Sunday just improving my mental stability so now on Monday, I actually feel a lot better about the situation that I've gotten myself into.

"I don't know, shouldn't we go out a little bit more first?" He wonders curiously. "Jensen, I literally have no idea what I'm doing right now, I don't know when I'm supposed to ask her."

I laugh at my best friend and wrap an arm around his shoulders. "You're so adorable, you know? I think that you should take her out again this weekend, nothing too fancy though. Maybe to a coffee shop or something, and ask her then."

"You don't think that's too soon?" He asks me hesitantly.

"Not if she really likes you," I tell him. "And she does really like you, it's pretty obvious."

"You think so?" He questions me again.

"Yes, Elliot, of course. What's not to like? She was completely ogling over you on Saturday. I've only met her once and I can tell that she has it bad for you. So just ask her out."

"Sure," He sighs, sounding kind of bummed out, which confuses me a lot because I thought that he'd be excited to make things official with the girl of his dreams.

"What's wrong now, El?" I ask him, sounding teasingly annoyed.

"Nothing, it's just that I don't want to wait until this weekend. I just want her to be my girlfriend right now," He explains to me as we get into the cafeteria and go to stand in line for food. "That sounds ridiculous, doesn't it?"

"It doesn't sound ridiculous," I assure him with a small laugh. "It just means that you really like her and that's romantic, what you just said. Just, you know, don't ask her over the phone. Call her right now and see if she's busy tonight."

"Are you sure?" He starts second guessing me again.

"Do whatever you feel like you want to do," I urge him. "She likes you because you're you, so just be yourself and do what feels right and she'll like it."

"Alright. I think that I'll go call her then," He states, nodding as if to give himself the confidence that he needs to go call Cara right now. I'm not sure if he'll actually ask her to be his girlfriend today or not because he has a habit of choking when he gets really nervous but in all honesty, I hope that he does ask her and I hope that she says yes. It'd make Elliot really happy and he's never had a girlfriend before so that'd be really cool for him.

It might sound a bit paradoxical to how I'd been thinking on Saturday when we went out for pizza but after I had time to throw myself a little pity party, I realized on Sunday that I was tired of just laying around feeling sorry for myself so I picked myself up on Sunday and told myself to get over it. Elliot is my best friend and that's it and I'm okay with that. I have to be.

"Good. Just be yourself," I repeat to him as I grab a garden salad from the line and some French fries before paying for my food and then I walk with

Elliot to our usual lunch table. He sets his food down at the table before telling me that he'll be right back. He grabs his phone from his jeans pocket and walks out of the cafeteria and into the hallway for some privacy to talk to Cara.

I feel a pang of jealousy for Cara, which is something that happens a lot, but I push it aside because I really am so happy for Elliot and even though I'm painfully jealous of Cara, I'm happy for her too, because she's found herself a really amazing guy and that's so great. I want it to be me that makes him so nervous that he doesn't know what to do but it's not me, and that's okay. I'll learn to get over it and I think that my "healing" process started yesterday, and it feels really nice to know that I'm getting over Elliot.

I'm about halfway through my fries when I remember that I have to find Beckett today and talk to him about the video getting such a big buzz about him. I don't really want to talk to him, especially after what happened last week but I know that if I don't talk to him, my mother will force me to because it's fair that he knows that the internet is buzzing about him right now. I know that he told me that he watches some of my videos but if he didn't watch the behind the scenes video then he may not have any idea about it.

I want to do it now before I forget and I also want to get it done before Elliot comes back because if he sees me talking to Beckett, I know that he won't be happy about it considering how much he hates the guy.

Glancing up at the door to make sure that Elliot isn't coming back yet, I stand up from the table, leaving my stuff there so that nobody tries to sit here while we're gone, and I search the cafeteria for Beckett. Seniors are divided into two lunch periods so he might not even have this lunch period and since I'm not in here all of the time, I don't really know if he is in here or not. However, after a minute of searching, I see his familiar head of dark hair sitting at a table across the room with a considerable amount of his friends. A few of them I recognize from my early high school days as they laughed at the sidelines of my Bethany-inflicted pain.

If there's a group at this school that remembers the hell that I went through freshman year, it's these guys. But I'm completely over all of that stuff, I tell myself, so I take a deep breath and push myself forward toward the table, winding through the cafeteria and all of the circular tables that are spread out through the wide open room.

Standing beside the table now, I quickly tap Beckett on the shoulder as he's listening to one of the other guys at the table talk about a sports game. Beckett turns to look at me but I notice that I grabbed the attention of some of the other people at the table too and that makes me a bit nervous but I look at Beckett and only him so that I don't have to look at anybody else at the table.

"Do you have a minute?" I ask him quietly.

He seems surprised that I'm over here talking to him and honestly, I'm surprised that I worked up the courage to walk over here as well but it's better than waiting until we're home because if I talked to him at home, we wouldn't have a time frame and who knows how long this conversation could last? But here at school, we have until the end of lunch which isn't a very long time frame and I need this conversation to be as short as possible.

"Hey, Jensen," I hear a girl at the table call my name and I look up at her despite my inhibitions about everybody at this table right now. "Great video last week- Marina and the Diamonds are my favorite."

I offer the girl, who I know is Kacey, a small smile and I hope that it doesn't look as awkward as it feels. She was really close to Bethany and Kelly when they were here and she usually had a front row seat to a lot of the torture that I went through, so it's really weird to see her smiling and complimenting me. "Thanks," I turn my attention back to Beckett in order to get away from this table as soon as possible. "Can we talk?"

"Yeah, sure," He nods, standing up from the table and he follows my quick pace away from the table and then into a small corner of the cafeteria that nobody occupies. I would talk to him in the hallway but since Elliot is out there talking to Cara, I feel like staying out of the hallway is the best idea. "What's up?" He asks me when we've got a bit of privacy in the open, loud cafeteria.

"I just wanted to ask you if you've heard about the blooper video that I put out last week," I say in a rushed voice. "Because you're in it for about a second. I didn't think it was a big deal but you're kind of blowing up on my channel right now."

"Really?" He wonders, his eyebrows raising a bit and a smile starts turning on his lips.

"Yeah, I'm really sorry about it. Like I said, I didn't think that it'd be such a big deal but if you want, I'll take the video down and I'll edit you out," I offer quickly. "I just wanted to let you know because it's just really weird, I guess."

"You don't have to take it down, I don't mind," He assures me with a one-shouldered shrug and then his smile grows a little bit. "What are they saying about me?"

My face flushes in heat and I hope that he doesn't see the blush on my cheeks. "Nothing very exciting. Just the normal fangirl type of stuff. They think that you're very attractive."

"That's nice of them," Beckett responds and I can tell that he's enjoying this a lot more than I thought that he would.

"Well, just... if you hear the term Benson, just completely ignore it," I warn him, fumbling with one of the denim loops of my jeans.

"What's that?" He wonders, quirking his head to the side curiously.

"It's nothing," I insist, wondering if I even should have mentioned it at all, which I probably shouldn't have done. "Just forget it."

"Wait, is that like what your fans do with you and Elliot? Except that it's you and me?" He wonders, now sprouting into a full-on grin that I just want to slap off of his face because he really is enjoying this way too much.

"You seem a lot happier about that than I'd imagine," I admit to him, not really able to hide my irritation with that fact.

"Oh, come on, Jensen, it's funny," He says, laughing.

"How is that funny?" I wonder incredulously.

"How is it not funny?" He refutes. "Like, every time a guy is mentioned in your videos, your fans just automatically assume that you're engaged, and especially now that it's with me, I just think that's really funny."

"I still don't understand how that's funny," I deadpan.

"Okay, so maybe it's not funny to you because the idea of you and I is probably pretty repulsive, but-"

"It's not repulsive," I say quickly, interrupting his sentence because I never said that the idea of me and Beckett is repulsive, even though it kind of is. It's just that when he says that, I think back to when Elliot had said that about Jelliot and how absolutely crushed I felt. I'm not saying that Beckett would feel really messed up about me saying that about Benson but I just would never say something like that about anybody. Even if it's Beckett.

"Really?" He quirks his eyebrow again and an amused smile sprouts on his lips.

I roll my eyes, getting a bit distracted from the subject at hand. "Look, I just wanted to tell you what was going on so now that I have, I'm going to go away. Have a nice day."

"You too, Jensen," Beckett says to me as I'm already turning away from the small corner of the cafeteria that we've been standing in and when I get back to the table, Elliot is sitting there with a nervous smile on his face.

He's facing away from where I was standing with Beckett so I'm assuming that he didn't see me talking to him.

"Where'd you go?" He wonders as I sit back down at my seat and finish eating my salad.

"Bathroom," I supply quickly. "And by the look on your face, I'd say that the phone call went well?"

"Yeah, we're meeting for coffee tonight," He nods at me. "And I'll ask her then."

"Good for you," I say with a chirp to my voice. "I'm so excited for you."

"Thanks, Jen. I'm pretty excited too. Painfully nervous, but excited too."

For the rest of the day, I'm sort of nervous for Elliot. If she says no, Elliot will be heartbroken. If she says yes, I will be heartbroken. There's no good way that this can end for me but there is a good way that this will end for Elliot so I'm really hoping that she says yes.

I'm jumping on my trampoline, playing the audio files that have been emailed to me from some musicians to try and decide what my next cover will be when Elliot arrives at my house with a wide grin on his face. Sara and Katy are there too, sitting in the grass and giving me their opinions on each of the songs too because they like to feel included in my YouTube stuff.

"How'd it go?" I ask him as he's running toward the trampoline and then he jumps on top of it without answering my question but by his actions, he basically already answered me.

"You are now talking to the official boyfriend of Cara Robitson," He informs me on a mock formal manner.

"Elliot, that's so great!" I exclaim, wrapping my arms around his shoulders but it's a really clumsy hug because I'm still bouncing and now Elliot is bouncing too so it's really hard to hug.

"What's going on?" Katy demands from the grass, feeling left out from my and Elliot's excitement.

"Elliot's got a giiirlfriend," I sing teasingly, letting go of Elliot so that we don't fall over on top of each other as we're jumping excitedly on the bouncing surface.

"Really? And it's not you?" Sara wonders curiously with her head cocked to the side.

"Mom is going to have a cow," Katy adds. "This throws off her whole life plan for you, you know. What is she going to do now?"

"Wait a minute," Sara speaks up as something dawns on her and her eyes go wide. "If Elliot is now taken, that means that Jelliot is dead... for now. And if Jelliot is dead, you know what that means, right?"

"I actually don't-" I start to say but before I can finish my thought, both of the girls are jumping to their feet.

"BENSON IS REAL!" They both shout at the same time, sounding way more excited about that subject than they really should be.

"No, it's really not like-" I try again to speak and I fail... again.

"We have to tell my mom," Sara says abruptly, dragging Katy toward her house but then Katy starts pulling Sara toward our house.

"No, we have to tell my mom," Katy refutes.

"We have to tell Beckett!" Sara shrieks, pulling Katy back toward her house and this time, Katy seems to agree with Sara because she gives up the fight and starts sprinting toward the Spears' house at full throttle to tell Beckett of their new delusion.

"I'll deal with them later," I sigh, returning my attention back to Elliot, who has stopped jumping. "But I'm really so happy for you. Why aren't you with her right now though? You should be making out in the back seat or something."

"Well, we did that," He admits sheepishly and I have to bite back a giggle at how embarrassed he seems about that. "But not for long because it is a Monday night and she has a project due on Wednesday. I can't believe that I actually asked her though, I was so nervous, Jen."

"You know what this means, don't you?" I wonder with raised eyebrows.

"No..." He trails off, looking a bit panicked.

"Now that you're a real couple, you better start thinking about proposals," I say with a teasing grin and he rolls his eyes at me once he realizes that I'm not being serious.

"Shut up," He mumbles, pushing on my shoulder and he stops me from being able to catch myself by tripping up my feet so I fall onto the trampoline with a loud squeal and then a long laugh. "Do you think that it'd be okay if she sometimes helps with the video stuff? She's really good at it all, she can really help out."

"Of course," I confirm before I can think of a good excuse to say no. Having her around during video shoots may be emotionally damaging on my part but practically speaking, it would be really nice to have an extra set of hands around. Especially if she's as talented as she seems with the video equipment.

"I think that you two can be really awesome friends and it'll be so much fun, filming with you and Cara because I'll have my best friend and my girlfriend and you'll have some awesome videos."

"You already make my videos awesome," I assure him softly just before I start jumping again.

"But with two people behind the scenes, they'll be even more awesome," He explains to me, jumping along with me. "And with this new Benson idea and if Cara shows up on some of the behind the scenes videos, maybe Jelliot will die once and for all."

"Right, yeah, it's a miracle," I respond dryly but of course, he misses my sarcasm because he's too happy and oblivious to notice. "Anyway, so are you going on an official date now that you're officially official and a real couple with labels and everything?"

"Yeah, I'm going to take her out this weekend to that water park about an hour south," He explains as I try to time my jumps so that I can bounce him higher into the air because I know that if I get it right, he'll fly up and it'll freak him out.

"Trying to show off your abs?" I wonder teasingly, poking his hard stomach which causes him to flinch a little bit because he's really ticklish.

"No," He mumbles and I know that I've unintentionally embarrassed him because he doesn't think that he's attractive, which is insane because I've seen him shirtless a lot of times when we go swimming or sometimes he doesn't wear a shirt when he's at home and even before I actually had a crush on him, I had to put a lot of effort into not staring at his abs or letting my mouth water. "It was her idea."

"So she wants to show off her bikini body," I say, still teasing him a little bit because it's just so easy to tease him. "Or she wants to see yours."

"Not everything is about sex, Jen," He tells me, still mumbling and adorably embarrassed.

"Okay, fine then, whatever you say," I sing just as I hear the backdoor of Sara's house open again and then the two little ten year old girls giggling their butts off, running back toward my house.

"Are you worried about what they told Margaret?" Elliot wonders as we watch them barrel toward us and then I notice that Margaret is coming out of the house as well, walking toward the house.

"Maybe a little bit," I admit, wondering how I'm going to tell Margaret that no, I'm not in love with her son and that it's just some major internet gossip.

"Hello, kids," Margaret greets Elliot and I with a friendly smile and a wave as she goes through the back door of our house and then the two giggling girls follow behind her without giving us an explanation as to what's going on.

I fall onto my back on the trampoline and Elliot starts laughing at me. "Elliot. It has now occurred to me that I am so screwed."

Chapter 16

For some reason, my mother and Margaret have this tradition where, for every Valentine's Day, they insist that we have a bonfire in our backyard. The attendance is mandatory for both the Spears family and the Cane family, save for Beckett's older sister, who is away at college and doesn't have time to come down for the weekend. Anyway, it's always the weekend before Valentine's Day and since Valentine's Day falls on this Wednesday, it means that the bonfire is going to be tonight, on a Saturday night.

They use to be really fun, these bonfires, because before high school, I was close to Beckett so we'd play together and roast marshmallows and all of that fun campfire stuff. When high school approached, though, and Beckett became an asshole, they weren't nearly as fun, they were just suffocating and painfully awkward.

When I became friends with Elliot, he started coming to the bonfires and that helped with the awkwardness because I'd make smores with him while Katy and Sara ran around playing soccer or tag or something while Beckett awkwardly sat beside his father and helped keep up the fire.

This year, everybody falls into their regular roles around the fire except for this year, things are a lot less awkward between Beckett and I, so that's nice.

My dad and Mr. Spears are both drinking beer and keeping enough wood on the fire to keep it burning, occasionally poking it just to see what'll happen. My mom and Margaret sit beside each other with glasses of red wine, giggling like high schoolers about their children's love lives. Once they've had enough to drink, I know that they'll start babbling about 'the good ol' days' like they always do. Katy and Sara are jumping on the trampoline, waiting for the hot dogs to be done that my dad is attempting to grill over the fire with the help and taunting of Mr. Spears.

I'm sitting between Elliot and Beckett and the newest addition to our campfire tradition, Cara, is sitting on the other side of Elliot. It's a Valentine's Day bonfire so my mother wouldn't have it if Elliot didn't bring his new girlfriend, it just wouldn't be right.

I can feel the tension between Elliot and Beckett, because I know that they still don't like each other and I'm not Beckett's biggest fan either but I don't hate him like Elliot does. Luckily, Elliot focuses most of his attention on Cara instead of Beckett though, leaving me and Beckett in a conversation about college- generic and easy to talk about. It's kind of awkward but at least we're able to hold a conversation, which is more than I can say about any previous Valentine's bonfire.

"Jensen!" My mother calls my name louder than necessary. "It'd be so wonderful if you played your guitar for us before we start the smores. A nice love song would be appropriate, don't you think?"

"I don't think that's a good idea," I say, shaking my head at my slightly intoxicated mother before taking a sip of my can of pop and then I sit it back down in the cup holder of my chair.

"You totally should sing for us," Cara pipes with an excited grin. "The one that you just put up is so cute and just really beautiful."

"See? You're outvoted," My mom sings. "Go get your guitar."

I immediately regret posting a video of me singing a love song that I'd been emailed by a singer in Montana. I'd put it up because it's a love song and Valentine's Day is around the corner so I felt that it was appropriate but now, that's obviously working against me.

I know that my mother is too drunk to be reasoned with and now, everybody is looking at me, so I just grumble and then stand from my seat by the fire to go inside and grab my guitar. When I get back outside, my dad and Mr. Spears have the hot dogs ready and everybody has a plate of hot dogs so before I have to sing in front of the two families, I grab a hot dog as well.

I'm not shy about my singing or my guitar playing so I guess it's not terrible that I have to sing this song for them, I just think that I'm kind of awkward when I have to sing in front of a live crowd. I don't know why, I just think that it's a little bit more nerve racking than it is when I'm singing on video without a live audience.

"Why are you so weird about singing in front of people?" Elliot wonders with a small laugh. "It's not like everybody hear hasn't heard you sing a million times before."

Swallowing the last bit of my hot dog, I give him a dirty look and grab my guitar. "Shush."

I know that I have all eyes on me from Beckett all the way around the circle to Elliot so I look away from all of them and stare at the blazing fire as I adjust my guitar and spend a quick minute tuning it before I clear my throat and start strumming my guitar and then, when it's time, I start singing the lyrics that I memorized for the video.

"To say 'I love you' is easy to do, But to mean it with all of your soul and be true. It takes the strength of a whole fucking army, To give myself like I've given to you.

You make me laugh and you make me cry, You've turned my tables, I'm wondering why. This doesn't really happen to people like me, You've kissed my soul and I'm flying so high.

Oh baby, I can feel the love in the air tonight, So fill your lungs and breathe it all in. I'll suffocate you in this love that I'm feeling, Baby tonight is our night so don't hold your breath.

The stars have aligned for us tonight, don't you see it, It's all for us, baby take it or leave it. But stay with me and hold me close, I can feel the love in the air tonight."

When the song is finished, I strum the last chord and then all nine people around me start clapping and I blush again, standing up to put my guitar on the porch so that it's not laying in the grass or anything.

"That was such a beautiful song," Margaret coos, leaning into Mr. Spears as he laughs and then wraps an arm around his wife's shoulders.

"Thanks," I mumble. "I mean, I didn't write it though, I'm just kind of the messenger."

"Well, you sang it beautifully," My mom pipes and my father nods his agreement.

"Can we make smores now?" Katy wonders, not seeming to be as into the conversation about my music as the older people are.

"Of course," Margaret pipes. "Josh, did you bring the marshmallows?"

The smores go by fantastically and it's kind of funny to watch Elliot stumble with his marshmallow because it almost catches on fire, which it does every year because he's so awful at roasting marshmallows and then I step closer to help him out like I always do but then I stop myself. Cara's here now, I remind myself. She's the one who gets to help him with his marshmallows.

"You're burning your marshmallow," Beckett informs me from my right, making me jump a little bit before I glance at him and then turn my attention back to the marshmallow at the end of the metal prong in my hand.

"It's not burnt," I deny, pulling my dark brown marshmallow out of the fire just before it turns black or catches on fire. "It's just well done is all."

"That's what people say when they've almost burnt their marshmallow," He says with a teasing smile and it feels weird to be joking around with Beckett but I'm in a good mood, despite the fact that Elliot and Cara are getting all cutesy to my left. The air is warm but not too humid and the sun is setting above us and there's laughter everywhere, coming from the little girls and our drunk mothers and our fathers rumbling about things that men rumble about.

"No," I argue, turning to the table with all of the smore stuff on it including graham crackers, chocolate bars, and some peanut butter per Elliot's request because he puts peanut butter on his smores. "That's what people say when they know how to cook the perfect marshmallow. As opposed to people like you, who are basically eating it raw. That marshmallow has barely touched the fire," I motion toward the marshmallow on the end of his stick and it's not even darkened, it's still cleanly white and uncooked but he's already taking it out of the fire.

I expertly squish my golden marshmallow between the chocolate and the graham cracker, forming a perfect sandwich and I watch as Beckett does the same. "It's cooked perfectly. Look," He presses the marshmallow between two graham crackers and it melts nicely between the two crackers like mine did. "See? It's melted, it just isn't burnt."

"Mine isn't burnt either," I say, laughing as I take a bite of my wonderful smore but I also try not to look like an idiot by avoiding getting marshmallow all over my face, which is hard to do considering smores are incredibly messy. "And I'm pretty positive that my smore tastes better than yours."

"And why is that?" He wonders with raised eyebrows, about to feel very defensive about his culinary capabilities.

I offer him a wide, victorious grin. "You forgot the chocolate, smart one."

He looks down at the sandwich in his hand and realizes that I'm right. In his concentration to prove my smores knowledge wrong, he had also forgotten to put a chocolate bar in his smore. I'd noticed it as he was putting it together but I wanted to be able to tease him about it so I didn't remind him before it was too late.

When he realizes that he doesn't have a great comeback for that, he just pokes his finger in the gooey marshmallow between his plain graham crackers and then wipes it on my nose before walking away to sit back down in his chair by the fire. I am almost tempted to poke him with some peanut butter in retaliation but then I remember that the Benson idea is still going around like the Swine flu and getting in a full blown food fight with Beckett will only amplify that idea, so I just wipe the marshmallow off of my nose and rejoin the fire with my smore.

I notice that Elliot is giving me a weird look so I return his weird look and say, "What?"

"Nothing," He says in response but I can tell that he doesn't look happy because he doesn't like that I'm talking to Beckett and that we're actually getting along. I know that it only upsets him because he cares about me, so I just pat him in the shoulder appreciatively.

"Don't overreact, El, it's no big deal," I assure him quietly before I go back to eating my smore.

He gives me an apprehensive look but doesn't persist and just takes his marshmallow out of the fire to make his smores.

Elliot leaves with Cara a little while after that because Cara has to get home and Katy and Sara start getting tired so they trod off into our house together with sticky hands and chocolate covering the lower halves of their faces but they seem too tired to do anything about it tonight.

"Well, Brian has work tomorrow, so we're going to head in for the night," My mother announces and my dad nods in agreement, helping my mom to her feet as she giggles. "And we're going to go to bed... if you know what I mean."

"Oh my God, Dad, shut her up," I groan, quickly cupping my hands over my ears so that I don't hear any more of my mother's drunken babble about my parents' sex life. Like most kids, I'm aware that my parents are married and in love and that's great but I like to pretend like they have vowed a life of abstinence but what my mother just said kind of pokes a hole in my desire to stay ignorant and I feel like I want to throw up.

"We're going..., goodnight everybody," My dad says, giving me an apologetic frown before he begins leading my mom toward the porch to get her inside.

Margaret, Josh, and Beckett all murmur a goodnight in response but I remain silent with my hands cupped over my ears until I'm sure that my mom is in the house and can't unveil any more disturbing information about my parents that I really don't want to know.

"I'm going to barf," I mumble, more to myself than to anybody around the fire but they all hear me and Beckett laughs beside me with sympathy.

"Oh, don't be so dramatic," Margaret says, dramatically rolling her eyes in my direction. "We might be parents but we're still young, okay? We can still have very enjoyable sex and-"

"Mom," Beckett thankfully interrupts his mother as she starts to slur along some drunken lecture about how middle aged people can have sex too. I don't care if they have sex, really, I just don't want to know about it. At all. "No. Stop. Now."

"You two are so touchy," She laughs at us and for some reason, I find myself blushing. "It's not like sex is an awful thing. I know for a fact that neither one of you are virgins, so you shouldn't be so prude."

"Mags, I think that maybe it's time for you to go to bed," Josh mumbles to his wife but I think that he's trying really hard to hold back some laughter.

"What?" Margaret ignores her husband and questions my and Beckett's matched looks of astonishment because the fact that she knows about our sex lives is really weird. I mean, it's understandable with Beckett because he's her kid but me? I guess it does make sense though, because my mom and Margaret talk about everything, I just never thought that they'd talk about my sex life. I don't even know how my mother would know that I'm not a virgin though, because it's not something that I've talked about with her. "You think that we buy you condoms for the hell of it? We count then, dummies. That's the oldest trick in the book."

"Okay, yeah, we're going to go. You kids have a good night, I hope that we didn't scar you too badly," Mr. Spears scoops his wife out of her chair and wraps an arm around her thin waist to lead her across the yard and into their house. With the way that Margaret is leaning into Mr. Spears, I'd say that they aren't up to any good either once they're in the privacy of their house.

"I can assure you that I'm plenty scarred," Beckett mutters to his dad before he's out of hearing range. I just wish Mr. Spears a goodnight and leave it at that, wishing that I could just erase the past twenty minutes of my life and pretend like they never happened.

After a few minutes of a slightly awkward silence, I clear my throat and say, "So I guess we're both kind of stuck for a while," I state considering neither one of us is willing to go into our respective houses right now, knowing what's happening in both of them. Just knowing about it and knowing that I'm so close to the scene makes me want to jump into the fire pit in front of us, I wouldn't dare go into my house for a good three hours, just to be safe.

"Yeah, well, on the bright side, they forgot the beer cooler," Beckett says, walking around to the other side of the fire where my dad was sitting with Mr. Spears with the cooler of beer between them.

"I am super thirsty," I agree, accepting a can of beer from Beckett as he takes one for himself.

"Exactly. And we can't exactly go inside to get something to drink," He reasons and I can't hold back a small laugh.

My mom lets me have a beer sometimes when we have these family gatherings and although I know that she wouldn't particularly agree with me drinking a beer without her supervision, I'm sure that even if they realize that we drank some of the beer, our parents won't necessarily be angry about it.

"So do you think that they do that every year? We would have noticed that before, right?" He wonders, starting the small talk that'll lead us all the way through until at least one in the morning, when we're sure that the coast is clear.

"I don't know," I say with a small shrug, taking a sip of the beer. "After these bonfires, I kind of just assume that they do, and I always go spend the night with Elliot."

"How's that going by the way?" Beckett asks me, which isn't something that I'm expecting but I'm in such a good mood that I don't really mind. "You and Elliot."

"We're awesome," I assure him. "I'm doing fine with everything. It sucks but... I'm a big girl, I'll handle it."

"That's good," He says, and then he's about to say more but, feeling hyped up on the campfire mood, I continue talking.

"It just sucks that she's so gorgeous and ridiculously smart and incredibly nice, so it's impossible to hate her and that just makes me want to hate her even more. It's a vicious cycle," I explain to him before I realize how weird it is that I'm talking about this with Beckett like it's a completely normal conversation. "Sorry. You don't have to listen to me rambling like this."

"I don't mind," He assures me. "I mean, if you want to talk, I can be a good listener."

"You don't have to feel bad for me, you know," I tell him abruptly, looking down at the glowing fire instead of over at Beckett because he's starting to make me nervous. "I'm fine, really."

"Feel bad for you..." He trails off, sounding confused and even though he doesn't say it like a question, it's still asking for an explanation.

"Yeah, I mean, I know I seem pretty pathetic right now but I don't need your sympathy and I know that you still feel guilty about everything that's happened, but you don't have to pretend to care about my predicament just because of what happened three years ago," I explain, taking a long drink of the cold beer in my hand.

"I'm not only nice to you just because I feel guilty, Jensen," Beckett assures me. "Don't you think that it's possible that I can be nice to you because I actually just genuinely care about you, and that I want to be nice?"

"I mean, I guess that's a possibility, I'm just saying that if you don't want to sit here and listen to my life's problems, you don't have to. I... I forgive you, you know. For it all. So you don't have to listen to me out of guilt."

"You what?" He wonders, seemingly surprised at what I just said.

I shrug, still staring at the bonfire. "I said that I forgive you. I mean, it was a long time ago and it's not like I can just hold a grudge for my entire life against my neighbor. It would be too exhausting. And I know that I seemed kind of harsh about it when we were in Brooks Town but that's not because I'm still mad at you. It's like somebody accidently hitting you in the head with a football or something. It hurts and I still remember it, but I've moved on. And I'm not your problem."

"You're talking like you want us to be friends," He says from beside me and even though I'm not looking at him, I can tell that he's smiling that childish smile of his.

"I'm talking like our parents have basically locked us out of our own houses for the next few hours and I don't know what else to talk about," I mumble before taking another sip of the beer. Other than a warming in my cheeks, I don't feel any effects of the beer and that's probably because just one beer won't get me drunk or anything, just a little buzzed maybe.

"Alright, fair enough," Beckett appeases. "But for the record, I really do care. It's not out of sympathy or guilt, it's pretty genuine, so that whole speech was kind of pointless."

"It was still a beautiful speech," I defend jokingly because I can tell that he's joking as well.

"It was," He laughs. "And I appreciate it. Really."

"Okay, well I've made this conversation too serious. It's your turn to think of something to talk about," I tell him, playing with the tab of my almost-empty beer can as I continue to just stare at the fire. I think that if I looked over at Beckett now, it'd make this awkward because I'm so used to feeling awkward with Beckett. Sitting here having this too-serious conversation with Beckett is too surreal and it only makes sense if I just don't look at him.

"Sure, well since you made it serious, I guess that I'll make it awkward. I find it really hard to believe that you're not a virgin and as my mother so kindly pointed out, you're not," He informs me and I wonder if he was sober and not going for his second can of beer, handing me one as well, if he would have brought this up. Probably not.

And if I wasn't opening my second can of beer, feeling the blushing buzz of the first one, I probably wouldn't have laughed like I do after he says that. It's a loud laugh but it's late, around midnight I think (no cell phones around the campfire, it's prohibited) so I cover my mouth with my hand to stifle the rest of my laughter before I'm calm again and then I say, "Have you been thinking about that this whole time?"

"Vaguely," He says with a chuckle. "I've never seen you with a boyfriend or anything around school and you seem pretty invested in your YouTube channel to have time for something like that is all," Beckett tries to explain.

"I've never had a serious boyfriend before," I tell Beckett with a shrug as I stand up and walk around the fire to the pile of logs that our dads had piled up before the night started and I put a few logs on the fire because it looks like it's going down a little bit. "I had a boyfriend last year though, it wasn't serious and he was kind of a pervert but he was kind of sweet. Until he broke up with me the night after we had sex. That part kind of sucked but like I said, we weren't serious and I wasn't all that broken up about it."

"Still though, that really sucks," Beckett tells me, his voice sympathetic and soft.

"Not really. I never looked at virginity as some little thing that needs to be cherished and protected and special. I think that virginity is not a thing, it's a concept that men created to label women to make them feel like crap. If you're a virgin, you're prude and if you're not then you're a slut. It'd all be so much easier if virginity just didn't exist. So after he broke up with me, I cried for a day and then I was over it. If they're counting my condoms though, they're going to be majorly misinformed because I've only used three of them myself but I gave a few of them to Elliot when he started dating Cara just to be safe."

"Three?" He wonders curiously.

"Three," I confirm with a laugh. "Don't act so surprised."

"I am surprised."

"I do have a life outside of my channel, you know," I tell him, rolling my eyes at Beckett and how naïve he's being. I mean, I'm sure that he doesn't spend a great amount of his time thinking about my sex life so I don't know why he seems so surprised to find out that I've done it three times which, to me, doesn't even sound like that much really. It's kind of comical though. "Anyway, who took your virginity? I always thought that you were having a secret love affair with Bethany, to be honest, because she was always so shady."

"Not Bethany," He negates my theory. "It was Kelly, sophomore year. We were drunk at a party."

"That's the best way to go."

"That's debatable."

I laugh again and I make the mistake of looking over at Beckett, who's slightly laughing too and it feels so strange to be sitting here, talking about something as private as sex with Beckett- of all things to talk about and of all the people to talk about it with. But the weirdest part is that it's so easy to talk to him, so easy to laugh about these things. It might be the beer but in all honesty, I think that I'm just losing my mind.

Chapter 17

"Jensen Cane," This is the response I get when I answer my ringing phone about a week later as I'm editing one of my videos so that I can upload it later tonight.

"Um. Wells?" I say to my English friend. "What's up?"

"I have some really cool news," He tells me. "Are you sitting?"

Now, I'm getting extremely curious. "Yeah, I'm sitting. What is it?"

"Heather's been conversing with me about a trip that she wants to take to come over here to London for the summer," He starts to explain. "And she's also told me that you want to tag along?"

"That's correct," I confirm. "What's the news part though?"

"You're impatient," He teases me.

"Well, now you've got me all curious and I want to know what it is," I defend myself, laughing a little bit as I step away from the computer to take a break while I have this conversation with Wells. I've been working on the video all day so a little break won't hurt.

"Sure, well we've also been in contact with a few other American YouTubers, and we're thinking about renting out this huge flat down the road from here so that you can all stay together and we'll all be really close. It could even be a thing, like Sumer of YouTubers or something with a title way more creative than that. Anyway, if you all share the rent, it's really affordable and the flat is really nice," He explains to me and by the end, my jaw is hanging on the ground. "So what do you think?"

"That sounds amazing," I babble, kind of shocked that this is turning into a real thing. I know that Heather mentioned London but I didn't really take it seriously but now that Wells is telling me about sharing an apartment with a bunch of people so that we can afford it, it feels more real. I have a lot of money saved up from my YouTube channel with ads and selling t-shirts and stuff like that so I can afford it most likely and I really want to spend my summer in London. "I can't believe that this is actually happening."

"Well, you should believe it because it's happening, So far, we've got Heather, Randal, Joseppi, Maria, Tasha, and Aiden. So with you, that makes seven and if we get one more, we can get two of the apartments because they're four bedrooms each. Do you want to bring Elliot or something?"

"I'm not sure, I'll ask him," I say, still reeling from this news because it still feels so surreal. Me. In London for a whole summer. Three whole entire months. That sounds so incredible. I mean, I love it here and I love my parents and everything but I want to get out of here, to explore the world some more and I think that London is a great way to start.

"Okay, cool. We haven't figured out all of the details yet, but once we get everything worked out, I'll let you know. It's just a baby idea right now but I just wanted to let you in on it," He explains to me.

"Right, this is so great. Wow, I can't believe this. I have to go tell my mom," I rant to him, still trying to picture myself going to London- not even just London, but I'll be flying without my parents, probably completely by myself. That's both terrifying and exciting to me because I've never done that before.

"Sure, little squirt. Talk to you later," He says with a laugh, making fun of my age even though I'm only three years younger than him which really isn't that much.

"Shut up," I say back as my defense before hanging up the phone and then sprinting downstairs where my mother is outside on the back porch with Margaret as Katy and Sara are jumping on the trampoline.

"Mom, guess what?" I shriek, going outside to catch her attention.

"Jensen, hey, what is it?" She wonders, looking up at me curiously as she's sipping on a can of pop.

"Wells is putting together a trip to London for a bunch of American YouTubers and do you know who's an American YouTuber?"

"Um. You are?"

"I am! And so he invited me to go to London for the summer. London. How amazing is that? I'll have to go shopping for London clothes and I'll have to get my hair cut so that I look like I belong in London, you know? I can't believe that this is really happening," I gush in excitement.

"That does sound like a lot of fun," My mom confirms with a nod. "Have you talked to your father about that though? He never was keen on you wanting to leave the country without adult supervision, especially at such a young age, Jen. It's a big deal."

"I know that, but I'm eighteen, and I can afford it with the money that I've made from YouTube, so it'll be fine. I can handle it."

"Congratulations, Jensen," Margaret grins at me. "Josh and I went to London for our five year anniversary way back when, and it is absolutely gorgeous. And you'll know people that live there so they can show you all of the cool places to go."

"Right? This is so great. Mom, come on, can't you at least pretend to be excited about this? I'll send loads of pictures," I say, nudging her shoulder with my own.

"I am excited for you, Jen, but I'm your mother- I'm worried about you too. Is Elliot going with you?"

"Probably not. I mean, I'm going to ask him but he'll probably want to spend all of his time with Cara anyway," I explain with a shrug with forced nonchalance. I have been getting better about dealing with Elliot and Cara. They are a cute couple and it's not like I'm completely in love with Elliot. I don't feel broken every time that he talks about her now and when he gets all excited about how much he likes her, I'm a lot happier for him than I used to be.

"Are they getting serious?" My mom wonders curiously, changing the subject from London to Elliot probably so that she doesn't have to think about me going all the way around the world without an adult. It probably makes her feel old when she thinks of her oldest child going out on her own.

"Yeah, I guess. It's only been a few weeks but he seems to really like her and Cara's awesome. So awesome, she's really nice," I explain to my mom with a nod. It still hurts though, to pretend like it doesn't bother me at all. I'm getting better, but it's going to be a slow process, I can tell.

"I like her, she does seem really nice," She nods in agreement. "And since you two obviously were never going to give in to our peer pressure to at least go on one little date, I suppose that dating other people is a good consolation."

"Yeah, it's about time that you gave up that delusion," I refute with a slightly forced laugh. "Anyway, I just wanted to let you know about that so I'm going to go call Elliot and let him know what's up too."

"Okay, but when your father gets home, you're the one that gets to tell him this awesome news because I'm sure as hell not doing it," My mom warns me as I go back into the house to call Elliot. He might still be with Cara but if he is, I'll just leave a message because he usually doesn't answer his phone when he's with her.

I grab a snack from the kitchen on my way back up to my room and I'm trotting up the stairs as I'm dialing his number.

"Hello?" He answers the phone relatively quickly, which makes me believe that he isn't with Cara anymore.

"Hey, are you busy?" I ask him. "Because I have some pretty great news."

"Oh, hey, Jen, no I'm not busy, why? What is it?" He wonders curiously on the other end.

I kick my door shut behind me and sit back down at my desk so that I can IM Heather to tell her that I've talked to Wells about the London trip. "I just got off of the phone with Wells, and he said that this trip to London can be a real thing."

"Really? That's awesome," He enthuses.

"Yeah, it's so great. We're going to rent an apartment for all three months of summer with a bunch of other American YouTubers," I explain to him, still feeling incredibly excited about the whole idea.

"Wow, all summer? It's going to suck to not have you around for three whole months, you know," He tells me but he's obviously not that torn up about it because he still seems pretty happy.

"Well, the thing is that they said that you can come too," I add quickly. "You don't have to, but it's just a thought. I mean, since it's going to be a YouTube gathering and you're a pretty huge part of my channel, I thought that it would be appropriate for you to get an invitation as well."

"That's very generous of you," He says with a chuckle. "But do you think that Cara would be able to go too?"

"Cara?" I wonder, feeling my chest deflate a little bit. "Um, no, there's only room for one more person. But you haven't even been dating that long, you think that it'd be okay to invite her on a three month vacation to London?"

"I don't know. I mean, once summer rolls around, we'll have been together for a lot longer than just a few weeks, you know. But I understand. I
don't think that I'd be able to go though. It's not just Cara, but my parents
would definitely say no considering it's my last summer home before I leave
for college. I'm actually surprised that your parents are letting you go too."

"I didn't exactly ask them," I admit sheepishly. "I kind of just told my
mom that I'm going- I'm eighteen, I can afford it, so yeah. I'm definitely
going. I'll send you postcards though. Especially that cheesy one where I'm
holding up the Leaning Tower of Pisa with my foot."

"That's in Italy, Jensen," Elliot tells me with a small laugh.

"Well, then I'll improvise with Big Ben or something," I refute. "And
there's the London Eye too, which will be so much fun. My dad's going
to freak but he'll get over it. This is so incredible. I can't believe this. Holy
cow."

"I'm excited for you," He says, obviously amused at how much I'm
freaking out right now. It's February now so there's still a while before
summer happens in June but I can't help but feel like I'm on top of the
world right now because I'm just so excited. A whole summer not only in
London, but with Heather and all of my YouTube friends. Granted, I'm
going to miss Elliot so much, it's going to be a blast.

"Okay, but anyway, how was your date with Cara?" I wonder, trying to
change the conversation so that I can calm down. I feel like I'm ready to
jump on a plane right now and go to London right now. Who needs to
graduate high school when you can go to London? Not me, that's for sure.

"It was fun," He confirms, laughing a little bit.

"You two seem to be moving kind of fast," I say as an observation. It's
only been a few weeks but he just said that he'd be willing to go to London
with her for three months, which is kind of a big deal. That worries me
because Elliot's never really done the relationship thing so I worry that he's

just going for it head first like a naïve little puppy, which makes him prone to heartache. And I know better than most that heartache is not a fun thing to experience.

"Yeah, I guess," Elliot says and I can basically hear him shrug through the phone as he tries to sound nonchalant about it. "I can't help it though, because she's so great and wonderful and I can think of about a bazillion other adjectives to describe her but that'd take a lot of time. Anyway, yeah, I really like her and... I don't know, maybe I love her."

"You don't love her," I negate his declaration very quickly.

"How do you know?"

"Because you're still in the honeymoon phase, where everything that she does is perfect and adorable and you're high on the romance. It's not real love until you realize her flaws and then you're okay with them. Have you found any flaws yet?"

"Nope. She's completely perfect," Elliot insists.

"That's exactly my point," I say with a small laugh. "Elliot, you can't know if you're in love or not until after the honeymoon phase, when all of the cutesy stuff starts to wear off."

"How do you know?" He questions me. "Couldn't it be one of those 'love at first sight' things? What's so wrong with that?"

"Love at first sight doesn't exist," I explain. "Look, El, I just don't want you to get hurt is all. If you give her your entire heart right now and things don't go as planned, you're going to get seriously hurt. You obviously don't have to listen to me and I guess it's not really my business but I just think that you should go a little slower and maybe not throw the word 'love' around just yet. It's only been a few weeks."

"Haven't you ever read Romeo and Juliet?" He counters again.

"I have," I confirm, spinning around in my chair a few times before I respond to Heather's IM back to me about London. "I read the whole thing, including the part where they both die at the end."

"Don't be so pessimistic, Jensen," Elliot tells me with an easy laugh. "You don't have to worry about me."

"I do have to worry about you," I insist. "You're so naïve when it comes to things like this and I have to look out for you."

"Have you ever been in love?" He wonders out of the blue and I think that I stop breathing for a moment. That question really takes the breath right out of my lungs. "I mean like really, really in love?"

"I love you," I remind him breathlessly and for a moment, I can't really believe that I just said that but I know that he won't take it the way that I sincerely mean it.

"I don't mean it like that, I mean romantically. I know that you've had boyfriends, but have you really ever been in love?" He asks me, doing just as I knew he would and remaining oblivious to emotions. I guess that's a good thing with this type of thing because it's really easy to hide this from him considering he's so easy to fool when it comes to this.

"Right," I say with a small sigh. "Well, no, I haven't then, I guess. I still know that it's too early to start saying that you love her."

"I appreciate your concern, Jen, but I'm not worried, I can handle it," He assures me, which makes me even more worried about him because he's just so confident in this relationship and although I really like Cara and I'm sure that their relationship will last, I'm still not feeling as confident about it as Elliot is. And that's my completely unbiased opinion. "Maybe when you find somebody that makes you feel like Cara makes me feel, you'll understand."

I roll my eyes at him, thankful that he can't actually see me. "You sound like a total sap."

"I know, isn't it great?"

"It's sappy," I decide. "And just because I've never really been in love doesn't mean that I don't know what I'm talking about- I still have common sense. But you do whatever you want to do, you're clearly too stubborn to listen to me anyway."

"Alright, we can agree to disagree," He decides and I go along with that because I don't know how else to convince Elliot that he's going too fast with Cara. And I mean, if he's happy then I guess I'm happy too. It's not that I'm upset about the relationship because of my sad crush on Elliot because I'm not that petty, but as his best friend, he's just worrying me right now is all.

"Right," I sigh in a mumbling voice. "So let's talk about the next video, because I have a really great idea."

As I'm discussing filming and stuff with Elliot, I'm instant messaging Heather online and she sends me a picture of her new bikini that she bought just for this trip to London. It's not on her because that'd be a little weird, but it's spread out on her bed and she's apparently already bought a lot of stuff for it- Wells had told her about the idea a few days ago but he told her not to tell me so that he could surprise me with it.

After a while of conversing with both Elliot and Heather, I hear the front door open and close downstairs, which probably means that my dad is home. And that means that I have to go downstairs and break the news to him that I'm growing up and that I'm going to London this summer. I don't want to have to pull the 'I'm eighteen' card because that sounds like such a childish thing to say but I feel like it's the only way that I'm going to get him to accept the idea of me flying across the world by myself.

"My dad just got here," I tell Elliot, IMing Heather to tell her that I'll be back soon and then I start walking out of my room toward the stairs to go down to the living room.

"Good luck with that," Elliot sings teasingly over the phone. "Let me know how this goes."

"Shut up, it'll be fine," I mumble, more to myself than to him. "I'll call you tomorrow."

I hang up and put my phone away in my jeans pocket as I trot down the stairs.

"Dad?" I call into the living room. I can hear him shuffling around in there, putting his briefcase down by the door and taking off his business jacket.

"Yeah, Jen, I'm in here," He tells me as I step off of the last step and walk toward him as he's doing his daily home-from-work routine.

"Hey," I say in a chirpy voice. "How was your day, Daddy?"

He sits down on the couch and loosens his tie as he lets out a tired groaning sigh. "It was fine. I have a troubling feeling that it's about to get a bit worse though. You're acting weird."

"I'm not acting weird," I deny, sitting down beside him on the couch with an innocent smile on my face. If I just remind him that I'm his oldest and best daughter, maybe he'll go easy on me for this one.

"What do you want, Jen?" He sees through my bullshit a lot easier than I was hoping he would, which isn't surprising because my dad is really good at seeing through my bullshit, which sucks.

"I can't just want to know how your day was without there being ulterior motives?" I defend even though we both know that there's something else that I need to talk about. My mom is still on the back porch with Margaret so we're alone in the house, which means that my mother definitely hasn't told him about London yet, which isn't a shock because she told me outside that she wouldn't tell him. I just wish that she had so that I wouldn't have to but I can tell by his attitude that he doesn't know yet.

"No, I don't think that you can," He says with a throaty chuckle. "Alright. Lay it on me, kiddo."

"It's good news," I assure him, just to calm him down a bit before I break it to him. My dad works a lot but even though he's gone most of the time, I think that I'm kind of a Daddy's Girl. I used to have him twisted around my pre-teen finger but now that I'm grown up, he's more of a protector than a giver. "I got a call from my friend, Wells, today. The one that lives in London."

"Continue," He urges me on, wisely sensing that there's more to the story than just a long distance phone call.

"He invited me to London for the summer," I say in a very quick wisp of words. Just rip it off like a Band-Aid, right?

"What?" Is his initial reaction.

"I-I mean, not just me. It's going to be a huge group of us going- Heather and a bunch of other YouTubers from the states, we're going to group together to rent an apartment and it's apparently a really nice apartment. Doesn't it sound awesome?"

"So you're telling me that you're going to be going to London for the whole summer without any adult supervision?"

"Well, technically, most of the people that I'll be staying with are adults," I pipe, as if that makes anything any better in this situation. "Come on, Dad, it'll be so much fun- it'll be such an adventure."

"How much will this cost me?" He asks, leaning his head against the couch behind him and closing his eyes as if he's the most stressed out person in the world.

"Not a lot, I don't think. I can pay the rent with my YouTube money but I wouldn't object to getting some spending money or something," I suggest, kind of surprised at how calm he's acting right now.

"And you're still going to college in the fall?"

I nod. "Of course, Dad. I'll come back before the semester starts. So you're okay with it?"

"Of course I'm not okay with it," He scoffs, opening his eyes again and looking over at me. "But I'm not going to fight it. Lord knows how useless that would be. I am going to need to speak to the guys that you'll be staying with though, just to make sure that you're in good hands. And you'll call home at least every other day. Is Elliot going?"

"Nope. I invited him but, you know, there's Cara."

"Right. There's Cara," My dad nods in agreement. "I think that a little time apart will be good for you and Elliot."

"Why do you think that?"

"Oh, I don't know," He sighs, leaning over and kissing my forehead before he stands up so that he can go greet his wife on the back porch. "It might be because you're not as good of an actress as you might think. Elliot is just a really oblivious dude.'

"I don't know what you're talking about," I mumble, standing up myself so that I can hurry upstairs to end this conversation. I'm relieved that his reaction wasn't as stubborn and ridiculous as I was expecting it to be, but now my face is flaming red and I'm wondering if the only person on God's green earth that doesn't know about my stupid crush on Elliot is actually Elliot himself.

Chapter 18

Wednesday is the only day that Cara is free to shoot the video. I need the video done by Saturday so that I can record the vocals for it but I guess when I told Elliot that Cara could be part of the recording process, they interpreted that into that I'm willing to work around her busy schedule so that she can be here for every step of the process.

She has yearbook on Monday and then student council on Tuesday, which is when I originally wanted to film. And then she has to volunteer at the nursing home on Thursday and Friday. So that left Wednesday. When Elliot explained this to me, he didn't really give me any room for debate, so I had to reschedule a dinner with my mother and maternal grandparents just so that we can film on the one day this week that Cara is available.

And if I sound annoyed, that's because I am. I love Elliot and I like Cara, but really.

So while Katy's at gymnastics practice and my mom is at dinner, my dad is at work, I get to setting up for the video. I rarely ever shoot music videos at my house but I figure it's easy and since it's during the week, we need it to be speedy. Behind the trampoline, I have a nice tree line so I tossed some Christmas lights into the pine trees to make it look pretty and then called it a backdrop.

Dressed pretty casually in a tan jacket, black tank top with a black and white rose on the front, and jeans with black bootie heels, my hair down and I straightened it and spent a lot of time right after school perfecting my makeup. I struggle through the grass in my heels to set up the video stands so that everything is ready when Elliot and Cara get here so that we can get this over with as soon as possible.

With so long to see Elliot falling unreasonably in love with Cara over the past weeks, it's significantly dulled my crush on him, so I'm glad that he found her and I'm glad that he's happy. It just still burns to see them together so I'm not too keen on spending my entire evening with the mushy couple.

As I'm making sure that the tripod is stable in the grass, I can hear footsteps coming from around the house so without looking up, I just assume that it's Elliot.

"El?" I call just to make sure.

"Yeah," He clears his throat when he gets closer. "I'm here."

"Do you think that this jacket looks okay with the shirt? Because I don't want to-" I cut off my fashion questions when I realize that Elliot's alone and I'm pretty sure that the only reason that we're shooting the video today is so that Cara could be here too. "Where's Cara? We can't reschedule this, El. I've already got a song picked out for the next video."

"Um, Cara's not coming," He mumbles, looking down at the grass instead of up at me and his upset frown is making my stomach ache with nerves. Something is definitely wrong right now and I have the sudden urge to run in the opposite direction instead of staying here to find out what that wrong thing is.

"Are we filming without her then?" I wonder, feeling a bit irritated if that's the case because, like I've made clear, we are only doing this today for Cara. I could be having dinner with my grandparents right now, who I rarely ever see because they live on the other side of town, but I canceled just to do this tonight.

"Sure, but I've got to talk to you about something first," He explains, his voice quivering and very quiet, which is how he gets when he's nervous but I've never seen him this nervous. It's incredibly unsettling.

"What is it, El? You're kind of starting to scare me," I tell him, giving him a concerned frown. My original assumption is that something is going awry in his relationship with Cara because she's not here and he is but then I decide that it's probably not a Cara thing because if it was, then he'd be way more upset than he looks right now. He doesn't necessarily look that upset right now, he seems just incredibly nervous.

"Well, you're not going to like it," He warns me. "Actually, I don't even like it. But you know how much I like Cara."

"Right..." I trail off, forgetting the tripod completely. Forgetting that we only have a few hours left of daylight to film with before we have to start getting out more light sources and lamps, which I don't want to do. He's looking so nervous right now that it's starting to make me feel sick to my stomach. "So what is it?"

"First of all, let me just say that Cara really likes you. She thinks that you're great and talented and inspirational. So this isn't personal, Jen. But she just thinks that we're spending too much time together," He explains to me, his voice still shaking and very quiet so I have to step closer and strain to hear him a little bit.

"Oh. Okay, well I can see that. You don't have to help out with every video, if you want to spend more time with her. I mean, it'll stink, but I think that I can mostly manage on my own. Maybe every other video or something? I mean, I do get you during school, so I don't mind giving Cara weekends or something," I shrug, hoping that that's the worst part of his bad news. Maybe he's just being overly dramatic about needing to rebalance his time commitments.

"It's not just that," He sighs, looking between the grass and the sky but not directly at me, which is really scaring me. "She doesn't want us to be friends at all."

"She doesn't..." I repeat his words, not really registering them in my mind.

"She doesn't," He confirms. "And you know that I really like her. Look, it's not as bad as it seems. We just need to take a little break and then in a few weeks, maybe a month or two, she'll realize that there's nothing to worry about between you and me and then everything will be fine again."

I blink a few times, still processing what's going on right now. "So... basically, you're telling me that Cara's making you choose between her and me. And you're choosing her?"

"When you put it like that, it sounds a lot worse than just taking a break," He says, his words mushing together in an almost-incoherent mumble.

"Friendship breaks don't exist," I say to him, focusing most of my attention on breathing so that I don't forget to do that. I still don't really understand what's going on though, because Elliot isn't the kind of guy to choose a girlfriend over a friend. He isn't the kind of guy that would give away our friendship of three-ish years just for a girl that he met a few weeks ago. He wouldn't do that. I mean more to him than that. I mean so much to him, he would never do that to me. "Friendship is a forever type of thing."

"Jensen," Elliot says my name and that's it, as if saying my name is going to make anything okay.

"What? What do you want me to say? That I understand?"

"I was hoping for something along those lines," He breathes, still not looking up at me.

"But I don't understand," I say, trying my absolute hardest not to cry right now. "You barely even know this girl but you're just going to give up everything that we've been through, our whole entire friendship, for her? Did you even have to think about it or did you automatically just know that she's more important to you than I am? Am I really that... that disposable to you?"

"No, it's not like that at all, Jen," Elliot denies and for the first time tonight, he looks up at me, our eyes meeting briefly before I look away, not able to stand looking into his eyes at all right now. "It's only a temporary thing. I might never get an opportunity like this again and I really don't want to blow things with Cara."

"It's temporary," I don't know why I'm repeating everything that he's saying but I think it's helping me with trying to understand the situation. "Do you think that I'm just going to sit around and twiddle my goddamn thumbs and wait until your girlfriend decides that she can trust you enough to allow you to be friends with me? Do you think that I'm that pathetic?"

"It's not-" He starts to say something but cuts himself off, looking like he's trying to find the right words to say but I don't think that there are any right words to say right now. There's absolutely nothing that can take away the sting of what he's telling me right now. "I don't want to hurt you, Jen."

"Okay," I sigh, trying now to both not cry and to move on from this conversation and to get Elliot as far away from me as possible. "Okay. We can do this. This can happen. Well, thanks for stopping by and letting me know. I'll drop off a box of all of your things this weekend. I'll find a new place to sit at lunch. I'll hire a camera man."

"This doesn't have to be such a big deal, Jensen," Elliot insists again, his voice and facial expressions painfully pleading for me to understand what's going through his mind, but I don't understand it at all. We've been through so much in these past few years, we have so many memories and laughs and adventures. And it's all over in the blink of an eye. In this one ten minute conversation, our whole friendship has crumbled to the ground from the size of a skyscraper. "Look, just keep my things, don't hire another camera. Just wait this out with me for a few weeks. That's it, and then we can go back to normal, like this never even happened."

"I'm not a second choice. I m not going to let you put me on the back burner and then come back in like nothing ever happened, like you didn't abandon me. I spent so long like that, living on the back burner. And I love you to death, Elliot, but I'm not going back. Not even for you. So if you're choosing her over me, even though there shouldn't even have to be a choice but that's between you and Cara, then that's your choice and you're going to have to live with that. I'm not going to be here for you when you come back."

Tears are running down my face, no doubt leaving black marks running down my cheeks made of smeared make up. I'm proud of myself for not giving into him though, even though I desperately want to. I don't want to lose Elliot but I won't let him treat me like crap. I can't do that or I'll lose my mind and it took me so long to get to this place where I can be confident in myself and not let people walk all over me. I can't go back. Not even for Elliot, I can't do it. But this hurts so bad and it's only just begun. I feel like my whole world is cracking in two, falling and crumbling into pieces as it splits around me.

"I don't want it to be like this," Elliot says in a whispering voice. "I don't want to choose."

"I'm not the one that's making you choose," I remind him, crossing my arms over my chest so that they don't start trembling. "I would never do that. And you were right, when you said that I've never been in love. But if this is love, you abandoning your best friend for a girl you just met, then

I don't want to have anything to do with it. It sounds like a disaster. And I was obviously wrong about you moving too fast with Cara."

"What do you mean?" He looks like he's about to cry and the angry part of me says 'good, let's see it' but the part of me, the bigger part, that still desperately loves him, wants to soothe him back to happiness like I always do. To comfort him and tell him that there's no reason to be so upset.

"It obviously doesn't matter how long you know somebody, they can still break your heart and the chances are that they will," I explain in a constricted, hard voice. "And if you're going then get out of here. I have a lot of shit to figure out."

He calls my name as I go into the house but I ignore him, not knowing what else he could possibly have to say to me right now after he just clawed his way into my chest and ripped out my heart, leaving it in the dirt out in my own backyard.

I watch out the front window as he walks back to the front yard and gets in his car, driving away from my house and leaving me feeling painfully lonely. My eyes are blurry with tears so I take off my black heels before I trip over something and break my ankle because it's just healing from when I had fallen off of the trampoline the last time that Elliot made me cry.

I let my jacket slide off of my shoulders and I toss it onto the kitchen table just before a loud, dry sob escapes my throat and it echoes through the empty house. My parents are gone, my sister is gone. Everybody is gone and this house has never felt so empty. I have never felt so alone.

I know that I'm not actually alone- I have Heather, my YouTube friends, my family, my fans. People care about me. But this house is so painfully empty and every loud sob that escapes my mouth echoes between the barren walls, just to remind me of how lonely I feel right now.

How is there Jensen without Elliot or Elliot without Jensen? We're a team, and we're a kickass team too. We've accomplished so much together.

We've created countless amounts of both videos and memories that I'm not ready to let go of. We were too wonderful to just be forgotten like this. How can this be happening?

Another sob. Another echo.

I can't be in this house anymore, I feel like it's swallowing me in its emptiness. I'm in no state to drive though and even if I could, where would I go? Find my father at work or my mom at the restaurant so that I can cry to them like I'm five years old? I don't have any other close friends except for Heather and I'm not about to drive all the way to New York on a school night.

But then I remember that Beckett might be home, and he's just next door. We may not be the best of friends but he's a good listener and he cares. He's said so. And I can't be alone or in this house any longer, so I don't give myself any time to think about it, I just grab my keys from my jacket pocket and try to clean off my cheeks a little bit and then leave through the front door, just to hurry through the yard and then onto Beckett's porch.

I know that this is probably a really bad idea and it's incredibly humiliating but I don't know what else to do right now so I don't give myself a chance to talk myself out of it, I just bang my fist into the door a few times and while I wait for somebody- hopefully Beckett- to answer the door, I try wiping some more runny mascara from my cheeks so that I don't look like such a mess.

For a few minutes, nobody answers the door, so I'm prepared to just go back home and figure something else out but just as I'm about to step off of the porch, I hear the door rumble and then it swings open. I turn around to see Beckett standing there with a confused look on his face.

"Hey," I breathe, sniffling as I do so.

"Hey," He repeats, looking me up and down as if to assess the situation. "Are you drunk?"

I shake my head, biting my lip so that I don't cry. "Not this time."

"Is everything okay?"

"Um, you know, now that you mention it, not really," I admit, pressing my palm to my lips to hold back a loud sob. "And I remember that you said that I could talk to you. Are you busy?"

"No, come on in," He assures me quickly, stepping out of the doorway so that I can come into the house. Beckett seems incredibly surprised that I'm here, which is understandable considering I rarely ever do willingly initiate conversations with him and I certainly don't come all the way over to his house just to talk to him. But desperate times and all of that. He shuts the door behind me and then walks into the kitchen, so I follow him. "What's up?"

"Elliot just broke up with me," I admit in one breath and when I say it, it finally sounds real. After a while of being able to deny what's been happening, it's settling in now and I'm feeling sick. "Cara... she made him choose between me and her and... obviously, he didn't pick me."

Beckett starts making a pot of coffee and then leans against the counter. "I'm sorry. That really sucks, Jensen."

"Yeah, it really does," I confirm, sniffling again. "And I'm sorry for barging in like this, I just didn't want to be alone in that house anymore. If I'm bothering you though, you don't have to put up with me."

"I don't mind putting up with you," He assures me with a slight smile. "Do you want something to eat or a tissue or ice cream or anything?"

"Do you have ice cream?"

"No, I don't think that we do," He shakes his head at me and if I was in a better mood, I would have laughed. Instead, I just sniffle again. Beckett walks over to the fridge and opens the top freezer part before saying, "Yeah, we don't have any. But if you want some, I can go get some- or my mom'll be home soon, she could pick some up on her way home."

I shake my head and slump against the counter, feeling the sobs start to overwhelm me again. "I don't need ice cream. I just... I think that I'm going to start crying again. Is that alright?"

"Uh, yeah, I guess," He nods before walking over to the coffee maker and he looks extremely unsure of what to do. "If you want to."

Of course I don't want to cry but I don't really have a choice at this point. I run my fingers through my hair as I start pacing in the kitchen and the tears start to bubble over my cheeks again. "I just don't know what I'm going to do," I rant and then I sniffle as Beckett pours two cups of coffee before pulling out the sugar and a thing of creamer from the fridge. "And it's not even the romantic thing, Elliot's my best friend. Or was, I guess now. I love him so much. I don't know what I'm going to do."

"You're going to figure this out," Beckett informs me, making his coffee. "You always do."

"But I always have Elliot with me to help me figure things out," I explain, losing more and more control over my emotions as my crying starts to get louder and my words get harder to understand. "He's always there. I don't... I don't know what I did wrong."

"You didn't do anything wrong, Jensen," He says, handing me the other cup of coffee and I use that to keep my hands busy so that they aren't shaking. I pour some of the creamer into the cup and then dump a little bit of sugar in as well. "It's not your fault, this Elliot kid is just extremely stupid."

"No, it has to be me. There has to be something wrong with me," I mumble, stirring the coffee and then my hands start shaking again and I try to get myself to calm down by pacing back and forth in the kitchen as

Beckett just leans against the counter sipping on his coffee. "There's just something wrong with me that makes people run the other way."

"That's not true," He denies, shaking his head as his eyes follow me back and forth in the kitchen. "Even without Elliot, you have millions of fans who adore you."

"But they don't know me," I argue. "They know my music and they know my online persona but they don't really know me. You knew me once upon a dream ago and then boom- you vanished in the blink of an eye. And then the guy that I fucked last year after homecoming, he saw the deepest parts of me, no pun intended, and he got the hell out of dodge. Elliot... he hasn't even known this girl for a month but she's clearly a better option than me. He loves her. Way more than he could ever love me. And again, it isn't the romantic thing but it's like he was just looking for an excuse to get away from me."

"I'm sure that he wasn't doing that," Beckett argues as I grab my full cup of coffee off of the counter and take a sip, letting the scalding liquid burn my tongue a bit before sliding down my throat. "He obviously cares about you a lot, Jensen. And there's nothing wrong with you."

"There has to be," I say but my voice is so weak now that it only comes out as a whisper and then that's the last of my energy because after that, I completely break down. Not just crying anymore, I'm in hysterics so I put the coffee down so that I don't spill it and then Beckett does something that I think surprises both of us. He steps closer to me and then a few steps closer until he's wrapping his arms around my shoulders. And then I do something unexpected in response, I hug him back and I bury my face in the soft fabric of his t-shirt as my whole body shakes with the sounds of my heart ripping apart.

Once I've finally calmed down again, Beckett gets me to sit down on the couch and he puts on a movie. I tell him to put on whatever he wants, just nothing that's romantic or sappy. He decides on a thriller but I'm not sure what it's called, I just sit down on the couch with my head resting on his muscly shoulder. I think that we probably look kind of like a couple because we're sharing a blanket too but I feel too defeated by the world to care about that right now.

Just feeling close to somebody is really all I need right now, even if that somebody is Beckett- of all people. And his arm is wrapped around my waist out of instinct- I don't even realize that he did that- but it feels so nice just to have somebody here.

"Hey, I'm home and I- Oh, hello, Jensen," Margaret comes through the front door about twenty minutes into the movie and I can feel Beckett tense up beside me but he doesn't move away. I assume he's waiting for me to move away from him because Margaret seeing us together will start a whole new Benson epidemic but I'm so exhausted by tonight that even my bones feel heavy, so I don't move.

I do, however, offer Margaret a polite wave. "Hi, Mrs. Spears," My voice is raspy from all of the crying but I think that my words were still coherent.

"Long night?" She wonders, sitting her purse down on the table in the foyer before walking through the living room and into the kitchen.

I let out a long, hiccupping sigh before I respond to her with, "The longest."

And I don't feel upset in the least about her thinking that Benson is a real idea, because it sure as hell beats Jelliot.

Chapter 19

The next day is Wednesday, and it's a school day, and it absolutely sucks. I'm so used to doing everything with Elliot that I have to remind myself not to go to him every step of the way.

When I go to my locker, I remind myself not to look around for Elliot, because he usually meets me there. When I go to lunch, I remind myself not to go to the AV room where we usually spend lunch together and instead, I eat by myself in the library. When I get an idea for a video to shoot, I have to remind myself not to immediately text the idea to Elliot.

I do text my mother to let her know that I'm alright because of course, when Margaret saw me with Beckett last night, she'd let my mother know that I was looking very upset and clearly, I was more upset than they'd ever seen considering I was going to Beckett for comfort. So my mother became worried about me and I told her what happened with Elliot last night when I got home after watching a few movies with Beckett in his living room. She offered me a day off of school but I shot that down because I don't want to run away from this, even if it'd feel really nice to just be laying in my bed right now, crying into my pillow.

I know Elliot's schedule so as I'm going to class, I actively avoid the hallways that I know he goes through. That might sound kind of crazy but I don't really care- I think that I'd lose the rest of my sanity if I ran into Elliot today, especially if he tries to talk to me or apologize about what happened yesterday. I don't want to see him, I don't even want to think about him but I'm not really having any luck in that department because I can't get my mind off of stupid Elliot and how stupid he is.

I keep replaying last night in my mind on a constant loop. Did I react wrong to the news? Maybe I should have just taken him up on his offer of just taking a friendship break so that I didn't lose him altogether. I mean, all he's really doing is trying to give himself a shot at romantic love because he doesn't think that he'll ever get a chance like this again. He just wants that chance. Maybe I was too hard on him.

But then again, I know that if I had to make the decision again, I wouldn't change my mind. I'd been bullied for so long, put through so much crap. My freshman year hurt a lot but I never hurt as badly as I did last night when Elliot told me that he'd picked Cara over me. And I can't get myself to believe that it's okay to do that to a person. I can't get myself to believe that it's okay for Elliot to say 'you're not important enough to me, so I'm going to ditch you but then when it's convenient for me, we can be friends again' and then for him to expect me to just be here, waiting for him. After he hurt me as bad as he did last night, he expects me to just forgive that and pretend like it's no big deal.

And maybe I should. Maybe that's the normal thing to do in this situation, I really don't know. But I won't do it. I can't let myself believe that it's okay to hurt somebody that bad and then just expect them to pretend like nothing ever happened. It isn't okay.

So yes, I'm going to miss Elliot like crazy. I'm going to cry a lot and I'm going to think about him and I'm going to remember all of our really amazing memories together. But then I'm going to move on, and I'm going to still remember him but I won't cry anymore. I'll be strong again at some point. I won't have Elliot anymore, but at least I'll have my pride and dignity- something that I worked so hard to build within the past few years.

After school is over, I get home just in time to drive Katy to gymnastics practice and then I have the house to myself. Nothing that exciting is going to happen though because I have a song video to edit and then I'll upload that. And since I'm feeling so emotionally whack today, I'll probably sing another song, something sad, to help me vent. Singing is the best remedy for me, so hopefully it'll help me today.

Once I log on to my computer, I suddenly realize that I actually don't have a video to edit. I was supposed to shoot that yesterday with Elliot and Cara but that obviously didn't happen, so I've got nothing. I'd offered to edit it so that Elliot could take Cara to the zoo or something but now I don't even have a video to edit. Awesome.

So I decide to use my venting sad song as my video to upload today because that's really the only choice I have. I grab my guitar from the corner of my room and set up my camera and light boxes across from the wall of my room that's plastered with fan mail including letters and drawings and then I study the guitar sheet music for the sad song that I want to play before I practice it a few times and then I give it a go with the camera recording the song.

As I'm singing the song, I can feel myself getting choked up because I'm thinking about Elliot and how he's usually behind the camera, studying me to make sure that the camera's angle is right. He's there to cheer me on, just by being there. But now he's not, and he never will be again. And it hurts so bad, just like I knew that it would. I focus most of my energy on making sure that my voice stays steady through the song but I can't stop a few tears from falling down my face. I guess that'll add emotion to the song, so there's a silver lining.

When the song is over, I barely finish the last note before I start breaking down into a fit of sobs again so I hurriedly turn off the camera and then put my guitar away so that I don't drop it in my fit of hysterics. It takes me a few minutes to recover from my crying fit and when I'm finally okay again, I put away my lights and tripod before carrying my camera to my computer desk so that I can plug it into my computer to edit the video. It shouldn't take very long to edit though, so I'll have a lot of time tonight to spend doing nothing at all. Maybe I'll go lay out on the trampoline and stare at the stars and listen to the song prospects for next week.

Before editing the video though, I go into the bathroom to wipe my face from all of the sticky tears. Clearing my face from all signs that I'd been crying somehow makes me feel a little bit better, like I'm washing away all of the sadness. That's obviously not true, because I still feel sad, but I don't feel as pathetic. I feel like myself.

Just as I'm about to edit the video down, my phone starts ringing beside my computer so I grab it and check the caller ID just to make sure that it's not Elliot or something and I see that it's Heather calling. With a sigh of relief, I push the green answer button and put the phone to my ear.

"Hey, Heather," I greet her in the happiest voice that I can muster.

"Hello," She sings in a chirpy voice. "So about this London thing, I'm thinking that isn't it legal to drink when you're eighteen in London?"

"Uh. I don't know, I haven't really thought about it."

"Okay, well let me Google that then because if it's legal, we are going to turn up!"

"I can't believe that you just said that," I say, forcing a small laugh but it comes out humorless and dry.

Unlike Elliot, Heather quickly picks up on my bad mood, which I was kind of hoping that she wouldn't. "What's wrong with you?" She wonders.

"Just some high school drama," I admit. "Have you found the drinking age yet?"

"Give me a second," She scolds before she pauses to type and then shouts, "YES! It's legal at eighteen- this summer just got a billion times better, you have no idea."

"Yeah, it's really going to be amazing," I agree with her but I don't sound nearly as excited as she does. I am really excited about London and about getting legally drunk sometimes but I just can't get myself to sound excited about it.

"It's too bad that Elliot can't come with us, I would pay great money to see him drunk," Heather pipes. "You should ask him again, maybe this legal drinking thing might change his mind."

"Elliot's actually the high school drama that I was talking about," I mumble. "We're not on speaking terms at the moment."

"Wait. What? Is that even possible?" She wonders incredulously after a moment of silence to process what I just told her. "What the hell happened?"

"Long story short: His new girlfriend made him choose between me and her. He chose her but he said that we could be friends again in the future, once Cara stopped being jealous about our friendship, but I told him no. I said that if he cuts off our friendship, then it's a permanent deal. So yeah, it's permanent and we're not friends anymore," I explain to her, trying to sum up the whole conversation without going into any details.

"That's so awful of him," Heather says. "He hasn't even known her for that long! What the hell is he thinking?"

"He's thinking that he's in love," I explain to her, sniffling just once and I try to do it quietly so that Heather doesn't hear it. "And that he'll do anything to stay that way. I know that I made the right decision, to tell him to stay away if he goes now but... I don't know with every hour that passes, I feel more and more like I made a mistake."

"You absolutely did not. He can't just walk all over you like that," Heather is quick to assure me. "Fuck him! I am going to send him a very strongly worded text message and then we'll see who's laughing. You know what I'm going to do? I'm going to send him a bunch of porn shots of just females from restricted numbers so that if Cara looks through his phone, and being the crazy bitch that she is she'll definitely go through his phone, she'll think that a bunch of girls are sending him nudes."

"You don't have to do that, Heather."

"I'm already doing it," She tells me. "He has no idea who he just messed with. But fuck him. How are you doing? Do you want me to send you some Edible Arrangements? A male stripper? Anything?"

"I definitely don't need a male stripper, but I appreciate the thought," I tell her, actually laughing this time despite my crappy mood. "I'm actually doing... well, I'm doing horrible to be honest but I'm getting through it. I had kind of a crush on him, if you couldn't tell-"

"I could tell, Jen. Everybody could tell. Except for Elliot, I guess."

"Right," I sigh. "Well, that's completely gone now, so that's good. I've been getting over it day by day since he started talking to Cara but after last night, it's just completely out the window. But even without the complication of the crush, he was my best friend and we've done so much together, I just... I can't believe that we're not friends anymore."

"Jensen, I'm so sorry," She tells me over the phone and I wish that Heather wasn't in New York right now, states away from me because I could really use a hug or something right now. Especially from Heather, who always has a way of cheering me up when I'm in a bad mood. "He definitely doesn't deserve you. I wish that I could be there for you right now."

"Me too," I mutter. "But it's okay, really. Believe it or not, I've been getting closer to Beckett and he helped me out a lot last night after Elliot left."

"You're not doing that just to spite Elliot, are you?" Heather wonders cautiously. "Because getting with one asshole to piss off another asshole is not the way to go, Jensen. It's just not healthy."

"I'm not doing it to piss off Elliot," I assure her. "Beckett's actually been really nice and it's actually kind of fun to hang out with him, I guess. He really isn't that bad anymore."

"Sure, whatever you say. I still don't like him but if he's making you feel better then I guess that I'll hate him a little less," She decides. "And I just sent that text to Elliot so now I'm going to go onto the lovely internet and find some promiscuous pictures to spam his phone with."

"Heather, you're awful," I say, laughing again at how insane she can be.

"No, he's awful. You're a bit heartbroken right now, so you can't feel the rage that's buried under your sadness but I can. I feel the rage. And soon enough, Elliot's going to feel my rage as well that little freaking punk," Heather explains to me. "And I still think that Beckett is awful too so you should give me his number so that I can send him angry texts too, while I'm caught up in my anger."

"I'm not going to do that," I decline her offer.

"Okay, fine. I'll stay away from your precious Beckett but if he ever hurts you at all- if he even looks at you the wrong way, you let me know, and I'll take care of it."

"I know you will," I laugh again. "You're the best, you know."

"I do know," She jokes. "That's why you love me."

"Do you think that the boys in London are cute?" I ask her randomly.

"Of course they are- haven't you seen Wells' friends? They're fucking adorable," She assures me. "And they're perfect for a rebound- even though you weren't dating Elliot, some rebound sex can still help- and they're also perfect for taking out some sexual frustration."

"I never said anything about sex," I remind her, although the idea doesn't seem too terrible. "But by the time that we get to London, I'll be completely over Elliot."

"That's alright, you can still sleep with one of the London boys," She pipes. "These American boys are shitty, we need some more variety. But before you start getting any ideas, the blonde one, Lyle, he's mine. We've been low key flirting ever since this London trip was created."

"Really? Why haven't I heard about this?"

"Because it's low key," She repeats. "And I thought that you were going to bring Elliot, but now that he turned into a complete and utter asshole who is only thinking with his dick, you can have any of them other than Lyle."

"I promise that I won't hit on Lyle," I assure her. "I don't even know if I'm going to flirt with any of them, I guess I'll just see what happens. It isn't for a while, so I have some time to decide."

"Just make sure that you pack a sexy bikini. You know, just in case," She reminds me. "But maybe also a conservative one so that if any of them get any ideas, you can shoot them down like the queen that you are."

"Right, I'll be sure to do that. Anyway, I've got to go get this video edited so I'll talk to you later?"

"Of course, darling. Call me if you need me. Seriously, whenever. Just call me," She assures me insistently. "I'll keep you updated on the Elliot-Sexting scandal."

"Sure. Thanks, Heather."

"Anything for you," She pipes. "Talk to you later."

I hang up the phone after saying goodbye and then start editing the video again which really doesn't take me that long at all. I long onto my YouTube account so that I can post it to my profile but just as I'm about to upload it, my finger freezes over the mouse and I'm suddenly unable to click the upload button.

I start thinking about how sad that I look in this video and I know that Elliot will watch it. He feels bad about ditching me like he did so I know that he'll watch the video just to see how I'm doing and then when he watches it, he'll see that I'm doing terrible. I don't want him to see what an effect he has on me. I know that it won't give him gratification or anything but I just can't stand the thought of him knowing how I feel about the situation. We're not friends anymore, I want nothing to do with him and that includes him knowing about my emotions.

But then I realize that if I don't post this video because I don't want Elliot checking up on me then I won't be able to post any videos because I'll be so paranoid that Elliot will watch it and then he'll know exactly how I'm doing. I don't want it to be so easy for him to just know how I'm doing or to see me making videos.

So instead of uploading the video, I get my equipment out again to make a completely new video. This one isn't going to be a song though, it's going to be a speech.

I sit in front of my wall again once my camera is ready with my soft boxes behind it and I push the play button. Once I'm ready, I clear my throat and then offer the camera a wave.

"Hello my favorite people," I greet the camera in a voice that's a lot less cheery than it usually is. "I'm afraid that I have some bad news for you today. The first part of the bad news is that I won't be uploading a video today but if you want to check out the girl that I was going to do a cover for, I'll put her information down below and you should go check her out because she's incredibly talented. Anyway, the other part of the bad news is that I don't think that I'll be putting out any new videos for a while.

"I don't want you to panic. I'm not completely done with YouTube, I'm still going on the London trip this summer, and I still love you guys so much. The thing is that I'm kind of going through something in my personal life right now. I know that I tell you guys almost everything but this thing is going to stay private for as long as possible, I think. Anyway, the problem with being famous on YouTube is that nothing that I do or say is private, obviously. Even people that I don't want to see my life can see it. And right now, I really need my privacy.

"Like I said though, I'm not completely done, I'm just taking a break. I'm really sad right now, I'm not going to lie, but I'm going to get through it. I have an awesome family and some incredible fans and I'm going to be okay. I've been through worse than this, I just need some time to myself. I can't do all that I need to do while on camera. I'll actually probably still film videos, I just won't be posting them, so the good part to this is that I'll be doing some rapid posting once I get back online.

"I'll also still be here, talking to you guys in comments and tweets and everything. I'm not just disappearing off of the face of the earth but I'm just not posting any videos. I'm really sorry, you guys, this is just something that I have to do right now. I love you all so much and this is extremely hard for me to do but I hope that you guys can understand. So yeah... that's really all that I have to say right now. I'll see you guys again, just... you know, not anytime soon."

Chapter 20

JustJensen is Offline

I stare at the news article in awe. I posted that video just a few days ago and now there's online articles on a handful of news websites and there's blogs and vlogs talking about it too like it's the end of the world or something. I didn't think that it'd be such a big deal, but it seems to be blowing up on the internet.

The article that I'm looking at now, on Friday right after school, is on Yahoo News which is a really big deal because a lot of people read Yahoo. I'd been informed of this by my friend, Maria, who is a YouTuber from California. She'd called me during my lunch hour today and told me that she went to check her email and my face was just there in one of the news stories.

The article is accompanied by a snapshot of me in one of my music videos and then under the article is the YouTube video where I announce that I'm taking a break for a little while. I haven't read the actual article yet though, because I'm kind of too nervous to do so. I don't really want to know what these people have to say about me because I don't take criticism well and I feel like they're going to criticize me.

I know that there are people out there who probably think that I did that just for the attention, but that doesn't make any sense because I didn't expect to get so much attention just for announcing that I'm going to take a break. I just stare at the article for a while, not reading it or anything, just staring at it until I'm shaken away from my computer screen by a loud knock on my front door.

Katy's at gymnastics and my parents are gone at work so that leaves me home alone, which means that I have to be the one to answer the door. I turn off my computer monitor and then hurry down the stairs to get to the front door. Looking through the peep hole, I see that it's Beckett and Sara standing outside, which is kind of weird.

I don't know why, but instinctively, I fix my hair a little bit before actually opening the door and offering them both a small smile. "Hello," I greet them. "Can I help you?"

"Yeah. We just came over to let you know that you're on the news. Which you probably already know," Beckett informs me.

"And he really wanted to see you," Sara pipes with a high pitched giggle.

"That's not true," Beckett says quickly as he shoves his little sister, only making her laugh some more. I too can't help but laugh just a little bit. "I just came over to make sure that you're doing okay, and Sara... I don't really know why she came with me."

"I just need to talk to Katy," Sara informs me.

I give her a strange look. "She's at gymnastics..." I say slowly, confused as to why she forgot that because she knows when Katy has gymnastics.

"Oh that's right, silly me. I guess that while I'm over here, we might as well take a selfie so that all of the people at my school know that I know you. For bragging purposes of course, now that you're on all of the big online news stations," She explains as she gets out her phone and steps closer to me before holding her phone up so that the camera is facing us. "Now smile!"

I barely have a chance to realize what's going on before she's snapping the picture and stepping away.

"Awesome. Thanks. Now I'll let you two love birds have your privacy and don't forget to use condoms," She warns us and I let out a shocked gasp but hide it behind an awkward coughing fit.

"You don't even know what that means, Sara," Beckett grumbles at his sister, who is now grinning at her older brother, who I think might be blushing.

"No, I don't," She agrees with him. "But it makes you all embarrassed and I think that's funny."

"Go away," He tells her.

She rolls her eyes at him and then looks at me and says, "Isn't he just so grumpy when he's in love?"

Beckett turns to his sister and glares before she's hopping off of the porch and sprinting toward her own house, leaving a fit of laughter behind her.

"Sorry about her," Beckett mumbles when she's completely gone.

"It's okay," I assure her but I can't hide a little bit of laughter. "I know how they can be. Do you want to come in?"

"Yeah, sure," He nods and I step away from the doorway to let him into the house. I haven't really talked to Beckett since Tuesday when I came to his house crying my brains out so this is a little bit awkward but I still want to be polite and invite him in and everything. I'm also not completely against the idea of hanging out with Beckett for a little while.

"So you saw the news stuff. Is it brutal?" I ask after I shut the door behind him and we both walk into the living room.

"No, it's not so bad. You haven't read any of it?"

"I haven't had time," I lie quickly as I sit down on the couch and he follows. "My friend told me about it just a little while ago but I never expected it to be such a big deal. I mean, I knew people would be unhappy about it on YouTube and Twitter but I never expected to get the attention of Yahoo or anything like that."

"You are pretty famous," He informs me.

"Yeah," I sigh. "I guess I just prefer to stay stuck in my little bubble of modesty so that I don't have to face that fact. It freaks me out too much. I just... I sing on the internet, I don't think that it's such a huge thing."

"You're a role model," Beckett says in return. "Not just a great singer."

"Right," I say with a loud scoff, leaning farther back in the couch. "Because my life is so put together."

"Nobody's perfect," He says with a shrug. "But you're still a really great role model for a lot of your fans- you've been through a lot and you came out alive, and that's what matters. Your life may not be so put together right now but the thing is that you'll put it together. And that's what makes you special."

I just stare at him for a minute, kind of surprised at what he just said because it was really nice but also incredibly unexpected. After a moment to process what he said, Beckett suddenly looks away from me and I feel like I really need to say something before this gets awkward again. "Uh. Thanks. I actually-"

I'm cut off when my phone starts ringing in my pocket, making both of us jump a little bit as I scramble to answer the phone, eager for an excuse to not have to think of something to say in response to that really generous statement from Beckett.

However, when I look down at the screen of my phone and see that it's Elliot that's calling me, I suddenly feel -1000% relieved. Before I can stop myself though, I look at Beckett and clear my throat. "Sorry, I have to take this."

"Sure, yeah," He confirms, nodding.

"Don't leave, okay? This won't take long and then we can... I don't know, hang out or something," I say quickly before I hurry out of the room to go into the kitchen to take the call. I don't want him to think that I think that what he just said was weird. I don't think that it's weird, I think that it's really sweet of him to say something like that. It was just so sweet that I had no idea how to respond to it is all.

Before giving myself time to panic, I answer the phone. "Hello?"

"Hey," Elliot sighs on the other end, sounding very relieved, and my breath catches in my throat because I haven't heard Elliot's voice since Tuesday and I really miss it and I miss him so much. I shouldn't have answered this call, it was such a bad idea but it's too late to turn back now. "I didn't think that you'd pick up."

"Well, I did. Is there something that you need?" I ask, trying to keep my voice as indifferent and monotonous as possible.

"I just... yeah. I..." He trails off, trying to figure out what to say and if we were still friends, I would laugh at how adorable he gets when he's nervous, how he loses the capability to use 90% of the English language. But we're not friends anymore so I don't laugh, I just listen to him babble for a minute on the other end until he finds his words again. "I wanted to let you know that you didn't have to go offline just because of what happened. I mean... if you don't want me to watch your videos, I won't. You love all of the YouTube stuff, Jen, you don't have to stop doing what you love because of me."

"I didn't do it because of you," I lie.

"Jensen, this is driving me crazy," He starts to rant. "I... I can't sleep at all and I can't stop thinking about what happened on Tuesday. I never meant to hurt you, I swear. You have to believe that. I love you to death and I know that you know that. This doesn't have to be a permanent thing. Just let Cara calm down for a little while and then everything can go back to normal. I just want everything to go back to normal."

"Nothing is ever going back to the way that it was," I say to him with a shake of my head even though he obviously can't see me. "And that's all bullshit because if she's going to make you choose now then she's going to make you choose forever. Deep down, you know that. And deep down, you chose her over me. Forever. That was your choice, so now you have to live with that. We all do."

"I don't want it to be like that though," He mumbles.

"That's not my problem!" I shriek into the phone. "I'm not the one who made it like this! I never made you choose, that was your bat shit girlfriend. So I'm not sure why you're whining to me about how things turned out because it's not my fault."

"Maybe if you talked to her, she'd realize that there's nothing going on between us," He offers up, sounding desperate now. "I tried to talk to her. I talked to her until my lungs were on fire but she wouldn't hear it from me but maybe she'll understand from you."

"I'm going to hang up now," I warn him, my voice shaking a little bit now. "And if you try to call me again, I'm going to block your number. I'm working very hard on getting over you, and you have no idea how hard that is because you're seriously the best thing that ever happened to me. But I'm doing it. And you calling me like this, it's making it so much harder. So goodbye, Elliot. I love you too."

I hang up the phone and wipe a few premature tears from my eyes before taking a few calming breaths and then returning to Beckett in the living room.

"Okay, sorry about that," I mumble, sitting back down on the couch and I turn on the TV so that we can watch something to give us something to do because I guess I'm hanging out with Beckett now. "Anyway, like I was saying, I really appreciate that."

Beckett looks over at me curiously and I can tell that he notices my dramatic change in mood from that stupid phone call. However, he does me a favor and he doesn't say anything about it. "Sure thing," He finally says.

"And I won't blame you if you ask for an autograph since I'm basically an A-Lister now, but it's going to cost you twenty dollars apiece," I warn him jokingly as an old episode of a cake decorating show plays on the TV.

"That's very generous, thank you," He chuckles, playing along with my joke. "I feel honored that you've even chosen to grace me with your presence."

"As you should," I respond, trying my best to forget about that conversation with Elliot. I think that maybe I was too harsh on him because he's really only trying to fall in love and to stay in love, which is something that he thinks won't happen again for him so if he loses Cara then he'll never get another chance again. Maybe I could go talk to Cara and tell her that nothing is happening between me and Elliot. But then I tell myself that it doesn't matter because I already hung up. It's over, so it doesn't matter if I made the wrong decision. There's no use in dwelling on it now.

"You alright?" Beckett wonders, shaking me out of my day dreaming.

"Oh. Um, yeah. I was just thinking," I say, trying to shrug to make it seem like no big deal.

"About what?" He asks me with his eyebrows raised curiously.

I shrug again. "I was just wondering if you have plans tomorrow," I state and when he raises his eyebrows at me again, I realize how flirty that sounds. "I mean... because I want to go to the beach. You don't have to if you don't want to, I can find somebody else to go with me, I've just decided that I want to go to the beach tomorrow."

"The beach sounds nice," Beckett says with a nod. "Kind of random though."

"I need a mental health day and I think that a day trip to the beach sounds so amazing," I explain with a small shrug. "We can bring Sara and Katy so that our moms don't start thinking that it's not just friendly."

"So we're friends now?"

I don't know why that makes me laugh because what he just said isn't funny and laughing kind of makes me feel like a lunatic but I still answer him with, "That is a very strong possibility. But you don't have to be my friend out of pity."

"Oh, well then never mind then," He says teasingly. "Because I really only ever talk to you out of pity."

"I am pretty sad-looking."

"It's incredibly depressing," He says and I laugh before rolling my eyes at him. "But I don't pity you, believe it or not."

"Good to know," I say with a small chuckle just as I hear the front door start to unlock from across the living room, telling me that my mother is probably home but she's a little early so I haven't been expecting her home for another hour or so.

"Jen, can you-" She starts talking once the door is open but when she steps into the house and notices that Beckett is also sitting on the couch with me. "Oh. You two are freaking me out."

"Why?" I wonder with raised eyebrows. "I thought that you wanted us to be friends."

"I do," She insists, walking past the living room and then into the kitchen to put down her keys and work stuff. "I think that it's great that you guys are getting along but it's just so random and weird and it's freaking me out. It's freaking Margaret out too."

"We actually started listening to you guys- it's a miracle," I reply sarcastically as my mom grabs a bag of her weird pretzel things and walks back into the living room, nibbling on the crunchy pretzels.

"Yeah right," She scoffs. "I don't buy that for a second. You guys are up to something."

"You're staring conspiracy theories now?" I wonder with raised eyebrows.

"Not a conspiracy," She insists. "Anyway, as I was saying, I'm home early because I have a doctor's appointment tonight- that one where they shove crap up where the sun don't shine- and I need you to pick up your sister from gymnastics."

"Yeah, fine. Speaking of Katy, I'm taking her to the beach tomorrow," I pipe.

"Really. Why is that?"

I just shrug innocently and lean over to take some of her pretzels. She gives me a dirty look but I just ignore it and eat her food anyway. "I just feel like the beach sounds like fun and I want to go. You and Dad have work though, so I didn't plan on inviting you."

"I don't have to work tomorrow," She tells me with a confused frown.

"Oh. Well, I'm still not inviting you."

My mother gives me a weird look before glancing over at Beckett and then back to me and then she grins and then laughs at something that probably isn't funny at all. "Oh, jeez, Jensen. You kill me. You just absolutely kill me."

"I didn't do anything," I remind her.

"Yeah, yeah," She sighs, standing up from the couch and she pulls her keys out of her purse to head back out the door to make her appointment. "Just, you know, don't get pregnant. I'm way too attractive to be a grandmother."

I know that she's joking, even though my mom is really pretty she isn't that vain, so I laugh and pretend like I haven't heard that joke a thousand times before. "Sure, Mom, I'll be sure to remember that while I'm completely single."

She laughs again and tosses a pretzel at me, causing it to bounce off of my shoulder and land on the soft carpet. "You're a dirty liar, Jen."

"I'm not lying, Mom," I insist honestly. "I'm pretty sure I've grown a gnome down there."

"Wouldn't the gyno just love that," She mutters, leaning down and kissing the top of my head from behind the couch as she starts to finally head toward the door again. "It's nice seeing you Beckett."

"Uh, you too, Mrs. Cane," Beckett says, looking like he feels pretty awkward about the conversation and really, I don't blame him because that is a pretty awkward conversation.

"And you two be careful at the beach tomorrow, and bring me back some fresh shrimp while you're there," My mom says just before opening the front door and then she disappears, finally leaving Beckett and I alone again.

"Why are our parents so weird?" I wonder, pretty much hypothetically as I turn my attention back to the TV.

Beckett laughs and then leans back into the couch some more. "The world will never know."

Chapter 21

"Elliot called this morning," My mother tells me just as I'm about to leave for the beach the next day.

"What'd you tell him?" I wonder, finishing the last few bites of my banana.

"I told him that you were in the shower and that I'd tell you that he called," She explains. "So just make sure to call him back when you get back home tonight."

"You do remember just last week that Elliot and I stopped being friends, right? If he calls again, tell him that he can stick whatever he wants to say to me right up where the sun doesn't shine," I mumble, grabbing my beach bag and tossing it over my shoulder.

"I know that you aren't friends anymore but it's just so awful. You two have been through so much and you were such great friends and I just hate to see it go to waste just because he's a little love struck," She explains to me. "Just... you know, maybe try to hear him out a little bit more."

"No," I say, trying to make it sound definitive so that she doesn't try to question my decision again. "And where's Katy? I'm supposed to meet Beckett in like, three minutes."

"She'll be down soon- she was having trouble picking out the right swim suit," My mother tells me and then starts sipping on her coffee. "So real talk- what's up with you and Beckett?"

"Nothing is-"

"Don't say that nothing is up because clearly, there's something," She states. "I'm not saying romantically, I'm just saying that I'm not so oblivious to you two and I know that you guys haven't really gotten a long that well since high school started but now that you aren't talking to Elliot, you're buddy-buddy with Beckett? I'm not against you two being friends, Jen, I just think that it's a bad idea to be friends with Beckett just because you think that he's a good substitute for Elliot."

"I'm not friends with him because I'm trying to substitute Elliot," I assure my mother. "We've been getting along better ever since the Brooks Town trip. When Elliot said that we couldn't be friends anymore, I kind of lost my marbles for a few hours and Beckett helped me out."

"I'm just saying that if you're going to be friends with him, that's great. Just make sure that your friends with him for the right reasons," She tells me from behind her coffee mug. "Friendship is not a take-what-you-can-get type of thing. Just because you aren't friends with Elliot anymore doesn't mean that you just have to be friends with the first person that's nice to you, Jen."

"Thank you, Dr. Phil. I'll keep that in mind," I mutter, looking back at the stairs to see that my sister is still not there. "Katy, hurry up!"

"I'm coming!" She shouts in response from upstairs.

"Anyway, just be careful," My mom warns me. "And have fun today. After the week that you've had, you deserve some fun."

"Sure, Mom. Thanks," I sigh, adjusting my t-shirt and then I start shuffling my black sandals on the tiled kitchen floor as if that makes me look busy so that my mom will stop talking to me about Beckett. It's not like I'm going to the beach as an excuse to spend time with him, because I'm not. It's just that yesterday, when I had decided that I wanted to go to the beach today, Beckett was there with me, so he's the one that I invited. Completely harmless.

Once Katy finally gets downstairs in her sundress and flip flops, my mom reminds us to wear sun screen and to have fun and all of that before I'm practically dragging Katy out of the house because now we're running late. Outside, I see Beckett leaning against his car on his phone but I don't see Sara out there with him.

"She forgot her sunglasses," Beckett explains when Katy asks about the whereabouts of her best friend.

"Oh no!" Katy gasps when she realizes that she too forgot her sunglasses at the house and she starts to run back toward our house but I grab her shoulder in a swift motion so that she doesn't get very far.

"I grabbed them for you," I tell her, motioning toward the big bag on my shoulder. I knew that she'd forget hers because she always does, so I grabbed an extra pair of mine for her to borrow while we're at the beach. I have a few things in my bag that I suspect Katy can possibly forget because if she does forget something that I don't remember then she'll start whining and throwing fits.

"The pink ones?" She wonders.

I shrug, knowing that the answer is no but if I admit that then she'll have to go all the way back to our house just to get the right pair of sunglasses and then she'll get distracted and then we'll be waiting on her for another twenty minutes and I'm not that patient. "Sure."

Just as Sara emerges from the house and starts hurrying toward the car, Katy says to me, "I don't believe you."

"Well, whether you believe me or not, we're leaving right now. With or without you, so you can decide if you want to go back for the right colored sunglasses," I inform her, giving her an impatient look so that she knows that I'm not kidding. Even though Beckett's driving and I'm sure that he wouldn't leave without my sister even if I ask him to.

Katy falls for it though and gets in the backseat of the car with Sara. Beckett opens the trunk so that we can put our stuff for the beach back there and then we get in the front seat before he backs out of the driveway and heads toward the freeway.

"So we've been thinking," Sara pipes from the back seat before I have time to start a conversation with Beckett, which is what I was planning on doing.

"Oh, right. We have been thinking," Katy agrees, nodding excitedly.

"That's dangerous," I mumble.

"Shut up," Katy responds before saying, "Anyway, so we've been thinking about you taking a break from your channel. Now that you don't have to work on your videos so much, you'll have a lot of free time. Is that correct?"

"Yes..." I trail off, not really sure where she's going with this but I'm pretty sure that I'm not going to like it.

"Well, that means that you have time to start dating," Sara pipes and then I realize that I was right- I don't like it where this was going.

"Exactly," Katy agrees. "And since you're not talking to Elliot right now, he's not an option. But you know who you are talking to right now?"

"Well, right now, I'm talking to you. And it's making me want to punch you in the face," I refute, looking out the window to avoid Beckett's reaction because they're obviously talking about him and I don't want to deal with this. I guess I should have thought this out better when I impulsively invited him to the beach and then impulsively thought that it'd be a great idea to bring our two romantic metaling sisters along. Now it's too late to change my mind and we're stuck in a car with them for an hour and a half.

"Let's not get violent here." Sara defends my little sister. "We're just suggesting that you have a lot of free time and Lord knows that Beckett has a lot of free time. All he does is hang out with his friends all of the time but they're annoying and unimportant. So it just makes sense that you both use your free time on each other and go on dates."

"We really want to be sisters," Katy explains. "Wouldn't that be so cool?"

"Has the thought ever crossed your mind that I don't need to date anybody?" I ask both of them with raised eyebrows as I turn to face both girls from the front seat. "Maybe I'm a lesbian. Or maybe I just want to be single. It's completely fine to just be friends with somebody of the opposite gender as me without it being romantic. Have you ever thought of that?"

The girls look at each other and then back at me and say, "No."

"Haven't you ever heard of the saying 'A girl needs a boy like a fish needs a bicycle'? Because I think that you both need to jam that concept into your brains," I explain to them, trying to nip this romanticizing of my and Beckett's relationship in the bud before it turns into something as big and annoying and harmful as the idea of Jelliot.

"You are absolutely no fun, Jen," Katy huffs, crossing her arms over her chest to show her displeasure.

"If you guys want to be related so much, you could just marry each other," Beckett adds and both girls make a disgusted face, which makes me laugh as I turn back around to face the front.

"Beck, we're serious," Sara sighs with a roll of her eyes.

"So am I," He says with a laugh. "I mean, you two are so keen on us ending up together, maybe we should start pushing it on you guys too."

"I like that idea," I pipe, grinning just because it's so much fun to tease our little sisters. "You know that Mom and Dad will wholeheartedly support your decision to come out of the closet, Katy."

"Shut up!" She shrieks at me. "We are not getting married! You're so stupid, Jensen."

I laugh at that because it's all fun and games for her and Sara until they're the ones in the spotlight. Maybe now, they'll shut up about me and Beckett but I highly doubt it. So now that we realize how buggy Katy and Sara get when we tease them about marrying each other, Beckett and I spend about a whole ten minutes on the road singing that "K-I-S-S-I-N-G" song from elementary school as they both throw a fit, kicking the backs of our seats and telling us to shut up like the ten year olds that they are.

Once they cool down, we stop singing but I'm laughing so hard at their hypocritical reaction that I have tears in my eyes. I know that Katy will tell my mom that I upset her when we get home but even if my mom lectures me a little bit on making Katy angry (she can pick on me but it's wrong when I do it back because I'm older- a role model) but it was so worth it.

Just as my and Beckett's laughing dies down, my phone starts to ring from where it's sitting on my lap so I look at the screen but I don't recognize the number. A few reporters have been calling me lately though (how they got my number, I have no idea) so I want to answer the phone because I don't mind answering a few questions for them to set the record straight on all of the weird rumors that have started to spread on my YouTube hiatus.

"Hello?" I answer the call.

"Hey, Jensen," A familiar voice answers so I know that it's not a reporter but I really wish that it was instead of this person.

"Marcus?" I wonder just for clarification because I've never talked to him over the phone before but it does vaguely sound like Marcus, Elliot's computer geeky friend that we used to hang out with at lunch. I mean, I'm sure that Elliot still hangs out with him during lunch but obviously, I've stopped spending my lunch with him and the other guys in the computer lab since Tuesday.

"Yeah. Um. What's up?" He asks awkwardly, clearing his throat to make it obvious that he's really uncomfortable right now.

"Not much," I mutter, silently sending a prayer to the heavens that Elliot isn't there with him, trying to talk to me through his friend because he knows that I won't answer his number or a blocked number. I know that the chances of Elliot not being behind this phone call are very low though, so I'm not hopeful. "Can I help you with something?"

"Right, yeah, uh, well you see the thing is that Elliot is kinda freaking out right now," He starts to explain. "And he's sitting in my room and I think that he's about to cry and-"

"Shut the fuck up, dude! Don't tell her that!" I can hear Elliot's voice in the background and it makes me flinch because I still miss him so much. I just wish that he'd leave me alone so that I could successfully ignore him until my missing him goes away.

"Okay, scratch that. He isn't crying. He's the manliest man that I've ever known," Marcus tells me. "Anyway, he wants to talk to you because he thinks that he made a mistake, so I'm going to give him the phone now."

"If you give him the phone, I'll hang up," I inform Marcus. "I'm not going to talk to him, no matter whose phone he calls me on. You can tell him to stop calling me and to stop having his friends call me and to stop bothering me because it's not going to do anything. You can also tell him that he can move the sun and the earth until his arms fall off but it's never going to be enough and I am not going to talk to him. I'm not going to forgive him. Tell him that and then tell him to leave me the fuck alone."

"You see, I would tell him that but I think he might go off the deep end," Marcus informs me slowly. "Can't you just like, you know, not be mad at him? I mean, really, what's the big deal? So he thought with his dick for like, one second. He's changed his mind now."

"He wasn't thinking with his dick, he was thinking with his heart," I correct Marcus and I try to talk quieter so that the girls in the back don't hear me say that D word. "And I'm tired of talking about this and I'm busy right now so I'm going to go. If you call me again because of Elliot, I'm going to punch you in your knee cap the next time that I see you."

"Yes ma'am," Marcus chokes out just before I hear a rustling around on the other side of the phone. I'm about to hang up but the ruckus makes me curious, so I stay on the line longer than I should have.

"I'm soooo so so sorry, Jen," Elliot's all of the sudden on the other end of the conversation, causing me to jump a little bit in my seat. Luckily, Beckett's having a strong debate with Katy and Sara about the radio station that we're listening to, so I don't think that any of them are paying attention to my phone conversation or my facial reactions. "I never meant to hurt you and I love you so much. Please don't hang up."

But I hang up anyway and I turn toward the window so that nobody can see how sad I look now because today is supposed to be relaxing and happy, not sad and pathetic. However, Elliot just has to ruin every single chance I get at trying to get over him.

"You okay?" Beckett wonders once he wins the radio debate and then realizes how quiet I've gotten.

"Yeah," I sigh, faking a yawn. "I'm just gonna take a nap before we get there. Wake me up when it's beach time."

"Alright," He assures me as I lean my head against the head rest and close my eyes. I probably won't really go to sleep but I just need to calm myself down and stop thinking about Elliot so that he doesn't ruin this beach day. The beach is an hour away so it's not an everyday thing that we get to do so I want to enjoy this as much as possible.

"She gets like this a lot now," I hear Katy saying when they all think that I'm asleep. "She likes to pretend like she's alright without Elliot but it's so obvious that she's sad. I can still hear her crying at night, it's so tragic."

"She's been through a lot," Beckett explains to Katy.

"I know that. I'm just saying that it's so sad what Elliot did to her, just traded her in like she's some trading card that those weirdoes always obsess over during lunch," Katy informs him. "And how she pretends like she's just fine with it. She's not fooling anybody though and somehow, that makes it sadder."

"Can you shut up? I'm not asleep, Kaitlynn," I mumble without opening my eyes or anything.

"What? I didn't say anything bad," She justifies.

"I'm not a sob story- I'm not a starving mother of fifteen in Africa. There is nothing tragic about my life," I inform her. "And mind your own business."

"She's grumpy," I hear Katy whisper but I think she purposefully stage whispers so that I can hear what she says. I just ignore it though and keep my eyes closed to just enjoy the bumps in the road.

The rest of the ride is uneventful and when we arrive at the beach, it's pretty busy but we got here kind of early so we should be able to find a spot in the sand before everybody starts showing up. Dragging my beach bag and a sun umbrella with me, I walk with Beckett and the two little girls as we walk out of the sandy parking lot and then to the beach.

We quickly find an empty area in the sand between a family and an old couple but far away from both sides that we aren't suffocating close to the strangers. After laying out our towels, Katy and Sara are eager to drop their sundresses and get sunscreen on to sprint into the ocean water. I remind them to stay close so that they don't get kidnapped and then I work on poking my umbrella into the sand so that I can lay down on my towel and not get the sun in my eyes.

"Do you want to go for a walk or something?" Beckett wonders after I get the umbrella into the sand to protect my laid out towel.

"Yeah, that sounds nice. Just give me a minute to put on some sun screen," I confirm, deciding that stretching my legs after such a long car ride will do me good before I lay down to tan a little bit. Before we leave our base camp though, I take off my t-shirt and my skirt-like sarong to put on my sun screen. I keep my sunglasses over my eyes not only because it's sunny, but I have to prepare for when/if Beckett takes off his shirt.

I remember when we went to Brooks Town and he'd been shirtless in the hotel room and it felt like the hardest thing I'd ever had to do to peel my eyes away from his chest. This time though, I'm prepared with dark sunglasses so that if the opportunity presents itself, I won't look like such a complete drooling idiot.

My bikini is black with some weird neon designs on it and it's kind of cute, I guess, and it matches my sarong which is mostly the reason that I chose to wear it today but the ruffles on the top make it look a little childish, they're fun though.

I pull my hair into a messy bun on top of my head to avoid a bad tan line and grab my sun screen. I lather my arms, legs, chest, stomach, neck, and face in the cool cream before I turn around to face Beckett and I immediately realize that he's shirtless, so I keep my eyes on his face just so that I can concentrate on my words.

"Hey, can you-" I start to ask him to do my back before I realize that I'm not the only one with a staring problem, because he's not looking up at my face, but down at my boobs. Maybe I should be embarrassed or angry or something but instead, I find myself smirking at him but I do blush. Hopefully, it goes unnoticed because of the hot sun. "Beckett, my eyes are up here."

"What?" He jumps a little bit and then his eyes jump to mine and I'm glad that mine are shielded by the sunglasses.

"You were totally checking me out," I tease him, still smirking a little bit because I can't help myself.

"What? No I wasn't," He denies as he takes the sun screen from my hand and I turn around so that he can get my back. "Okay, so I was but you have no right to get all smirky because I know that you were checking me out back at the hotel in Brooks Town."

"No I wasn't," I lie but I laugh loudly just to make it more convincing.

"I know that you were," Beckett assures me with a small laugh as his hand runs down my back with globs of sunscreen. "I just didn't say anything because I was being nice."

"I guess you're nicer than I am," I refute with a genuine laugh this time.

"I guess I am," He agrees with me, laughing as well.

Once I'm covered in sun screen, I put my dark blue sarong back around my waist and then we start walking down the shoreline of the beach. I feel a pang of disappointment when Beckett doesn't put on sun screen and need help applying it to his back because I really wouldn't mind getting a poke at his back muscles. After only a second or so with that thought in my mind, I quickly push it away because that's not a good thought to have. We can't go far because we have to keep an eye on our sisters but we still have a small-ish stretch of the shore that we can walk along while still being able to turn around and see Katy and Sara in the water.

"So Elliot's still giving you a hard time?" Beckett wonders as we start walking.

"Yeah. I mean, I'm handling it, but it's still really annoying," I sigh, kicking my feet through the soft sand. "He feels really guilty about everything but I'm not really sure what he wants me to do about that. Like, it's not like I was the one who made him choose between me or Cara. So even if I did forgive him, it wouldn't change anything. Cara will still be there, making him choose, and he'll still choose her because he's a sucker for romance."

"Maybe he's changed his mind and he broke up with that Cara girl," Beckett suggests optimistically.

"I highly doubt that," I say with a humorless laugh. "He loves her."

"Oh. I didn't realize that they've been together for that long."

"They haven't! That makes all of this even more aggravating. I mean, maybe he does really love her but he barely even knows her and he's just going to throw-" I pause in the beginning of a rant when I realize that I don't want to spend my vacation day thinking or talking about Elliot and how stupidly gullible he is. "You know, it doesn't really matter. Cara sucks. Elliot sucks. It's whatever."

"That's a good attitude," Beckett says with a nod. "I mean, you're pretty famous and you can have just about any friend that you want so Elliot just gave up a major opportunity and the joke's on him because you're pretty great."

"I'm hardly famous," I shake my head at him. "I mean... kind of, I guess. But it's not as glamorous as it may seem."

"No?"

"Not really. It's mostly just me being at a computer screen editing video or talking slash singing into a camera and reading feedback from tiny people who have no idea what they're talking about. I love what I do though. I love singing and touching so many people via the internet- and I know that sounds really creepy but you know what I mean. It's amazing, but it's not very Hollywood."

"That meet and greet at Brooks Town was pretty Hollywood," Beckett reminds me.

"True," I agree. "But I don't do stuff like that very often. I've done interviews though. A few of them over the phone lately now that I've shut down for a little while. Most of the interviews are about freshman year though."

"I can see that," He nods in confirmation and then he clears his throat so I think that he feels awkward now that I brought up freshman year.

"I'm inspirational, apparently," I add.

"You are inspirational," He agrees.

"I guess," I say with a small shrug. "I didn't really think of it like that when it was happening though. I mean, it wasn't like I woke up one day and I was like 'I'm going to say no to bullying today and stand up for all of the kids who can't' or anything, which is what a lot of people think and to be honest, I usually just go with that story. In all honesty though, I came home from school one day and I had a complete emotional breakdown and I couldn't take it anymore. Doesn't sound as noble or inspirational when I say it like that though."

"It's still pretty amazing," He counters. "Being a role model doesn't mean that every part of your journey had to be beautiful. Especially considering your position at the time, I think that an emotional breakdown is very understandable."

"That was very deep."

"Oh, I'm always full of wise words," Beckett assures me teasingly.

"Of course you are," I say in a sarcastic voice and then that's the end of our serious discussion. As we turn back toward our sisters so that we don't lose sight of them, we start talking about lighter subjects such as the amount of fish feces in the water and the likelihood of a shark attack.

It's really easy to talk to Beckett, despite the awkward history between us. He's really funny when he isn't giving me his wise words of advice and I'm just pretty glad that we're friends. I just hope that it doesn't end badly because with my luck as of late, this seems like it's just a recipe for disaster. But I'm optimistic.

Chapter 22

After the random trip to the beach, a whole month passes and I start to fall into a comfortable routine. Elliot has stopped trying to contact me, which is really nice for me because it makes it so much easier for me to forget about our friendship. Well, I mean, not forget about it, because I'm never going to forget about but I am moving on and that's all that I can ask for. As for Beckett, we're friends but that doesn't really mean much because we don't really hang out that much.

Us putting the 'friend' label on our relationship pretty much just means that when we're together when our families are gathering, things aren't awkward and when we see each other in the hallways, we smile and wave at each other. We are comfortably aware of each other but we aren't avidly great friends now that we've bonded over some emotional trauma.

With my break from YouTube still in effect, I've been focusing most of my energy on graduating high school and then the trip to London for the summer. Graduation is only a few months away so I'm making sure that all of my grades are staying up and that I'm ready for final exams to happen. I've only made two videos other than the sad song I'd sang right after Elliot ended our friendship and in my downtime, I edited those two videos together so that they look nice and when I go back online, I'll have a good startup.

"Wells said that he's going to take us to some parties," Heather is explaining to me on a Friday morning as I'm getting ready for school by doing my makeup, putting my phone on speaker phone and sitting it on the dresser in front of me so that my hands are free. "So make sure you have some cute party dresses packed."

"I'll be sure to do that," I assure her. "I think that partying will be really good for us, considering that we're both hopelessly single. It'll be fun."

"Just fun?" She wonders hysterically. "No. It'll be unforgettable. Re-markable. Amazing. Stunning."

"Sure, it'll be all of that," I agree with Heather but I'm really putting more focus into making sure that my eyeliner is even. "I'm going shopping this weekend with my mom to get some stuff for London so I'll be sure to grab a cute party dress or two while I'm out."

"And killer shoes, of course."

"Of course."

"You know, there's still an extra bed in our apartment," Heather explains to me. "Can you think of anybody else to invite?"

"No, we've gone through just about everybody," I remind her. "Doesn't somebody else that's going have like, a friend or a boyfriend or girlfriend that can tag along?"

"I don't know, we just need to fill this bed because if we do, it makes rent cheaper," She explains even though I already know that. "Well, since you've been so buddy-buddy with your new pal, Beckett, maybe you can invite him."

"I'm not going to do that," I say with a small laugh as I finish up my makeup and put the caps back on all of my stuff, leaving everything laid out on my dresser as I start brushing through my hair again. "We're not buddy-buddy and you know that. We're friends but we aren't close or anything, we just talk sometimes. We aren't nearly friendly enough for me to invite him to London for an entire summer."

"Maybe things will change before we get to London," She suggests jokingly.

"Or maybe not," I refute. "Why are you so keen on the idea of Beckett and I being friends all of the sudden though? I thought that you hated him."

"I do hate him."

"Then why would you want to spend all summer with the guy?" I ask her. "That doesn't really make that much sense, you know."

"Well, I hate him but I know that you don't hate him so if you want to bring him, I'm just saying that I'd be okay with it is all," She explains to me as I'm slipping my shoes on and I leave my room, grabbing my school bag and my keys. Checking the time on my phone, I have twenty minutes to get to school.

"That's very generous of you, but unnecessary. I'm not inviting him," I say again. "I'm sure that we'll find somebody to go to London with us though. If anything, we could do like, a contest to give the last room away to a fan or something. I mean, not give it away because they'd still have to pay rent but that might be an idea, right?"

"It is an idea. You should run it by Wells and see what he thinks," She agrees. "I don't really care who's in that room, I'm just so excited I can't even stand it. I wish that these last few months of school could just vanish so that we could be in London tomorrow."

"That would make life a lot easier," I laugh at her as I get into my car and toss my school bag into the passenger seat. "Anyway, I've got to get to school so I'll talk to you later."

We say our goodbyes and then I make my way to school where I park in the normal parking lot and get into the school. On my way to class, I text Wells about my idea to give the last room to a fan so that I don't forget to do it later and he responds quickly by telling me that they'll consider it if we get desperate enough to fill the last room.

I let myself wonder to an alternate universe for a minute, thinking that if Cara had never come into the equation, then Elliot would have easily filled that last spot to London. Even if we were still friends and he was still dating Cara, he wouldn't have come to London so she would have to be wiped out of the equation completely for it to be possible.

But then I remind myself that for that to happen, I'd probably still be hopelessly in love with a boy who wouldn't even think twice about me in that way. And that's no way to live. After Elliot left and I've gotten over my stupid feelings for him, I've felt a lot freer with myself and more in control of my emotions. And that's an amazing feeling. I miss my best friend like crazy, I'm not denying that, but it just feels like a breath of fresh air for me to not be pining over somebody that I knew would never love me back in the way that I wanted.

Without any romantic feelings for anybody, I feel like my life is mine and mine only. Not Elliot's or some other useless boy, it's just mine. And when I go to London, it's going to be just mine and I'm going to have so much fun with all of my YouTube friends being just me.

Now, without being tied down to Elliot, I can go find somebody that I love insanely and that, most importantly, loves me insanely in return. Loving somebody is such a magical thing but to be loved back is a rarity that I have yet to experience. Maybe in London, I'll get the opportunity.

When lunch comes around, I don't go to the cafeteria like I usually do now. For my next video, I want it to be a pretty fancy video and I'm not talented enough to pull it off myself. The last time that I felt that way, I went to the AV group and they gave me Elliot and it was the best decision I'd ever made. This time, I won't be so stupid. Instead of getting human help, I'm just going to go to the art room because I know that the art teacher can help me get the effects that I need. I took an art class last semester so the teacher knows me and she's really nice so I'm sure that she won't mind helping me out.

As I walk into the art room though, I notice one sickeningly familiar face sitting on the edge of the left side of the room. There's three computers sitting on the counter and at the middle computer, Elliot is sitting with his back to me working on the computer in the art room.

"Can I help you dear?" The art teacher wonders from her desk. There's nobody else in the room so I assume that this is either her lunch period or her grading period.

"Yeah," I clear my throat and turn my attention to the teacher when the only thing running through my head is 'of-fucking-course he'd be here right now' but then I tell myself to remain calm and then I remind myself of why I came in here. "I need some help with a video idea that I have and I was wondering if you could help."

"Of course, Jensen, what can I do for my favorite celebrity?" She wonders with a grin and in my peripheral vision, I can see Elliot pivot in his chair to look at me but I keep a firm gaze on Miss Turner so that I don't create eye contact between us to make this situation even more awkward. If I'd seen Elliot in the room before entering, I could have just turned around and come back next week instead of walking in all the way and getting Miss Turner's attention after it was too late to back track.

And now that it's too late, I just go with it. I start explaining my idea to Miss Turner and then I tell her my ideas on how to tackle the plan and she just stands there, nodding at me as she thinks about the best solution to get the effect that I want.

"You know, I think that I have the perfect idea for this," Miss Turner tells me. "Just give me one second to go find a working computer, the ones in here have been screwy all week. I've had tech guys in here all day to try and fix the problem. Anyway, just sit tight and I'll be right back."

"Okay," I say, pursing my lips because in actuality, I'm screaming at her in my head not to leave me alone with Elliot. I listen to the pound of her feet as she leaves the room and then the room grows silent. The awkward silence is almost so unbearable that I consider just walking out now and going to lunch but I don't do that because I know that it'd be really rude to Miss Turner. I'm going through all of the options in my head to try and think of a way to get out of this situation while also not standing up Miss Turner, who is going to help me with my video out of the kindness of her heart, when Elliot clears his throat and I know that he's going to say something. I cringe.

"Hey, Jen," He greets me awkwardly but he's typing away at the computer, so he's not looking at me. At least I have that one thing going for me right now. "How are you?"

"Fine," I say, keeping my tone and vocabulary civil. I'm not mad at Elliot anymore for the choice that he made last month because I've spent a lot of time getting over it and moving on. That doesn't mean that it doesn't hurt to see him around school now, knowing that we aren't friends anymore. It just sucks a lot. "You?"

"I'm doing well," Elliot tells me. "You're still going to London for the summer?"

"Yeah. We've got the apartment and everything," I confirm slowly, trying not to overthink the conversation. We're allowed to talk without it having detrimental effects on my sanity, right? It's been a month, I'm fine now. It's actually kind of nice to be able to catch up with him a little bit. "Uh, well, how's Cara?"

"She's really good," He says and I think that he's about to elaborate on the subject but luckily for me, Miss Turner returns from wherever she went and starts going into her suggestions for getting the effect that I need in my video. I think that I can only talk to Elliot for a good few minutes at the most without losing my mind so Miss Turner showed up just in time. I shouldn't have asked him about Cara though because I don't want to hear about her. I just panicked and needed something to talk about and she was the only thing that popped into my mind, so that's another reason that I'm so thankful that Miss Turner showed up when she did.

After Miss Turner gives me what I need for my video, I thank her profusely for her help and then I leave the room as quickly as possible to escape the awkwardness of being in the same room as Elliot. The irony of this situation does not go unnoticed by me at all- at one point, Elliot was my friend and we were so comfortable each other but every time that I saw Beckett, I was blinded by awkwardness. Now though, the roles are reversed because I can hardly stand to be in the same room as Elliot but I'm completely fine with holding a conversation with Beckett.

I miss the old way though and I wish that we could go back.

I blink away that useless thought before it evolves into a full mental monologue and then find myself sitting back down in the cafeteria with a salad in front of me but I'm not very hungry so I'm kind of just randomly stabbing at the lettuce and nibbling on the soggy croutons.

"Hey," Beckett randomly greets me, inviting himself to sit down across from me at the empty section of the table that I'm sitting at. "Are you busy this weekend?"

I give him a curious look because it's kind of weird that he's asking me that question but I answer him anyway, "I have a thing on Sunday but nothing tomorrow. Why do you ask?"

"A thing?" He wonders, cocking his head to the side to add emphasis to his curiosity.

his curiosity.

"I'm going shopping with my mom," I elaborate, stabbing my salad again absentmindedly as I bite back a short laugh. "Why do you ask?"

"There's a party tomorrow night," He explains to me quickly, in one breath of air as if he's afraid of saying what he just said. "It'll be kind of lame but they all want me to invite you to make it less lame."

He nudges toward his lunch table full of people that I know to be his friends as a way of explaining who 'they' are and then I look back at him with a confused look. "Are you telling me that those people over there want me to hang out with them? Because they think that I will make their party better?"

"Well, and I want you to come. I'm not just asking because they want you to go," He adds with a charming sideways smile. "It'll be fun and there will be free food and beer."

"I appreciate the offer, but no thanks- it's a little bit too much irony for me," I say to him with an apologetic frown.

"What do you mean?"

"I mean, that blonde girl right there in the green sweater pushed me into the guys' locker room when the baseball team was showering and thought that my mortification was just the funniest thing in the world. That guy with the Under Armor shirt told our whole class that I was a regular at an abortion clinic. So I think that it's rather understandable that I don't want to spend my Saturday night hanging out with them."

"Yeah, but people change," Beckett defends. "I changed, remember?"

"I know that. And it's so great that you aren't an ass hat anymore, I really appreciate that," I tell him with an assuring nod. "But I refuse to believe that everyone at that table has grown a heart of gold since freshman year. But thanks anyway for the invite. Have fun at your party."

"Okay, I can understand that. If you don't want to go to the party though, how about something just me and you?" He wonders, raising his eyebrows at me.

With a nervous laugh, I look back up at him as I flick a cherry tomato around in my salad with my plastic fork. "You just said that you have a party to go to tomorrow."

He shrugs at me and when he doesn't look away after a long moment, I clear my throat and look away myself. "They won't miss me too much. They'll be disappointed when I tell them that you won't be able to make it- they were really hoping for a celebrity appearance."

"So you'll skip your party just to hang out with me?" I wonder for clarification because I don't really understand why he would do that. Like I said, after last month when we agreed to be friends, we haven't really talked all that much so I feel taken off guard a little bit by him asking me to hang out tomorrow night.

"Yeah. It's not going to be a great party anyway," Beckett informs me. "We could go to that grilled cheese restaurant that just opened up down-town—I've heard good things. Have you been there?"

"No," I say slowly, still confused but not complaining because I don't really mind that Beckett is talking to me right now and I don't mind the idea of hanging out with him tomorrow night.

"Cool. I'll see you tomorrow then," He says, offering me a friendly smile as he stands up from the seat that he's sitting at to go back to his group of friends on the other side of the cafeteria.

"Sure, I'll see you tomorrow," I agree, laughing now at how ridiculous this day has turned out for me. Not necessarily bad or good... just strange. I watch as he walks back to his table and then tells them all the bad news- that I won't be attending their party tomorrow. When they all start looking over in my direction, I look back down at my salad and then down at my phone to have something else to look at.

But I have to admit that even though it's kind of petty, it's really hard to keep a smile off of my face. In a way, I kind of feel like I've won. The girl that they had pushed around for a whole year, called names, mercilessly tortured and scarred—that girl has changed for the better, so much so that they want me to hang out with them. They think that I will make their party better. Me. That girl that absorbed all of their hatred when I was nobody.

I wonder if they think about all of the times that they ruined me when they look at me now, or when they hear my name. I wonder if they watch my videos and go back to when I was being mocked by the whole baseball team in the shower room. Or if they see my name in the news and remember how they'd nearly drown me in a mud puddle.

I wonder because I know that's how it is for me, when I see them sitting at the table across the cafeteria from me, or when they're walking down the hallway near me, it's all that I see. It's the only thing that I can think about, and I know that that will never change. And I also know that I won, and it feels so good.

Chapter 23

"This is really good grilled cheese," I state as I sink my teeth into another bite of my mushroom and bacon grilled cheese. "Now, I understand the hype over this place."

"I know," Beckett agrees. "It's like eating your own personal slice of heaven."

"Jesus probably wouldn't appreciate that," I tell him. "Is this worth missing your big party for?"

"Definitely," He says with a quick nod. "It's hardly even a party to be honest. All they're doing is getting drunk and dancing to awful mashups because one of the guys is trying his hand at being a DJ and nobody has the heart to tell him that he sucks."

"Wow, now I'm feeling bad that I turned down the offer to join them, that really sounds amazing," I joke with a small laugh before I take another bite of my delicious sandwich.

"Yeah, it's just a blast," Beckett tells me sarcastically.

"Personally, I'd rather just sit around in my pajamas and watch American Beauty."

This makes Beckett laugh with a big bite of food in his mouth, which in turn makes me laugh. "I've never seen it."

"You've never seen American Beauty?" I say, adjusting my black crop top to make sure that I'm not making a mess on my shirt because my sandwich is really large and I feel like something might fall out of it and if that happens, I want it to be on the plate and not on my black shirt or my lap.

"Nope, I don't think so."

"Kevin Spacey and the girl from Hocus Pocus... ring a bell?" He just looks at me with a blank stare for a moment and I take that as a no. "Well, anyway, it's a really great movie. Incredibly intense and fucked up though."

"My kind of movie," He says with a grin and I laugh again, rolling my eyes at him. "Sounds kind of like Beetlejuice."

"I wouldn't know, I've never seen it."

"No," He gasps dramatically and then a wide grin spreads across his face and I can't help but think that it's a beautiful grin. I know that I shouldn't think that though, so I quickly look down at my half-eaten sandwich so that I'm not looking up at him anymore. "That's impossible."

"It's not impossible, that movie always creeped me out so much that I just never got the courage to watch it," I shrug, eating some of my fries now. "The guy in the black and white striped suit still freaks me out."

"That movie is iconic," He informs me, still pretty shocked about my uncultured mind.

"That movie is terrifying."

"It's not even scary, it's funny. I mean, of course it's a little twisted—it's a Tim Burton film," Beckett explains to me. "You know what, I have it at my house so when we're done here, we have to go back to my house so that you can watch this movie."

"I don't want to watch it though," I tell him with a small laugh. "But I appreciate the offer."

"No, you are culturally unfit to walk the streets of America if you have not seen this movie. If I let you go on with your life knowing that you haven't seen this movie, it will be a public injustice."

"Okay then," I say with a small laugh at how dramatic he's being just over this ridiculous movie. "I guess I don't have anything else better to do."

"Nothing will ever be better than the introduction of the Tim Burton era," Beckett assures me.

"I've seen Tim Burton films before, so it's not really an introduction," I inform him just before taking the last few bites of my sandwich and then I start digging into my fries.

"You haven't really seen Tim Burton until you've seen Beetlejuice," He tells me with a shake of his head and I laugh again just as I feel a hand on my shoulder and both Beckett and I turn to see three middle-school aged girls standing by our table with wide grins on their faces.

"Ohmygoodness, you're JustJensen, aren't you?" The one in the middle asks me.

I glance back at Beckett, apologizing with my eyes because I know that this is interrupting our dinner and our very interesting 'debate' about Beetlejuice, and I feel bad because I know that this is rude but I don't have the heart to just tell my fans to go away because I'm busy. Beckett just shrugs at me with a small smile, silently telling me that it's okay and then I turn back to the girls and smile politely at them. "Yeah, that's me. How are you ladies doing today?"

"Oh, we're great," The girl to the left says and it looks like she's about to cry, which I find to be awkward, when fans cry because they're meeting me, but it's also adorable and flattering too. "You look so much prettier in person, by the way. I-I mean, not that you look ugly in your videos but just... wow. I can't believe that we're really meeting you right now. How is this even happening?"

"Can we take a picture with you?" One of them ask before I can respond to the crying girl.

"Of course," I chirp and then I stand up and the girl in the middle hands her phone to a grown lady that's standing behind them, one of their parents, I assume, and I stand with the girls and wrap my arms around their shoulders, which is my ordinary candid fan picture pose.

"Do you know when you're going to end your hiatus from YouTube?" One of the girls asks me. "Because living without your videos is like living in the Sahara Desert without any water."

"I'll be back soon," I assure her with a small nod. "But I appreciate your patience."

"Really? Like, how soon?"

"Nyla, shut up!" The girl beside her whisper-shrieks and then subtly elbows her side before looking at me and grinning. "Can we get an autograph? Just really quick, please?"

"Sure, of course," I confirm and then I dig into my purse and pull out a Sharpie that I keep with me at all times now because I've met girls that will start crying hysterically when they meet me but have no pen for me to autograph something with and it's pretty tragic.

So they each give me a napkin to sign because it's not like they brought something to be autographed when they came out to dinner tonight and I add a little message to each of them- Nyla, Kenzi, and Rian are their names and then when that's done, they each give me a strong hug before their mother pries them away from me and then they leave the restaurant.

With a long sigh, I sit back down with Beckett. "I'm sorry about that. But we should probably get our check now because there's a strong possibility that we're about to get mobbed with people asking for autographs."

"That happens to you a lot?"

I shrug. "Not incredibly often but sometimes. I just know that once one person recognizes me, it grabs everybody's attention and then everybody is gathering for a picture. I'm going to go to the bathroom really quick, and then we should probably get out of here."

"Alright, that sounds good."

I give him another apologetic look before I stand up from the table again and take my small striped satchel with me so that I can go into the bathroom and put on an extra dab of makeup so that if anybody else does catch me for a picture, I can look nice.

When I return from the bathroom, I see that Beckett got the rest of our dinner packed up in to-go containers and he says, "Alright, we're all set to go."

"We have to pay," I remind him as I start getting my wallet out of my purse.

"I already paid," He tells me.

"Oh..." I mutter slowly. "I was going to pay for my dinner though."

"It's not a big deal, Jen," Beckett tells me with another easy laugh and then he starts leaving the restaurant, so I follow him through the tables to the big glass doors that we entered from a little while ago.

"Dinner and a movie," I say jokingly. "How charming."

He offers me a boyish grin as we get in his car. "I'm just full of surprises."

I just roll my eyes at him and I tell myself not to think much of it. Even though it's kind of date-ish to pay for my dinner and now we're going to go back to his house to watch a movie, probably just the two of us, and I don't mind that much because I like hanging out with Beckett. He's funny and pretty easy to talk to and he's really nice but I just don't want him to get the wrong idea about us because I just want to be friends.

"So you told that girl that you're going to start your YouTube channel up again soon. Are you really?" Beckett asks me on our way back to our neighborhood.

I nod. "Yeah, I'm thinking about it. I'm not repulsed by the idea of Elliot watching my videos anymore and I really miss posting videos. I have a few that I'm ready to post because I've been working on them through the month, I just didn't post them so I think that it's time that I get over myself."

"That's good. Not getting over yourself, I mean, but that you're going to start up your channel again. Are you going to find somebody to be your camera man or are you just going to wing it on your own?"

"I haven't decided. I'm thinking that I'm just going to do it by myself until graduation and then when I get to London, I'll be with a bunch of YouTubers who can help me out with the tech stuff. When I come back for school though, I think that I'm going to actually hire a professional video team."

"That's ambitious, especially if you have college stuff going on."

"Well, if I practice the song during the week, I should be able to go into a studio and film and record everything over the weekend so I think that it'll work out," I explain to him.

"Do you know where you're going for college yet?" He asks me curiously.

"Nope, I'm still absolutely clueless. I've got all of my acceptance letters back though, so I just have to decide which one of the acceptance letters that I want to accept. What about you?"

"I'm waiting for one more acceptance letter and then I'm going to decide. I really want to go to the one that I'm waiting for though," He explains.

"Which one is that?"

"Duke, up in North Carolina."

"Yeah, I know where Duke is," I say with a small laugh. "When we were talking about college when we were at the bonfire, you never mentioned that you applied to Duke. That's huge, it's such a good school."

"Right, I haven't even told my parents that I applied there. It's such a good school that I just highly doubt that I'll get in. I don't want to jinx it by talking about it too much."

"That's very superstitious of you," I laugh and I open my mouth to tell him that I think that his superstitious beliefs are kind of adorable but then I remember that we're just friends and that it's going to stay that way, so I don't actually tell him that. Even though I do think that it's adorable.

"I know, but I'm not taking any chances," He says. "My sister goes to Northwestern though, which is a really good school, so I have to beat that."

"That's taking sibling rivalry a little far, isn't it?"

"Maybe, but I need some bragging rights here. And like you said, it's an amazing school," He explains to me.

I'm about to add something else about Duke when we pull onto our street and I see a car in his driveway. "Are your parents home?" I wonder curiously even though I don't recognize the car as either one of his parents' cars.

"My mom's home but that's not her car," He tells me as he pulls into his driveway and we both curiously walk up to his front porch but then right before he opens the door, Beckett jolts to a stop. "Oh! Shit."

"What is it?" I wonder, feeling a little alarmed at his sudden reaction and then I look around for something that looks alarming but I'm not seeing anything.

"Um, nothing, it's just that I remembered something. And maybe we shouldn't watch that movie today. Some other time would be better," He explains to me, glancing back at the car and then to his front door, making it clear to me that he's just now realized who that car belongs to and he doesn't want me to find out.

"Alright then..." I play along because I don't feel like being invasive and if he doesn't want me to know who it is then I won't persist about it- it's none of my business. "I'll see you-"

I'm interrupted when the front door swings open and Margaret is standing on the other side of the threshold with a wide grin on her face. "Hey, kids! Beckett, you'll never guess who decided to stop by for a visit."

Before Beckett has time to answer, a familiar face appears behind Margaret and I suddenly feel dizzy. "Hey, sport," Kevin greets Beckett. He looks way older than I remember him to be from freshman year but it's clearly him, I recognize his evil-looking green squinted eyes and that gooey voice that used to drown me. I feel like I'm going to vomit.

"Hey, Kev," Beckett mumbles, glancing quickly to me and then back to him and then to his mother, but my eyes are glued to Beckett's shoulder because he's standing in front of me, between me and Kevin, and if I looked anywhere else, I would probably pass out.

"And this is Jensen, right?" Kevin wonders, causing a knot to tighten in my stomach. He passes Margaret and then steps onto the porch and extends his hand for me to shake but my hands are wrapped around my midsection, hugging myself so that I don't fall apart, and I don't have enough strength inside of me to move, to act polite for Margaret's benefit. It's what I should have done so that she won't get suspicious but I just can't get myself to move. "You're looking really good."

"I didn't realize that you two knew each other," Margaret pipes.

"Oh, we go way back. Don't we, Kev?" My freshman sarcasm starts flowing out of my lips without my consent and I feel like I'm in the hallways of our school again, being pushed against a locker, being called a freak. And I feel like I have to fight back and that I can't cry because that was always my number one rule. "And as much as I'd like to stay and catch up, I have things to do at home, like putting my face into a blender or something else that's less painful than this reunion."

I start backing off of the porch but before I get very far, I hear Margaret call after me, "Jen, are you okay, sweetie?"

However, I have the feeling that if I open my mouth again, vomit is going to come out, so I don't respond to her, I just fumble my way down the few steps of the porch and start heading toward my house. I hear Beckett follow me though, and when I feel a hand on my shoulder, my freshman instincts kick in like an old habit- like riding a bike- and I push him off of me as violently as I could.

"Don't touch me!" I snap at him, louder than necessary and my breathing ragged both because of how scared I feel right now and because of how hard I just pushed Beckett. I know that I shouldn't feel scared because even if Kevin is still a giant bully, I know that nothing would happen with Margaret there and I also know that I can handle myself physically now so he can't hurt me, even if he wanted to. But my mind won't believe me, and I'm finding it hard to breathe.

"Jen, I'm sorry," Beckett says quietly so that his mother can't hear what he's saying. "I didn't know that he'd show up like this. Are you okay?"

I don't answer him because I'm too terrified of what'll come out of my mouth if I tried so I just turn back around and speed walk as quickly as I can back to my house.

Once I'm back in the safety of my own house, I lock the door behind me and then go up to my room. My parents took Katy to a gymnastics meet so there's nobody else home, which is fortunate for me because I go into the bathroom and make a lot of noise throwing up the amazing grilled cheese that I'd just eaten at the restaurant and then I start clutching my chest because I feel like my heart's going to beat out of my chest.

At first, I'm thinking that I'm having a heart attack and then I realize that it's most likely a panic attack which I learned in psychology resemble heart attacks sometimes. Without having the energy to move, I just lay on my bathroom floor and hyperventilate for a few minutes with tears falling off of the sides of my face and my hands trembling as if there's an earthquake shattering my entire being. The pure terror running through my veins is enough to keep me on the floor for a good five minutes before I can sit up again and catch my breath.

All of the horrid memories from freshman year come flashing through my head like some sick flip book of nightmares—memories that I've spent the past three years of my life trying to get over, and I've been doing a pretty amazing job at it too, if I do say so myself. But I guess that if Kevin can still get to me like he just did then maybe I haven't actually gotten better at all, I've just been able to trick myself into thinking that I have.

To get myself out of my weird panicked daze, I stand at the sink and splash some water on my face and focus on my breathing so that I'm not gasping for breath anymore.

"Jensen?" I hear Beckett on the other side of the door before two loud knocks echo through the small bathroom that I'm in. My whole body jumps at the sound because I didn't expect him to follow me and I also didn't expect him to be able to get into the house considering I locked the door. "Hey, are you okay?"

"I'm fine," I assure him quickly, turning off the running sink water to respond.

"I wouldn't have invited you over if I thought that Kevin was going to stop by," He says through the door. "I'm really sorry. He isn't an insane dick anymore though, he's not going to mess with you or anything."

"I'm not worried about Kevin," I lie. "I haven't talked to him in years, I'm so over it. So thanks for checking up on me but it's not necessary. How'd you even get in my house?"

"My mom was worried so she gave me the spare," He explains. "What should I tell her?"

"Tell her the truth. That the grilled cheese didn't sit right with me and I didn't want to blow chunks on her porch," I explain, only half-lying. I really didn't want to puke on her porch.

"Right," He sighs, obviously not believing me but he doesn't question it. "Do you want some help? Or should I leave?"

"I can handle myself," I tell him, covering my mouth to silence a sniffle. "But thanks."

"Are you mad?" He wonders. "Because I feel like I shouldn't leave if you're mad at me."

"No, I'm not mad. I mean, why should I be mad? Of course you guys are still friends, he never destroyed you."

"Okay, I'll-"

"Just forget it, Beck," I say quickly. "I'm sorry. I'm being dramatic, I know, but I really just want to be alone right now."

"Okay," He says again. "Okay, I'll call you tomorrow."

I don't respond and then after a minute, I hear his footsteps as he walks away from the other side of the door and then descends the stairs and then, thankfully, I'm alone again.

Because that's when the tears start.

24- Red Flags

"What happened yesterday?" My mother asks me the next day as I'm going through all of the clothes in my dresser.

"Nothing happened," I say, trying to sound as convincing as possible even though my mother has an unbreakable built in lie detector so I know that it probably won't get past her.

"Margaret said that you freaked," She explains. "Well, she used kinder words, but she was worried about you. She said that you seemed spooked by Beckett's friend."

"They aren't really friends," I say quickly as if that makes my situation any better. "I mean, they used to be but they stopped being friends when Kevin graduated after our sophomore year. He just stopped by for old time's sake or whatever but they aren't like, close anymore or anything."

"You don't like Kevin, I take it?" She wonders, stepping into the room to continue this interrogation even though I really wish that she wouldn't.

"No, I don't. He's a creep."

"He seemed nice, I thought," My mom tells me, sitting on the bed as I'm kneeling on my carpet by my dresser, continuing to fiddle with my folded up t-shirts.

"You met him?"

"Yeah, we all went to breakfast this morning before you woke up. He's in town for his sister's wedding and wanted to stop by to say hi to Beckett. I thought that it was sweet that they still keep in touch after so much time has passed," She explains. "Did something happen between you and Kevin back when he went to your school or something?"

"No," I say quickly. "Mom, I just don't like him. It's not a big deal."

"Okay then," She sighs, appeasing me and just dropping the conversation. "What are you doing to all of your clothes?"

"I'm just deciding what I want to take to London with me," I tell her with my back still facing her as I talk.

"You're planning out what you're going to pack for London?" She wonders incredulously. "Sweetie, you still have two months before you leave, I think you have some time."

I know that I have a lot of time before London but in all reality, I'm only doing it to keep my mind off of what happened yesterday. I've spent all day just trying to keep my mind off of last night's events. When I woke up, I organized my room and then I studied my song entries for my next video and chose which song I'm going to do next week and then I made sure that all of my homework was done before I started going through my clothes to mentally pack for London because I couldn't think of anything else to do.

"I just want to be prepared," I say instead of explaining all of that to her because if she sees really how perturbed I am by Kevin's reappearance, I know that she'll be able to make the leap and figure out that Kevin was one of the bullies from my freshman year and when that happens, I think that it'd be an easy assumption to make that Beckett was involved as well.

"I think that you need to calm down," My mom says. "Take a breather and tell me why you're acting so jittery."

"I'm not jittery," I argued and then focused on slowing down my motions to try and seem steadier and more in control of my movements because I did feel kind of jittery, I just didn't want her to notice so much.

"Jensen," She says my name in a way that tells me that she's not falling for my crap and that I need to explain to her what's going on. "You can talk to me, you know."

"I know, Mom," I assure her. "I just don't have anything to talk about."

"I think that you're lying and I think that there's more to this Kevin thing than you're telling me," She accuses me as she stands up from my bed again and starts walking out of my room. "But you're upset and I don't want to push it right now so I'm going to go but I'm not through with this conversation so don't think that you're off the hook yet, alright?"

"Sure, fine. Have a nice evening," I mumble to her, still not looking up from my clothes.

After she leaves, I realize how ridiculous I'm being, going to such an extent that I'm messing up all of my folded up clothes so I stop messing around with my shirts and I shut the dresser drawer. I want to go for a run or something but I'm afraid that if Kevin is still hanging out at Beckett's house that I could run into him again and that's about the last thing in the world that I want to happen right now.

So instead of getting all of my pent up anxiety out over running like I should do, I just grab my guitar and go for the second best remedy for this type of anxious feeling. I lay on my back on the floor of my bedroom because that's just the kind of mood that I'm in and I rest my guitar on my belly as I just start moving my fingers around, playing random chords that kind of sound good together and then I fall into playing an actual song. I don't sing or anything, I just play the music for it.

After a while of just laying on my carpet, staring up at my ceiling while strumming the notes to various songs, I hear a knock on my door and I assume that it's my dad because my mom doesn't even knock, she'll just walk right into my room. He's probably coming in here to talk to me about what's going on because my mom forced him to because she does that sometimes, forces him to ask me the same questions that she's asked me thinking that he'll get a different answer.

"Come in," I call to him over the quiet notes from my guitar.

I hear the door open but I don't look up because I'm really comfortable on the ground right here and if my dad wants to lecture me on worrying my mother with my emotions, he can do it while I lay down and stare at my ceiling.

"Hey," When he speaks, however, I realize that it's actually Beckett and not my father. Which makes this situation ten times worse.

"Hey," I respond, still not getting up from the floor.

"What're you doing?" He wonders curiously, stepping farther into the room and then he shuts the door behind him.

"Just practicing," I respond which is kind of a lie because I'm not practicing the songs that I need to practice or anything, I'm just randomly playing the songs that I already know by heart. He doesn't need to know that though. "What's up?"

"I just wanted to stop by to make sure that you're okay," He explains, clearing his throat at the end which means that he's feeling awkward right now because I've heard him clear his throat many times through our few years of awkwardly existing together. I don't feel awkward anymore, I just feel tired of talking to Beckett and tired of thinking about Kevin.

"I'm fine," I assure him with a long sigh.

"You don't look fine."

"How would you know what I look like when I'm feeling fine?" I ask him with raised eyebrows even though I still don't look up at him due to my high level of comfort.

"I don't think that anybody who's feeling fine just lays on their bedroom floor playing sad music," Beckett informs me with a quiet laugh under his breath.

"This isn't sad," I argue, strumming louder on my guitar as if that proves my point. "And I'm actually really busy right now so can you come back some other time?"

"You're busy?"

"I'm practicing," I remind him again, strumming my guitar again just to prove my point.

"I feel like you're mad at me about what happened yesterday," Beckett informs me instead of just leaving my house, which is what I was hoping that he'd do. He is very stubborn sometimes, I'll give him that.

"Why would I be mad at you?" I wonder dryly.

"Well, I know that you aren't Kevin's number one fan but I really didn't know that he was coming over. He didn't call or anything, he just showed up," He starts to explain.

"I'm sure it was a pleasant surprise for you to see such a near and dear friend of yours after so many years," I respond, my voice soft and dull because I don't want to come off as offensive and yet, I kind of do because it makes me a little sick to think that I was hanging out with Beckett at the same time that he was conversing with Kevin.

I know that Beckett was a grade A asshole at the beginning of high school but I've only been able to get over that because he was so passive about it all, he didn't actually instigate the conflicts. I know that it doesn't make it okay at all but it's better than how messed up Kevin was to me- instigating everything, taunting me every day, just generally fucking me up inside and out.

"He really isn't a bad guy," Beckett says in a quick breath and that's the sentence that finally grabs my attention enough for me to stop absent-mindedly strumming my guitar and to actually sit up and look at Beckett and I look at him as if he's just grown two heads. "I-I mean, I know that he was a jerk in high school but he's been through a lot and-"

"You're defending him? To me?" I wonder incredulously just to clarify what's happening right now because I didn't think that Beckett would be stupid enough to try and make me feel sympathy for the guy who ruined most of my high school career. What Kevin and Bethany started during freshman year will haunt me for so many years, probably even into adulthood, and he did it with a smile on his face and I know that it was a long time ago but that crap isn't something that I'm just going to get over just because I got over it with Beckett.

"No, that's not what I'm doing at all."

"Yes it is," I argue, leaning my back against my dresser as I'm still sitting on the floor and Beckett's sitting on my bed so I have to look up to him and now I'm making it obvious to him that I really am angry. I try my best to glare daggers into his cheeks with laser vision or something. "That's exactly what you're doing. Jeez, Beckett, just get the fuck out of my house, alright? The absolute last thing that I need right now is to hear you tell me about what an absolute saint Kevin is now that he's grown up."

"Why is it so hard to believe that he's changed since then?" Beckett wonders with raised eyebrows, not in a defensive manner but his voice holds a curious tone to it. "You've been able to see that I've changed, what's so different about him?"

I give Beckett a pensive look before putting my guitar down beside me and stretching out my bare legs and then I shrug one shoulder. "I don't know, maybe I don't really believe that you've changed at all."

"What do you mean?"

"I mean that I've been so desperate for some sort of friendship that I've just so easily lied to myself, told myself that you're a better person than you used to be but what would give me real proof that that's true? That you've really changed?"

"Are you serious?" He asks me. "Jen, come on, we legitimately hung out for like three hours yesterday."

"So? Just because you're nice to me now that I'm kind of famous doesn't mean that you're not such a shallow prick anymore. For all I know, you're still knocking kids down in the hallways and stealing their lunch money," I refute, defensively crossing my arms over my chest.

"Kevin being here is getting into your head too much," Beckett decides. "I don't even talk to him that much anymore, we just text sometimes but it's not like we're still close friends or anything. I'm really not the same person that I was freshman year. You know that."

"I don't know that," I deny with a shake of my head.

"Well then what can I do to prove it to you?"

"Why does it matter to you? You have a lot of friends, you'll be just fine without me around to force your weird movie obsessions onto," I mumble to him. "Anyway, I'm not mad at you or anything and as far as freshman year goes, I really do forgive you for everything that happened. I forgive everybody, Kevin and Beth and all of them. But that doesn't mean that I'm over it. Because I'm not, obviously. And the whole idea of us being friends is kind of a joke. Who were we fooling anyway? We have too much awful history to ever be anything more than acquaintances."

"That's not true," Beckett denies as I stand up from the carpet and I grab my guitar to put it back in its case because he's obviously not leaving and I'm obviously not going to be playing my guitar for the time being. "You're only freaking out because Kevin showed up, you were fine with us being friends before that so let's just forget that he ever even showed up."

I hold my hands on my hips to show him that I can be just as stubborn as he is and that I'm not just going to give in that easily. "You didn't answer my question," I tell him and now that I'm standing up and he's sitting on the edge of my bed, he's the one looking up to me now.

"What question?"

"Why does it matter so much to you?" I repeat and I think that I stop breathing for a moment because I'm so nervous about what his response is going to be. I probably really don't even want to hear what he's going to say but I have to ask.

"I don't know," He sighs. "Because you're really cool to hang out with."

"You have a lot of friends," I state the obvious. "You have tens of other people to hang out with."

"Yeah, but-"

"Please don't say that I'm different or that I'm cooler than your friends because that is way too... cheesy and ridiculous," I interrupt him because I can sense that that's what he's about to say, which is not something that I want to hear right now so I might as well just save us both the trouble of having to hear/say it. "Seriously. You'll have to be more sincere than that."

Beckett sighs again and then runs his fingers through his hair, looking slightly stressed out as he really thinks about what comes out of his mouth again. "Because you're honest, and funny and brave and just a really awesome person to be around. And I really have grown up since freshman year, just like you did—just like everybody does."

I purse my lips, trying to think of a response that was neither angrily mean nor nice and forgiving because I wanted to be in the middle of those two things. "I still don't think that-"

I stop talking when Beckett abruptly stands up from my bed as if there is a fire under his ass and I wait for him to say whatever it is that made him stand up so abruptly but he doesn't say anything for a long time and he's just staring at me. Getting a bad feeling about this (even though I can feel a buzz start to grow in my stomach), I look down at my shoes and I pinch my lips together so that if his intent is to try to be romantic, he can't kiss me.

However, after an even longer silence, I can't just be silent anymore so I release my lips from their hiding spots and look back up at Beckett, who is still staring at me and I wonder if that's really why he stood up, if he's really going to try to kiss me. Maybe that's just me being too vain or too into the sappy romantic movies where the guy just abruptly gets up and goes for it.

Finally, I break. "What're you-"

And again, he interrupts me and just like in the movies, he goes for it. A little bit of a delay there at the beginning, which threw me off, but sure enough, his lips are now attacking my lips. At first, I'm completely prepared to push him off of me and to yell at him again because I'm still mad at him and he has no right to just kiss me like he is. I even lift my hands up to his shoulders and tell myself to push but I can't get myself to let go.

When I don't pull away from him like I think that he expects me to, his arm wraps around my waist and he pushes his lips tighter against mine. I try again to tell myself to pull away, but again, it just doesn't work.

I blame it on the buzz in my stomach that is now taking over my whole body like a virus and how warm and soft and slightly perfect his lips feel against mine. Despite him being Beckett- the guy who was a passive mega-jerk, the guy who put me through high school hell for a whole school year. Because yeah, we do have that past and it sucks but we also have the present, where Beckett is sweet and easy to talk to and funny and there for me and an amazing kisser and absolutely hot as hell.

But even with all of those great qualities, I know that I shouldn't be doing this. I don't like Beckett as more than a friend even though I think that he's one of the most attractive people that I've ever met. Physical attraction does not equal an emotionally romantic bond, and I don't have that with Beckett. So even though he's really fun to kiss right now, I worry that I'm leading him on by not stopping this. And yet, I'm still not pulling away.

Just as he's about to deepen the kiss, I hear my door swing open and then a high pitch squeal reverberate through the room before I can jump away from Beckett and he can do the same.

Looking toward the door, I'm slightly relieved that it's not my mom but I'm also incredibly mortified that it's Katy.

"We weren't-" I start to say something to my little sister but before I can start to beg her not to tell our parents, she's already disappearing from the doorway and running toward the stairs.

"MOM!" She's shouting as she's running and then I'm chasing after her through the house in hopes of catching her before she finds our mother and then I can threaten her to be quiet about what she just saw.

"Katy, get back here!" I snap at her but she probably can't hear me over her incessant shouting for our mom, who is tending to her small garden out front of our house. When I see Katy run out the front door before I can get to her though, I give up on trying to catch her and go back upstairs. Still not breathing steady from the mind blowing kiss, I wait outside my door to catch my breath for a minute before I prepare myself with a mental pep talk and then I go back into my room where Beckett is standing just about where I left him.

"We can't do this," I blurt quickly, shutting the door behind me and leaning my back against it to stable my quaking knees. I inwardly smile because I'm proud of myself for really saying that so that he knows that it can't happen again, even though my lips are already feeling a slightly desperate ache to feel his again.

"Right, I'm sorry, I shouldn't have done that. I'm sorry," Beckett starts to apologize.

"I just mean," I start to say quickly and I can tell that my will power isn't as strong as I'd like it to be. I really have no pride at all. "Because my mom is downstairs."

"Oh," Beckett pipes, looking slightly relieved at my statement and I feel ashamed at myself for giving into that buzz inside of me but at the same time, I don't regret it. Having a little bit of fun won't hurt anybody, I suppose. "Well, I mean, my house is empty. If that matters or anything."

"Okay," I decide in a split second and I turn to leave my room in hopes that if we move fast, I'll avoid my mother who undoubtedly is learning about our previous kiss right now as we speak. "Let's go."

Chapter 25

"Hello my favorite people! JustJensen here and as you can obviously see, I am back! And I have a lot to say today so I'm sorry that this video is really long but I just want to update you guys on everything that's happening with me and why I took that break and all of that. So most of you all know and love my best friend in the whole wide world, Elliot, but I am sad to say that he will no longer be part of the show. He's found better things to do with his time. But I'm okay with that now. I wasn't okay with that for a really long time, which is why I had to take a break from the public eye for a little bit and just spend some time with myself. But a friend of mine has recently made me realize that I'm totally okay without Elliot and I don't want my old crush on my best friend to hold me back from doing what I love, which is playing my music for you guys".

"Anyway, I'm still going to London this summer, as promised, and I'll be posting new videos again. Let's hope for every other Wednesday, I think that I can manage that. I'll open up my email account again so if you have an original song that you want me to listen to and cover, just email it to me and I'll try to get through all of the songs that are sent to me so that I can pick my very favorite songs to cover every other week. Also, as you can see from the wall behind me, my fan wall has been updated because I've been getting so many supportive drawings and letters from you guys in the past month, which was just so awesome and I tremendously appreciate every single fan mail that I get from you wonderful people".

"Okay, and now I think that this is the last thing that I have to say. I'm going to post a music video right after I get done with this video because I miss letting you guys hear my music so much. And my unfortunate falling out with Elliot inspired this song- I actually recorded it right after we went our separate ways, so all of the emotions were really raw in this video- and I think that it's obvious once you watch the video because I'm like, half-crying all the way through it. I just want to say that if you're going through a tough time, don't ever think that it'll be like that forever. Stay strong, stay positive, and stay true to yourself and I know that everything will work out for you".

"And now I'm done talking. I told you that this was going to be a long video. Okay, so I'll see you guys next Wednesday with a new cover just like old times. Bye for now!"

With a deep breath, I upload the video with the title "I'm Back!", and then it's official. My break from YouTube is officially over and all of the hard work is going to start up again, which is really fortunate right now because I need as much distraction as possible from the shit storm that has become my life. I mean, that's me being dramatic but it isn't that bad. With Elliot gone (even though I'm mostly over it, it still sucks that he's not around), and now with all of the Beckett drama that I've brought on myself, my life is getting a lot more complicated than I care to admit.

After I successfully post my announcement video, I re-watch my recording of me singing Break by Artist vs. Poet, which is the song that I had sang to myself right after my falling out with Elliot and I really am such a mess in the video with tears running down my face and my hands shaking so hard that it's almost impossible for me to get the notes right on my guitar.

It's almost hard for me to watch, actually, because it takes me back to when I was so vulnerable and so lost without Elliot. Honestly, I still feel a little bit lost but at least I can function normally now without thinking about Elliot every step of the way. In all honesty, I've barely thought about him in the past week or so except for when I see him in the hallways at school.

Especially with all of the crap that happened between Beckett and I on Sunday. It's only Wednesday now so I've only had a few days to mull over that in my mind and the more time that goes by, the more that I'm beginning to disapprove of my decision to go so far with kissing Beckett. I don't regret it because what happened happened and regretting it isn't going to change anything, I just have to live with it and move on. But it just wasn't my proudest afternoon.

We didn't do anything too awful, we just spent a few hours going back and forth between intense making out and when we needed a break to breathe, we'd just lay side by side on his bed but I wasn't up for conversation, so I didn't say anything and he didn't either so it was just silence when we weren't kissing. But it wasn't awkward or anything, it was actually kind of nice just to relax and to kiss, which was incredibly enjoyable because Beckett's an unfairly good kisser.

However, the more that I think about the event, the more surreal it feels because the idea of kissing Beckett just seems so ridiculous to me, which it is. It's so ridiculous that I let my hormones get the best of me, especially because it was Beckett and our history is too awful for me to let myself lose self-control.

And yet, my house is empty and after I've uploaded the Break song video to YouTube, I can feel my hormones getting the best of me yet again. Even though I'm sitting here, telling myself that Sunday was a mistake, that it shouldn't have happened, I'm thinking that it also wouldn't be an awful thing if it happened again. After all, history is in the past so it's not like we can't just move forward from that, right?

We also don't have school tomorrow and it's not really hurting anybody if we just mess around a little bit out of horny boredom. It's completely harmless if I don't let it go any farther. Just one more time wouldn't hurt anything.

I know that I'm just making excuses for myself so that I don't feel guilty when I pick up my phone and text Beckett, asking him if he's busy. I know that it's wrong, that it's a terrible idea, that it's going to cause so much drama that could be prevented if I just don't invite him over.

But the thing is that I can't help myself because ever since that first kiss on Sunday, I kind of can't stop thinking about Beckett's lips and how much I want to feel them on mine again. So even though I know that it's an awful idea, I do it anyway.

He messages me back that he's just doing homework.

This is my last chance to make the smart decision here and to ask him if he wants to hang out somewhere public like going out to lunch or to a movie or something so that we can't do what I really want to do. Or to just talk to him via text instead of in person. This is my last chance to be smart and again, I don't take the opportunity. I invite him over but I make sure that I don't sound too eager about it.

Just minutes later, I hear a knock at the door and I'm hurrying downstairs to answer it. Still unable to comprehend what's really happening right now, I swing the door open and see Beckett standing on the other side so I offer him a friendly smile but I don't step aside to let him in yet.

"Before you come in, I have to talk. So just listen really quickly," I tell him as my brain tries to keep up with my mouth because I don't really know what's going to come out of my mouth before it's actually being said.

"Okay then," Beckett nods his understanding.

"About what happened on Sunday, I just want to say that it was fun. And I don't mind messing around like that, I actually really like it, but I don't want this to get complicated. I don't want a relationship or anything and I don't want anybody else to know about it. Also, I'm not having sex with you today. Is all of that okay?"

"Yes," He says with a small laugh. "I agree with the terms and conditions."

"So funny," I breathe sarcastically before stepping aside and then Beckett walks into the house and then we're both rushing up the stairs and then into my room to make some more regrettable decisions that shouldn't be made. But we're young, we're stupid, this is the perfect time to make mistakes in our lives so we just have to go for it. Right?

The next morning, I'm woken up by my doorbell blasting through the house. Whoever is pushing the bell is pushing it frantically because it keeps repeating the first dinging noise as if the bell is stuttering. With a loud groan, I stand up out of my bed wearing only Beckett's t-shirt and panties and I look to my alarm clock to see that it's ten in the morning, which means that my parents are at work now and Katy's at school so if I don't get the door, it probably won't stop because nobody else will answer it.

I pull on a pair of short shorts because they're the closest thing to me and then I hurry downstairs, leaving a sleeping Beckett alone in my room to figure out who's at my front door right now abusing the doorbell.

I shouldn't be surprised when I see that it's Elliot standing on my front porch and yet, my half-awake self lets out an audible gasp when I see my ex-best friend standing in front of me wearing a deep frown on his face. It suddenly occurs to me that I uploaded those two videos yesterday and I'd talked about him a lot in them so that's probably why he's here. I suddenly feel a lot more awake than I did two seconds ago.

"Hey," He says, his voice barely audible to me when he speaks and then he's looking down at his shoes instead of at me.

"Hello..." I say slowly, playing dumb as to why he's here because I don't want to make any assumptions until he admits that he's here about the video like I think that he is. "Can I help you with something?"

Elliot in all of his adorable innocence glances up at me and I see him look over my outfit of an oversized shirt and because it's big on me, the shorts are hidden underneath of it so it looks like the shirt is the only thing that I'm wearing. "Yeah, I just wanted to let you know that I saw your video yesterday."

"Over half of a million people have seen that video already," I tell him, crossing my arms over my chest. I don't want to be a bitch to Elliot but I don't want him to think that I'm sorry for putting up the video or that I want to be his friend again so I want to be as distant as possible with him. Not bitchy, although I think that it comes out that way, just distant. "But I'll be sure to note that one of those views is from you. I appreciate the contribution. Is that all?"

"I know that it was about me," He blurts, his hands squeezing into fists by his side, which is something that he does when he's nervous and it's so hard to stay indifferent toward him when I just want to pull him into my arms and to tell him that he has no reason to be nervous. I want him to be okay, but on the other hand, I don't and I want him to squirm a little bit for what he did to me. "And it sounded kind of romantic and you also said that you had a crush on me. I know that you said it because I've watched that part of the video about twenty times already just to make sure that I heard it right."

"Well that's absolutely crazy," I respond dryly. "I was like a sister to you, that'd be disturbing, wouldn't it?"

"Holy shit, Jensen," He mumbles, obviously detecting my sarcasm for the first time ever. "Holy shit."

"It's not like I like you like that anymore," I defend myself, stepping into the house and motioning for Elliot to come in as well because I don't want to stand outside anymore, looking as indecent as I do and Elliot isn't going to leave without some sort of explanation. "And it's not a big deal, so it's really stupid that you drove all the way over here just to tell me that."

"Not a big deal?" He wonders incredulously and it almost looks like he's actually about to cry, which I didn't think would happen and I really don't want to see him cry. "Jensen, I totally... I know that I really hurt you with what I did but now. Now, I think that I broke your heart. I did, didn't I? I didn't mean to do that. I didn't mean for any of this to happen but definitely not that."

"Well, it's over now, isn't it?" I remind him. "No use in worrying about it now, the damage is done."

He puts a hand over his mouth and starts shaking his head back and forth frantically and then he starts running his fingers through his hair in a stressed manner. "This is all so fucked up."

"What's fucked up?" I wonder with raised eyebrows as I lean against the couch.

"Just... all of that time, you just didn't say anything. You just let me talk about it like it was the worst thing that could happen in the world," Elliot starts to rant. "But the whole time, you were..."

"Dying inside? Yeah, I remember. I was there."

"Why didn't you tell me?" He asks me, stepping closer to me but not too close.

"Well, like you just said, you were always going on about how repulsive the idea was and how disgusting it would be for us to be more than friends. That alone was enough to keep me quiet about it. I was fine though, I would have gotten over it after a little bit of time so it wouldn't help anything if I told you what was going on."

"And what I did to you for Cara," He adds and I almost physically cringe at that awful memory. "Now I get why it hurt you so much. I didn't think that you'd mind so much but now, it all makes so much sense."

"No it doesn't," I argue. "If you think that I was so upset about that just because I was secretly in love with you then you really still don't understand why I was so hurt by what you did."

"What do you mean?"

"Okay. Do you know what you're problem is, Elliot? You put too much emphasis on romantic relationships and feelings. You chose Cara over me because she was your girlfriend and I was only your friend but just because we were only friends doesn't mean that we didn't really love each other. At least, I really loved you. And not just romantically, I loved you as my friend. And that's so special, you know? So either you didn't love me as much as I thought that you did, or you just assumed that your romantic relationship was worth more to you just because of the romance part. And it's so ridiculous to just assume that a friendship is less important than romance.

"I was not so hurt by your rejection because I was in love with you, I was hurt because you weren't my friend anymore, and I absolutely loved being your friend. And if you keep just assuming that your girlfriend is more important than your friends, you're probably going to fall in love—or maybe you already have—and you're going to get married and it'll be a fairy tale. But then you're going to look around and realize that other than your Cinderella, you're absolutely alone. Because when it comes down to it, you're such an asshole. And an idiot. And I want you to get out of my house now."

"I just..." He trails off, trying to comprehend my whole speech before he says something else, choosing his words carefully. "I just wanted to know what it felt like, the whole dating and the falling in love and all of that. And

I know that if my relationship with Cara doesn't last then it'll probably never happen for me again and I was terrified of losing that."

"I know," I sigh. "And you'd rather lose me than that chance at love. Whatever, I got it."

"But I didn't think that you wanted that type of thing... with me."

"You thought that I didn't want it?" I wonder incredulously and I hear movement upstairs so I'm assuming that Beckett's awake now. I wonder if us talking is what woke him up and I silently will him to stay upstairs because if he comes down here and Elliot's still here, it'll make this situation a billion times worse. "You were always the one who said that Jelliot was repulsive and disgusting and that we were basically siblings and all that crap."

"I only said all of that stuff because that's what I thought that you wanted to hear," Elliot says quickly and his voice is starting to rise to my level and we're on the brink of shouting at each other now.

"Well maybe you shouldn't worry so much about what you think that other people want to hear and actually say what's on your mind," I snap at him, feeling annoyed at everything right now. Annoyed that Elliot is here right now, annoyed that we might have had a shot if he would stop worrying about what I wanted, annoyed that he's telling me all of this five weeks too late.

"I just-"

Footsteps coming down the stairs cut off Elliot's speech and this time, I really do physically flinch because I have no idea what'll happen but I do know that I really don't want to find out.

"Is everything okay?" Beckett wonders as he steps down the last few steps.

I clear my throat and I hold my shoulders up straighter in an attempt to not seem affected by Elliot seeing Beckett coming down from my room. "Yeah, everything's fine. You remember Elliot, right? He's just leaving."

"Wait... what's he doing here?" Elliot asks me, glancing at Beckett, who is now standing right beside me, and then back to me for an explanation, as if he deserves one or something.

"Oh, come on, El. I know that you're naïve but you can't be that naïve," I say to him even though Beckett and I really didn't have sex last night (although we did just about everything else), I'm so annoyed at Elliot right now that I want him to believe that we did. I know that it's petty and wrong but I just want to get under his skin right now, just to spite him for throwing away anything that we could have been. Granted, it was my fault too because I could have told him how I felt but I would have told him the truth if he didn't start spewing all of that crap about us being like siblings.

"I'm going to go make some coffee," Beckett pipes awkwardly, deciding that he doesn't want to be part of this conversation.

"Is this some sort of trick to piss me off or something?" Elliot asks me once Beckett is gone and in the kitchen, out of view.

"Yes, Elliot," I snort sarcastically. "Because I had a psychic vision that you were going to come to my house this morning so I decided to sleep with Beckett just to piss you off. Because really the only purpose of a vagina is to try to make other people jealous or angry or whatever it is that you think that I was trying to make you feel. Believe it or not, I can find happiness, even if it's not with you. At least he doesn't call me repulsive."

"I never meant it like that and you know it," Elliot says, glaring at me now. "And I know that you can be happy without me but why that guy? After everything that he's done to you."

"Beckett can throw me into a million lockers but it'd never hurt as much as what you did," I fire back. "And you don't get a say in who I talk to, or who I fuck, and you don't get to lecture me or pretend like you care. We're not friends anymore. You finding out the truth doesn't change anything."

"It changes everything," He argues.

"No it doesn't," I deny with a shake of my head. "So please get out of my house because I'm tired of talking to you now and I have better things to do."

"Come on, just give me like, five more minutes. Please, Jen," He pleads.

I cross my hands over my chest again and give him an intense stare before stepping closer to him and then I say just about the worst comeback that I could have thought up. "No. Ironic, isn't it? It's almost as if I'm choosing Beckett over you. And now you're the one left in the dust. You know how much I love irony."

Even a twelve year old could come up with something better than that but it's the only thing that comes to mind on the spot and luckily for me, it gets Elliot to give up on whatever he was trying to say to me.

"Okay. Well, I guess that I'll see you at school, Jensen."

"I guess you will."

I hate how broken and defeated he looks because most of me still cares for Elliot so much and I just want him to be okay. I don't want him to hurt or to feel as broken as he looks right now and I don't want to be the one hurting him. But I'm still angry at him for everything and I don't want him to know that I feel so bad for hurting him, even though he hurt me so much worse. So I let the door shut behind him before I let just a few tears fall down my face.

I quickly wipe them up though, and tell myself that it's going to be okay. Just forget about Elliot, he's old news. I pick myself back up and then I join Beckett in the kitchen for coffee.

Chapter 26

I know that I deserve this, because I brought it on myself, but this really sucks. Beckett, Elliot, London, YouTube. Graduation. All of these things are taking over my mind so badly that it's almost impossible for me to focus on anything else at all. I can barely focus on getting through breakfast without worrying about how to face Beckett at school on Monday or what I'm going to pack for London.

"Jensen," My mother says my name to snap me back to reality on Saturday morning as I'm reliving my night with Beckett and then my ugly morning with Elliot and the amount of indecision that I'm feeling about both of them is starting to put some uncomfortable pressure on my chest.

"Yeah, Mom?" I wonder, standing up and rinsing out my bowl of cereal. I hope that she doesn't notice that I've barely touched my cereal before I throw it all away.

"What's on your mind? You seem so out of it," She tells me with a concerned frown.

"Nothing."

"Is it about Kevin again?" She wonders as she finished the raisin toast that she was eating for breakfast and then she stands up and starts walking closer to me.

"No. It's really nothing. Just with my channel coming back up and graduation around the corner, I've got a lot on my mind but everything's fine. I promise," I assure my mother, not lying to her but still not telling her the whole truth.

"Okay, well I have to get to work but we should talk tonight, alright?" She tells me, leaning over and kissing the top of my head in her motherly way. "I love you, Jen."

"Right, sure. I love you too, Mom," I assure her as she walks away to get her stuff ready for work and I hurry to go upstairs, not wanting to give her any more time to interrogate me about my off mood because I know that the more she questions me, the harder that it will be to lie to her about it.

Yesterday was the first day of school after my confrontation with Elliot and I spent the whole day avoiding Elliot's route through the hallways through the whole day and if I saw that I was about to pass Beckett, I'd duck my head and speed walk passed him so that he didn't have time to recognize me to stop me for a conversation. This avoidance strategy is also my plan for today as well because I don't know what to say to either of the guys.

I think that everything's been said between Elliot and I that needs to be said. We had our friendship, now it's over. That's it. The end of our story, it's done. I know that Elliot disagrees though, which is why I'm avoiding him to the best of my ability, because I don't know what I'd say to him and I don't want to find out.

As for Beckett, I don't really know what to say to him either. Although, our situation is completely different for obvious reasons. After Sunday morning, we spent a lot of time together that day and most of it was just kissing and messing around and doing things that we definitely shouldn't have been doing. Between the fooling around though, we had breaks where we'd actually talk and it was a really fun time. He really helped me get my mind off of Elliot in more than a few ways.

The problem, however, is that I know that feelings are starting to grow. I know that after Thursday, I could start to feel myself start to like Beckett as more than a friend or even a friend that I kiss. And having a crush on Beckett is just not okay with me at all. So the only way to not get a crush on Beckett is to not kiss him anyway, which will be really hard for me because he's so much fun to kiss. And I know that I'll have to tell him this much the next time I talk to him, and I'm not so sure that I know how to phrase it in a way that makes sense to other people.

I know that I brought this Beckett drama on myself because I let him kiss me in the first place and then on Wednesday, I invited him over on my own free will. I knew what I was doing, I knew the risks. And our little fling didn't last very long but I know that I have to nip it in the bud now before it gets out of hand. I have to say no to his physical perfection, no matter how hard that will be for me to do.

Up in my room, I listen to my mother leave for work and I hear Katy in her room with her music blasting as my sister and Sara are hanging out doing I-don't-know-what in her room which is making it even harder for me to think straight. I try to distract myself from everything going on around me by doing my weekend homework but I don't have a lot of that so it's done within thirty minutes and I need more to do.

I have my videos done and I really don't feel like starting a new one so to pass time today, I grab a book from my bookshelf and start reading one of my favorites. It's a cheesy teen romance type of thing and I don't know why like it so much but I've read it a billion times and it always calms me down in a tough spot.

Unfortunately, I don't get even three chapters into the book when there's a knock on my bedroom door and then Katy screeching at me through the door. "Jenny, Beckett's here! He wants to see you!"

I grumble out loud even though I don't mean to and I almost tell her to tell him that I'm not here or that I'm sleeping, but I know that she'd just tell him 'she told me to tell you that she's sleeping, but she's not so I'll take you to her room' or something like that to make the situation even worse, so I don't say that.

"I'll be down in a minute," I tell my sister instead, closing my book and trying to contain my inner turmoil about what's about to happen. I still have no idea how to confront Beckett about what happened on Wednesday and Thursday and I have no idea how I'm going to tell him that we can't do it anymore. I also fear that when I see him in person again, my logical thinking and personal resolve will fall apart again when he flashes me a grin and then purses his lips. I have to keep myself together no matter what.

Going downstairs, I try to plan out in my head what I'm going to say but even as I get down to the living room where I see Beckett and the two little girls sitting on the couch, I'm still coming up blank.

"We're going to give you guys some privacy," Katy informs me as she and Sara stand up from the couch when they see me emerge from the staircase. "But before we go, I just want to say that I did see you two kiss and that I'm not crazy. Sara doesn't believe me but it happened."

"It didn't happen, Katy, now go away," I demand, giving her a dirty look to scare her to move faster toward the stairs.

"We're going," She huffs at me, mirroring my dirty look back at me. "But you're a dirty liar."

Once the girls are gone, I sit down on the love seat beside Beckett and offer him a slanted smile. "What's up?"

"I swear to God, Sara, it happened!" I hear Katy shriek from downstairs and I can't help but let out a small laugh.

He just shrugs and smiles at me in return. "Well, you weren't answering your phone and I think that we need to talk. You know, about what's going on."

"I agree," I say with a nod as I start ringing my hands together on my lap to try and clam myself down.

"Good. Yeah, okay, you go first," He urges me, leaning forward so that his elbows are resting on his knees.

I look up at the ceiling as if the words that I need to say are painted up there like a script so that I knew what to say in this moment. Knowing that I have to at least say something, I open my mouth to speak but words escape me and I fall flat, closing my mouth again. And then after a moment of floundering for words, I start to feel words bubbling up my throat and I don't know what I'm saying until after it's being said. "It needs to not happen," I blurt.

"What?" Beckett wonders, obviously confused.

"Yeah. Whatever it is that we were doing, it can't happen," I look down at my hands now because I know that if I look up at Beckett, I'll lose my resolve and I might just take back what I said. "I mean, we can be friends but that's it, just platonic friends."

"Oh. Is something wrong?"

"No, not really. I don't think so. It's just that... I didn't want to involve feelings but you're being really sweet and everything so I don't think that it can work out without feelings happening," I explain to him, trying to word it as best as I can and I hope that he understands, although he looks really confused so I don't think that he's really understanding.

"Okay. What's so bad about feelings though? Would it be so bad if you liked me like that? We could go on dates and be a real couple or something, that could really happen," He tells me with a frown on his face.

I shake my head at him in the negative and again, I try to plan out what I want to say in my head and then I pray that it'll make sense when I say it out loud. "It's just that I don't want that type of thing right now. And this whole thing was stupid and just a lack of judgment. I should have never let you kiss me and I shouldn't have texted you on Wednesday, and I'm sorry that I was... I don't know, leading you on? But I wasn't really because I told you that it wouldn't turn into anything. I don't know, the bottom line is that we're not going to start messing around like that because it's not okay."

"So you just regret it all? Is that what you're saying?" He asks me, raising his eyebrows at me. This isn't going as well as I'd planned in my head.

"No, that's not what I'm saying. I'm saying that I have a lot going on right now and I need to cut out any excess stress and this relationship is just too stressful for me to deal with right now," I explain to him.

"It wouldn't be stressful if you'd just let me take you on a date or something," He informs me persistently.

"That can't happen," I stubbornly say again.

"Why not though? You just said that you like me like that and I obviously like you like that so what's wrong? You don't have to make things so complicated."

"Because I can't..." I trail off, stopping before I say what I need to say because I know that it's too harsh but it's the truth and I think that it needs to be said. After a long moment of hesitation, I decide to really say it so I keep my eyes locked on my hands because I don't have the guts to look him in the eye when I say this. "Because I can't give my heart to somebody who once destroyed it."

He looks taken by surprise by what I say and then after he realizes what I mean, he pinches his lips together and looks up at the ceiling before looking back at me.

"I mean," I keep talking, not letting him respond to my harsh truth. "I still have nightmares about what freshman year and you're in every single one of them and I know that I said that I forgive you, and I totally do, but I don't forget it. I can't forget it."

"Oh. Yeah, okay, I can understand that," He mumbles, looking kind of sad so I look away again because I feel bad for making him feel sad even though I'm not sure if I should or not. I don't know if he deserves that or not, or who's wrong here or if neither one of us is wrong. I don't know what's right or wrong anymore, I just know that I have to do this or I'll go insane. I have to be honest and I have to end this relationship before it gets out of control. "I guess I lost my chance three years ago, I should have seen that."

"I'm really sorry," I say, my voice weak and almost a whisper now. "I wish that I could get over it because you're really sweet and I think that we could be awesome but it's just..."

"I know, I get it, Jen. You don't have to keep explaining yourself," Beckett assures me, standing up from the couch. "And I'm going to go now. Maybe I'll see you around or something."

"Sure, it'd be really cool if we stayed friends or something," I suggest lightly but he's already walking toward the door.

"Yeah, maybe," He agrees halfheartedly just before opening the door. He gives me a short goodbye wave and a weak smile before he opens the front door and disappears out the door in the blink of an eye, leaving me alone in the living room. I take a deep breath and mentally pat myself on the back because I'm proud of myself for not backing down. He didn't really put up a fight, which was fortunate because I know that if he fought hard enough for me to give him a chance, I might have done so. There's just something about Beckett that drives me crazy but there's another part of him that triggers my PTSD and it's not worth that.

"What was that about?" Katy wonders as she quietly steps down the stairs with Sara following her.

Rolling my eyes at my stupid little sister, I lean back in the couch. "It's none of your business, Katy, go upstairs."

"So you aren't dating my brother?" Sara asks me for clarification with her voice quiet and timid as if she can sense my bad mood and is attempting not to make it worse.

"No, I'm not dating your brother. We never dated."

"But I saw you guys kiss," Katy reminds me as if that proves my statement wrong.

"Jeez," I groan in annoyance at my sister even though I'm not really annoyed at her but she's here and she's being persistent on the matter so now, she's going to get my annoyed wrath. "Yes, we kissed, okay? That doesn't mean that we're dating, Kaitlynn. It means that we misjudged the situation and made a mistake. There is no way on earth that we'd work out as a couple, you know. Not in a million years would Beckett and I be a functioning couple in this lifetime. So please shut up. And go upstairs. And leave me alone."

"Okay, calm down. All I'm saying is that I think that you two would make a cute couple," Katy informs me, not listening to me by going upstairs and leaving me to pity myself in peace.

"You don't really know anything about my relationship with Beckett, so just drop it," I mumble to her, looking over to glare at her to show her that I'm not in the mood for her pre-teen crap right now.

"I know that we don't know everything," Sara pipes. "But we aren't that young, Jensen, we do know some stuff. And we think that you are saying no to true love right now."

"That's the same thing that you said about Elliot," I remind them.

"Yes, and we will keep saying it until you listen to us and actually date the boy that you like," Katy refutes. "I mean, we're hopeful about the next one because you know what they say: Third time's a charm."

"Why are you so invested in my nonexistent love life anyway? It's really weird, you know," I tell them both before standing up from the couch to go into the kitchen to make a pot of coffee.

"Because... I don't know, it's just cute," Katy tells me with a shrug. "And everybody deserves to fall in love."

"It's not as beautiful as you think that it is, Katy," I inform my sister. "Love actually sucks a whole lot and I suggest that when you girls are older that you stay as far away as possible from the whole thing. You'll thank me in the long run."

"That's so negative of you," She tells me.

"Yeah, well it's realistic," I refute. "And if you're such a romantic when you get into high school, you're going to be absolutely doomed. Both of you. You both just need to get you stuff together in the next four years before things start really getting whack for you."

"I think that you're just upset about Beckett, and you're taking it out on us," Sara tells me as I start the coffee and lean against the counter, facing away from them in hopes of that being a hint for them to go away.

"Well, I told you to leave me alone like five minutes ago so whatever I'm saying to you right now is completely and entirely your fault," I defend myself. "So you should leave now before it gets worse."

"Okay, okay, we're going back upstairs now. For real this time," Katy tells me and thankfully, she starts heading toward the stairs in the living room and Sara follows her.

Once they're completely gone, I take a deep breath again, trying to calm down my terrible nerves. I tell myself that everything's going to be okay now. I'll make it out of all of this just fine. I'll be okay. Everything will be okay.

Even as I feel as calm as possible, I still feel the gnawing feeling in my chest that I want to talk to somebody about all of this, and I want that person to be Elliot, because I used to tell him everything and our friendship is a tough habit to kick. I know that that's not going to happen though, so I pick up my phone and I call Heather and I tell her everything.

Chapter 27

On Sunday, I'm woken up by the insistent ringing of my phone on my nightstand. I try my best to ignore it for as long as I can but it eventually cracks me and I wake up and answer my phone.

"Hello?" I answer the phone in a grumbling tired voice.

"Jensen," Elliot replies and I immediately regret answering the phone instead of just turning off my phone or putting it on silent so that I could just keep sleeping. "I know that you hate me now but you gotta listen to me. Go to your YouTube channel right now."

"Why? What's going on?" I ask, not really sure that I want to know the answer.

"Um. You'll see. I'm on my way over by the way."

"What? No, don't-" But I stop talking when I realize that Elliot has already hung up so me telling him not to come over is useless now.

Instead of trying to call him back to tell him to leave me alone, I just go to my desk and sit at my computer, turning it on to go find out what on earth he was talking about. It must be something bad if Elliot thinks that he needs to come over here to see me.

Once I've logged onto my YouTube channel, I don't see anything out of the ordinary. My most recent videos are posted on my home page just like they always are and my design is the same so I'm not sure what Elliot was talking about. Still curious, I check my emails and see that I have a lot of Twitter notifications so I log on to my Twitter and I see a lot of people mentioning me in tweets, which is normal, but what they're tweeting me about seems kind of strange.

Poor @JustJensen ! Beckett is such a jerk! Hang in there, we all love you!

He messed up but at least he admits it, @JustJensen ... I think that he deserves a second chance, he seems sweet.

At least he's trying to make things right, but this was the wrong way to go. Good luck, @JustJensen , you're going to need it.

@JustJensen We're here for you <3

I still have no idea what's going on right now but I have a horrible feeling about it because they're mentioning Beckett and I've never talked about Beckett in my videos except for that one time when he was in the behind the scenes for the Primadonna video.

Scrolling down the tweets far enough though, I see one of them with a YouTube link and again, I'm getting a horrible feeling and I don't want to click the link but I know that I have to see what's going on. Holding my breath now, I click the link and it pops up a YouTube video with the title "My Apology to JustJensen" and then when the video loads, I see Beckett's face pop up in the video. It's a crappy laptop camera and it looks like he's sitting in his room. I also notice that he's wearing the same shirt that he was wearing yesterday.

In a panic, I press the pause button before he starts talking so that I can mentally prepare for whatever is about to happen in this video. I take a few deep breaths and then remind myself that I have no choice. I have to watch this video. Pressing play again, I forget how to breathe as I start listening to Beckett talk.

"Okay, uh, well hi there. I don't really know how to make a video but I think that it's the best way to get Jensen to listen to me, because she's always making videos like this. Anyway, I'm Beckett. I've lived next door to Jensen, or JustJensen as you know her I guess, for pretty much our whole lives. We've gone to school together forever and we've pretty much grown up together. We were kind of friends from elementary school to middle school, which is kindergarten through eighth grade. When we started high school though, things went south. If you've watched Jensen's videos, you'll know that the beginning of high school was rough for her. She was bullied a lot by some of the upperclassmen at our school and it was really bad, but she stayed strong through the whole thing and I admire for that and I always will.

"The part of the story that people don't know, however, is that the people who were bullying Jensen were my friends. I'd met the guy through shared friends because I was in baseball and he was in basketball, so I joined the big group of athletes at the school and I guess they were the popular kids. During the summer before freshman year, we'd hang out after practices and it'd be really fun because they'd always make me feel so included and they laughed at my jokes and then when school started, I was popular because of these guys and I didn't want to lose that feeling.

"So when one of the girls in our little group of friends decided that Jensen needed to be 'put in her place' or something like that, I didn't stop her. And when everybody else started going along with her, I still didn't stop them. I just went along with it, I let them hurt her because I was afraid that if I tried to stand up for her that they'd turn on me. The girl, her name was Bethany, she didn't like Jensen because Jensen's dad is a lawyer and he had put Bethany's dad in jail just a few years before school started. It was petty and stupid but just for that reason, a whole group of kids decided to pick on Jensen and then it grew and grew until we were all just making her miserable for no reason other than Bethany decided that she would be their target.

"We were throwing her around into puddles, shoving her against lockers, calling her names, locking her in locker rooms and closets. We were making her afraid of life. She was afraid of going to school every single day, afraid to open her eyes in the morning. But she never lost her resolve in front of people. She always fought back as much as she could, she was always tough when there were people around. What she doesn't know though, is that I knew that it was really hurting her even though she wouldn't let other people see it. From my room, I'd see her sitting on her front porch after school and she'd cry.

"I guess that makes me worse than the others because I could see how much it was killing her. I watched her go from a lively, bright girl in eighth grade and then within a few months, she just deflated. She was quieter, more timid, anxious. But none of the others saw that change or how much it really got to her, and I think that it makes me worse than the others in some ways.

"I'm making this video because I don't deserve the secrecy that she's given me these past years. I know that she doesn't want people to know either because it'd hurt more people than just me, and I know that Jensen won't appreciate this video. But it has to be said and I don't have the guts to do it in person. I know that Jensen's parents are going to blame themselves for pushing us together for all of these years because they were unintentionally trying to force Jensen to be friends with one of her biggest bullies in high school. I know that my parents are going to blame themselves for not seeing what a coldhearted asshole they had raised.

"I can think of a long list of people that this video will effect if it gets out but it needs to be said. This is the way to move on, for both me and Jensen. I don't know if this will fix things between us or not, but I'm really hoping that it'll help in the long run. Maybe not right now but once everybody adjusts to the truth, I think that we can move on. Because we won't be able to be anything until we move on from this history. And I really want to move on from this so that I don't lose Jensen altogether. I love her, and this is my last ditch effort to not lose her.

"Because she's seriously great and incredibly brave and smart and funny and she's more of a person than I ever will be, than most people ever will be. And there's nobody else like her on earth. But I messed up my chance. In fact, it seems like everybody that gets a chance with Jensen messes it up, which is so ridiculous because people should really realize how magical she is and how much she shouldn't be taken for granted.

"So that's the end of what I have to say. I should say that I'm sorry for what happened, because I am sorry, but I don't think that words can really describe how sorry I am for treating Jensen the way that I did at the beginning of high school. But I'm not going to get into that on here because the only person that needs to really understand how sorry I am is Jensen, and she probably won't even watch this all the way through."

He leans forward and turns of the camera, ending the video after that and then I'm left alone in my room to process what I just watched, and the shit storm that it's going to throw at me very soon if the wrong people see that video. I sit in my chair feeling paralyzed for a good five minutes before I get the sense to look at the view count and I feel like I stop breathing when I see that it already has a little over 200,000 views.

Trying not to freak out too much, I stand up from the chair with wobbly knees and walk toward the door to my room so that I can go downstairs to see if my parents have seen the video yet and if they haven't, to make sure that it stays that way.

Standing at the top of the stairs, I hear my mother talking downstairs so I stop before they can hear me and I eavesdrop on whatever she's saying.

"I just don't understand how this could happen," She's saying, probably do my father.

"Jensen just didn't want you to find out," I hear another voice and I'm kind of surprised that it's Elliot. Even though he said that he was on his way, I didn't think that he'd stop downstairs to talk to my mom, who has obviously seen the video.

"But if we knew, we wouldn't have put her and Beckett together so much. We would have protected her."

"She knows that," Elliot tells her. "She just really didn't want you to find out because she was worried that it'd hurt you more than anything."

"We could have helped her," My dad interjects.

"She's over the whole thing," Elliot adds. "She's even friends with Beckett now, or I think that she is."

I don't really want to hear any of this anymore so I step down the stairs and I make sure that my steps are loud so that everybody who's downstairs can hear me coming. Everything falls silent downstairs as I step slowly into the living room, looking warily around the room to see both of my parents sitting on the couch and Elliot sitting in the chair across from them.

"Hey," Elliot greets me, standing up from the chair that he's sitting in and he starts walking toward me. "I know that you probably don't want me around but I had to make sure that you knew, and that you were okay."

"Jen, honey, are you okay?" My mother interrupts, standing up as well and looking at me with a worrisome look.

"Yeah, Mom, I'm just fine," I assure her but I sniffle, giving myself away. "I just... I'm really sorry."

"Oh, sweetie, you have nothing to be sorry about," She says and my father starts nodding his agreement. "We love you so much and it just kills me that we had no idea. That Beckett has basically been part of this family all of this time when in reality, he had been hurting you like he did."

"If you would have told us, we would have done something about it," My father adds.

"I know," I say quickly. "I didn't want you guys to get involved, that's pretty much why I didn't tell you. All of that is over now and Elliot's right, I'm actually friends with Beckett now. All is forgiven."

"All is not forgiven," My mom argues. "With all that he-"

"Can we talk about this later?" I interrupt her, not really able to stand hearing her go on a rant about how angry she is at Beckett or whatever she's about to go on a rant about. "I'm still kind of processing what's going on right now."

"Okay, sure, sweetie. We're going to go over next door to talk to Margaret and Josh," She tells me, stepping forward and she kisses my forehead.

"Have they seen the stupid video too then?"

My dad nods in affirmation and then steps forward as well, pulling me into a tight hug. "He did the right thing by coming clean about it."

"Was it the right thing to blast it publicly as well?" I wonder irritably.

"Probably not. But we're going. You're sure that you'll be alright here by yourself?" My mom wonders as both of my parents start walking toward the front door of the house.

Glancing at Elliot, who is still standing beside the chair, I turn back to my parents and nod. "Sure, I'll be just fine."

"We love you, Jensen," My mom says just before they're both out the door, leaving me alone with Elliot in the living room.

I don't want to need him, I want to be able to just push him out the front door and to tell him thanks for the help but no thanks. Get out. We're not friends anymore. I want to not need him, and it pains me that I do. Elliot is the only person that really knows what's happening to me right now. He knows that Beckett was one of my bullies, he knows that my parents continuously urged us to become friends, he knows that they had no idea and he knows that I never wanted them to find out. And no matter what the situation, he always knows how to make me feel better, and I need that right now. I need Elliot.

"Thanks for coming," I tell him, not moving from my position by the stairs and my voice is quiet, barely above a whisper. "I, uh, I really appreciate it."

"Really? I mean, yeah, it's no problem at all. I just thought that if I talked to your parents first then maybe it'd help when you talk to them, to get them to understand a little bit more, I guess," Elliot explains to me, awkwardly rubbing the back of his neck.

I step forward, tentatively, afraid of taking down the boundaries that we've built in these past weeks. But like I just said, I need him. But I know that I can't just pick and choose when I need him, so if I give in to him right now, I can't go back to being mad at him. That isn't fair for either one of us.

"Does Cara know that you're here?" I ask him because I do want him back in my life but I don't want him to be gone again tomorrow because Cara said that it wasn't okay for us to be friends anymore.

"She doesn't," He denies. "But I'll tell her. And she'll deal with it."

"She might not take it so well."

"She'll deal with it," Elliot repeats. "I'm going to be here for you if that's what you want, no matter what."

"For how long?"

"For as long as you want," He tells me. "Hopefully forever, if you don't get tired of me."

"I don't know what I'm going to do," I mutter to him, my voice still quiet and almost whispering and then I walk toward him and lean my head on his shoulder for comfort. He wraps his arms around my waist and pulls me close as I start to cry, finally letting out all of the pent up emotion that I've been holding in since I saw that video.

"We'll figure it out," He assures me. "Your parents aren't mad at you, they're just trying to adjust to the news. Just let them adjust for a little bit and then talk to them tonight about it. Everything is going to be okay, Jen."

"I don't want to talk to them about it though, that's why I never told them. I just wanted to move on from it, I don't want to have to go through all of this again, to relive it all," I mumble, clearing up my tears as I wipe my face with Elliot's t-shirt and I step back from him.

"I know," He sighs. "But if you don't want to talk about it, I don't think that they'll push you to do so right now. They'll give you time to adjust too."

"Why is my life so complicated?" I wail. "And since when do you have all of the answers?"

"If I had all of the answers, we wouldn't be in this situation in the first place," Elliot responds with a soft smile tugging at the corners of his lips. "Because then I wouldn't have left at all and then Beckett wouldn't have had the chance to get close to you at all and then he wouldn't have had the urge to do the right thing."

"I can't believe that he did that," I mumble, going back to the video that has surfaced. "How have so many people seen it already anyway?"

"He posted the link on Twitter and tagged you in it, and it just kind of spiraled from there," He explains. "I can go over there and try to get him to take it down if you want."

I shake my head at him. "No, it's alright. The damage is already done."

"It'll work out, Jen. Everything's going to be fine," Elliot tells me again. "Just give it some time, this will all blow over and then everything will go back to normal."

Back to normal. That sounded so nice. Avoiding Beckett at all costs, being best friends with Elliot without Cara existing at all. Normal. But I knew that our old normal isn't going to come back because now, Beckett is unavoidable and Cara does exist and Elliot knows what was once my deepest secret ever. Normal is changing, and we can't go back to the way that it used to be. But I guess that the smart thing to do would be to learn to adjust to what's happening right now, to make it the new normal, but I have no idea how to do that.

"Everything's falling apart," I find myself whispering and then just as I start to fall apart again, Elliot pulls me into a hug to keep all of my pieces together. I cry into his shoulder for a few minutes before I eventually get my shit together enough to step back and find even breaths again.

"Your parents are going to be fine," Elliot says as he walks us over to the couch and we sit down beside each other. "They're going to adjust to the news and then they're going to move on and it'll be okay. You just have to talk to them, and wait out the storm right now. But it will go away, I promise."

"I know," I breathe. "I just never thought that this would happen. I thought that we were passed all of this. I just want to get passed it."

"I think that this is the best way to get passed it, with the truth being out there. It was ridiculously stupid of that jackass to put it on YouTube to make it a public thing, but now that your parents know the truth, I think that it'll be easier for everybody to move on from what happened," Elliot starts to explain to me.

"I can't believe that he did that," I say, shaking my head in disbelief.

"Well, he's an asshole," He mumbles.

"No he's not," I disagree with a sniffle. "He's just trying to do the right thing. He's an idiot though. I'm going to go call him."

"Are you sure that you want to do that?" Elliot wonders, raising his eyebrows at me as I stand up from the couch to go upstairs to get my phone so that I can talk to Beckett without having to walk over to his house where they're undoubtedly talking about the video and about everything that's happened.

"I'm sure. I'll be right back," I say, disappearing upstairs.

I grab my phone from my desk and find Beckett's number in my contacts. With a shaky breath, I press the green 'call' button and then put the phone up to my ear, not really so sure that this is what I want to be doing anymore. I don't change my mind though, because I need answers and Beckett's the only one who can give me an explanation.

"Hello?" He answers the phone after a few rings.

"What the hell was that?" I hiss into the phone, sounding a lot angrier than I had intended to sound. But I am angry. I'm not really angry at the fact that he came clean about the bullying but I am pissed off that he felt like it was a necessary thing to do on YouTube, in front of the world instead of just our families. "What on earth were you thinking?"

"Hey, Jensen," He mumbles softly. "I was thinking that I couldn't keep it a secret anymore. And I'm sorry, because I know that you didn't want it out in the open but at least we can really move on now, right?"

"And the only way for you to get this off of your chest was by broadcasting it to my whole fan base?" I wonder hysterically.

"I know that it wasn't the best way to handle things, but I didn't know what else to do."

"How about just telling them face to face? Writing a letter? Emailing your mom? A text? I can count off tens of better ways to come clean than the bullshit that you just pulled," I snap at him. "And now my parents are freaking out thanks to you and everything is getting so screwy. Or screwier than they've already been, at least."

"Yeah, I know, I can hear all of them talking downstairs," He tells me.

"Well, you've successfully caused a shit storm- I hope that your mission is accomplished," I mutter sarcastically to him.

"The mission won't be accomplished until you let me take you on a date or something, because honestly, that's why I did it. Because I really like you, and I want you to be able to like me too," He explains to me.

"This wasn't the right way to go about that," I tell him coldly and I remember that in the video, he had said that he loves me, which I don't really know how to feel about at all.

"I'm hoping that you'll change your mind," He says.

"I don't love you back," I say in a fit of rage, just feeling so pissed off at the boy on the other end of this phone call that I just start going on a tangent. "I don't know if you were expecting a romantic confession or something, but it's not going to happen."

"I know that."

"And it was incredibly stupid and selfish of you to post that video like you did. And I can't believe that you're such an idiot. Because I'm going to be the one that has to deal with the aftermath of this, not you. I'm going to have to deal with blog interviews and my fans demanding more answers and it's all bullshit because if you just kept this within our families, things would be so much simpler right now. You're such an idiot."

"I know," Beckett says. "And I'm sorry, Jen."

I open my mouth to say something else but I don't really know what to say, I'm out of my rant and I'm out of words to yell at him, so all I say is, "I'm sorry too," And then I hang up.

Chapter 28

Sunday night, I have decided, is going to be the worst night of my life. After this morning when everybody saw the video that Beckett oh-so chivalrously posted online, we've all been given enough time to process it on our own so my mom and Margaret have both decided that now it's time for us to process it as a group.

They want to have dinner, all of us together. My parents, Beckett's parents, Marianna, and then Beckett and myself. Katy and Sarah are going to a friend's house so that they don't have to be part of this. It feels like a scene out of a horror movie, one of my worst nightmares. And I don't want this to happen but my mother has kindly made it clear that I have absolutely no choice in the matter.

So at around four o'clock, I say goodbye to Elliot with a promise that once this Beckett crap blows over, we will talk about what's going on between us, if we're friends or not and whatever else there is to talk about but I can't make my situation even more complicated without uncomplicating part of my life first. And then I start preparing a reaction video to Beckett's announcement so that my fans have an explanation on my side of the story as well, which has to happen soon but I don't want to do it today. I just scribble down an outline of what I should say as I'm getting dressed for dinner.

I'm wearing a slightly fancy light blue blouse with white skinny jeans and brown sandals so I kind of look nice. I guess that I just want everybody at this stupid dinner to see that I'm actually not falling apart, and that I'm okay. So I even put on some makeup and braid my hair before I hear my mom call my name from downstairs that it's time to go because we're all going over to Beckett's house for dinner. Margaret is cooking.

Before actually leaving my room, I take a few deep breaths to give myself some confidence that I sorely need right now. I wipe some lip stick from the corner of my mouth and then head downstairs where both of my parents are waiting for me.

"You look nice," My mother comments with a forced smile. "Are you ready to go, Jen?"

"I will never be ready for this," I grumble, passing both of them and leaving through the front door.

"This will be good for all of us, Jen," My dad assures me and it sounds like something that my mother has told him because they sound more like her words than his. I wonder if my dad is just as unexcited about this dinner as I am.

"I vehemently disagree," I tell them, feeling my heart begin to beat faster in my chest than I'd like it to be beating.

My mom doesn't have time to tell me once again that this is a good thing, to have this dinner to talk about our feelings, because we're quickly on the Spears' porch and only seconds after knocking on the door, it's being answered by Marianna with a smile on her face.

"Hello," She beams at us before moving aside to invite us all in. "Thanks for coming, we're glad that you guys could make it."

"Hi, Mari, it's so nice to see you again. How's school?" My mom wonders as we all walk as a group into the dining room where Beckett and his dad are talking in the corner of the room and I can hear Margaret moving around in the kitchen.

"Oh, it's going okay, it's just school," She says with a shrug.

"Well, I'm going to go help your mom in the kitchen," My mom announces as she flashes me a fleeting smile and then heads into the kitchen.

"I'll come too," Marianna pipes, following my mom into the kitchen. Way to set women back thirty years.

That leaves me, Beckett, and our two fathers in the room but when our dads start a conversation about their jobs to avoid the awkwardness in the room and the awkward dinner that's about to happen, that basically just leaves Beckett and I. I'd prefer it if we stayed on opposite sides of the dining room but of course, Beckett disagrees because he starts making his way over to me, where I'm leaning against the wall with my arms crossed to make it clear that I'm unhappy about this situation.

"Hey," He greets me under his breath. I notice my father glance over at us and he looks protective, like he doesn't want Beckett to talk to me but I just return his look and offer him a shrug, letting him know that I'm alright talking to Beckett. He cautiously goes back to his conversation with Josh but I can tell that he's keeping an eye on us as if anything is going to happen.

"Hello," I respond in a clipped tone.

"This dinner thing wasn't my idea," He says quickly. "And I really tried to talk my mom out of it. Just so you know."

"What did you think was going to happen?" I wonder with raised eyebrows. "That they'd just shrug it off and call it a day and then forget the whole thing? Our parents are nerds, they're going to want to sit down and talk about our feelings and shit."

"I know, I just wanted to let you know that this whole dinner thing, it just wasn't my idea," He repeats. "And I know that you're mad at me right now but I really do think that this is the right thing to do, for them to know what happened."

"I'm not mad at you for telling them," I tell him in a quiet voice so that our dads can't hear our conversation. Nothing is a secret anymore, but

I just don't want them to hear what we're saying. "I'm pissed at you for telling the world."

"Yeah, I got that. I took the video down, by the way, now that all of the people that need to see it have already seen it. If that makes anything better."

"It doesn't."

"Okay. Well, this dinner is going to go terribly."

"Agreed," I confirm. "And for the record, I think that it's kind of sweet, what you did. I mean, I'm still pissed about it and everything, but I know that you risked a lot by putting that video out there, and you only did it because you're into me, I guess."

"Yeah?" He wonders, a smirk tugging at the side of his mouth.

"Yeah. All I'm saying is that you've potentially ruined my reputation and possibly even my life, but I appreciate the reasons behind it, even though I'm still incredibly pissed about it," I explain to him, feeling like I have absolutely nothing to lose anymore so I'm just going to be honest about it all. "And although it's practically impossible to not jump your bones only based on physical features, I want to make it clear now that I don't like you like that. You're just a really great kisser and you have abs to die for, but all of that stuff that happened between us, it wasn't because I have romantic feelings for you."

"I kind of figured that," He says. "Not the abs thing, but that last part."

"And after all of this blows over," I continue. "There's a sliver of a chance that we can be friends. Maybe with benefits, or we'll actually get together. I don't know what's going to happen in the future but I'm also saying that there is going to be a future because we're going to get passed this. Maybe not together, even as friends, but us as individuals will survive this shit storm, it's inevitable."

"That's a nice speech."

"Thanks, I just kind of winged it," I say with a shrug just as both of our moms and Marianna come out of the kitchen with dinner and we all take our seats around the dinner table for the World's Most Painful Dinner Ever.

"Alright, dinner is served," Margaret pipes, causing both Beckett and I to walk toward the table. Beckett sits down first, so I have the option to sit by him or to completely avoid sitting by Beckett. I decide that although I don't want to sit down beside him, I should sit by him to give our parents the impression that we get along now, despite our rocky history.

"How are you doing, Jensen?" Josh, Beckett's father, asks me as we're all getting seated and piling Margaret's homemade food onto our plates.

"I'm great, thanks," I say, offering everybody at the table a wide grin just to confirm that I'm not a sad, damaged girl anymore which I'm thinking that they think that I am now that they've found out that Beckett was involved. If I convince them that I'm happy, maybe they won't make this such a big deal. "How about yourself?"

"We aren't here to talk about us, Jen," My mom reminds me, taking a bite of her chicken after she speaks. "Are you two getting along?"

Beckett looks over at me and I turn to look at him but I realize by the way that he's looking at me that he's going to make me answer this question. "For the most part," I say, turning back to my food to start eating.

"I have to say that when we saw that video, we were just devastated to hear what had happened. We never thought that Beckett was capable of anything like that," Margaret explains and I know that it's polite to look up at her because it's obvious that she's talking to me, but I can't really seem to face her, so I just stare down at my dinner. "And both Josh and I are deeply sorry about everything."

"Well, it's not your fault," I respond lightly. "And I've gotten over it."

"Can I just say how fucked up I think that this is?" Marianna speaks out and I'm grateful because at least she probably won't start firing questions at me. "Because I know that you were originally only popular at that stupid school just because I was kind of popular when I went there. And if I knew what kind of piece of shit you were going to turn into, I would have turned the school against you before I left."

"Marianna," Margaret says in a warning voice.

"Sorry for the language," She mumbles in response. "But really. What on earth were you thinking? How do you justify making somebody's life miserable for an entire year? That's not what popularity is about. It's about being liked, not feared. As if high school popularity means anything at all, which it doesn't."

Everybody, including myself, turns to look at Beckett to see what he has to say to that. "I'm not trying to justify it, Mari," He tells her, his voice quiet and awkward.

"Well then why did you do it in the first place?" She asks him.

Again, everybody watches Beckett for his response. "I don't know, I gave into peer pressure, I guess. I was afraid that they'd turn on me if I didn't do what they wanted."

"That's just so terrible of you, Beck," Marianna adds with a disappointed frown.

"I know," He sighs.

"The fact that we didn't know about this makes me absolutely sick," Margaret explains and I just want to shrink into nothing so that I don't have to sit here and listen to what they're saying right now. I'm sure Beckett feels the same way tenfold. "If we had any clue that this was happening, we would have never pushed you guys to be friends for all of these years."

"Well, it's okay because we actually are friends now," I pipe. "And the whole this is behind us. It sucked, it was hell, but I'm over it now so we can stop talking about it."

"We can't stop talking about this, Jensen," My father argues, shaking his head at me.

"We have so many questions," My mom adds and then everybody save for Beckett nods in agreement. "Like, when did this even start?"

"About when freshman year started," I say, hoping that all of these questions will be so easy to answer, although it's doubtful. "One of the upper classmen immediately decided to hate me."

I don't tell them that she decided to hate me because my dad prosecuted her dad because then I think that my dad would feel guilty for letting his job cause so much trouble and I don't want that to happen. Although I'm sure that somehow, that part of the story will leak, I'm hopeful that I can keep at least parts of this stupid story to myself.

"And why didn't you tell us before? Like, right when it started happening? Or even after it was over, we would have done something to help you," My mom explains to me.

"I didn't want you to know because I didn't want it to get out of hand," I tell her. "I handled myself fine, I turned out fine. And I didn't want you to know afterwards because I didn't want this to happen," I say, motioning toward the dinner table to explain that this dinner is the thing that I've been trying to avoid at all costs. "I mean, I lived through it once, I don't want to do it again."

"We don't want you to relive what happened," Margaret says quickly, shooting me a sympathetic smile and I look away. "We just want to understand how any of this happened."

"Well, I certainly don't understand how this happened so I feel like this dinner isn't for me," I explain to them, feeling absolutely desperate to get out of this dinner without talking about the past. I'm positive that my mom will start crying or something. "Because I sure can't explain any of it more than any of you can."

"Jensen," My father says and he gives me a 'be polite' look but I don't understand that, because I'm trying my best to be really polite.

"What?" I raise my eyebrows at him. "I survived it but that doesn't mean that I understand it. I know that you guys want to know what happened, how much Beckett really had to do with everything that happened. Why else would I be here?"

"We thought that it'd be a good idea to sit down with everybody here to make peace with everything," Margaret explains to me.

"I've already made peace with it," I assure her, trying not to lose it. I know that they don't deserve for me to start ranting, but I feel like if they keep wanting to talk about this (which they will) then that's what's going to happen because I can't take this at all. "We're friends now, me and Beckett, everything is in the past."

"But we haven't," My mom adds. "And we need some answers before we can move on from this."

"Well, I don't have any answers," I inform her with an unapologetic shrug. "All I can tell you is that as far as the bullying went, Beckett wasn't the worst one. Out of the main four people, he was the easiest out of the four. He just watched mostly, chased me around sometimes, but he wasn't that terrible."

"You started hanging out with the basketball team, didn't you?" Marianna wonders, turning the attention back to Beckett. "They were always such assholes."

"Kevin was on the basketball team, wasn't he?" Josh asks.

"You started hanging out with Kevin?" His older sister gawks at Beckett and he just weakly nods at her. "Well, that explains just about everything. That kid was a psychopath."

"So it was Kevin that talked you into hurting other people?" Margaret asks.

"Um. Yeah. I guess so," Beckett mumbles.

"That explains a lot about why you were acting so strangely when Kevin came to visit," My mom adds, talking to me now, putting those pieces together in her mind.

"Yeah, I'm not his biggest fan," I sigh.

"Wait, so that day in May when we found you on the porch and you told us what was happening, Beckett did that to you?" My dad enters the conversation as he remembers the day that I got beaten almost to a bloody pulp and then dumped on our porch for my little sister to find all muddy and unconscious.

"No," I say quickly. "Well, I mean, kind of. He never physically hurt me, but he was there. A bystander, I guess."

"That's still horrible," Margaret says and I can see that she's tearing up now, which means that my mom is soon behind. "She ended up in the hospital, Beckett. Because you couldn't do the right thing. We raised you better than that."

"I know, Mom," He mumbles softly, unsure of what else to say.

"And you should have told us sooner," She adds with a sniffle.

"He didn't tell you because I didn't want him to," I add, trying to make the situation at least a little bit better.

"Does Elliot know all of this?" My mom asks me and I can see her chin wobbling, which makes me cringe because it is so weird to see a parent cry. Maybe it's just me, but I think that it's awkward and weird and I'd wish that she wouldn't cry right now.

"Yeah, he knows. That's why he hates Beckett so much," I confirm. "And before you ask why he didn't tell you, it's because I didn't want him to. Because this dinner where we sit down and talk about our feelings is literally the worst thing that I could ever imagine. And everybody who knew the truth before that stupid video knew that, so they didn't tell anybody."

"Why do you think that this is so terrible, Jen? Nobody's mad at you or blaming you for anything, we just want to understand," My mom insists as I take a bite of my chicken and force it down even though I'm not feeling necessarily hungry.

"Because I don't want to think about. I don't want to think about Kevin or getting beaten up or Beckett being an asshole or anything about freshman year. I just don't want to think about it at all and I think that it's pretty obvious why that is. I just want to move on, and I have, and I don't want to start digging up crap that happened three years ago," I say quickly.

"We're not trying to upset you," My dad says as if that's not obvious. I know that they aren't trying to, they just are. "Do you have anything to say, Beckett?"

Beckett looks up from his plate and then glances to my dad before looking to his mom and then to me before he decides on what to say. "I think that everything that can be said about it has been said. Jensen knows how sorry I am, I know that she's done all that she can do to forgive me. And I know that it's harder than just forgiveness because it's something that really haunts her and I know that it's going to be pretty impossible to get over that. So I'm not going to apologize anymore—I'm not sure what else you guys want me to say."

"Do you even realize the magnitude of what you've done?" Josh asks his son.

"Yes, I do," Beckett confirms. "And obviously, I'm doing all that I can to make it right."

"See? So are there any more questions or can we talk about the weather or something now?" I say, stabbing my piece of chicken with my knife in an attempt to cut it.

"Are you truly happy now, Jensen?" Margaret wonders, looking at me curiously and then all eyes are on me, expecting a quick response. "After everything that happened, are you absolutely happy?"

"Yes," I say quickly. "I mean, I wouldn't say that my happiness is absolute, but life isn't so bad. I mean, I have Beckett, and we're kinda friends. And I have Elliot, although that's complicated. And I have YouTube, which is absolutely awesome. So, I guess my life is painfully complicated right now, but I've been worse."

They all look at me like they're satisfied with that answer and I offer them an awkward little smile in return, hoping that that's enough to get them to forget that this whole thing ever happened. For good.

Epilogue

My mom has always been a big party thrower. For any little event, there's a party to be had in our backyard with her closest friends with me, awkwardly standing to the side and answering the same questions repeatedly for all of her friends. I don't mind it really, because her friends are nice and it's nice that they're so interested about my life. It is a little boring though, considering they all answer the same questions and they're such typical questions.

This party is no different.

Well, it kind of is. This party is worse, because I have jet lag and I only got four hours of sleep last night so I don't have much of a patience level today.

The smell of the barbeque from my father's and Josh's attempts to make hamburgers keeps me going though, because they smell ten times better than I know that they'll taste and I'm starving. I step out into the backyard by myself wearing a simple lace dress and my hair up in a ponytail to keep it out of my face.

This party is for me after all, so I have to look nice. It's my welcome home party and just in case I forget that, there's a huge banner on the back of the house that reads 'Welcome home, Jensen!' in big colorful letters. I guess when your daughter spends three months away in London, a welcome home celebration is in order. For my mom it is, at least.

"Jen, honey, smile," My mom tells me, approaching me on the wooden patio with a platter of finger sandwiches balanced on her hand.

"Sure, but Mom, you know that you're a host, right? Not a waitress. Put that plate down somewhere and go enjoy the party. If they're hungry, they'll come get the food," I tell her, taking the large plate from her and I sit it on the table with all of the other little snack foods before we walk together down the steps of the patio and then into the grass where people are sitting around in foldup lawn chairs mingling with each other and preparing their mundane questions to ask me about my trip.

"The party girl is here!" My mom announces my arrival as if I'm the birthday girl at a sweet sixteen or something. Being totally anticlimactic, I yawn and then awkwardly wave to the people in the small circle that consists of two people that my mom work with, one of their husbands, and Margaret. Sara and Katy are jumping on the trampoline in the background.

"Hello, Jensen. How was London?" Margaret asks me, sounding very excited to hear the stories that I have to tell about London.

"It was amazing," I say honestly. "I met a lot of great people and it was really a great blast."

"We've been watching all of your videos and collaborations and everything," My mom adds. "And it looks like you've been having the time of your life over there."

"Yeah, it was great. All of the other YouTubers were just absolutely amazing and it was really cool to be able to spend so much time with them," I continue my spiel although all of this is true. I can't tell them a lot of the stories that I have from London because a lot of them just aren't very family friendly.

It's not like I went badass over there in London, but we did go out a lot and we got drunk often (but not too often because we were still making loads of videos for our separate channels and everything) and I hooked up with a few London boys (and by a few, I mean two). They weren't exactly one night stands, but it was complicated. Stuff like that, I'm obviously not going to tell these people because that'd be really awkward and I'm too tired to think of any G rated stories to tell them about my trip to London.

"And living with Heather was amazing, because she's one of my best friends," I add, glancing back at Margaret and realizing that I don't see Beckett here, which makes me start to silently wonder if he's coming.

I know that Margaret wouldn't force him to come if he doesn't want to, unlike how she used to force him to come to these gatherings before she knew that he was one of the biggest antagonists in my high school nightmare. However, for the last two months that I was home, after everybody found out due to the video that he put out, Beckett and I were okay. We hung out sometimes, we texted frequently, and when the sunset looked particularly pretty, we'd go jump on the trampoline together and I'd pretty much have to force myself not to kiss him.

Because no, I really didn't like him romantically but yes, he was physically perfection and it was just so hard to not just rip his clothes off sometimes. Now that I haven't seen him in three months though, I feel like the desire to rip off clothes is going to be ten times worse, which is why I'm hoping that he's going to be at this party or that our first reunion is at least something public so that I don't even have that option.

We've stayed in touch for the entirety of my London trip via Skype and texting and sometimes, we'd talk on the phone. I don't know why but Beckett's just really easy to talk to. And I really like talking to him, so he's a really good friend.

"So when are you leaving for college?" My mom's friend from work, Rebecca, asks me curiously which effectively snaps me back into the conversation. "I don't even think that I know where you're going."

"I'm going to the University of Virginia," I tell them all. "And I'm leaving in two weeks."

"Yeah, she's getting home just in time to unpack from London and then pack up again to move four states away for college," My mom pouts, giving me a sad frown even though I've already chosen my college and I'm not going to change it now, so I don't know why she's giving me the pity look.

"Why did you choose Virginia? That seems kind of random," Margaret wonders.

"I chose it with Heather, so that we can go to the same college. It's almost halfway between here and where she lives in New York and it's also a really great school. We're even rooming together in the dorms, which I'm really excited about," I tell them all.

"Isn't Virginia kind of close to North Carolina?" She asks me and I know that she's referring to where Beckett is going to school come this fall, which is Duke University because he's kind of brilliant.

"I don't know, I haven't thought about that," I lie. I wasn't considering Beckett's location when I made my college decision but after Heather and I had decided on UVA, I realized that it's actually about 150 miles away driving, which is about three hours, which isn't really that bad considering it'll take about 11 hours to drive from my campus back here to Florida. "Where is Beckett though?"

"He should be on his way out, I think he overslept. He said that he was coming out though," Margaret explains, motioning over to her house. "Sara! Go tell Beckett that Jensen is here."

Sara stops jumping, lets out a loud groan, and then both her and Katy hop off of the trampoline and then make it a race to Sara's house to go find Beckett for me.

"Oh, speaking of Jensen's problematic boys, look who just arrived," My mother coos, motioning toward the gate that leads from the front yard to the backyard, which is how most of the people here arrive so that they don't have to go through the house. Elliot is walking through the gate now with a purple gift bag hanging from his fingers. "Jen, go say hi."

"I'm going," I hiss at her before I start to walk forward to greet Elliot. I'm kind of surprised that he's here at all.

After the video was released and then everything calmed down with my parents and the Spears family, I did talk to Elliot about our friendship and we agreed to be friends again but in all honesty, it just wasn't the same anymore. He was still dating Cara, so he couldn't hang out a lot and even when he was free, I didn't feel up to hanging out with him but he did help out with my videos for the time that I was still home, and we had fun when we did hang out. It was just a little bit awkward with everything that had happened before. I'm not sure if he felt it too or if I was just imagining it, but I had always felt awkward.

"Hey," I greet him with a grin once I'm standing in front of him. "Thanks for coming."

"Hi, Jensen. You're welcome. I, uh, I got you this," He says, handing me the gift bag that he'd been holding. "And welcome home. It's good to see you. How was London?"

"It was fabulous," I tell him, even though he already knows that because we've been talking while I've been away as well. Not very much, but every once in a while, I'd drunk text him and then I'd have to call him the morning after to explain myself and it'd lead to a conversation. "I had such an amazing time with everybody. You'd absolutely love Wells, he's just hilarious."

"He seems like a cool guy," He nods.

"Anyway, how was your summer? And how's Cara?" I ask Elliot as I'm taking the pale green tissue paper out of the bag to reveal a teddy bear sitting inside of the bag.

"Actually, we broke up," He informs me.

"Oh, you're kidding. Seriously? When?" I wonder, looking away from the teddy bear and up to Elliot out of shock of the news that he just dropped on me.

"Yeah. It's recent. She finally had too much of me being friends with you, and I think that you coming back to Florida kind of set her off," He explains. "But I told her that I wouldn't stop being your friend and I realized that she has a complete lack of ability to trust me, so I broke up with her. It's a long, complicated story but I guess that's the general idea of it."

"I'm so sorry," I say, giving him a sympathetic look even though I'm internally shouting at him 'YOU DON'T SAY?!' and just say, "But hey, you'll find somebody new. There's loads of hot girls at Carnegie Mellon."

"I'm sure there are," He chuckles at me and then nudges at the bear in the bag. "Open the present."

"Sorry," I say quickly, bending down and pulling out the bear and I can't hold back a laugh when I see that the bear is wearing a little Carnegie Mellon t-shirt and it's a really cute looking bear. "I love it, El."

"Good. So when you're away in Virginia, you won't forget to root for us Scottish Terriers," Elliot says jokingly.

"You know, the school sounds so much more awesome if you don't mention the mascot," I tease him.

"Yeah, well the cavaliers aren't that much better. Do you even know what a cavalier is?" He raises his eyebrows at me as I put the bear back in the bag so that I don't get it dirty.

"No, but I'm sure that it's cooler than a tiny little dog," I defend with a small laugh and I love how normal this conversation feels, like the past seven months never even happened. Maybe it feels more natural because I know now that Cara isn't looming over my shoulder, making sure that

I'm not trying to steal her boyfriend, or maybe I just needed a break from this place to remind me how much Elliot truly means to me. But this conversation feels really good. "Are you all packed for your flight to Pittsburgh?"

He shakes his head. "I still have a week."

"So you've done nothing?" I wonder, laughing again.

"I've packed some stuff," He defends. "But yeah, I have a long way to go before I'm ready to leave. What about you?"

"I haven't even unpacked from London yet," I scoff. "But I have two weeks, not one. And I've been in another country, so I have an excuse for my procrastination."

"Yeah, yeah. I just don't think that I'm ready to leave this place yet. I'm going to miss you," He tells me.

"I've already been gone for three months, it's like I'm already gone," I remind him.

"Right, but I've just got you back and now we're moving away from each other again. I'm going to miss you like crazy," He says, pulling me into a tight hug that almost surprises me. To me, things are still awkward between us and I don't think that it'll ever change. I want to tell him that I already miss him like crazy, I miss the Elliot that used to be my friend, before he traded me in for Cara. I've forgiven him, put it in the past, but we will never be able to go back to how we were before Cara happened, and it still breaks my heart.

"You're going to make me cry," I mumble breathlessly into his shoulder. "I'll get you a UVA bear if that'll make it better. And we'll only be five hours away so we can make that drive sometimes. We were still friends when I was in London, we're still going to be friends when we're only five hours away."

"I know," Elliot sighs, pulling away from me. "We're just growing up a lot is all."

"Yeah, I know, it's like they've been saying 'ready, set...' our whole lives and now it's go time," I mumble.

"Ready or not, here comes the future," He adds.

"But we've been through worse. We'll be fine," I assure him. "And you're going to absolutely love Carnegie Mellon. You'll be amongst other computer nerds and everything, it'll be great."

"It will be great," He agrees.

"And-"

"Hey, Jen," Beckett arrives at the party and both Elliot and I turn to look at him.

"Oh, hey," I grin at him, giving him a tight hug as he approaches and I'm very glad that there's so many people around so that I don't feel the urge to attack his lips with my lips. I don't know why, but I just feel a magnet attraction to him but I think that it's just physical. I think that if I did stay here during the summer, we probably would have had a friends with benefits type of relationship because it's so hard for me to deny that attraction and with everything figured out with Elliot, it would be guilt free. Now that we're both going to different schools, it'd just be a bad idea to start anything now.

"Welcome back," He says, glancing to Elliot and then to the teddy bear in the gift bag. "Sorry I'm late. I didn't get you a present."

"That's okay, it wasn't a requirement," I assure him. "We were just talking about how unprepared we are to go to college to be on our own. I mean, it's not like we're going to stop being friends or anything, because Elliot is five hours away and you're going to be three hours away so we can still occasionally visit each other."

Elliot and Beckett are looking at each other apprehensively because while I'm friends with both of them, they don't particularly get along very well still. I don't know if it's still just because of my ugly past with Beckett or if it's something else, but Elliot just really doesn't like Beckett and I don't think that Beckett likes Elliot either. It sucks that I can't hang out with them at the same time but in the two months that I had with them, I learned to adjust.

"And I'll still be making videos," I add. "Maybe not as much, but I'll still be making them. So if you're ever missing my gorgeous face and unforgettable sense of humor, you know what my channel is."

"And no shortness of confidence either," Beckett adds teasingly.

"Of course not," I shoot back.

After a little bit more conversation, we all go sit down with my mom's friends, which takes away some of the tension between Beckett and Elliot but the disadvantage of sitting with other people is that they start asking about my relationship status. And whenever I assure them that yes, I'm single and that no, I'm not into anybody right now, I can see both Beckett and Elliot shift uncomfortably in their chairs. Which makes things a big awkward for me.

I know that I've had romantic-related feelings for both of them. Elliot, I was in love with and Beckett, I'm in lust with. And Beckett might still like me but I haven't asked because I'm too afraid of the answer, so we just don't talk about it. Maybe Elliot likes me like that too, but I'd like to think that he doesn't. It's a bit too late or that anyway.

No matter what, it doesn't matter who is romantically into me because I'm not getting into a relationship right now despite Elliot's handsome face and comfortable personality and Beckett's stunning body and sense of humor. I'm about to go to college, to discover myself even more than I already have. I need to focus on myself and my YouTube channel and my friendship with Heather and the other girls that we meet in Virginia.

I don't need a boy, I don't need a boyfriend or a crush or a complicated relationship with anybody. My life is not a romantic comedy or a fairytale with a 'happy ever after' it's messy and it's complicated and it's real. And I'm learning to adjust to that. I just need myself and my guitar, my family and my friends. Maybe there's a future with either Elliot or Beckett, I have no idea, but that isn't important to me right now.

What is important is that they're both two of my closest friends and I love them dearly, and I need to focus on them as my friends right now, because friendship is more important to me than finding somebody to sleep with at night.

Myself, my guitar, my family, my friends. That's it. That's all that I have, and I'm happy. And in the end, that's really all that matters.

www.ingramcontent.com/pod-product-compliance
Lightning Source LLC
Chambersburg PA
CBHW070756190726
48292CB00002B/555